Seeking
Sasha

Seeking Sasha is a work of fiction. Names, characters, places, and incidents are the product of the author's imagination or are used fictitiously. Any resemblance to actual events, locales, or persons, living or dead, is coincidental.

Willow River Press is an imprint of Between the Lines Publishing. The Willow River Press name and logo are trademarks of Between the Lines Publishing.

Copyright © 2026 by Laura Frost

Cover Design: Morgan Bliadd

Between the Lines Publishing and its imprints supports the right to free expression and the value of copyright. The scanning, uploading, and distribution of this book without permission is a theft of the author's intellectual property. If you would like permission to use material from the book (other than for review purposes), please contact info@btwnthelines.com.

Between the Lines Publishing
1769 Lexington Ave N, Ste 286
Roseville MN 55113
btwnthelines.com

First Published: February 2026

ISBN: Paperback 978-1-965059-61-6

ISBN: Ebook 978-1-965059-62-3

Library of Congress Control Number: 2025944473

The publisher is not responsible for websites (or their content) that are not owned by the publisher.

Seeking Sasha

Laura Frost

To my husband, Ryan, who always believed in me,
even when I didn't believe in myself.

Chapter 1

April

Heavy clouds and rotting fences loomed as she forced her legs to keep moving. Every scurrying cat, flittering bird, and tree swaying in the wind was a monster ready to strike.

Suck it up and shove it down.

A gnarled branch grabbed her hair. Ensnared in the limb's grasp, she wound her fingers around her locks and yanked herself loose. Strands of hair, forever imprisoned on the branch, waved as she left a piece of herself behind.

You can't be Bryn anymore. Find a new name.

The drone of traffic crept into the air while her burning lungs begged for a reprieve. The wooded pathway opened to a two-lane highway, and she staggered to a halt, certain each approaching vehicle was the black BMW. Pulling her hood over her head, she weaved between honking cars and trucks as her oversized pack clung to her back.

She paused on the sidewalk for only a moment, then she scurried across the parking lot and vanished in rows of towering semis. A chameleon in the shadows, she snaked between the parked rigs.

Steadying herself against the sandpapery grime on the cab of one, she peered out from between two trucks.

Shrubbery dotted the edges of a restaurant.

People lounged behind windows.

Slowing her staccato breaths, she crept towards the building. Her fingers pressed onto the glass, leaving smudged prints as she peered in from the shadows. A man sat at a table near the window, stuffing down meat, fries, and vegetables boiled until they were floppy and the color of death. He glanced up. Their eyes met. He turned back to his plate.

She inched along the side of the building, bushes scraping their claws along her pack as wind whipped hair in her face. A man with a giant gut pushed open the door and stepped from the restaurant. The smell of fried food and bleach floated through the air as she hovered behind a shrub.

Ask him.

He walked towards a rig, climbed in, and rumbled away.

Another man pushed open the door, but her throat was closed tight. *Suck it up and shove it down.* She opened her fist to a crumpled ten dampened with sweat. Crushing her fingers around the bill, she drew in a breath that tasted like diesel. *You can still go back...*

"You all right, love?"

She spun on her heels, bracing her legs to run. A woman, middle-aged with graying hair, stood in front of her. Swallowing tears that begged for release, she bit her lip and shook her head.

"Is there something I can help you with?"

"Is there any chance you can give me a ride somewhere? Anywhere?"

The woman looked her up and down as she zipped up her coat. "What's your name, love?"

"It's... Deb. I mean, Del. Delilah. My name is Delilah."

"You have no one?"

"No, ma'am. I need to leave town. Please. I have to get away or else... I'll... He'll... I'm sorry I only have this to give you." With a shaky hand, she thrust the crumpled ten at the woman.

"Keep your money, love. I'm heading to Lashburn, and you can join me if you wish."

"Lashburn? There's nowhere else?"

"I'm on a schedule and can't change the route but I'd be happy to have you keep me company."

She looked around the parking lot, every car the BMW. Glancing at the kind face of the woman, she hugged her arms around herself and nodded. "Thank you."

Traffic flew by as the truck lumbered down the highway, and her stomach clenched when she saw another mileage sign bearing Lashburn's name. With each passing mile, she was fleeing from one life only to be barreling towards the life she had already fled.

Chapter 2

September

Hayley scraped dirt from under her nail as the elevator slowed to a stop. Tugging her ponytail tight, she stepped into the hall painted yellowish-orange with sunlight. A woman in a pantsuit smiled as she walked past, her high heels clicking a steady tap dance. As Hayley strolled up to the office at the end of the hall, she glanced at the nameplate on the wall: *Craig Patterson, Public Works.*

"Hey, Craig," Hayley said, rapping on the open door. "Can I grab my final paycheck?"

Craig, hands deep in a file, looked up from the filing cabinet. In jeans and a golf shirt, he stood apart from the pantsuits and ties that filled other offices on the floor. "Just grab it from the cubby. Accounting has me searching for an invoice and I'd rather not lose my spot in this mess."

Shifting the bag on her shoulder, Hayley followed the path worn into the carpeting and scanned the faded Dymo labels affixed to each square hole jammed with envelopes and memos. When she found "Grounds," she plucked the stack of envelopes from the hole and flipped through them.

"So," Craig said as his fingers skimmed page after page in the cabinet. "What are your plans for the fall?"

"I'm going to head back west. There's a greenhouse outside of Ellison that I worked at a few years ago and the manager wants to hire me again."

"Ellison, hey? Say hi to the ocean for me. When do you leave?"

Hayley leaned against the cubbies, her shoulder crushing a memo that was sticking out of the *Sanitation* nook. "I have to call them to finalize details but I'm hoping for later this week."

"Lashburn is going to miss you. If you happen to be back in the city next summer, I'd love to have you on the crew again."

Having spotted the name she was searching for, Hayley dumped the rest of the envelopes back into the nook. "Thanks for the offer but I'm planning to stay west for good."

"If you change your mind, let me know by spring and I'll hold a spot for you."

Hayley fiddled with the envelope, its crisp edges digging into her skin as her gaze landed on a map of Lashburn on the wall behind Craig. The more she stared at it, the more it grew, as though it was trying to swallow her up. "I'll keep it in mind."

Hayley waltzed down the street with the paycheck clutched in her hand as cooing pigeons walked their tightrope overhead. A scattering of yellow leaves swirled past a fire hydrant, through the legs of a sniffing dog, and came to rest in a puddle.

Following the cracks in the sidewalk, Hayley turned towards the blinking "Money Place" sign that stood out between the laundromat and pawn shop and pulled open the door. Peeling mustard-yellow walls met a scuffed brown floor while a staticky Rod Stewart ballad hummed from somewhere in the ceiling. Hayley glanced at customers slouched at plexiglass panes and took her place at the last window where an employee picked her nails.

"How can I help you?"

Sliding the check under the glass, Hayley said, "I need to get this cashed."

"ID?"

Hayley dug through her bag. Her fingers brushed her sunglasses and a forgotten guitar pick before they found the plastic baggy. "Here," she said, pulling out the card and tattered birth certificate.

The woman's eyes narrowed as she studied the documents, then relaxed to their previous bored state. "Here you go," she said and slid the pieces back under the window. "It'll be about ten minutes."

"Do you have a phone I can use while I wait?"

"On the table in the corner." The woman pointed across the room while clicking the mouse, her glazed expression lost in the computer screen.

As Hayley sauntered towards the deserted waiting area, she stole glances at other customers and the door. She tossed aside a year-old Reader's Digest and settled into a chair with frayed fabric pulled taught around foam crushed to a pancake.

The calling card grinned at her through the creases in the plastic baggy.

She closed her eyes; her lips moved slightly, silently. As she released a cleansing breath, her eyelids drew open, revealing a sparkle, and her mouth turned up at the corners. She slid the hair tie from her ponytail and shook waves of hair over her shoulders.

Bracing the receiver in the crook of her neck, she studied the numbers scrawled in blue ink on the inside of her wrist and tapped out a disjointed rhythm on the phone's dial pad.

"Primrose Greenhouse. This is Gail."

"Hi, it's Crystal Cooper. You asked me to call about starting work."

"Your timing is perfect. Are you in town already?"

She glanced over her shoulder at the jingle of bells carrying from the door. "I'm in Lashburn for a few more days but I can probably start work on Wednesday."

"Let's see if that'll work…"

She scanned the space. A man, fat and ponytailed, took his place in line. The bored woman clicked her mouse behind the plexiglass.

"I've got deliveries coming Wednesday morning," Gail said, "but I should be done with those by eleven. How about you come in after lunch and we can get the paperwork completed as well as a quick refresher on your responsibilities."

A smile stretched across her face, and her fingers and toes tingled. "That would work beautifully."

"Make sure you bring a void check so I can pay you by direct deposit."

"Is it okay if I just pick up my checks?"

"We work with direct deposit. It's easiest for everyone."

"It's not…" She pinched the bridge of her nose and focused on what needed to happen. "Picking up my checks is what's easiest for me. My green thumbs are excited to help streamline your seed collecting and cleaning, plus I want to share my pest control experience, but that means picking up my checks."

The line was quiet for a moment before Gail spoke up. "We'll figure something out, okay? I'll see you Wednesday."

As she returned the receiver to its base, a giggle tumbled from her, and her feet danced under the chair. "Yes," she said and wrapped her hair back into its ponytail.

Magda's lips quieted from their silent mantra as she turned up the walk that was more weeds than concrete. Conquering the busted front steps, she rattled the screen door, but it stayed jammed shut. "Damn screen."

"Hey, Mags." Gina took a swig of beer and looked through the warped screen.

"I can never get this piece of shit to work," Magda said, brow furrowed as she madly shook the handle.

With a sigh, Gina put her beer on the peeling linoleum and reached for the door. "I keep telling you, you need to push the button in and then lift up on the handle or else the bottom of the door sticks." Gina jiggled the door from the inside. It shot open and smacked Magda on the forehead.

"Son of a..."

A fit of laughter erupted from Gina. She reached for her can and, between snickering breaths, took another gulp. "Not so smooth, Mags," she said, wiping beer from her lip.

"Maybe if you'd ever get that door fixed."

"And are you willing to pay more?"

Magda glared at Gina while rubbing the red mark above her eyebrow.

"I didn't think so. Anyway, there are a couple of sweet parties tonight that me and Ian are going to. You gotta come."

"Nah." Magda shifted the bag on her shoulder and headed for the stairs. "I could use a night in for a change."

"That's lame. You're coming. I've already decided."

Magda huffed as Gina tipped her head back and shook the last drops into her mouth. "I'm not going. I'm tired."

"You're going to waste your life being boring?"

"Boring?" Magda's eyes narrowed as something inside of her tightened. "Have you already forgotten last night?"

Gina turned towards the kitchen and lobbed the empty can at the sink. It bounced off the edge with a tinny bang and rattled to the floor. "Last night—now that was epic. We need a repeat, Mags. You *have* to come."

The stairs that led to her room tried to steal Magda's attention.

"I'll give you a beer if you come," Gina said.

"I don't need a beer."

"Your mood says you do."

"Fine," Magda said, flipping her hair over her shoulder. She dragged her feet to the kitchen and kicked Gina's empty can aside while a fly snacked on globs of drying Cheez Whiz on the countertop. After snagging the beer that Gina pulled from the fridge, Magda popped the top with a cracking hiss and slurped the rising foam. "I'll go to the stupid parties. Knock on my door when you're ready."

Magda jogged up the narrow staircase and hopped over someone's jeans, then sidestepped a frying pan with crusty cheese glued to the bottom. Leaning her shoulder into her door, she worked the key until it turned and clicked. She slipped through the crack, pressed the door closed, and checked the lock.

Her jacket fell from her shoulders and onto the floor as she sucked back a mouthful of beer. She pushed through the bitter hops and yeasty undertones and forced the alcohol down.

Magda tossed her bag on the mattress, kicked aside a damp towel, and picked her way to the doorless closet. Balancing on her toes, she reached to the back of the dusty shelf until her fingers found the tampon box. It sat thick and heavy in her hand as she pulled it from hiding.

Beer in one hand and bulging tampon box in the other, she settled into the lumpy mattress. A slice of sunlight tried to break through the grime on the window, but Magda was too absorbed in her task to notice.

She placed her can on the floor and pulled a handful of bills from the baggy secreted at the bottom of her bag. Tucking her legs under her, she opened the top on the tampon box and eased the wad of cash from within. The money's inky-linen smell wafted up as she unfolded the stack.

The yellowed walls and shouts from downstairs disappeared as Magda lined the bills in symmetrical piles: fives, tens, twenties, fifties. She dumped coins onto the mattress with a clinking song, and her fingers flew through the pile, sorting and counting at the same time.

When the last coin was added to the total and when she straightened the three stacks of twenties, Magda leaned against the wall and sipped her beer. "I've done it," she said as she took in the display before her. "Thirty-two hundred." As her teeth grazed the lip of the can, her eyes crinkled in a smile. "Goodbye, Lashburn. And good riddance."

Chapter 3

Magda stumbled across the dance floor, the living room spinning like she had just stepped off a Tilt-A-Whirl. As the strobe light pulsed, she searched the faces that flickered in and out of view, but Gina and Ian were gone.

A guy, spikey-haired with half a dozen piercings stuck in his face, sprang in front of Magda and started dancing. With a flip of her hair, Magda smiled and moved in rhythm to the thumping music, her arms over her head, her body like a cobra being charmed. Alcohol swam in her veins and turned the flashing lights into colorful streaks while she floated an inch above the floor.

The guy's hands found Magda's hips as partiers jostled her on all sides. Body odor hung in the air. He gyrated his hips against hers, his beer breath hot in her ear.

Magda's smile faded to a scowl. "I've got to go find my friends," she shouted over the music, squirming from his grasp.

"But we're just getting started." He tightened his hold and slipped a hand into the back pocket of her jeans. His pelvis thrust against hers while bodies knocked into her in the tightening circle.

"I've got to go." Magda pried herself from his grip and shoved him away.

Breaking from the dancing throng, Magda scanned the room, but she was alone. The guy was in the middle of the dance floor, his hands all over another girl. "Asshole," she muttered as she stumbled towards the cooler. She plunged her hand into the icy water, fished out a beer, and popped the tab. Gulping malty beer down, she spun around and slammed into a body.

"Sasha?"

She froze. A cold sweat washed over her, like her outermost layer of skin was dissolving and washing away. She lifted her gaze and when her eyes met his, her knees buckled.

"Sasha. I can't believe it." His arms were instantly around her, holding her like he would never let go. "My Sasha."

Her vision blurred and doubled. The room tilted on its end. She pushed Cole away and stumbled backwards as though she had been punched in the stomach.

"Sasha, it's Cole. Cole Dawson."

Her eyes were locked on his as if under a spell; the beer trembled in her hand. Sasha bit her quivering lip and tasted blood. "Cole... I... Wow. I never in a million years would have expected to bump into you tonight."

"Me neither. I thought you were..." He reached for her, but she stepped back, just out of reach. "What happened to you? Where have you been?"

Sasha's mouth dropped open, words and explanations from deep inside not knowing their way out.

"Magda. There you are."

Run. Sasha's fingers tingled with adrenaline. Her eyes darted from Cole to Ian to the exit.

"We're heading to that other party." Ian puffed his chest out and narrowed his eyes at Cole. "Are you going to join us?"

As the men hovered over her, Sasha curled in on herself, a crocus closing its petals under a dark sky. *You're Magda, you're Magda. You. Are. Magda.* Fingers denting her beer can, Magda opened her eyes and looked at Ian. "I think I'm going to head home."

"Whatever," Ian said, glancing at Cole before heading into the crowd.

"Magda?" Cole said.

"Oh… yeah…" Her limbs became jelly again as she studied his brown eyes and lopsided smile. Leaning in close, she shouted, "Magda is a nickname that Ian gave me. It's a long story. One of those inside jokes between us, you know?"

"No, I don't know. What…" Cole looked around the room before returning his gaze to Sasha. "I just can't believe… Can we talk? Maybe head outside so we can actually hear each other."

Sasha glanced towards the door then to Cole's eyes, warm and steady. "Yeah, let's get out of here."

Cole wrapped his hand around Sasha's. His warmth radiated up her arm and into her core as they left the muggy beer-sweat air behind.

"That's so much better," Cole said as they stepped into the crisp night. "I could barely hear myself think in there."

Sasha slipped her hand out of Cole's and pulled her arms around herself, refusing to meet his intense stare.

"Mags!"

Her heart stuttered. She tucked her chin to her chest and hid behind her beer.

"Scored yourself a hottie, did you?" Gina said as she hip-checked Sasha.

Blood pulsated in Sasha's ears. She scanned the yard and considered diving into the lilac bush and never coming out. "He's an old friend who I haven't seen in a while."

Gina's smile turned into a pout while she analyzed Cole. "Me and Ian are heading to the other party. You coming?"

Sasha looked sideways at Cole. The thumping music from inside the house matched her heart's rhythm. "I'm actually going to hang out here."

"I don't blame you," Gina said, her eyes lingering on Cole's face. "Catch you later, Mags."

As Gina skipped down the steps, Sasha glanced again at the lilac bush.

"I thought Magda was a nickname between you and Ian."

"It is. He calls me that all the time and other people picked up on it and started calling me that too. It's dumb. Sorry for the confusion."

Cole furrowed his brow and studied Sasha. "That makes sense, I guess. It's just weird to hear people calling you by a different name."

"Yeah... I guess..."

Cole's searching eyes would not leave her. Sasha guzzled the sour beer but choked and sputtered. Beer shot from her mouth like a faulty fountain and dribbled down her chin. "Oh my gosh," she mumbled and wiped her face with the back of her hand.

"Here." Cole swept his thumb across Sasha's cheek, leaving a tingling heat. "You missed some."

Swallowing hard, Sasha looked at Cole. A thread of guilt oozed up from deep inside. She dropped her gaze and toyed with the tab on the can until it popped off.

"I still can't believe you're here. Where have you been?"

"I... uh... I just needed to–" Sasha crashed into Cole. Beer sloshed out of the mouth of her can and doused the front of his shirt. Cole wrapped his arm around Sasha and held her to his chest. His arms, scent, nearness... A thousand memories burst from where Sasha had been keeping them locked away. Two men continued to push each other around and slammed into Sasha again.

"Watch where you're going!" Cole said as he shoved the men away. With his arm locked around Sasha, he steered her down the steps.

"You okay?" he asked, pushing past partiers.

"I'm fine." She wriggled out of Cole's embrace and glanced towards the house where more men had joined the growing melee. She took another swig of beer and cringed at the taste.

"Leave your beer and let's go. This party is getting out of hand."

Sasha squeezed the can, the cold aluminum a grounding rod. "I'll take my beer."

"Actually, you need to leave it. It's against the law to have open liquor in public."

"You're seriously going to make me leave this?"

"Yeah, I am. Now let's go. I don't want to be here anymore." Cole pried the can from Sasha's grip and tossed it on the lawn. Taking her hand, he pulled her down the sidewalk. With his hand wrapped around hers, long forgotten images of her and Cole as kids flashed through her mind like old home movies.

The noise of the party started to fade, Cole slowed his gait, and Sasha wriggled her hand free. Crossing her arms, she studied the collection of tiny moles on Cole's forearm. Her face warmed as she remembered how she used to tease him, saying they looked like a smiley face. She tucked a piece of hair behind her ear and matched her breaths to his—steady and even. Picking at a hangnail, she watched his canvas shoes move under the glow of the streetlights.

"So," Cole said. "I was asking you where you've been for the last decade. You just kind of disappeared. I tried to track you down on social media, but I couldn't find you. It's like you vanished."

That was kind of the point, Sasha thought as she chewed her lip. "I'm not on social media. I'm not into technology and I'm guessing no one would be interested in following my life anyway."

Cole glanced at Sasha. "I would be."

Sasha shrugged as their shadows swelled and collapsed in the streetlights. "I headed to the coast. My aunt lives there so I moved in with her. I just needed to get away from here, you know? There are so many more gardening jobs out there. They don't get winter the way Lashburn does." She peered at Cole to gauge his reaction, but he just stared ahead at the empty streets.

"I spent the next few years bouncing from town to town, working at orchards, vineyards, landscaping… that sort of thing." She looked again at Cole. His silence was excruciating. "Eventually," she said, "a friend suggested I try life up north, so I headed there."

"How far north?"

A breeze picked up and Sasha wrapped herself in a hug as goosebumps ran across her arms. "You know… north. Tundra and stuff."

"I never pictured you in the tundra. What community were you in?"

"Community? Well… I… It was just a bunch here and there. Tiny places you likely haven't heard of. I'd have to show you on a map… if they even show up on a map. Like I said, they're pretty small. But enough about me and my boring life. What have you been up to?"

Cole shoved his hands in his pockets and kicked a pebble across the sidewalk. "After you disappeared, I kind of lost my focus. I started college but soon realized I was meant to help others, so I joined LPS."

"What's that?"

"Lashburn Police Service."

Sasha stopped. She stared at Cole, half expecting a badge or handcuffs to pop out from nowhere, like he was a magician with a gun. "You're a cop? Wow. I guess I shouldn't be surprised. You always wanted to save the world."

With a shrug, Cole picked up the pace. "It's not all that I imagined it would be. I mean, I love the job but there are so many technicalities that people can get off on and a lot of bad people are protected from the law for a variety of reasons. And don't get me started on the paperwork. If I could spend as much time on the streets as I do at my desk, I could help a lot more people and put a lot more bad guys behind bars."

"That sucks," Sasha said, cringing as the words flopped out of her mouth. *Sasha's pathetic. Come on, Magda. Where did you go?*

"I make policing sound worse than it is. I love being a police officer and I think I make a pretty good impact. It's just not quite the job that idealistic twenty-year-old Cole thought it would be." Cole turned to Sasha and dissected her with his eyes again. "So, you're back in Lashburn now, hey?"

A car turned onto the street a few blocks ahead. Sasha narrowed her focus as the headlights pointed at her. "A friend put me in touch with Lashburn's Public Works department and I was offered a summer job landscaping around the city."

"You've been here all summer?"

Sasha glanced sideways and squeezed herself in a tighter hug. "Uh huh..."

"Gawd, Sash." He kicked another pebble with enough force to send it bouncing halfway across the street. "Now that summer's over, what are you doing?"

"Oh. Ah... I mean, Craig was so impressed with my work this summer, he asked me to stay on year-round. It's a typical Monday to Friday gig with a lot of office work. It's all right, but I prefer to be outdoors."

"What about a boyfriend? Husband? Kids?"

As the oncoming headlights drew near, Sasha positioned herself behind Cole. Thumping bass reverberated in her chest. As the Nissan passed, Sasha's shoulders relaxed. "I'm not really girlfriend material. Definitely not wife material and most definitely not mom material."

"Why not?" Cole asked, bumping his shoulder into Sasha's as tall buildings rose around them. "You're nice, smart, funny... What else do you need? Unless... Oh hey, are you gay?"

"What? No. I just meant it's not the kind of life I see myself living." She sucked in a steadying breath, forced a smile, and turned to Cole. "What about you? Girlfriend? Wife? Kids? Boyfriend maybe?"

Cole laughed. "No. None of the above. Some of my colleagues say I'm married to my job, and I guess that's good enough for me."

A strong breeze swept Sasha's hair from her shoulders, sending a fresh wave of goosebumps down her back.

"We're about to get really wet," Cole said, glancing skywards.

Shimmering stars dotted the sky while a darker mass loomed beyond the skyscrapers. "Those clouds are still far away."

"My mom always said that when the first strong wind picks up, you have exactly five minutes to take shelter. Those clouds might look tame, but there's a lot of rain in them."

Sasha looked at the sky again as Cole grabbed her hand and yanked her forward. "What's your plan?" she asked. "Everything around here closed hours ago."

"I know somewhere."

The wind ruffled their shirts as they rushed past darkened banks, bistros, and shops. A smile broke through Sasha's worry lines, and she relaxed her fingers into the spaces between Cole's.

The once-distant clouds were blotting out the stars and the first drop of rain hit Sasha's cheek. A minute later, the downpour was upon them. "I thought you were going to find us shelter," she yelled over the pounding rain. She splashed through rapidly forming puddles, water squelching in her thin canvas shoes.

"It's not far. Only four more blocks."

Heart pounding, Sasha scrambled to catch her breath. She shivered, her clothes heavy and glued to her skin. Raindrops rolled down her face and over her lips, finding a home on her tongue where dewy freshness mingled with bitter beer aftertaste.

Cole steered them to the outskirts of downtown. He finally slowed to a stop in front of a building and pushed open the glass door. As they stepped from the deluge, the door eased closed behind them; the silence of the vestibule dampened the drumming rain.

"Where are we?" Sasha said, a puddle forming under her shoes.

Cole smiled and wiped the rain from his face. "My place."

"Your place?" Glancing through the second set of glass doors into the lobby with its fresh vinyl plank flooring, neat grid of stainless-steel mailboxes, and couch opposite the elevators, Sasha turned to Cole, her mouth agape. "You live *here*?"

Chuckling, Cole fit a key into the lock and pushed the door open with his shoulder. "Yeah. Come on up and we'll dry off."

Sasha looked around the lobby as she squeezed water from her hair. "This is really nice."

"It's all right," Cole said and pushed the elevator button. "A place to lay my head."

The doors closed them in. As the elevator moved under her feet, Sasha wrapped her arms around herself. Her wet shirt clung to her body like shrink-wrap and her pounding heart echoed in the small space. She focused on a gum wrapper lying in the corner and wondered if Cole was looking at the same piece of garbage. Sasha lifted her eyes and studied him, finding glimpses of the boy she had known beneath stubble and toned muscles. As the elevator slowed to a stop, Cole met her gaze. She tore her eyes away.

"It's down this way," Cole said as he turned out of the elevator. At number 726, he fit his key into the lock and pushed open the door.

The warmth and peace of Cole's home enveloped Sasha like a warm cup of coffee on a cold day. Her muscles tensed. She hovered in the doorway.

"Come on in. We can warm up by the fire."

"You have a fireplace?"

"Of course I do," he said and pulled Sasha inside. The door closed behind her with a deafening click. "Follow me. I'll grab you a towel." He kicked off his sopping shoes and disappeared around a corner.

"I'll leave wet footprints on your floor," Sasha called after him. A fierce round of shivers rocked her body. She hugged herself with one arm while the other hand found the doorknob.

"I don't really care about a bit of water on my floor. Now come get a towel before you freeze to death."

Her grip tightened around the knob, and she closed her eyes. *You are Magda.* Her eyes opened to Cole's effervescent face poking out from around the corner.

"Come on, Sash."

Pursing her lips, Sasha's hand fell away.

As she padded down the hall, her eyes darted between dust bunnies and discarded socks. Cole was at the end of the trail, pulling a fresh towel from the linen closet.

"I barely ever have house guests and figured the extra towels my mom gave me were just taking up space, but I guess they're coming in handy today." Cole grinned and handed Sasha a fluffy towel. "Hang on a sec and I'll get you something dry to change into." He disappeared into the bedroom and came out a minute later with folded clothes. "Like I said, I don't get house guests, and I have no need for women's clothes, so this is the best I have to offer." Cole held the clothes out, but Sasha just stared at them.

"You can't stay in those wet clothes; you'll freeze to death." Cole marched past Sasha and tossed the clothing onto the bathroom's vanity top. "I'm guessing the last thing you want to put on is my t-shirt and boxers, but it's all I've got that has a chance of fitting you. Toss your wet stuff into the hall and I'll pop it in the dryer."

Sasha's teeth chattered as she stared at Cole staring back at her. Reluctantly, she stepped into the bathroom and closed the door.

Eyes squeezed shut, she pressed her back to the door. "What are you doing here? Sasha's dead. You *have* to find Magda."

The wet clothes stuck to her skin like a leech as she worked at peeling them off. After rubbing the plush towel over her body, Sasha fingered Cole's boxers. She pulled them on. Their silkiness caressed her thighs and sent a rush of pink to her cheeks.

As Cole's shirt fell over her head, she caught her reflection in the mirror. Her hair was clumped and stuck to her face and neck. The boxers sat low on her hips, barely staying on, and her chilled breasts lifted Cole's shirt from her belly.

She buried her face in her hands.

"You going to stay in there all night?"

Sasha jumped at the eager knock. "No... Just about done." Avoiding her eyes in the mirror, Sasha adjusted and readjusted the fall of the shirt.

Hugging her arms around herself, she inched out of the bathroom. As the gentle rumbling of the dryer carried down the hall, Sasha tried to push the thought from her head that Cole had picked up her wet bra and panties from the floor.

"Can I get you something to drink?" Cole asked from the kitchen. "I have beer, Coke, water, orange juice, milk... That's about it. I didn't expect company."

"What are you having?"

"A beer."

"I'll have one too, please."

Beer in hand, Cole walked towards Sasha. The corner of his mouth curled up like it always had when he was about to tell her a secret.

"Thank you," she said as she took a bottle from him. His fingers brushed hers. She pulled away.

The thumping of her heart overshadowed the drum of rain against the patio door as Sasha followed Cole to the living room. "You have a really nice place."

Cole shrugged as he flicked the switch on the fireplace. "It does the job."

As the flickering flames tried to cut through the chill, Sasha's eyes drifted around the room, from an open gym bag in the corner, to a framed pencil drawing on the wall, to a blanket lying on the couch. She pulled up the collar of the shirt that had slipped off her shoulder and glanced at Cole. He stared back. She looked away.

Swallowing in the silence, Sasha looked down at her chest—her nipples poked through the cotton. As she hugged her beer, a water droplet escaped from her hair and rolled down her back, sending a fresh round of shivers through her.

"Let's get you warm," Cole said, taking Sasha by the hand. Settling her on the couch next to him, he reached for the blanket and let it fall over them.

Sasha pressed the mouth of the bottle to her lips and stole a sideways glance at Cole. He gazed at her with a sweet smile. She tipped the bottle farther back. His eyes still on her. She reached under the blanket and yanked the loose boxers up on her hips before pulling the blanket over her chest. Her elbow bumped his arm and tiny electric currents radiated through her. She gulped the beer. *Please help, Magda. Sasha's a loser.*

"You warming up?" Cole said. He pulled the beer from Sasha's hand and set it next to his on the coffee table. His fingertips tickled the fine hairs of her cheek as he peeled a piece of wet hair from her skin.

"A little, I guess."

Sasha fixated on the beer sitting on the coffee table a galaxy away. Cole eased his arm behind her and rested it around her shoulders. He was warm and oddly familiar, yet Sasha stayed stiff as she stared at her beer.

"You know," Cole said, "they say a great way to warm up is with body heat."

"I'm sorry?"

"There's even a theory that for best warming, skin-to-skin contact is ideal."

Her face flushed and she turned to Cole. His eyes locked on hers, his warmth and strength pulling Sasha in.

As she stared at Cole, his serious expression cracked, and his easy laugh bounced off the walls. "You should have seen your face. Priceless. You've always been so easy to tease."

Sasha sucked in a breath as Cole's quirky sense of humor drifted from the recesses of her memory. With his arm stretched behind her, his finger traced an invisible line on her arm, leaving heat in its wake. His other hand found Sasha's under the blanket. He laced his fingers through hers and caressed her skin with his thumb.

A thousand memories rushed into her.

"All jokes aside," Cole said, his voice growing quiet, "I am really happy we bumped into each other tonight. I still can't believe that after nine years of silence you're here in my home. I searched and searched for you but had given up hope of ever seeing you again. It's like you're back from the dead." Cole shifted closer to Sasha; his eyes locked on hers. "My friend—my Sasha—is home."

I can't do this. I can't be here.

Cole grazed his fingers across her cheek and slipped them through her hair.

Sasha closed her eyes. *Suck it up and shove it down. You are Magda and you are with a different guy. You are Magda.* Slowing her breathing and repeating her mantra, her jitters steadied, and her shoulders relaxed.

In the quiet of the home, with her body pressed close to a man's, Magda gave in as his lips touched hers.

She cracked her eyes to an unfamiliar ceiling, strange couch, unknown walls. As she blinked the sleep away, the weight of Cole's arm smacked her back into reality. In the stillness of the space, the drum of her heart reverberated off the walls while her disjointed breaths clashed with his rhythmic ones.

Sasha's gaze shifted around the dark room and landed on the floor. The discarded t-shirt and boxer shorts that she had borrowed lay limp, like a skin a snake had crawled from. The t-shirt and pajama pants that Cole had been wearing were in a soft pile, fresh but used.

Cole's arm was like floppy lead as Sasha shifted it off her. He stirred and settled.

With the t-shirt and boxers in her arms, she scampered to the laundry room where she pulled her clothes from the dryer and dressed. They hung off her, dull, thin, and worthless.

Sasha tiptoed down the hall, a lump jammed in her throat. As she slipped her feet into her soggy shoes, she looked at Cole's sleeping form. "Sorry I let this happen," she whispered. "But you don't know who I am anymore."

Chapter 4

Sasha burst from the building, holding back tears before they broke to the surface. The streets were dark. A blood orange hue from the rising sun reached around high-rises like poison slowly tainting the world.

And Sasha ran.

Her feet pounded on the pavement, her wet shoes leaving hints of footprints that marked her escape.

Suck it up and shove it down. Don't you dare cry.

She flew past a man setting up a sandwich board outside a bakery, a woman unloading a stack of newspapers from a truck, a stray cat looking for a home.

The rolling grumble of a bus carried through the air. Sasha staggered to a halt and, searching the streets, spotted a bus stop ahead. She hurried towards it but caught her toe on a crack and crashed to the sidewalk.

Sasha's wrists were on fire as blood oozed from the scratch marks. She touched her knee—a fresh hole was torn through her jeans, the fraying edges tinged with red. *You're not allowed to cry.* She scrambled to her feet and hobbled to the stop as the bus slowed.

Sasha spilled a handful of change into the fare box, stumbled down the swaying aisle, and collapsed into a seat. As the bus rumbled down the road, she tucked her legs to her chest and buried her face in her hands. "You weren't supposed to be there," she said to her knees. "You weren't supposed to meet me again."

As the bus rocked Sasha, the feeling of Cole's lips on hers—warm and sweet—crawled out from her lockbox of memories...

...*The sky had been bright blue, the sun high over the school's track field. Sasha sat on the lonely bleachers as Cole paced the track, his chest heaving. He waved at Sasha and bounced up the bleachers two at a time.*

"Hey," he said, plopping down beside her. "Thanks for coming. That was my best time ever."

"It's fun to watch you run. You're kind of gross afterwards, though," Sasha said, wrinkling her nose. She moved a wet piece of hair from Cole's forehead and wiped her hand on her shorts.

"You mean this?" He laughed and shook his head. Droplets of sweat flung out from his hair in all directions, splattering Sasha.

"Eew! You're disgusting. Go shower before you touch me again."

Cole looked down at the field where athletes stretched and guzzled water. "The guys are razzing me because you're here. They say you're only watching me so I'll ask you to prom."

"Oh really?" Sasha laughed. "Friends aren't allowed to watch?"

"That's what I told them. But it got me thinking." Cole picked at a scab on his knuckle. He pursed his lips and turned to Sasha. "Maybe we should go to prom together."

"You mean... you and me?"

"Yeah, you and me. What better way to finish off our school career?"

Sasha searched Cole's eyes, her brow wrinkling.

"Look, if you don't want to go with me that's totally fine—no hard feelings. But there's no one I'd rather go with. Plus, you will probably look really sexy in a dress."

"Cole!" Sasha said and shoved him away. "I'm not sexy."

"Sorry to tell you, Sash, but you are hella sexy."

"Oh my gosh, Cole." Her face flushed, and Sasha focused on the football team running drills on the adjoining field.

"I'm not saying we go as a couple, but you're the one I want to go with."

Sasha picked her nail and looked sideways at Cole. "You really want to go with me?"

"Well… yeah," he said, his lip curling up on one side. "I just… I dunno. It feels right, I guess."

Sasha bit her lip, but a smile snuck through as a breeze swept her hair into her face.

Cole tucked Sasha's hair behind her ear and smoothed the strays into place. "I want to go with my best friend."

The hoots and hollers from the field below vanished. Cole's dark eyes pulled Sasha in and would not let go. "With me?" she said.

He leaned in and paused. With the hint of a lopsided smile, he brushed his lips to hers. "Of course, you."

Sasha's lips tingled. A salty sweetness danced on her tongue and her stomach flipped. As Cole brought his lips to hers again, the tingles that swept through her body solidified to ice. "Cole," she said, pressing her hand to his chest. "I can't do this."

"You can't or you don't want to?"

Tears hovered in her eyes. "I can't. You know that."

"You're eighteen. You can do what you want."

"But… I… I can't be here." She fumbled for her schoolbag as a tear rolled down her cheek.

"I'm sorry. I got caught up with all this prom talk. Forget the whole thing."

"I gotta go." Sasha slung her backpack over her shoulder and took off across the bleachers, their metallic rattle following her trail.

"Sasha, wait!" Cole called and bounded after her. "I'm sorry. I'll ditch out of practice, and we'll walk home together. Give me five minutes to shower. Please."

"Leave me alone."

Sasha's stomach searched for something to digest as the bus rolled through the waking city. She hugged her arms around her knees and leaned her head against the clattering window as gray clouds choked Lashburn.

I'll leave today, she thought, her eyes glazed and unblinking. *There's got to be a bus to Ellison today. I have everything in order. I can just go. And then I'll be Crystal and life will be okay again, and the world won't have to be burdened with Sasha.*

As the bus turned onto her street, Sasha pulled her head from the window and closed her eyes. *You are Magda. You are strong and tough, and no one can push you around.* Her shoulders relaxed and her lips fixed into a confident line.

Magda left the bus behind and marched down the sidewalk, stepping over a discarded slushie cup and around a garbage can knocked on its side. When she turned up the walk, she groaned at the door. "Damn thing better work today." She mashed the palm of her hand to the button and winced. "Son of a…" A fresh smattering of blood oozed from the scrapes on her hand. Gritting her teeth, Magda slammed her hand to the button again, then lifted the handle and pulled. "Stupid piece of…" she muttered as the door slammed behind her.

Urgent panting drifted down the stairwell. Magda dragged her feet up the stairs, sidestepping the same cheesy frying pan. As she wandered down the hall, the rhythmic grunts became louder. "Cut it out!" Magda yelled and slammed her fist to the door as she passed. The sounds stopped.

As Magda pressed her bedroom door closed, the cries resumed, only more intense. She grabbed a book from the floor and lobbed it at the wall. It hit with a bang and dropped to the floor. The moaning continued.

"Screw this place," Magda said as she pulled her pack from the closet and jerked it open. The room next door quieted, and a giggle passed through the thin wall.

Magda tore through the room, stuffing shirts, dishes, and food in her bag. When she was done, the floor was naked, baseboards seeing light, and wire hangers dangled from the rod as though frozen in time. Only the bare mattress remained. She cinched the drawstring, strapped her water bottle to the side, and clipped the buckles.

"Let's do this," she said as she balanced on her toes and swept her hand across the closet shelf. Her fingers brushed the tampon box, and she fumbled it into her grasp.

The weight was wrong. The box was not bulging.

Magda's breath stuck in her throat as she pulled the feather-light box from the shelf. She blinked hard as she stared inside, then blinked again.

"What the hell?"

She stuck her hand in the box and pressed her fingertips to the corners. She tore into it, ripping the cardboard to shreds. Wheezing, she stared down at the box bits that littered the room.

Magda choked down a sour mouthful of bile as she heaved her pack across the floor and dropped it by the closet. Balancing on its soft unevenness, she gripped the lip of the shelf. She scanned the surface, corner to corner. It was a barren land, thick with dust, dead flies with legs pointed at the sky, and an unyielding tampon.

"Where is my money?"

Magda rushed across the room, flipped over the mattress, and examined every crack and corner.

The palms of her blood-crusted hands dug into her knees as she gulped for air and focused on keeping herself upright. Stars danced at the edges of her vision while her body tilted and swayed. Using the wall for support, Magda lowered herself onto the mattress. As she stared at the shreds of her cardboard safe, she collapsed onto her side and clutched her stomach.

The moaning started up again.

Chapter 5

Jane pulled her windbreaker over her hoodie and zipped it up to her chin. The scent of oil and spices stuck in her hair, and her fingers were pruned from hours swimming in gray dish water.

As she wandered from the quiet kitchen to the entryway of the darkened restaurant, she glanced outside. Snow crystals hit the window in gusts and neon signs reflected a distorted array of color on the growing snowdrifts.

"I'm all done in the back," Jane said, stopping at the till where a neat stack of menus in another language were stacked.

Mr. Chen nodded and popped the register open. *"Liù shí měi yuan,"* he said as he collected three twenties and handed them to Jane.

The promise of another month with a bed released some of the tension in her shoulders but relief was stifled with the rumble of her stomach. "Mr. Chen…"

"Yes." The word came out like a command rather than a question, every letter thick with his accent.

"Could I get an advance? This is enough to cover the rest of my late rent but that leaves me with nothing else. Even twenty dollars will do."

The corners of Mr. Chen's mouth dipped, and he looked at her like she was an important puzzle to solve.

"I've been a great employee these past few weeks. I'm always on time, I do the job thoroughly, and I sometimes stay late to finish up. Please. Just this one time. I need to buy food."

"Food? Yes, food." His face having brightened, Mr. Chen hurried to the kitchen and picked up the leftovers that Jane had scraped into a box.

"Thank you," she said, fumbling the box and the handful of fortune cookies that Mr. Chen was shoving into her arms. "I really appreciate the extras, but I need money. Cash." As she held the bills out to Mr. Chen, a fortune cookie tumbled to the floor.

"Liù shí." He pulled the bills from Jane's hand and counted them out one by one, Mandarin sounds following his motions, then handed the bills back to Jane. "Liù shí."

With a sigh and a nod, Jane pocketed the money. "Thank you," she said and collected the lost cookie. "I'll see you Tuesday."

"Yes." With a smile, Mr. Chen opened the door. A blast of icy wind hit Jane in the face as her boss ushered her outside and closed the door behind her.

Jane glanced at the dark streets. A taxi rolled past, snow whipping up behind it, and vanished around the corner. As Jane pulled her hoodie over her head, tucked the leftovers close to her chest, and pushed into the weather, her persona crumbled away like flakes scattering into the wind.

She passed markets, restaurants, and nail salons, all windows unlit and neon signs cut to black, while power lines stretched overhead. As she turned out of Chinatown and pressed towards home, her thoughts turned to the impossible screen door, sketchy roommates, and the cheesy frying pan that now housed a dirty sock.

The rumble of a bus through the frozen air caught her attention and she glanced up to see a bus lumbering towards her, the digital display singing, "Library."

Her shoulders relaxed and a warm glow filled her chest.

"Can't," she mumbled, and pressed on through snow that was beginning to pile up. But as the bus grew near, an image of Gina pouring beer down her throat and begging for another party swelled in her mind.

Before she could convince herself otherwise, she was across the street, standing at the stop. "I have enough... I have enough..." she said as she dug in her pocket while balancing her dinner in her hand. "I just won't buy wine this week."

The bus slowed to a stop and the doors eased open, presenting a world of warmth and security. She climbed aboard, forfeited change to the farebox, took the transfer slip from the driver, and collapsed into a seat that felt like a cozy armchair.

As the bus pulled away from the curb and put more miles between her and home, she relaxed into the wall and fished a fortune cookie from the collection in her pocket. She snapped it in half, catching precious crumbs on her tongue, and eased the slip of paper out.

Ask yourself if what you are doing today is getting you closer to where you want to be tomorrow.

"But I'm allowed a break every now and then," she muttered and shoved the cookie in her mouth. As she popped the lid on her dinner, the aroma of the restaurant wafted out, circling around her and drifting through the bus. She slid the chopsticks from their sleeve and dug into the fried rice and noodles.

The bus turned into the downtown core, the start and stop of the ride lulling her in her seat. When the library came into view, she collected her things and returned to the frigid world.

Wind blasted her and knocked her hood off her head. She tucked her chin to her chest, scurried up the steps, and slipped into the warm, bright space.

Shelves upon shelves of books towered over her and she breathed the scene into her lungs. The air smelled of worn pages and fresh ink, fantasy worlds, biographies of fascinating people, and stories of love. The only sound was the quiet murmur of a librarian giving a guest a computer tutorial.

With a smile, she bounced up the stairs and around the corner. "Please be there…" She turned down her aisle and searched the far end of the third shelf on the left. Her treasure was there.

She lifted the novel from its home and found her favorite lounger in the corner, empty and welcoming. With a deep breath, she cleared her mind and set her space: boxed food tucked into her lap, away from onlookers and strict librarians; the novel on the armrest, page 134 waiting for her; and a quick glance at the bus transfer ticket that showed she still had seventy-eight minutes of freedom.

Tucking the transfer into her pocket, she turned to her food but paused. A book on a nearby table watched her, the words on its spine digging into her memories.

She chewed her knuckle and stared at the anthology. Thought about the words within.

And she was drawn towards it.

The book was heavy in her hands, the spine old and worn, the pages impossibly thin, and she rested its secrets on her lap. Knowing exactly where to find the passage, she flipped though musty pages and stopped.

I celebrate myself, and sing myself, and what I assume you shall assume.

She ran her fingers over the words. Despite knowing them by heart, seeing them in black on white helped them sink in. "Maybe Mr. Fortune Cookie is on to something…" A lump jammed up her throat.

Shaking thoughts from her head, she fanned the pages and paused at a random poem.

Sometimes with one I love I fill myself with rage…

"No!" She slammed the book closed. As the word bounced off the library walls, her hand flew to her mouth, and she threw the book on the table as though it had caught fire. "Suck it up and shove it down."

The anthology took up the entire table. It swallowed the library in its pages as Curtis's words echoed in her mind: *"It belongs on the shelf."*

Breath in… breath out…

"It belongs on the shelf. Now."

Her heart squeezed and tears tried to set themselves free, but she clenched her teeth and clamped her fists. "You want it on the shelf?"

She glared at the book. With a quick motion, she grabbed the anthology, marched to the middle of the long bookcase, and shoved it between books about scorpions.

A wicked smile curled her lips, and she collapsed back into her chair. As the poetry book stuck out amongst science and nature volumes, she popped the lid on her dinner and glanced at the clock—seventy-two minutes left.

She collected a chicken ball in her fingers and plunged it into the viscous sauce, a red that no food should harbor. She bit into the cold ball, glanced again at the out-of-place Whitman, and smiled before turning to page 134 in her novel.

Legs curled under her, she turned another page and another, her entire being captured by the characters as though she were a member of their traveling party. The empty Chinese food box—sauce container licked clean—rested on the floor.

"Just a reminder that the library closes in ten minutes, miss."

With those eleven words, she was sucked out of her fictional journey. Her head snapped up to see a long skirt disappear behind a row of books.

"No."

She scrambled from her seat and knocked over her dinner box, her eyes glued to the clock. "No, no, no."

The novel went back to its place on the shelf, page 209 waiting for another day. She pulled on her jacket, dumped the garbage in the nearest bin, and launched out the doors.

The air was an ice wall, hitting her in waves as she hurried down the steps. Crystals stung her face, and her thin shoes vanished under the snow with every bound as she searched the ghostly streets for a bus despite knowing hers was already halfway home.

She huddled in the windbreak of the tiny bus shelter and peered through the smudged plexiglass; her eyes trained on the snowy road ahead. Her mind whipped with calculations of bus times, and, like clockwork, a bus turned down the street eight minutes later.

Scrambling up the steps and into the bus, she handed her transfer ticket to the driver and fell into a seat. She sunk into her hoodie and tugged the hood over her blown hair.

"Hey," the driver said, turning around.

She peeped out of her hood as her face sank lower into the fabric.

"This is an expired pass. You can't use this."

Like a turtle coming out of its shell, she withdrew her face just enough to speak. "I don't have bus fare. I lost track of time. It's only twenty minutes past expiration, anyway."

"It's expired. You need to pay full fare or get off the bus."

She looked out the window. Snow was piling up along doorways and signposts, and a plastic bag flew down the street like it was running from something. "It's freezing out and I don't have bus fare."

"I can't let you ride."

Mr. Chen's sixty dollars plus the thirty-eight she had brought from home—all her money in the world and the key to another month of secured rent—sat heavy in her pocket. As she stared at the transfer in the driver's hand, a well of anger bubbled up. "But it's freezing. And it's barely expired. I'm not paying."

"Then get off the bus. I'm not a charity."

"But…"

"Off. I have a schedule to keep."

Huffing and collecting herself, she stormed off the bus. The warmth of fumes as the bus pulled away was like a final hug before the blizzard rushed into the breaks in her clothing. As the bus turned the corner and the howling wind blasted her, a rock settled in the pit of her stomach.

"I can walk." She cinched her hood and pulled her hands into her sleeves. As she started down the sidewalk, snow collapsed towards her feet, stinging her ankles with icy fire. "I can walk."

She plowed though snow, careful to pick her feet up rather than push through the deepening banks, but after only three blocks, she was already searching for warm places to take a break.

"It's only four miles," she said to the sidewalk. "That's easy. Just walk faster."

She picked up the pace as her feet continued to numb. A beam of light broke the dark sidewalk—a convenience store shone brightly, the inside lights casting a radiant glow on the blizzard.

With her hand tucked inside her sleeve, she pulled open the door, the rattle of overhead bells a welcome sound. The shop was small, decorated in junk food and barred windows, but its heat enveloped her like a sauna and started its magic of thawing her freezing bones. She breathed into her hands and glanced at the cashier. He stared at her, not breaking his glare.

Still breathing warmth into her dulled fingers, she turned up one tiny aisle then down the next while she inspected candy bars and bags of chips as though they were priceless works of art. The cashier stared on.

When she had scoured the entire store, she started again, creeping up one aisle and slinking down the next.

"Can I help you find something?"

"No... Just looking..."

Her skin tingled where it thawed; her shivers quieted.

"Are you going to buy something?"

She looked at him, then away.

"This isn't a hangout. You have to leave."

"But..."

"Do I have to call the police?"

"The what?" *Cole.* His image jumped into her mind and stared her down. Shaking his face from her thoughts, she said, "I'm just shopping."

Without losing eye contact, he picked up the phone.

"Oh my gosh. Fine." Putting the junk food treasures and grimy sauna air behind her, she re-entered the storm that had turned the city into a ghost town. Street crossings and sidewalks had become one long snowfield with no breaks to tell one from the other. She set her internal compass and pushed against the weather while it pushed back.

A bus emerged from the squall like a guardian breaking through the storm, the number and location advertising an unknown route. She ran towards the stop, snow finding hiding places between shoes and socks, and when the bus doors pressed open, she stepped aboard. "How close does this bus get to the Sax?"

"This is about it."

The seats beckoned her with their plasticky plushness. The stale air pumping out recirculated heat hugged her, and she knew the rocking motion would lull her to sleep for hours. "Is this bus running all night?"

"This is my last run. Once I pull into the Southbend Station, she's parked until five-thirty in the morning."

The rock in her stomach gained another pound. She stepped off the bus.

A blast of wind whipped the hood from her head and sent her hair flying as though it were caught in a tornado. She pulled the hood up again, but the tornado blew it off.

"Okay," she breathed, eyes darting around the quiet streets. Roads were empty. Businesses were dark. Even the moon dared not come out.

Her rock weighed her down and the shivers deepened.

A beacon of light the next street up called to her, and she hurried towards it. As she drew near, the bright neon "Open" sign of the café was like a friend, happy to see her. She opened the door just a crack and slipped inside; the roaring gale was instantly deadened. Sinking her face into her jacket, she slid into a chair in the corner like a ghost.

Coffee aroma enveloped her while Jim Morrison warned about *The End*. The barista turned from dish duty, wiped her hands, and leaned across the counter. "Can I get you something, hon?"

"Hm?" She glanced up, arms hugging her shivering body. Her rent sat like a brick in her pocket. "Oh. Yeah. I don't really have any money on me. Can I stay anyway?" She glanced out the window, then back to the barista.

"We close in half an hour, but you are welcome to stay until then."

The warmth of the barista's words filled her with more glow than the furnace pumping out heat. A moment later, the barista placed a steaming cup of coffee on the table. "It's on the house. Cream and sugar are at the counter."

Her eyes grew wide, and tears pricked at the corners, then slunk back into hiding. "Thank you." She slid from her seat and poured in sugar until the coffee tasted like dessert. She slurped back a quarter of the mug, the piping liquid burning her tongue, and topped it up with as much cream as it would take.

Settled in her seat, she warmed her hands on the mug, filled her nose with the smell of coffee, and stared out the window at the storm that was only growing worse.

She huddled in the entryway of the coffeeshop and pulled her hands into her sleeves. The neon "Open" sign beside her shut off and the café's interior lights blinked out, plunging her into darkness. Halos of streetlights undulated in the storm as the wind whipped snow in every direction.

"What are your options?" she said, looking like she was talking to a shadow. "Catch a bus if you see one and hope that it runs all night or hitch a ride." She shivered at the thought. "But you have to walk until either of those options present themselves." Yet, as she ran the plan through her head again, her body stayed tucked away from the squall.

With a whisper of silent words and a nod of her head, she tightened the hoodie, balled her hands inside her sleeves, hugged her arms around herself, and stepped into the blizzard.

Her hood was instantly knocked off her head, so she tugged it back on, but it was whipped off again. She pressed her hands to her ears, which had numbed too fast. Tucking her head down, she stomped through drifts of snow, some reaching her knees. She stumbled, righted herself, stumbled again, and fell into a bank. As she pushed herself to standing, she looked at her fingers. Red skin peeked out from snow.

She pressed on.

She passed under dozens of streetlights, storefronts, and parked cars hiding under blankets of snow until it all began to look the same. She studied street signs, but the numbers no longer made sense. Was she getting closer to home, or had she made a wrong turn and was walking away? Another blast of wind whipped her icicled hair and, needing a moment of reprieve, she slipped into an alley.

The wind was calmer but the cold just as piercing. *Just a rest.*

Back pressed to the brick wall, she slid down and collapsed into a bank. Snow pressed into her wet socks, but it did not feel cold... or hot... It just was.

She tried to make her eyes dart around the alley and down the street, but it was more of a slow scan. She was alone in the cold—a slowing soul becoming more ice than human. Icy hair hug in her face but when she tried to brush the clumps back, her hands would not move the way she asked them to. She figured she should be hyperventilating as the reality of her situation engulfed her, but her breaths teased her with their lethargic pace.

I'm going to die. And it's okay.

She blinked slowly, tiny icicles on her eyelashes kissing her cheeks. She blinked again and saw it—a sign she remembered from a month ago. A bank, its windows decorated with letters promising investment growth while painted leaves of orange, red, and yellow circled the words.

Cole's building was right around the corner. Not three blocks away.

Her limbs were lead, her joints in desperate need of oiling, yet she staggered to her feet, which felt like blocks. With every ounce of strength she could muster, she pushed out of the snowbank and stumbled down the street, painted leaves pulling her forward.

Chapter 6

Cole lay on the couch in his pajamas, the remote loose in his grip. *"...the Rockets taking the win against the... ...with temperatures well below seasonal average... ...Beavers are known for building dams, lodges, and..."* Eyes heavy, he killed the TV and tossed the remote to the side.

As Cole picked his way to the kitchen in the dark, another gust of wind slammed against his window and pelted the building with snow pellets. He pushed the blinds aside and looked out. The streets were white, the air was white, and Cole could barely make out the building across the street. Like a television screen that had lost its signal, swirling gusts of ice crystals hypnotized him. He stared into the squall and saw Sasha's face. He could still feel her arms around him, tears ready to spill from her eyes...

...The music had been pumping out dance tunes while rainbow lights swept figure-eights across the ballroom floor. Cole leaned his shoulder against the wall as his classmates, dolled up in gowns and suits, bounced to the music.

"I know you said you needed to leave after the grad dinner, but you have to stay for prom," Cole said, returning his gaze to Sasha. *"It won't be the same without you."*

"Cole..." Sasha let out a rush of air and hugged her arms around herself.

"I know. You can't. I'm sorry I keep pushing you." He glanced across the ballroom and watched her father watch him. "I'm just happy you were able to make it to the dinner."

Sasha pressed her back to the wall, the simple gown hugging her waist before spilling to the floor. "Have you ever wished life was different?"

The smell of lavender floated into Cole. He pulled his eyes from Mr. Cooper's stare and pressed his nose to Sasha's hair. "The world is at our fingertips, Sash. College, careers… We are about to forge our own paths in life." He found a break in Sasha's fist and nestled his fingers around hers. "Maybe we can scrounge up enough money and get our own place. Be roommates. Be our own bosses."

Sasha sucked back a sniffle. "I don't want to talk about the future. I just want to hold on to this moment." Relaxing her fist, she slid her fingers into the spaces between his.

"I was right, you know," Cole said as he ran his thumb across the back of Sasha's hand.

"About what?"

"You look damn sexy in a dress."

"Oh my gosh, Cole."

"You do."

Across the room, Sasha's parents pushed back their chairs. Her dad's eyes were still on Cole.

"Cole." Sasha's grip stiffened around his hand. "I'm not ready to leave yet."

"Then stay."

Sasha's eyes fell closed and she stuttered in a breath. Her shimmering glossed lips whispered silent words. As she brought her eyes to Cole's, she blinked back tears. "I have to go."

"Then go, my Sasha. It's okay. Just promise me you'll do something special for yourself tonight and I'll see you tomorrow."

Sasha's arms were suddenly around Cole, and she hugged him like she was never going to let go. Her breath warmed the space between his suit's collar and his neck as her voice broke. "You are the best friend anyone could ever have. I wish I could stay, but I have to go. I'm sorry. Please understand."

"I know, Sash."

With a deep breath, she released her grasp. Her hands slid down his arms, over his hands, and with a final squeeze, lifted away...

Two short rings pierced the air and knocked Cole from his trance. Like a lighthouse's beam slicing through a storm, Cole's phone sent out a beacon from table to ceiling. The light dimmed and Cole furrowed his brow. The same rings cut the air again, as the beam reached skyward once more.

Cole grabbed the phone. "Hello?"

Silence.

"Hello?"

"It's m-m-me."

"Who is this?"

"S-S-Sasha. Can I come in?"

The phone fumbled from Cole's hand. He stumbled over a chair as he scrambled to find his phone in the dark. "You still there? I'll be right down."

He shot across the condo. As he shoved his feet into his boots, another gust of wind slammed into his building. "Freaking Sasha," he said as he bounded down the stairs. "She rises from the dead once again."

Cole pushed through the door to the lobby and stopped. With eyes closed, lips blue, and hair thick with icicles, Sasha looked like a shuddering corpse propped against the wall.

46

Cole raced to the doors as his mind scrambled to make sense of Sasha's state. "Sasha, what happened?" He wrapped his arm around her and steered her to the elevator.

As the doors groaned shut, Cole enfolded Sasha in his arms. She was stiff and her body shook against his. "You're freezing," he said as an icicle melted on his cheek. Her iciness pressed through his t-shirt as her shallow breaths warmed a spot on his chest. "What were you doing out in the storm?"

Her body was lead, her legs spaghetti, and she slumped into him.

"Don't do this." Cole adjusted his stance as Sasha sagged to the side. He scooped her up in his arms and pictured her body shattering into a million pieces at the slightest touch. As he pressed his lips to her forehead, a shiver ran through his body.

Stumbling into his condo, Cole maneuvered Sasha onto the couch. "Easy... easy..." he said as he knocked off her snow-covered shoes, peeled away her ice-encrusted socks, and brushed crystals from her hair. "You've got to stay with me, okay?"

Cole tore his shirt off and eased Sasha's over her head. "I may have been kidding before about the body heat thing but I'm not kidding about it now." He pressed his chest to her body of ice and wrapped them in a blanket. His teeth chattered as he buried his face in her hair. "We'll warm you. You'll be fine... You'll be fine."

With the glow of the fire warming the room, Sasha's shakes subsided to mild quivers. "How are you doing?" Cole said as his hands pressed into her back.

"Still cold but not as bad."

"Then we're on the right track." Cole eased Sasha to the rug and tucked her shirt over her head. The skin of her stomach was like silk as his fingers fumbled with the fabric. He slid a pair of his socks over Sasha's toes before guiding her arms into one of his hoodies. As Cole fit the zipper together, he searched Sasha's blank expression, but her gaze remained locked on the floor.

"We need to warm you from the inside," Cole said and dashed to the kitchen. A moment later, he pressed a steaming mug into her hands. He adjusted the blanket around her shoulders and tried to read her vacant face. "You scared the crap out of me. Why were you out in the storm?"

As though the weather had frozen her in place, Sasha stared unblinking at the mug in her hands.

"What happened?"

"I only wanted an hour."

"An hour of what?"

Flickering flames cast dancing shadows over Sasha. She pulled the blanket around herself like she was building a cocoon, and hid in her mug. "Next time I'll listen to the fortune cookie."

"The what?"

"Nothing."

Sporting a lopsided frown, Cole moved a clump of Sasha's hair from her face. "You're soaked. How long were you out there?"

"Does it matter?"

He pursed his lips and studied Sasha—the new way she parted her hair, the old way she chewed her lip when something was bothering her. "If I had Oreos, we'd be deep into the package by now."

She met his gaze, the barrier in her eyes breaking for a moment. "I think this needs at least three boxes."

"We've got you and me in my little hideout of a home, and a blanket around your shoulders. We can do it without the cookies. Tell me what's going on."

Her lips parted. Her chest rose, air filling the space in preparation for a long story.

And she tore her gaze away. As her eyes gently closed, her lips fell into a whispering rhythm.

"Sash?"

Sasha's face scrunched and she brought her hand to her ear.

"Are you okay?"

"It's just my ears. They burn a bit."

"I'm not surprised. May I?" he said and reached out to her. Cole pulled back Sasha's curtain of hair to expose whiteness on the tip of her ear. "I think your ears are frostbitten."

"They'll be fine," she said and hid her face in the mug.

"How are your feet?"

"I dunno. They kind of tingle."

"Tingling is good. It means they are getting circulation back. May I take a look?"

Sasha peered over the mug. "If you think it's necessary."

Keeping his eyes on Sasha's hair-obscured face, Cole slipped his hand into her pant leg and glided it up her calf until his fingers brushed a fringe of cotton. As he rolled down the sock, he studied the straight line of Sasha's mouth, the taught muscles of her eyebrows. Cupping her foot like it was a precious sculpture, Cole grazed her icy toes with his fingers. Her toes came to life in his grasp and a giggle broke her hardened features.

"Still ticklish, hey?"

Her smile vanished. "No." Sasha pulled her legs from Cole and tucked them under the blanket. Shifting flames threw lights and shadows over her face as she picked up the mug and focused on her drink.

"I'm glad you came here."

"I didn't want to. But I saw your street and... I'm sorry I'm bothering you when you should be sleeping."

"You are not bothering me. If you didn't come here…" A familiar heaviness squeezed Cole's heart as an image of Sasha's body, stiff in a snowbank, battered his mind.

Sasha peered through her hair at Cole. Her almond-shaped eyes of ocean blue matched dozens of sketches he had drawn from memory, but their sparkle—her mystery that shone from her core—was something that had always eluded his pencil. As he analysed the way the dancing flames played with the darker flecks of blue, his silent promise to her over a decade ago knocked around in his brain. He slipped his hand around hers and found the space where their fingers melded perfectly. The lingering warmth from the mug on her skin faded, leaving her hand cold in his.

"But I'm fine." Sasha tore herself away and cocooned in the blanket.

"Yeah…" His eyes drifted to the framed sketch on the wall as his mind whirled with questions. "What happened to you tonight?"

"…nothing."

Another gust of wind shook the patio door and snow peppered the glass. The furnace clicked on, and the hum of warm air was piped into the condo. "Are you in trouble?"

Sasha moved only her eyes from her tea to Cole. He held her gaze and tried to see past the mystery and secrets, but she had built a wall.

"Whatever it is, you can tell me. Wandering around in a blizzard in the middle of the night in summer clothing is freaking weird. You weren't mugged or anything, were you?"

Her eyes flew open. She thrust the mug at Cole, hot tea sloshing over the side. "Oh my gosh. Where's my jacket?" Dumping the blanket on the floor, Sasha popped to standing and spun around in frantic circles. When her eyes landed on her jacket in a pile on the floor, she dove for it.

Like a vulture over carrion, Sasha curled over her jacket and pulled a worn plastic baggy from within. She flipped through the bills and counted the loose change, ignoring the two—or was it three—plastic cards in the bag.

With a nod and a releasing breath, Sasha tucked the cash back into the baggy and secured it in the pocket. She plopped down in front of the fire, pulled herself into the blanket, and collected the mug from Cole as though nothing had happened.

Cole glanced towards her crumpled jacket. "I guess you weren't mugged."

A strand of hair had fallen into Sasha's face. She twirled her finger around the piece, staring at it as if it would do something.

"Where'd you get all that cash?"

"Cole, please..."

"Do you not use a wallet?"

"Can we just sit here without you interrogating me like one of your criminals?"

"Sorry." As shadows and light danced on Sasha's face, Cole tried to estimate the amount of cash she had, and what those cards were.

"Do you know the bus schedule around here?"

"The bus?" Cole said, pulled from his investigation. "No, but I can look it up for you. There's probably not much running in the middle of the night, plus with the storm... It's best you spend the night."

"Thank you."

"Where's your car?"

"The bus serves my needs."

He opened his mouth, dozens of questions on the tip of his tongue, but as he watched Sasha stare into her mug as though doing a tea reading of her future, he pulled back. "Don't worry about the bus. I'll drive you."

"It's not necessary."

"I want to."

"Of course you do."

Cole pulled his hoodie off as the room warmed to that of a sauna, yet Sasha remained tucked inside the blanket. She sipped her drink, taking bigger gulps as it cooled.

"Can I ask you something, Sash?"

"No."

"Why are you dressed the way you are? Where's your winter clothing?"

"Gosh, Cole." She groaned and shook her head.

"It's a perfectly reasonable question, considering the circumstances."

Sasha breathed deeply and closed her eyes. Her lips moved silently, like she was casting a secret spell. In the next breath, her eyes popped open. She sat up straight, released the death grip on the blanket, and flipped her hair over her shoulder. "It's just that I spent most of the last decade on the coast and you don't really need winter clothes for the type of weather they get. I keep meaning to buy stuff for winter, but I never get around to it."

"It's about time you got around to it. How about tomorrow? What time do you work?"

"I have tomorrow off."

"I thought you work Monday through Friday."

"Oh... right." She paused and focused on the flames. "I took tomorrow off. I needed a break."

"Then it's set. Tomorrow, we shop." Glancing again at her jacket, Cole said, "My gift to you."

"No, thank you," Sasha said as she traced her finger around the rim of the mug. "I'm not... I mean... Spend your money on yourself. I'll go on my own."

"No way. I have a decade of gift giving built up for you and I won't take no for an answer. It'll be like old times. You and me spending the day together, goofing around."

Sasha glanced at him, eyes brightening yet narrowing, then looked away.

"I have so many new jokes to tell you."

With her eyes on the floor, a hint of a smile poked through. "Fine, but under one condition—we shop at a thrift store. I'd feel better knowing you didn't spend an arm and a leg on me."

"Deal."

As flames flickered and the furnace hummed, Cole ran his hands over his face and stared at Sasha. She was picking pieces of lint off the blanket and tossing them into the empty mug.

"Are you okay? Life in general, I mean."

"What?" she said, a sudden smile plastered across her face, a speck of lint crushed between her fingers. "Yeah, I'm great. Why wouldn't I be?"

"I haven't seen you in so long and I want to make sure you're doing okay."

Sasha blinked at Cole, her smile weakening to a blank stare.

"You just seem... I don't know... What about right now? Are you still cold?"

"I'm chilled to the bone. I don't think I'll ever be warm again."

"You're not shivering, and your lips are nice and pink again, so I think you'll be okay."

Tucking a piece of matted hair behind her ear, Sasha swiveled her body to face the fire head-on. Cole crawled in beside her and studied her face; it glowed like she was an angel come to deliver a message. "I'm glad you're here," he said, leaning his shoulder into hers. She sat encapsulated in herself and stared into the flames.

Pursing his lips, Cole pulled his shoulder away. He busied himself with a loose thread in the rug as he stole sideways glances.

As his face warmed, Cole's brain worked the past hour over and over again. He kept glancing at Sasha, but she never turned from the fire, barely blinked, hardly moved. The blanket hung off her in cascading folds—the same folds that had lain abandoned on the couch like a used condom the morning after the party. Cole's eyes drifted to the gentle curve of her exposed collarbone and a tingling warmth rushed to his lips. "Why did you sneak out last time?"

Had it not been for the occasional blink of her eyes, Sasha would have been a statue.

"I thought we had shared something special. When I woke up and saw that you were gone, it tore me up inside."

Silence.

Cole turned his body towards Sasha, but she only stared ahead. His muscles strained and twitched, and he wanted to grab her by the shoulders and give her a good shake. "If you regretted what happened between us or if I did something to upset you, you should have told me. The way you walked out is simply cruel and I have a right to know why you did that to me."

Staring into the flames, Sasha whispered, "I wasn't myself that night. I wasn't thinking straight."

"Come on, Sash."

"You're so good and so kind. You don't need someone like me in your life."

"Don't be like this."

"It was shocking to bump into each other, and we had fun reminiscing. One thing led to another… but believe me, you don't want me."

Cole bit his tongue, a multitude of swears begging to fly out. "Go on and tell me what I want." Shaking his head, he raked his hands through his hair. "Gawd, Sash. You didn't even give me a chance. You just left. Unannounced. Again."

She shrugged.

"A shrug. Real nice, Sasha. Classy as always."

With the blanket pulled tightly around her body, she said, "Leave me alone."

"Maybe I need to do that." He stared at Sasha, waiting for an answer to pour from her lips, but she only gazed into the fire.

"We used to lean on each other. We used to talk. What happened to you? Where did my friend go?"

She stared ahead.

"You want me to leave you alone? Fine," he said and pushed himself from the rug. "This time maybe show some respect and stay the night rather than sneaking out like a coward."

Sasha lifted her head from her knees and looked up with glistening eyes. "I'm still chilled. Aren't you going to stay and keep me warm?"

As Cole steamed towards his bedroom, he called over his shoulder, "You're no longer hypothermic; you're just cold."

Chapter 7

Cole hugged his pillow as threads of a dream—Sasha with blue lips and ice in her hair—swirled through his mind.

His eyes flew open. "Sasha."

He stumbled out of bed and, after untangling himself from the sheet, dashed to the living room. Upon seeing the blanketed lump on the couch with Sasha's face barely visible amid the soft folds and splayed hair, Cole let out a rush of air and collapsed against the wall.

Peace and stillness settled into Cole despite the waves of wind playing outside. After another peek at Sasha, Cole moved to the balcony window to assess the storm's damage. Corners of patio furniture poked out from under snow and a drift was piled against the sliding glass door. Ice crystals swirled in a gray landscape and came to life in a dazzling array of sparkles as a slice of sunlight broke through the clouds.

Cole turned to his coffeemaker and as he scooped grounds from the bag, the smell of coffee beans floated through the kitchen. The air was charged with a fresh energy and every sound, from his footsteps on the linoleum to the opening of a cupboard, seemed magnified.

With his mug filled and steaming, Cole settled on the rug beside Sasha. A smile crept onto his face as his eyes traced her glowing skin, sweeping eyelashes, slightly upturned nose, and faintly downturned mouth. As he smoothed her hair away from her face, he pictured her hair tangled in a cedar twenty years earlier…

…Cole twisted the branch until it snapped and fell from Sasha's hair. With a smile, he grabbed her hand and continued through the shrubbery. "Come on, Sasha. It's just through here."

"What are we doing?" Sasha tightened her fingers around Cole's as waxy leaves brushed their faces.

With one more stumble, they landed in a clear patch between greenery and brick. "So?" Cole said. "I found a secret hideout. What do you think?"

Sasha gaped at the wall of trees, solidity of the house, and peaceful space in between as she hugged her doll to her chest.

"Come here." Cole yanked on Sasha's hand. She flopped next to him on a blanket spread on the dirt as Cole reached for a plastic bin tucked against the house. "I've got everything we need: flashlights, coloring books and crayons, an extra blanket, paper to write out our secret plans, and cookies."

"Cookies?"

"Of course." Cole shoved his hand into the box and pulled out two Oreos. "A secret hideout always needs cookies."

Sasha took a cookie from Cole and twisted the wafer from the cream. "This is really cool," she said and pressed her tongue to the icing.

"We can come here any time we want, and it doesn't have to be together. Even if I'm not home and you need to come here, you can. It belongs to both of us."

"Really?"

"And the best part is…" Cole brandished a Batman action figure he had stashed at the base of a cedar. "Batman put a forcefield around the whole thing, so we're safe when we're in here. Nobody can get in but us."

"Nobody?"

Cole stuffed his hand into the box and pulled out two more cookies. Handing one to Sasha, he smiled. "Nobody..."

Warm Arabica notes played on Cole's tongue as Sasha's eyelashes fluttered. Stretching her arms over her head, she yawned. She blinked awake and, as her vision focused, she jolted backwards like a spooked cat.

"Good morning, sunshine," Cole said with a chuckle. "You have a good sleep?"

"Oh my gosh, Cole. Don't do that," Sasha said and pulled the blanket over her head, blending into the cushions.

Cole placed his mug on the coffee table and slid the blanket from Sasha's face. "Let's see how those ears are doing." Brushing her hair back, he frowned. "They're pretty red and you have a small blister on one. They're definitely getting circulation back, but they may bother you for a while. Try not to touch them. How about your fingers?"

Sasha brought her hands out from under the blanket. As Cole stroked her skin, his thumb bumped over rough calluses. He slipped the socks from her feet and Sasha giggled as Cole caressed her toes. "Looks good. Do they still tingle?"

"No."

"Are you still cold?" he asked as he tucked Sasha's feet back into the socks.

"I warmed up through the night."

"And how did you sleep?"

A shy smile spread across Sasha's face. "Really well, thank you. Thank you again for taking me in last night."

"No thanks needed. We're friends—Cole and Sasha, Sasha and Cole—like it's always been."

"Mm-hm."

"Sorry I got upset last night. I just... After last time..." Cole reached for his coffee. "I want you to know that you are welcome any time, day or night. I like that you're here."

Sasha ran her fingers along the hem of the blanket. "I'm sorry I left last time," she said. "I figured you'd wake up regretting what happened, and I was trying to spare you from having to face me in the morning."

Cole tried to hold Sasha's gaze, but she was lost in blanket threads. "Zero regrets. I can handle you telling me if you don't want to be with me or if I upset you or something, but I can't handle being left in the dark."

Sasha nodded and looked away.

"Do you drink coffee?" Cole said, tugging on a piece of her hair.

"You have coffee?"

"Of course I have coffee." Cole half-laughed and pulled Sasha from the couch. "Let's get you a big cup."

After filling a mug, Cole turned to the fridge and reached for a carton of eggs. As he pulled a pan from the cupboard, Sasha dumped three spoonfuls of sugar into her coffee and dribbled in milk until a creamy blend hovered at the brim.

"Do you still like eggs?"

Her lips were glued to the mug's lip. She slurped back coffee until it was no longer in danger of spilling over. "Yes, thank you."

"How do you want them?"

"Cooked."

"No kidding, cooked. I meant, are you still into fried to a crisp?"

"Oh. Um... however you like yours is fine by me." She snuggled into Cole's hoodie and wrapped her hands around the mug as a ray of sunshine lit her up, then darkened just as quickly. "The coffee is delicious, thank you."

"You're welcome," Cole said and cracked eggs into the pan. "Toast?"

"Yes, please."

The popping of eggs frying in butter filled the kitchen as Cole stole glance after glance of Sasha. With the hood pulled over her head and the mug obscuring her face, she had all but disappeared.

"Help yourself to peanut butter and jam," Cole said as he placed the breakfast in front of her. "Would you like some orange juice?"

"Yes, please."

He set a glass of juice on the table and paused as Sasha smeared an obscene amount of peanut butter on her toast. Biting his tongue, he sank into his chair. "You mystify me."

"I mystify you?" Sasha looked at Cole as she plopped the knife into the jam jar. "What's that supposed to mean?"

"I don't know. You've always made me look at the world in a slightly different light."

"Sorry."

"That's a *good* thing. You're fascinating yet mysterious."

A slight smile snuck out of Sasha as she stuffed egg into her mouth. Within minutes, her plate was clean.

"Can I make you more?"

"I don't want to be a bother," she said as her finger cleared a trail through the crumbs on her plate.

"Stop it, Sash. I'll make the whole carton of eggs for you if you want, but you need to stop thinking that you're somehow bothering or burdening me. Now how many eggs would you like?"

"Can I have two, please? And another piece of toast?"

"For you, anything."

Sasha devoured her second helping. When Cole noticed her mug and glass were empty, he topped them up and she sucked them dry.

"More eggs? Toast? Juice?"

"No, thank you. I think I've had enough."

Leaning against the counter, Cole crossed his arms over his chest and studied Sasha. She stared into her empty mug as her finger traced the rim in never-ending circles. As Cole's gaze drifted past her and out into the blustery world, he slipped into his chair and wrapped his hands around hers. "What do you say we get you some mitts to protect these hands?"

Cole scanned the shelves as row upon row of footwear stared down at him. The jarring voice of a radio deejay cracked through the overhead speakers while a teenage boy mopped wet footprints at the end of the aisle.

"How about these?" Cole asked, reaching for a pair of size eights. "They look warm and have a waterproof exterior."

Sasha shook her head and pulled down a pair of worn hikers. "These are four dollars cheaper. I'll get these."

Cole studied Sasha's serious expression as she ran her fingers along the scratched leather. "Sash."

She stayed stuck in place.

"Sasha."

Only her eyes moved, meeting Cole gaze.

"I can handle four dollars. Those hikers would be great for long walks in the summer, but they're not built to keep your feet warm." He pulled the boots from Sasha's hands and shoved his choice into her arms. "Try these. If they don't fit or you don't like the style, we'll look for something else, but they will keep you warm and dry."

Sasha bit her lip and slipped her feet into the boots. She fingered the wool-like lining that hugged her calf and smiled as she shuffled down the aisle. "They are nice. Really cozy."

"Good. They're yours. Keep them on as I'm not letting you back out in the cold with your shoes." Cole picked up Sasha's canvas slip-ons, using the hole in the heel as a handle.

"But the four dollars..."

"Tell you what. If you prefer the hiking boots, we'll get those. But that means I'm going to have to follow you around with a cordless hair dryer, blowing warm air on your feet all day long. I'm guessing one of those will set me back at least forty, fifty bucks."

Sasha stared at Cole before her body relaxed into a grin. "Oh my gosh, Cole," she said, pushing him away. "You are such a dork. Fine. I'll get the winter boots."

As they weaved their way out of the footwear maze, Cole hip-checked Sasha. "On to hats?"

"On to hats."

"This is amazing," Sasha said, looking like a marshmallow in her winter layers as wind and snow swirled around them outside the thrift store. "My fingers are toasty, my ears feel snuggly, and snow isn't pressing into my ankles. I guess I kind of forgot what real winter was like. Thank you."

"You're welcome, my Sasha."

As though caught in a lie, the smile dropped from Sasha's face. Her eyes darted from his parked car to the bus pulling away across the street.

Cole moved a stray hair from her cheek and tucked it under her hat. She flinched but stood her ground, her gaze lost in the swirl of snow kicked up by the bus.

"I'm here for whatever you need."

"Yeah."

As Cole opened the passenger door for Sasha, he said, "It's good to have friends you can lean on."

She flopped into her seat and focused on the stitching of one of the mitts. As the car hummed to life, the warm air pumping through the vents was not enough to thaw the ice wall that Sasha had created.

"Sash?"

"Hm?"

"I need to grab a few groceries."

"Oh... okay." She closed her eyes and spoke silent words.

"You all right?"

"Hm?" Opening her eyes, she turned to Cole. "Yeah, I'm good." She rested her forehead on the window; her silence sucked the energy from the air as they drove.

As Cole pulled into the parking lot, he studied Sasha from his periphery—the zipper on her coat took all her attention. "Think about what groceries you need," he said.

Sasha's fingers froze on her zipper. "I don't need any groceries. My fridge is jammed full."

Cole looked sideways at Sasha as he eased into what he guessed was a parking spot in the snow-packed lot. "I've already decided I'm spoiling you today, so you're just going to have to come up with a list of groceries you want. I'm not taking no for an answer."

Pulling the fur-lined hood over her head, Sasha sunk low in her seat.

"Sasha?"

"You're so freaking stubborn."

Fluorescent lights hummed overhead and a call for a cleanup in aisle ten blared from the speakers. Cole maneuvered the shopping cart through the produce section and grabbed apples, carrots, and a cucumber while Sasha lagged behind.

"I'd tell you a joke about a potato," Cole said as he reached for a bag of Yukon Gold, "but I don't know where to starch."

"Oh my gosh," Sasha mumbled as she added bananas to the cart.

"I heard they're not going to grow bananas any longer."

She turned to Cole with raised eyebrows. "I'm sorry?"

"Apparently, they're long enough already."

With a groan, she wandered off ahead.

"You know what, Sash?" Cole said as he caught up with her. "We make a great pear."

Sasha pursed her lips, but the corners of her mouth twitched as she stared at the pear that Cole was holding out to her.

"We do," he said with laugh. "We always have. You can't deny it."

"You're such a dork," Sasha said but a giggle broke through, smoothing the hard lines on her face and adding a familiar sparkle to her eyes.

"I knew you were in there, my Sasha. You could never resist my jokes."

"You're remembering wrong. Your jokes are terrible." Sasha rolled her eyes but as her gaze met Cole's, another laugh bubbled out of her.

The cart slowly filled, with Cole's groceries towering over Sasha's pile. "Are you sure you don't need anything else?" Cole asked as he steered into the checkout line.

"No... This is all I need." Tucking a strand of hair behind her ear, Sasha reached for a gardening magazine. Her face relaxed into a smile as she traced the pink contours of a foxglove.

"I like this coat," Cole said, adjusting the fall of the faux-fur hood around Sasha's shoulders. "It's a good color for you."

"Mm."

The cashier scanned their purchases, and Cole loaded the bags into the cart. "Sasha, grab a couple of candy bars, my treat, would you?"

"What kind?"

"I'm happy with anything, as long as it doesn't have coconut in it."

"Do you still like Twix? Or Snickers maybe?"

Sigh. "Just grab something."

Hugging her arms around herself, Sasha turned to the candy rack. Cole snuck his peanut butter and cheese under her bag of tortillas.

As warm air pumped from the vents, the windshield slowly defogged. Cole dug around inside one of the bags in the backseat and tossed a candy bar to Sasha. "What do you want to do now? I have no plans for the day. We should do something."

Sasha opened her mouth as if to say something but closed it and dropped her gaze. "I really should get going. I've got a lot to do today."

"It can't wait? I'd love to hang out more—get to know each other again."

"No." Sasha flipped up the hood of her coat and turned to the window. "I need to go home. Now."

Cole frowned as he examined Sasha's profile. He bit into his bar, but the peanuts were stale and the caramel tacky. Pulling the wrapper closed, he sighed. "Where is home?"

"It's uh… The Maples."

"The Maples? Seriously?"

Sasha glanced sideways at Cole. "Yeah, the Maples."

"Sorry. As talented of a landscaper as I'm sure you are, I didn't expect you to live in the Maples. How's the rent? Is it pretty steep?"

"Actually, I own the house. I lived cheap out west and saved a ton of money. When I came back to Lashburn, I bought the house, and the mortgage is supplemented by the rent I charge my roommates. I've always dreamed of living in the Maples, so I found a way to do it."

"Hey, sorry. That's awesome that you've been putting away money." Cole half-smiled and turned out of the parking lot.

The drive to the Maples dragged, with Cole glancing sideways at Sasha who sat like a prisoner being transported to death row. As he pulled to the curb in front of a Victorian house, he let out a slow whistle. "She's a beaut," he said, gawking at the grandiose home with the sprawling yard and large trees. "You did well."

"Thank you."

"Let me help you with your bags."

"No!" Sasha turned to Cole with wide eyes.

"I'm just offering to bring your bags in for you. I'll be out of your hair right away."

Sasha breathed deeply as if steadying her nerves. She closed her eyes for a moment before she returned her focus to Cole, her features softened yet her stare hardened. "I appreciate your offer but there are only a few bags. I can manage on my own."

"It's no trouble."

"I know, but I'm good. Anyway, I was going to do some stuff outside before I go in. I'll just leave my groceries on the front steps for now."

Cole looked through the windshield at drifts of snow building on the sidewalk and swirls of ice crystals being thrown around by wind gusts. He flipped open his wallet, grabbed a chewed pen from the console, and scrawled his cell number on the back of a business card. "Fine. You win. But here's my card, and I wrote my cell number on the back."

Biting her lip, Sasha reached for the card. When her fingers brushed Cole's, he grasped her hand. Her eyes met his; her forced smile quivered.

"Promise you'll call if you need anything. If you need help with something or need a place to crash or just want some company, please call. No matter the time or distance, I'll come for you. I'm used to shift work, so calling in the middle of the night is no problem."

She wiggled her hand from Cole's and stuffed the card into her pocket. As she stepped into the storm, Cole called, "What about your number?"

Wind whipping her hair in her face, Sasha leaned into the car. "I don't have a phone. I'm not into technology."

"You don't have a phone? Not even a land line?"

"There are enough phones in this world that I don't have to bother owning one of my own."

"How do people contact you?"

"They don't." Sasha closed the passenger door and gathered her bags from the backseat. "See you around," she said before slamming the back door and turning to the house.

Drumming his fingers on the steering wheel, Cole waited for Sasha to go up the front walk, but she stood frozen in place. He unrolled the window which sent a cascade of snow tumbling onto the passenger seat. "Aren't you going to put your groceries on the steps?"

"Aren't you going to leave?"

Cole clenched his fists around the wheel and forced himself to combat breathe. *In, two, three, four... Hold, two, three, four... Out, two, three, four... Hold, two, three, four...* With a groan, he rolled up the window and put his car in gear. Waving to Sasha's back, he pulled from the curb and turned down the next street. He took the next left, then the next, until he was driving towards the Victorian house again. As he edged towards the quiet intersection, he spied Sasha marching down the sidewalk with her bags in tow.

He inched his car forward, keeping pace with her, following a block behind. "Where are you going?" he said as he popped the chewed pen in his mouth. He could not believe her obstinacy as she kept walking, block after block in the blowing cold. When she turned right, Cole bit into the pen. "Please, no. Get on a bus, just keep walking... Anything."

Sasha turned.

"Sash, what are you doing?" Swallowing hard, Cole crept past the house where a man had cracked two of his girlfriend's ribs on one occasion and burned her ear with a lighter on another. He glanced right, down the alley where a stabbing victim had spit blood in Cole's eye. Up ahead loomed the house that Sanchez from Narcotics suspected was a meth lab. Sasha trudged past them all, shifting the bags in her arms as she shuffled down Saxton Lane.

The pen splintered in Cole's teeth. "Dammit," he said, wiping ink from his lips. His fingers drummed the wheel as he tried to avert his eyes from the scene sprawled out before him: broken down houses with old appliances littering their yards; teenagers in track pants, shivering in the cold, passing a cigarette around; ravens scavenging from a trash can, garbage scattered around them; a woman up ahead viciously kicking a car door. Cole rubbed the back of his neck. His car was too polished for this neighborhood, and it started to turn heads.

Cole trained his eyes on Sasha as she turned up a walk. "Sasha, no." He bumped over a pothole and Sasha disappeared behind a busted door. His stomach clenched as his foot jammed down on the gas pedal. Turning out of the Sax, he watched the destitute neighborhood fade in his rear-view mirror as he left Sasha behind.

Chapter 8

Cole staggered up the stairs of the police station as images of Sasha being swallowed by the busted house whirled through his head. He pushed past officers and fell into the chair at his desk.

"You do know what it means to have a day off, don't you?"

Cole yanked his hand from the mouse and spun around. "Oh hey, Sandy. I thought of some stuff regarding a file, and I knew that if I didn't deal with it today, I'd go crazy during my days off. I'm not staying long."

"Sure, sure." Sandy laughed as she shifted the court packages under her arm and turned from Cole. "That's what you always say."

Cole's eyes followed Sandy as she crossed the bullpen and sat down at her desk. Phones rang and officers' voices droned, but Cole's mind was humming with thoughts heavy enough to kill all sounds. Turning back to his computer, he popped a pen in his mouth and reached for the mouse.

The keys felt stiff, like they were fighting back, as Cole began entering passwords. The input screen opened, and Cole hesitated, his fingers hovering over the keyboard.

With a steadying breath, he punched Sasha's name into the system. The screen filled in. Five entries stared back. The pen flattened between his teeth.

Disturbing the Peace... Disturbing the Peace... Domestic...

He scanned the dates, and his shoulders relaxed when he saw that the last file was created over a decade ago. As he reread the list, his jaw clenched at the memory of Sasha's dad being led away in handcuffs, and the next day when Sasha showed up at school, hair parted to the left and falling over the makeup-covered bruise on her cheek.

The cursor hovered over the first entry. The noose of guilt tightened around Cole's neck.

He closed out of the system.

Pulling up the search engine, Cole typed in *Lashburn Public Works*. He glanced around the bullpen and waited for two officers to pass before he reached for the phone. His leg bounced as the ring tone buzzed in his ear.

"Public Works. This is Craig."

"Mr. Patterson," Cole said. "This is Officer Cole Dawson from the Lashburn Police. I'm working on an investigation and am looking for some information on an employee of yours."

"Oh?"

"Sasha Cooper." Cole glanced around the room again, the hammering of his heart drowning out the chatter of officers.

"Sasha Cooper? The name sounds vaguely familiar, but she doesn't work in my department."

"What?" Cole fell into the back of his chair like he had been shot. "What about this summer? You had additional staff for landscaping and grounds work, correct?"

"Yeah, I managed twenty-two seasonal workers this summer."

"Was Sasha on your summer staff roster?"

"Not a Sasha. I had a Hayley Cooper. Solid worker. Nice gal. But no Sasha Cooper."

Cole snatched the pen and chewed it feverishly. "I'm sorry to have troubled you, Mr. Patterson. If you happen to recall where you may have heard Ms. Cooper's name, please give me a call." With a groan, he ripped the pen from his mouth and hurled it at the corkboard above his desk.

Pulling up the police database again, Cole typed in *51 Saxton Lane*. His stomach knotted as the screen filled with entries. Domestic Assault. Disturbing the Peace. Drug Possession. He scanned the dates—at least two years old—and let out a rush of air. *Her house is safe. Her house is safe. Her house is...* The phone jumped to life.

"Officer Dawson."

"It's Craig Patterson. We spoke just a moment ago."

Cole bolted upright. "Mr. Patterson. What can I do for you?"

"That name—Sasha Cooper—it was bugging me as I'm sure I've heard it before. I looked into my old employee files and Sasha did in fact work for me this past summer. Her file lists her legal name as Sasha Cooper, although everyone knew her as Hayley. Even I forgot about the name as only accounting used her legal name to issue her checks."

"Hayley? What the..." Cole scrambled for a pen with an intact ink chamber and jotted down *Hayley*. After a pause, he added *Magda* and *Sasha*.

"Do you still have Sasha's—Hayley's—application form?" Cole squeezed his eyes shut as his breach of policy smothered him.

"I'm looking at it now."

"What does she list for prior employment?"

"It's actually pretty impressive; she was an easy hire. It's all out near the coast. Fruit picker at Delburne Orchards, head gardener at Primrose Greenhouses, vineyard worker at Oasis Wines, seasonal landscaper with the town of Stanley, and again with the town of Prairie Roots. She's got experience. I hired her on the spot. Her knowledge is solid, and she works hard. I told her she has a job next summer if she wants one."

"And what did she say to that offer?"

"Not interested. She moved back west after the summer was over. Said she had a job at a greenhouse."

"But she…" Cole rubbed his eyes as the house in the Sax took center stage in his mind. "And for her employment history, did she list any northern communities?"

"No. It's all out west."

"What did she list as her most recent employment?"

"That'd be Delburne Orchards near Ashton. February to September of last year."

Cole scrawled the information down, his mind trying to grasp dates of when Sasha worked out west and when she must have returned to Lashburn. "What was her employment period with you?"

"She started April twenty-fourth, and her last day was September twenty-second."

"What about her contact information?" Cole said, glancing around again.

"Address is Two-Thirty-One Magnolia Street in Lashburn."

Shaking his head, Cole jotted down the address as well as the phone number that Craig was rattling off.

"Did she list an email address?"

"She left that field blank. She also didn't list anyone as an emergency contact. I should have flagged that field and tracked Hayley down for the information, but the spring was so busy, I didn't get around to it and then I forgot about it until just now."

"Anything else out of the ordinary on the application?"

"That's the gist of it, other than her Social Security number. Do you need that? I can scan and email the application to you if it helps."

"No, but thanks. You've been more than helpful." The guilt stuck like tar in the pit of his stomach.

"Officer," Craig said, "Hayley's not in trouble, is she?"

"Not in the least. We just need to get in touch with her about something, but I appreciate your concern. Thank you again for your assistance."

Picking up the phone again, Cole punched in the phone number that Sasha had written on her Public Works application. A moment later, he was listening to an automated weather report.

Cole plunked his coffee on his desk and reached for the files that had stacked up during his time off.

"Mornin', Daws."

"Mornin', Frankie," Cole mumbled as he flipped through the top file.

"You have some good downtime on your days off?"

"Not really."

"Looks like you're going to be a lot of fun to be around today. Want to start the day with a patrol?"

"Yeah, sure." Cole tossed the papers on his desk and shrugged his jacket on. "Let's go." He followed Frank out the back door of the building and trudged through the parking lot where police cars were lined up like soldiers ready for battle.

"What's gotten into you?" Frank asked as he pulled the car onto the road.

The cold had already breached Cole's patrol jacket and raised goosebumps across his chest. "It's freaking cold today," he said and cranked up the heat.

Frank glanced at his partner.

Cole powered up the in-car computer and jostled the radio from its mount. "Control, this is Echo-Four-Five. Martinelli four-four-six-two and Dawson five-two-one-nine are ten-forty-one." As Control confirmed the message, Cole slipped his gloves from his hands, flipped open his notebook, and scrawled the date and time at the top of a fresh page.

"Out with it."

"With what?" Cole said as he tucked his notebook into his vest pocket.

"It. Whatever *it* is."

Stuffing his hands into his gloves, Cole sunk into his seat. He rubbed the back of his neck and stared out the window at office workers and shoppers filing in and out of tall buildings. "I have a friend. I think she's in trouble, but I don't know how to help her."

"What kind of trouble?"

"She's… I don't know." Cole ran his hands over his face as various names pinged around in his head. "She doesn't know I know about her problem. In fact, she's doing everything possible to keep me in the dark, and I keep going back and forth about what I should do."

Frank glanced at Cole as he took a right at the museum. "Is she doing something illegal? Or dangerous?"

"No. She's completely clean when it comes to the law, and although she's not doing anything dangerous, her situation has the potential to become dangerous."

"And she doesn't want you to know?"

"She's going to great lengths to keep me in the dark."

"Then how do you know about her situation?"

74

Turning to Frank, Cole furrowed his brow. "I'm a police officer; intuition and investigation is who I am. Plus, I've known her my entire life and can see through her."

"And she's a grown woman with a stable mind?"

"Yeah."

"And what might happen if you tell her that you know her secrets?"

"I don't know." Cole leaned his head into the headrest. "She's vanished twice before with no trace and I'm worried that if I upset her, she'll run again, and her problems would only compound. She's put herself off the grid, so finding her would be nearly impossible if that's what she wanted. I have this nagging feeling I'm all she's got."

"You're all she's got, yet she's withholding information from you?"

Cole closed his eyes and nodded.

"Do you think maybe you're overthinking this?"

"No. I mean..."

"As a police officer, you *are* investigation and intuition, but you are also programmed to serve and protect. Do you think maybe your need to help is overshadowing *her* needs?"

Cole shook his head as he watched a woman struggle with a grocery cart loaded with garbage bags. "It's not like that. She needed me when we were kids, and I failed her. Popping back in my life is my chance to do for her what I couldn't do when we were little."

"My point exactly. From the sounds of it, she wants to be left alone. It might be wise to simply be there as a friend who she can turn to rather than calling her out on something she is trying to keep private. Why'd she vanish twice, anyway?"

"I don't know. She had a screwed-up homelife growing up, so my guess is she wanted a fresh start. That was the first time she disappeared. The second time was, well..." Cole shifted in his seat as he felt the heat of Sasha's breath on his neck, her hands on his body. "I don't really want to get into it. It's not important."

Slowing to a stop at a red light, Frank shook his head and chuckled. "Daws, you are a terrible liar."

Chapter 9

Jane breathed in a blend of oil, seared meat, and bleach as she scraped leftover eggrolls and ginger beef into a box. A peaceful silence had replaced the clattering of pans and shouts from the chef, and the kitchen rested in wait for tomorrow's rush. Turning back to the sink, Jane dumped the final wok into the soapy water and started to scrub.

"Two more weeks," she said to the greasy water. "If I work another six shifts..." The numbers rolled through her head. "...then I should have enough. But..."

Jane's gaze drifted to her new coat—a warm friend waiting on a hook by the back door. Her mouth turned up at the corner as she pictured Sasha strutting down the thrift store aisle in a hideous rainbow jacket while Cole clutched his stomach, laughing.

"No," she said, plunging her hand into the water. "Stick to the plan. Sasha sucks, anyway." Tensing her hand around the scrubber, Jane scoured the dark spot left from thousands of orders of Szechuan beef. "Six more shifts and then you're free. But..." She paused and stared at the cement wall in front of her. "Maybe nine more shifts..."

The dish water gurgled down the drain as Jane stacked dried pans into precarious towers. As she draped the wet cloth over a hanger, she glimpsed Mrs. Chen playfully tap Mr. Chen on the bottom with her broom. Jane pursed her lips as an image of Cole swatting Sasha on the butt with his backpack welled up from her forbidden memories...

"...Aced it," Cole said, swinging his backpack over his shoulder.

"I knew you could do it." Sasha looped her arm through Cole's and led him out the school doors. "You need to have more faith in yourself."

"Easy for you to say. Math comes easy to you. Thanks for helping me study. As a thank you, I will treat us to slushies on the way home."

"With soft serve on top?"

"That's disgusting, Sash. But for you, anything..."

"No." Jane shook her head and marched towards her coat. As her fingers curled around the faux-fur hood, she hesitated.

"Mr. Chen," she called, spinning on her heels and scurrying across the restaurant. "Mr. Chen, may I please use the phone?" Sasha pointed to the phone, then to herself. "Phone? Please?"

"Ah, yes, yes."

Sasha grasped the receiver, and her finger hovered over the numbers like they might bite her. Forcing her finger to the pad, she punched in Cole's number. The ringing reverberated in her ear as she hugged the phone to her face and stared at the tile floor. "You can't do this," she said and pulled the phone from her ear, but a voice through the air made her pause. Squeezing her eyes shut, Sasha brought the phone back to her ear.

"Hello?" His voice was like a light switch in a dark room.

"Hey. It's me. Sasha."

"Oh hey, Sash. How's it going? It's great to hear from you. I was starting to think you lost my number."

"It's all right," Sasha said, blinking back unexpected tears.

"Are you okay? Do you need me to come get you?"

"No, I'm good, but thanks."

"Because if you need me, or need anything, I'll come for you."

"You're so nice," Sasha said, rubbing her eyes. "I'll be okay. I'm okay. I promise."

"You're just calling to chat? Or…"

"I don't know. I guess I just wanted to say hi. What are you up to?"

"Me? I'm at work."

"Oh my gosh. I'm so sorry. I didn't think… I'll let you go."

"Don't hang up. I'm happy you called. Yeah, I'm at work, but I'm just at my desk, cleaning up some files. Honestly, I'm free to talk. If I get a call I'll have to go, but until then I can talk."

Sasha faded into the wall as quiet Mandarin chatter floated through the air.

"Where are you calling from?"

"I'm at a restaurant. I was just about to leave but thought I'd call you first."

"A restaurant? Nice. Which one?"

"Just a little Chinese place. They make the best eggrolls."

"And how are you getting home?"

"Walking. It's only a few blocks from my place. I'll be fine." Sasha straightened menus into a neat stack while she listened to dead air.

"I'll come get you. I don't like you walking alone in the dark."

"No!" Sasha's eyes went wide, and the menus slipped from her fingers. "I'm here with one of my roommates and we're walking home together. It's a nice night and we're looking forward to the fresh air."

"Sasha…" A groaning sigh carried over the line. "I'll come get you and your roommate and I'll take you both back home. Or I'll drop her off and you can stay at my place. For a change of scenery, I mean. It's an option. If you need it. Or want it." Dropping his voice, Cole added, "I'd like it if you stayed over."

Sasha closed her eyes. Every molecule pulled her towards Cole's warm home, safe walls, and calming smile. "No, really. Gina and I are good on our own, but thanks for the offer. I don't really know why I even called you. Gina's waiting and I should get back to her."

"Wait. What are you doing tomorrow?"

"Tomorrow? I work."

"I'm on nights this week. If you can get a break from work around three, I'd love to take you for a late lunch. Meet you for lunch. Whatever. I can pick you up from work if you like."

"That's not why I called. I can't. I just…"

"My treat. I'm excited to see you again and I'd love to take you out."

Her body suddenly lead, Sasha slumped against the wall. The memory of Cole's hand wrapped around hers sent a glow through her. She picked up a fortune cookie from the basket by the till and cracked it open. As she nibbled a piece of cookie, she slid the paper from the other half.

A thrilling time is in your immediate future.

"These dang cookies," she said under her breath.

"What was that?"

"Nothing." Tucking the fortune into her pocket, Sasha said, "I guess I could do that. I'm supposed to work until four, but I can probably end my day at three and just make up the lost hour another time. Craig's usually pretty good with stuff like that."

"Sasha, can you just please…"

Sasha stared at the floor. The hushed air was broken by a heavy sigh. "That sounds great. Can I pick you up from work?"

"I'm actually doing research for work at the downtown library. How about we meet there? I'll be waiting on the front steps at three."

"I will be there. I was worried that you'd never call. Thank you for calling. And are you sure I can't give you a ride tonight? I'd feel better knowing you weren't walking home at this hour."

"I'll be fine, but thanks for the offer. I'd better let you get back to work."

Cole sighed again. "Okay. I'll see you tomorrow. Three o'clock at the downtown library. Take care, my Sasha."

Sasha returned the phone to the wall as lights around her went out one by one. With the boxed dinner hugged to her chest and the rest of the cookie stuffed in her mouth, she pulled her hood over her head, nestled her face deep into her coat, and heading for the bus stop. As snow crunched under her boots, her eyes darted down dark alleys and into shadowy doorways of shuttered buildings.

Her mind whipped through calculations—two weeks versus three weeks.

Her hand curled around the frayed business card that she clutched inside her mitt.

Cole drummed the steering wheel and glanced at the clock again. "Come on, Sash. Don't leave me hanging."

The library doors opened a crack, and half a face peered out before the door drifted closed. Crossing his arms over his chest, Cole furrowed his brow and locked his eyes on the door. The sunlight's reflection shifted on the glass, the door cracked again, and Sasha slipped out.

"Hey," she said as she popped open the passenger door. "Sorry I'm late."

"No worries. You get tied up with work?"

"Yeah. I was going through a mountain of material and lost track of time."

"It can happen," Cole said as he pulled from the library. "Where do you want to go for lunch?"

"I don't care. You pick."

"Have you been to Juicy Burger? They make huge patties, and you can put whatever you like on your burger. It's one of those create-it-yourself types of places. Every order comes with a mountain of fresh-cut fries."

"Mm. I love burgers. I haven't had one in… I have no idea how long. Burgers sound great, but I feel bad that you're treating me again."

"This was my idea and I'm happy to pay, so please don't worry about it."

Nodding, Sasha looked out the window. "This is nice."

"It is nice." Cole reached across the seat and squeezed Sasha's hand. "I'm glad you could come."

Cheeks pink from the cold, Cole and Sasha stomped snow from their boots as they breathed in grilled meat and fried onions. A man behind the counter restocked tomato slices in a silver tray while a table of teens erupted in laughter in the far corner of the restaurant.

"What are you going to get?" Cole asked.

"I don't know," Sasha said as her eyes flew over the chalkboard menu. "What are you getting?"

"I always get The Works, except I leave out the pickles and double the jalapenos. You can basically build whatever burger you want."

"I guess I'll do that, but I like pickles, and I don't like spicy food."

"What about a drink?"

"I'm okay without. Or whatever you want to get."

Stifling a grimace, Cole said, "Why don't you find a table and I'll get our orders going."

"Where do you want to sit?" she asked as she scanned the restaurant.

"You pick. Just leave me the chair facing the door."

Cole watched Sasha shuffle around tables and plop down by a window. Turning to the man working the counter, he said, "I'll get two of The Works. One with pickles and one without, and neither with jalapenos."

With burgers prepped, Cole balanced the trays and made his way to Sasha. "Dig in," he said and slid her food towards her. He wriggled a piece of lettuce out from his burger and laid it beside her fries.

"What's with the lettuce?"

"Lettuce romaine friends forever."

"Oh my gosh, Cole. You really are a dork." Shaking her head, Sasha picked up the lettuce and slid it under her bun. "Joke's on you—I now get your lettuce."

"Fair enough. So, are your plans to stay in Lashburn for good now?" he said as took the top bun off his burger and dumped ketchup on the innards.

"I don't know," Sasha said and stuffed an escaping pickle back into her burger. "There are more of my kinds of jobs out west, with a longer growing season. I can find indoor work if I have to, but I don't like it as much."

"How are you enjoying being back in Lashburn? Besides the work, I mean."

Sasha shrugged and bit into her burger. She looked at the ceiling as she chewed, like she was a contestant on a game show searching for the right answer. "There's not as much for me to do here in my down time. Out west, I'd go for a hike at least once a week. I also love the ocean. I could spend hours there, either walking the beach, trying to find things that had washed up, or I'd just sit and watch the shorebirds chase the waves. It's easy to find places with no people around on the coast. In Lashburn, I really like the library; it's the biggest one I've been to. The parks are nice too, but there's too much concrete and way too many people."

"If you do head back, can you promise you'll tell me this time? It almost killed me not knowing what happened to you after prom. I actually thought maybe your dad did something to you."

Sasha froze, her fingers indenting her bun.

"Sash?"

A low growl emanated from Sasha. "Can we please change the subject?" she said, staring at her fries.

"Sorry. What uh… What are you researching for work?"

"Just stuff." She sucked in a lungful of air and let the breath slowly leave her. "Plants and stuff. Landscaping ideas for next year. Craig is thinking of changing up some of the planters and beds around the city and wanted me to look into ideas that other cities have tried. I don't want to bore you with the details. Let's talk about your job. I'm sure it's loads more exciting than putting some plants in the ground."

Cole put his burger down and smiled. "I always loved watching you in your little garden. I'd spend hours at my bedroom window with my sketchbook while you tinkered. Planting might not give you the sudden rush of adrenaline that tackling a criminal to the ground does, but there is something special about what you do. I wouldn't belittle it."

Reaching for the salt, Sasha tucked a strand of hair behind her ear and smiled before losing herself in her lunch. As she worked through her burger, a comfortable silence settled between her and Cole.

"I've been wondering something, Sash. After so long on the coast, what brought you back to Lashburn?"

As salt pounded her fries like a tiny hailstorm, Sasha's smile dropped from her face. "A guy."

"Oh," Cole said, his body wilting. "You followed a guy here?"

"I came here to get away from a guy."

The chatter from other tables, the sizzling of beef, the ringing of the till all faded as though a bubble had formed around Cole and Sasha. "What do you mean?"

"It's nothing."

Cole searched Sasha's face, but she was lost again. "What guy did you need to get away from? And why?"

Sasha sipped her root beer until the final drops slurped up the straw. She pulled her lips away and shook the cup, the rattling of ice cubes piercing the stuffy air.

Cole dropped his mangled fries and slid his hand around Sasha's. Her fingers were cold and damp, and Cole rubbed her hand as he spoke. "What happened? Please tell me."

"It was nothing, really. Just a guy I was with. I thought he was the best thing ever. He was really good looking and had loads of money, and I couldn't believe it when he showed interest in me."

"And?"

"And what?" Sasha slid her hand away and reached for a fry.

"What happened that made you need to get away from him?"

"I'm probably blowing things out of proportion," she said as she chewed. "He was great, actually. He treated me like a princess. I moved in with him and I actually thought he was the one I was going to spend my life with."

"But..."

Sasha nibbled potato skin while staring at the Juicy Burger logo on her napkin. "But then things got weird. He got weird. Maybe he was weird from the start, and I just didn't see it. Anyway, one day something happened that made me need to leave, so I did."

Cole stared at Sasha's gentle features, and his hands curled into fists. Forcing his voice to remain soft, he said, "What happened? What did he do?"

Sasha shrugged and, reaching for another fry, turned to the window. Snow had started to fall and heavy snowflakes smothered the cars in the parking lot. "He got mad. It was my fault as I did something he told me not to do. Anyway, he got mad and… Well, after that, I needed to get away."

"What did he do to you?"

Keeping her eyes trained out the window, Sasha grabbed another fry and stuffed it in her mouth.

"Sasha." Cole glanced around the restaurant before leaning in close. "Did he hurt you?"

Sasha lifted her eyes and locked them on Cole's. He searched their perfect blueness; she narrowed her eyes as she stared back. "It was only once but it bothered me enough that I decided to leave."

"This is not right." Cole shifted to the seat next to Sasha and wrapped his arm around her. "Did you report it to the police?"

A single laugh fell from Sasha as she reached for her empty cup and sucked up the little bit of water from the melted ice. "It was no big deal, plus it was kind of my fault as I made him upset. It was only the one time and then I left, so there really was nothing to call the police about. Not like the police would do anything anyway."

"It was absolutely not your fault. If someone strikes you, it is never your fault. *You* know that. And he assaulted you, so there is definitely reason to call the police."

"Let's just drop it."

"What's his name?"

As though a storm had erupted inside, Sasha slammed the empty cup to the table and shrugged out of Cole's embrace. "I shouldn't have told you. I'm sorry to bother you with my boring life."

Cole grasped her hands. She stiffened and her eyes darted to the exit.

"I'm glad you told me. What's his name? Where does he live?"

"I don't want to talk about it anymore," Sasha said and ripped her hands from Cole's. "It's in the past and I've moved on, so can we please just drop it? I shouldn't have told you. I don't know why I did."

"This is serious. You need to report him, and if you're not comfortable talking to me about it, then you should talk to someone else."

"I've got to go." She spun in her chair and fumbled with the sleeve of her coat.

"Sasha, don't."

Breathing like she had just hiked a mountain, Sasha stood from the table. "I have to go."

"I'm done talking. Stay. Just for a little longer. Please, my Sasha."

Sasha paused. With one coat sleeve on, she looked at Cole.

"Please."

She glanced at the exit again before sinking into her chair. Swiveling in her seat to face the window, Sasha grabbed her burger. A glob of ketchup landed on her jeans, leaving a red stain. She ignored it as she watched the snow fall and demolished her food.

"I had breakfast only a couple of hours ago," Cole said, poking at his burger. "Do you want the rest of my food?"

"No, thank you. It's yours."

"It's too hard to eat a burger on shift. You can have it. If you don't want it, I'll just toss it."

Sasha stared at Cole's food like it was abandoned treasure. "That's being wasteful. If you're just going to throw it out, then I may as well take it." As she pulled his burger towards her, she ran her finger through a dollop of ketchup and stuffed more fries in her mouth.

"How about dessert?" Cole asked, tapping her foot under the table.

"We should go."

"I don't work till seven. We have time to do something else if you want."

"We've had a long enough visit. I need to go."

"A long enough... what? What's that supposed to mean?"

Hugging the leftovers to her chest, Sasha stumbled from her seat and hurried towards the exit.

"Sasha, wait," Cole called, catching up to her. "Sorry. If you have to go, then we'll go. To the Maples, I take it?"

"I'm going to head back to the library and finish up my last hour of work."

"Sasha." Cole grabbed her arm and spun her around. He held on tight even as she pulled against him. "Let me take you home with me. For a place to stay."

"No," she said as she wrenched herself away and pushed through the door. "I can't."

"Why not? Talk to me."

Sasha shook her head as she marched through the parking lot. "Please take me to the library. Or I can walk."

"Okay, fine," Cole said, throwing his hands up. "You win. Off to the library we go."

As Cole drove through light downtown traffic, Sasha kept herself pressed to the door, her lips making silent words. The moment Cole slid the gearshift into park, Sasha's hand flew to the handle.

"Wait," Cole said and grabbed her arm.

Her mitted hand stiffened on the handle.

"I'd really like it if you called me again, either just to talk or to meet up. And if you ever need help of any kind, remember that I'll always come for you." Cole glanced at the melting snowflakes that landed on his windshield before turning back to Sasha. "I'm sorry if I brought up difficult memories. I'm just trying to get to know you again and sometimes our conversations lead the wrong way."

Sasha shook her head and popped the door open. "Thank you for lunch. And for the ride. But you probably shouldn't get to know me again."

Chapter 10

Magda shimmied from the soft spot on the mattress, causing a small avalanche of bills to leave their stacks spread out before her.

"Six-hundred and eighteen dollars and ninety-five cents," she said as she returned the rogue bills to their piles. "It's enough. Plus, with two more shifts before the end of the month…"

After sweeping the money into the plastic baggy, Magda tucked it under her pillow. She shifted again when a wire spring jabbed her in the bottom, but a hollow spot pitched her to the side. "Stupid piece of…" She rolled to the floor with a thud.

With a warm bottle of Lucky Duck pressed to her lips, Magda grabbed an outdated gardening magazine from under a dirty sock and flipped it open. *I wonder what Cole is doing…*

"Get a grip," she said, wiping her lip with her sleeve. "You're Magda. You don't care about him."

As she skimmed an article on xeriscaping, the corner of the baggy poked out from under her pillow and whispered to her. Magda glanced sideways at the baggy before returning her attention to the magazine. She put the bottle to her lips and sucked back a mouthful, but the money called to her again. Narrowing her eyes, she looked at the baggy. "Six hundred," she murmured, forehead wrinkling, "minus the cost of the bus ticket. And what if hostel prices go up in December…" She swigged the wine, her eyes still on the bag. "…And how easy is it to find work just before Christmas…"

Magda yanked the pillow over the baggy and turned a page, tearing the magazine. "Stick to the plan."

Glancing over an ad for fertilizer, she reached for the last of Cole's cheese from the gap in the frozen window and nibbled on it as she turned the page. The wine bottle slipped from her grasp and her hand flew to her face as she stared at a swan gliding through still waters. She was back in the bedroom in Ashton, her cheek stinging as Curtis stood over her, his hands balled in fists.

The magazine bent under her grasp as wine glugged from the forgotten bottle onto the floor. "Leave me alone, Curtis. I'm not Bryn anymore." She chucked the magazine across the room and buried her face in her knees.

"You're useless!"

Bryn's eyes few open. Muffled shouts filled the air, and a loud thump shook the shared wall. Cheese squished in her fist.

"This is easy! An idiot could do it!"

Bryn sprang to her feet, a puddle of cheap wine soaking her sock.

"I'm sorry. I wasn't thinking!" A woman's stifled cries were a sword through Bryn's guts, twisting and screwing.

Bryn grasped the window frame and waited for the spinning room to steady. Musty air stuck in her lungs, and she strained to breathe. Jamming the cheese in her mouth, she grabbed the baggy of money, shoved it into her coat pocket, and slipped from the house.

Bryn scurried down the darkened streets, her hooded head down. As she bustled past a group of men, a skunky smell stuck in her nose.

The men laughed, hooted, and whistled. "Where are you going, gorgeous? I've got a warm place for you."

The sweet rumble of a bus drifted down the street. Forcing down tears, Bryn hurried across the road as the bus doors sighed open. "Does this bus go downtown?"

"It does, but it'll be a while," the driver said. "We go through the Maples, Brookview, and down Caraway before we head downtown."

With the baggy secreted deep in her pocket, Bryn's fingers counted out the right change. The bus pulled from the curb, leaving the Sax behind. She stumbled down the aisle and crumpled into a seat as the voices and thumping from the house buzzed in her head.

Burying her face in her mitts, Bryn saw Curtis again: his eyes, smile, and hands. Memories swarmed her mind and sent her heart racing as Curtis's aftershave burned her nose, and his voice whispered in her ear...

... *"Perfetto," Curtis whispered as he fastened the necklace around Bryn's neck; goosebumps raised beneath his touch. He pressed a kiss to the soft curve where her neck met her shoulder...*

... *"Dammit!" he roared. The bottle of raki exploded into hundreds of pieces when it hit the wall. Curtis grabbed a chair and launched it across the kitchen. A piercing crack echoed throughout the house...*

... *"I'm not going to stop spoiling you, pumpkin. You are mine forever." Bryn squealed and threw her arms around Curtis. He nuzzled her neck while balancing the drink in his hand.*

... *"Why are you not wearing the clothes I bought for you, Bryn?" he said as he pressed her against the wall. "Do you not appreciate my gifts? You are my swan, and swans do not spend time in a vegetable patch, they do not rake leaves, and they don't wear jeans with holes." He tightened his grip on her wrists and forced his thumbs into the soft spaces between tendon and bone...*

The rattling of the bus jolted Bryn. The buildings of downtown Lashburn rose around her, the streetlights casting flickering patterns across her face. "How close does this bus get to One-Oh-Six Street?" she called to the driver.

"This is about it. I head down One Hundredth and then we leave downtown."

Scanning the empty streets, she waited a few more blocks before scuttling off the bus.

High-rises towered over her as she trudged through the snow, her face burrowed deep in her coat. As Sasha slipped through the door, the tension in her shoulders released.

Sasha punched Cole's number into the keypad. One ring. Two rings. Three and four. Voicemail. Shoulders slumping. Tension returning.

"Hey," Sasha said into the air. "It's me, Sasha. I'm at your place. I don't know why. I guess I didn't feel like being home tonight and I didn't know where else to go. Maybe you're not home."

Leaning against the wall, Sasha tried the number again, the metal buttons cold and hard under her fingertips, Cole's recorded voice detached and distant. Keeping the tears jammed deep inside, she ended the call.

Sasha shoved her hands into her mitts and slid down the wall until she hit the floor. Her lids were heavy as sandbags as Curtis's eyes, voice, and scent infected her mind. *Leave me alone. I'm not yours anymore.* Tucking her legs in close, she rested her forehead on her knees and waited.

Chapter 11

Cole rounded the corner, streetlights sweeping across the hood of the car, and cranked the volume on Queen, but an onslaught of curses and insults drowned out the lyrics. He glanced in the rear-view mirror at the man rocking around in his backseat as he steered the police car down deserted streets and past the occasional frosted car parked for the night.

"You're a tough guy, are you?" Frank yelled as he scrawled notes into his notebook.

Adrenalin shakes starting to subside, Cole steadied his breathing as the taste of iron lingered in his throat. "Keep at it," he said. "The more energy you burn off now, the easier it'll be to haul you into your cell."

As Cole entered the downtown core, the police radio crackled to life. "We have a report of a suspicious person loitering at One-Oh-Six-Eight, Ninety-Two Avenue. Are there any patrols in the area?"

Frank looked up from his notebook. "Isn't that near your place?"

"That *is* my place. If it wasn't for our friend in the backseat, I'd be all over that call."

"This is Echo Five Four," a voice buzzed over the radio. "We'll take the call."

"Murph?" Cole asked, raising his eyebrows and glancing at Frank. "Murph."

The darkness of the sleeping city was left behind as Cole pulled the car into the station's bay. Florescent lights screamed down on him as he slid from the vehicle and waited for the overhead doors to seal them in. "Okay, buddy," he said and popped open the back door. "Let's find you a bed for the night."

The handcuffed man fought against Cole's grasp and curses bounced off the concrete walls. Cole's muscles were on fire as he applied a wrist lock and dug his heels into the floor. "Stop resisting!" As they stumbled through the doorway, the man went limp.

"We've got a fighter, do we?" the cells Sergeant said as he helped the officers pull the flaccid noodle to his feet.

The profanities and the Sergeant's voice disappeared down the hall. Straightening his uniform, Cole dragged his body up the stairs behind Frank.

Like the rest of the world, the bullpen was quiet, other than the clicking of a keyboard from an officer on the far side of the room. Cole slumped into his chair and slid his notebook from his vest just as his shift cellphone rang.

"Officer Dawson."

"Hey, Daws. It's Murphy. Did you hear the call regarding the suspicious person at your building?"

"Yeah. What's that about?"

"Well, it's a young woman who was sleeping in the vestibule. She says she was waiting for you to come home."

Cole's heart spiked, and he bolted upright. "Is she okay?"

"So, you know her."

"It's Sasha, right?" Cole stumbled from his chair and motioned to Frank.

"That's what her ID says, although it's been expired for over two years. Initially she kept insisting her name was Magda. If she's some weird stalker or something, just say the word and I'll get rid of her, but I figured I may as well call you first."

"Keep her there. I'll be right over. Is she okay?"

"Yeah, she's okay. Nice enough girl, but nervous as all hell. Like I said, I can deal with her. I just wanted to check her story."

"I'm coming," Cole said and pushed through the door. "I'll see you in a few."

"What's going on?" Frank said as he slid into the passenger seat.

"It's my friend—the girl I've been telling you about. Murphy's at the call with the suspicious person, and that person just happens to be Sasha. She was sleeping in the vestibule, waiting for me to come home."

"Is she all right?"

"Murph says she's okay, but I have no idea why she showed up at my place. I forgot my phone at home and if she's been trying to reach me all night…"

With police lights pulsing atop his car, Cole cranked the wheel, pulling the car from its tail slide as he swerved out of the lot.

"Take it easy," Frank said as his eyes shifted between Cole and the streets. "Sasha's not going anywhere, and you won't be any good to her if we don't make it there."

Cole veered around another corner and trained his eyes on his building. A police car was parked out front, blue and red lights dancing on the snowbanks. Cole pulled to the curb and, looking past the officers, locked on Sasha. Only her eyes poked out from layers of winter clothing, and she stared at Cole as her breath condensed in the night air.

"Thanks, Murph. Thanks, Gibbs," Cole said as he joined the trio. "I've got it from here."

Pressing his hand to Sasha's back, Cole guided her out of earshot. "I'm sorry I forgot my phone at home. Did you try calling?"

Eyes wide, Sasha looked Cole up and down. "You look really good."

"What?"

"That uniform. You look a lot bigger in it. Taller too, somehow. And really good."

Cole searched Sasha's face. "Are you okay?"

Dropping her gaze, Sasha hugged herself and stepped into a shadow. "I'm really embarrassed. I shouldn't have come here. I didn't feel like staying at my house tonight, so I got on a bus and found myself here. I'm sorry I'm bothering you guys."

"First of all, you aren't bothering anyone—this is our job. Secondly, I don't blame you for not wanting to stay at your house. I wouldn't want to, either."

Sasha shot a glance at Cole before withering into her hood.

"I'm glad you came here. I hate it that you only call every few weeks because I worry about you, and when I got a call that you were here... I didn't know what to think."

"This is stupid. I'm mortified that the cops showed up and then they had to call you and now there are four of you here, just because I felt like dropping by. I'm sorry. I should go."

"Don't go. You needed to come here, and I want you to stay. I'll take you upstairs and get you settled, but I can't stay as I'm on until seven. We can visit tomorrow, and you can spend another night if you want."

Tiny muscles between Sasha's eyebrows crinkled. "Why are you so nice to me?"

A frown crossed Cole's face, and he tried to read Sasha's poker face. "Because I care about you. You came all this way, so you may as well stay."

"I just... I don't..." Her eyes locked on the snow-packed sidewalk. "Okay."

"Give me a sec," Cole said, turning away. "Frankie," he called, "could you stay with Sasha while I chat with Murphy and Gibbs?"

With a smile, Frank sauntered over.

"Frank," Cole said, "this is my friend, Sasha. Sasha, this is Officer Martinelli, but you can call him Frank. I'll be right back, okay?"

Sasha nodded as Cole squeezed her hand.

"What's her story?" Gibbs asked as Cole joined the pair.

Cole rubbed the back of his neck. "She's a friend of mine from a ways back. She's had some struggles lately and I'm trying to help her get back on her feet. She's a good person, just lost right now. What'd she tell you?"

"Well," Murphy said, "we had to wake her as she was sleeping in the vestibule. She said her name was Magda and skirted all our other questions. When we asked for ID, she said she didn't have any on her. She kept insisting she was waiting for her friend to get home from work, so we asked about her friend. Again, she was skirting questions. I called her bluff, so she finally gave us the name of the person she was visiting. What was that name?" Murphy asked, turning to his partner.

Flipping a page in his notebook, Gibbs read, "Curtis Schakal."

"Right. So, she says she's waiting for her friend, Curtis Schakal. We looked his name up on the tenants list but, surprise-surprise, no one of that name lives here. We started hauling her to the PC but then she blurted out your name. Shocked the hell out of us. I told her I'd call you to confirm her story, and that's when she said her name was Sasha. By this time, we were tired of her stories, so we were going to stuff her in the PC at which point she conveniently remembered she had ID on her, although it's well past expired. Anyway, that's when I called you, and you basically know the rest."

"She has an ID?"

Gibbs slid a card from his vest pocket and handed it to Cole. With his flashlight making Sasha's stoic image glow, Cole analyzed the identification—it looked perfectly legitimate despite it no longer being valid.

"What do you want us to do with her?" Gibbs asked.

Cole looked back at Sasha who was hiding a smile while Frank chatted. "I'm going to take her upstairs. Get her settled in my place, then I'll finish my shift."

Murphy and Gibbs exchanged a look. "Seriously?" Murphy said. "You're taking her up to your place and leaving her there?"

"Yeah, why?"

"She's nice and all, but the way she was giving us false names and skirting our questions... She just doesn't strike me as the type of person you'd leave alone in your place."

"She's had some tough times and some bad luck, but that doesn't make her a bad person; it just makes her someone who needs a friend."

"All right," Murphy said. "I can conclude this file?"

"Yeah, I've got it from here." Cole kicked at a pile of snow before turning towards Sasha and Frank.

"Hey, Frankie. I'm going to take Sasha upstairs. I'll only be a few minutes."

"Sure thing. It was nice to meet you, Sasha."

"Come on. Let's get you inside," Cole said, pocketing Sasha's ID as he held the door open. "You can't be carrying around expired identification, so I can't return it to you. I highly suggest you get a new ID. I can go to the DMV with you if you want."

As they waited for the elevator, Sasha sunk into her coat and stared at the floor. "You look really good," she murmured.

Cole slipped his finger into the break between Sasha's mitt and coat sleeve. Her wrist was soft and smooth, exactly as it had always been.

The moment the elevator doors closed behind them, Cole had his arms around Sasha. "Stay with me," he whispered, his nose pressed into her winter hat. She was a solid rock as the floor moved beneath their feet. As the elevator cracked open, Cole pulled himself away.

Every sound was magnified in the quiet hall in the dead of night: the swish-swish of their pants as they walked; the clunk of their boots on the floor; Cole's baton that bounced in his duty belt; the keys jingling in the lock.

"Sorry I can't stay," Cole said as the door clicked closed behind them, "but I want you to make yourself comfortable. Use my bed; it's more comfortable than the couch. If you're hungry, help yourself to anything in the kitchen, and I mean it. Make yourself an entire carton of eggs if you like."

A pink hue painted Sasha's cheeks, and she looked away.

"There are fresh towels in the linen closet if you want a bath or shower. I'll try to be back in a few hours."

She sucked in a breath and curled her arms around herself.

Meeting Sasha's gaze, Cole adjusted the hat on her head. "You can trust me, you know. If you need help or if you want to tell me something, I'm here for you. There's nothing you can say that will turn me away. Do you believe that?"

Dropping her eyes, Sasha focused on the badge on Cole's chest. "This is hard for me."

"What's hard? Tell me. Let me help."

Beneath the folds of her puffy polyester shell, Sasha's body stiffened. "I just wish Sasha would stay dead," she barely whispered. "The world is better without her."

"The world is... *what?*"

"Nothing."

"It's not nothing."

Sasha bit her lip and tears formed in the corners of her eyes. Shaking her head and clearing her throat, she said, "I'm fine. I just didn't want to be alone tonight, that's all."

Cole pulled Sasha into a hug and rested his chin on her head. "I'm happy you're here. I always feel better when you're here rather than in... the Maples. Just tell me and we'll fix it together. I promise I won't be upset, and I won't judge you."

Sasha melted into Cole's arms and tightened her grip around him, but her lips stayed clamped shut as silent minutes ticked by.

The stillness of the darkened condo was broken when a staticky voice blared over the police radio. "Sorry, Sash, but I've got to go. Frankie's waiting. Make yourself at home. I expect to find an empty fridge when I get back." Smiling at Sasha, Cole traced the line of her jaw. She sucked her lips in and stared ahead at his chest.

With a final hug, Cole slipped into the hall and bounded down the stairs. He pushed open the door that led to the outside world and breathed in a lungful of crisp air.

"How's she doing?" Frank said as Cole fell into the passenger seat.

"She's all right. Stubborn as you can get, though. I practically told her I know she has secrets and that she can trust me with them, but she pretended like nothing's going on."

Frank flicked the signal light and pulled from the curb. "She's a nice girl. You're a good friend."

Cole crossed his arms and furrowed his brow as images of Sasha and the Sax, and a carton of eggs tumbled through his head.

Cole fit his key in the lock and listened for the click. "Be here. Please be here," he whispered. As he eased the door closed behind him, he glanced at the couch. Sasha was curled up under a blanket as fire danced in the fireplace. His heart swelled and a smile relaxed across his face. "Thank you."

After throwing on pajamas, Cole pulled the blanket and pillow from his bed and laid them on the living room floor. He settled onto his makeshift bed and gazed at Sasha—eyes closed; mouth turned down at the corners. As he tucked her blanket around her shoulders, the once-familiar sound of Sasha's door crashing open rung in his ears...

...*Cole jumped to his feet, knocking his science textbook into the garbage can. He pressed his hands to the window as Sasha vaulted off her deck, her dad hot on her heels.*

"My Sasha." Cole burst from his room and tore down the stairs. As he stumbled out the patio door, he caught a glimpse of Mr. Cooper disappearing back into his house.

Under the light of the moon, Cole crept across the deck and peered into Sasha's yard, but everything was dark. Everything was still.

"Sasha!" he whispered, gripping the railing and trying to find a solid shape amongst the shadows. His heart thundered as he slipped down the steps and through the wall of cedars. "Sasha?"

She was curled in the corner, sobs shaking her body.

"Hey, Sash." Cole settled beside her and enfolded her in his arms.

She collapsed into him, her tears soaking his t-shirt. "Stop wasting your time on me. I'm not worth it. You heard him."

"He's so wrong, Sasha. And I'm not wasting my time on you. Not even close. Even when we're wrinkly and gray, I'll be here for you."

"I'm a mess," she said, wiping her eyes and pulling herself from Cole. "I must look pathetic."

"You're beautiful."

"And you're delusional," she said with a sniffle-laugh.

Melding his fingers with hers, Cole steadied his breath. "Did he hurt you?"

"Doesn't matter."

"Of course it matters." His fingertips brushed the fringe of Sasha's hair, but she curled away.

"What about your mom?" Cole said as he tugged the blanket from the bin. It settled over them, a warm barricade against the cold. "Where is she when your dad gets like this?"

"You know she's sick. When she gets one of her headaches, everything's just so..." Sasha pulled the blanket to her chin and wiped her eyes.

"Sick enough that she can't stand up for her kid?"

"Leave her alone. You have no idea."

"And why don't the police do anything? I saw them at your place again a few weeks ago."

"Geez, Cole!" Sasha threw the blanket aside and rummaged through the bin. With a box of cookies gripped in her hands, she said, "Why is this so hard for you to understand? Yeah, he gets mad, but he's not a bad person. Maybe if he didn't have to put up with me."

"It's horseshit. You deserve so much more."

"I deserve what I deserve..."

Cole's eyes cracked open. Sticky with sweat, he spied the flickering fire and pushed himself to sitting. The blanket sat neatly folded on the couch. "Sasha?" he called, scrambling to his feet. "Sasha!"

Cole searched the condo, but she was gone. All that was left of Sasha was the scent of her hair on the folded blanket and a note left beside the coffeemaker:

Sorry I'm not here anymore but I had to go to work, and I didn't want to wake you. Thank you for your kindness and sharing your home with me again. I hope you don't mind, but I took a couple of bananas and granola bars. Also, please apologize to the other cops that I kept them from helping someone who really needed it. I feel terrible, I'm embarrassed, and I want them to know I'm sorry I caused such a commotion. I'll call you soon. Thank you for putting up with me.

— Sasha

Cole crumpled the paper in his fist.

Chapter 12

Cole held his head in his hands as though it would self-combust if he let go.

"I'm so sorry, Cole. I feel terrible."

"Sash, seriously. Nobody's upset. This honestly isn't a big deal."

"But because of me, I took up the time of four cops who could have been helping someone else."

"It's fine. I promise. It's been a week and you're the only person who's still thinking of that night. Let it go."

"I can't."

The conversation looped through his head like a hamster in its wheel, never tiring. He flopped back in bed and rubbed his eyes.

"Let's go for lunch. Dinner maybe. Stay the night. Please."

"No."

Pulling up the search engine on his phone, Cole squinted and dimmed the screen. "Give me something to work with, Sash," he said as he typed in *Chen's Noodle House Lashburn*. Only a Yellow Pages listing popped up.

Groaning, Cole tossed his phone to the side and yanked the blanket over his head. "Why do you keep calling from the same restaurant?" he said to the covers. "Are the eggrolls really that good?"

Cole tossed the gnawed pen on the floor of the police car to join its fallen brothers. He looked at the Noodle House sign outside his window and steadied his voice. "I'll grab the food which will give you some time to work on your notes."

"Sounds good," Frank said as he slid the gearshift into park.

As Cole slipped from the car, an older woman bustled past, her foldable cart bouncing off packed snow while a skinny Santa clanged a bell beside a Salvation Army sign. Cole wrapped his fingers around the cold metal handle of the restaurant's door. "Forgive me, my Sasha, but I need to know."

As Cole cracked the door, he was hit with warm air that smelled of oil and seasonings. Tables were filled with diners talking and laughing, their chopsticks lifting veggies and noodles from plates, while a Christmas tree shimmered in the corner. With a quick turn of his radio's knob, Cole quieted the police chatter.

A man approached him with a smile. "Yes."

"I'd like to order takeout but I'm also looking for some information on a friend of mine. She's called me a few times from your restaurant and I'm trying to figure out why she's here so often."

The man looked blankly at Cole. "No English."

"Sasha," Cole said slowly. "A lady. About this tall."

"No, no English."

"Sa-sha," Cole said. The man stared on.

Planting his hands on his hips, Cole scanned the restaurant. Chinese characters on vertical banners lined the walls; a map of China, labeled with a foreign alphabet, hung near the door; and diners chatted in a language Cole could not understand.

Stifling a groan, Cole caught the movement of the kitchen doors. A teenage girl stepped from the kitchen, bowls of rice balanced expertly on her arms. She glanced towards the front of the restaurant and when her eyes met Cole's, she froze. A moment later, as though someone had hit her reset button, she set the bowls on a table and weaved towards the entrance.

Smoothing her apron, the girl smiled at Cole before turning to the man. A disjointed mix of pauses and lilts flew between the two as Cole tried to follow an incomprehensible discussion.

The man nudged the girl. *"Wèn tā xiǎng yào shénme."*

With a nod, she turned to Cole. "Hello, and welcome to Chen's Noodle House. Can I help you with something? Are you here for food or for... something else? You're welcome to look at our menu for takeout."

"Uh, yeah." The creases across Cole's face smoothed; the sunshine streaming through the windows brightened.

Cole flipped open a menu and glanced over the selections, one side in English and the other with Chinese characters. "I hear your eggrolls are amazing. Also, I'll get a number twenty-four and a forty-six."

"Is that everything?" the girl asked as she scribbled on a notepad.

"That's it for food, but I also have a question about a friend of mine you might know, or at least recognize."

"Let me put your order in, then I'll be back." Spinning on her heels, she scurried through the restaurant and disappeared into the kitchen.

Cole adjusted his stance and smiled at the man who stared up at him. "Busy," Cole said, gesturing to the diners.

"Ah, yes," the man said and motioned towards an empty table. "Sit."

"No, no." Cole took a step back. "I'm getting takeout. I said it's busy in here. Lots of people. Business is good?"

"No English."

Shifting his weight, Cole moved to the map as though it were the most interesting thing in the world. When the girl pushed through the kitchen doors, Cole breathed relief.

"Excuse my father," she said as she joined the men, "but he doesn't speak English."

"Your father is the owner? Mr. Chen?"

"Yes. This is our family's restaurant."

"I don't want to take much of your time. Maybe your father can help me with my problem regarding my friend, if you are able to translate."

"What is it you would like to know?"

"Her name is Sasha. Sasha Cooper. Do you know her?"

"No, I'm sorry."

Mandarin words rolled off the girl's tongue, mixing with her father's shrill speech; Sasha's name jumped out amongst pitches and timbres. Mr. Chen shook his head, and the girl turned back to Cole with a shrug.

"She's twenty-seven years old, this tall," Cole said, holding his hand up again, "light brown hair just past her shoulders, blue eyes... She's called me a few times from your restaurant, and it's always been on a Tuesday night shortly after eleven. Does she happen to work here?"

"Do you mean Jane?"

"Jane?"

"I don't know if it's the lady you are asking about, but we have someone who washes dishes for us three nights a week."

"And she matches the description?"

"Sounds like her. She works hard but doesn't say much—not that there's anyone she can talk to besides me. My brother is the only other one who speaks English but he's not at the restaurant when she is."

"What hours does she work? And how long has she been working here?"

"She starts at six and usually works until eleven, although she sometimes works later if we have late diners. I think she's been here for a month or two."

"Do you mind me asking how much she– Actually, never mind. Thank you for your time. Please don't tell Sash– I mean Jane that I stopped by."

"Sorry I took so long, Frankie," Cole mumbled as he pulled himself into the passenger seat and dropped the bagged food at his feet.

"You all right, Daws?" Frank asked, tucking his notebook into his vest. "You look a little frazzled."

Cole rubbed his eyes and leaned his head against the headrest as he felt the car pull into traffic. "You know those days when you look for answers and all you find are more questions? And even if you do get the answers, there's nothing you can do about the situation anyway? And what you initially hoped would lead you out of a dark tunnel only casts you deeper into it? Well, Frankie, that is my day. That has been my whole freaking life."

Chapter 13

Magda glared at her pack lying in the middle of the barren room, its seams ready to burst. "Go," she said, narrowing her eyes. "You're ready."

Her feet were glued to the floor as air rushed in and out of her nose like a bull staring down a matador. "Don't let Sasha keep you here. Stick to the plan and leave her behind."

Thunderous pounding on the door tore Magda from her stance.

"Mags!" Gina roared through the door.

Scowling, Magda turned her attention back to the bag.

"I know you're there, Mags. You better hand over December's rent or I'm going to send Ian after you."

Magda's fingers curled around the baggy in her pocket. As she stared down her opponent, she said, "No one tells Magda what to do."

Chapter 14

Cole stared out the window as he swirled rum and eggnog in his mouth; it stuck to his tongue like runny custard flavored with turpentine. The trees outside his parents' home cast shadows of monsters on the snow, the glint of Christmas lights their eyes.

And Sasha squealed...

...Ten years old, she bounded through the snow as Cole pelted her with snowballs. She collapsed in laughter and Cole pounced on top of her. Chest heaving, Sasha rolled over and smiled up at him. Her eyes sparkled like the snowflakes that dotted her hood. "What name are we going to give today's snowman?" ...

"Hey, Cole. Can I get you a drink?"

The voice jostled Cole from his trance. He tore his eyes from the frozen world to see his dad smiling at him from across the living room.

"Still working on my eggnog, but thanks."

Rubbing his eyes, Cole dragged his feet through the house and found himself hovering outside his old bedroom. The glow of the hallway lamp lit a path through his nephews' dump trucks and plastic animals. Cole settled into the window seat, knees bent, and feet cramped. As he sucked creamy turpentine into his mouth, he looked at

Sasha's old backyard. Like staring into the snowy front yard, images flooded Cole's mind: Sasha, as she crawled under the deck, hugging her dolls; Sasha, tinkering in her little garden; Sasha, a ghost inside her house, yet Cole would wait for her to emerge as he filled sketchbooks with drawings. Sasha. Sasha. Sasha...

...Sasha, bent over her small garden, eased weeds from between flowers, beans, and peas. Two dolls were propped up on the grass, leaning into each other with forever smiles while they watched her work.

The crash of Sasha's back door flying open and hitting the outside wall jolted Cole from his sketchbook; a deep line of lead cut through the gray sunflower on his paper. Sasha's father, a ball of rage, stormed across the yard. Shouts, swears, and words that made Cole's stomach turn cut through the open window. Mr. Cooper's hand curled around a bean plant and ripped it from the earth. Pea vines and flower buds landed beside it, leaves torn and wilted.

Once the hurricane had disappeared back into the house, Sasha collected the limp foliage and fallen petals. She dug up the roots and pulled seed packs from her pocket. Parting the earth, Sasha dropped seeds into the soil in perfect rows. She swept dirt overtop and pressed down, smothering the seeds into safety, preparing them for life above soil...

"Oh, hey. There you are."

Wiping away tears, Cole turned from the window. His sister peered at him from the open doorway.

"What are you doing in here with the lights off?"

"Just looking at my old view," Cole said and pushed himself from the window seat.

"You okay? You've been quiet tonight."

"I just have a file on my mind. I guess it's kind of weighing on me."

"Anything you want to talk about?" Lori asked, stepping into the room.

"It's confidential." Cole looked out the window again at the empty yard and snow-covered boulders where there used to be a garden.

"Why do you do this to yourself? You get so wrapped up trying to make the world right and you end up a ball of stress. You're allowed to give yourself a night off from being Batman."

As Cole drowned his potatoes with a gravy tsunami, his family talked and laughed while they carved turkey and passed plates. Candles flickered and steam rose from dishes. Cole slumped in his chair and ripped apart a bun.

Smothering thoughts that ravaged his mind, Cole pulled himself upright and forced a smile. "So, Mike. How's work?"

"Actually," his brother-in-law said, "we're starting a new project in January that I'm really excited about."

As Mike talked about bridge abutments, piers, and piles, a gentle vibration buzzed in Cole's pocket. He slid his phone out just enough to see the name on the screen—Chen's Noodle House.

"Sorry," Cole said, knocking his chair backwards, "but I have to take this. I'd love to hear more about the project in a few minutes." With a grin plastered across his face, Cole excused himself.

"Hello?"

"Hey. It's me. Sasha. Merry Christmas."

Cole's smile widened and he leaned his shoulder against the wall in the hallway. "Hey, you," he said, trying to keep his voice low. "I've been wondering about you. I haven't heard from you in weeks."

"Yeah, sorry. I've been busy."

Cole glanced into the dining room where Lori sliced turkey for her son. She looked up and her eyes met Cole's.

"I'm glad you called," Cole said, pulling his gaze from Lori's. "You brightened my day."

"I brightened your day? It's Christmas. Shouldn't your day already be bright?"

"I guess it is, but now even more so."

"You're a strange guy, Cole Dawson."

Cole could hear the smile coming through Sasha's words and felt a warm glow within, like he was full of hot cocoa and Baileys. "I don't think it's strange to have your day brightened because someone you like calls to wish you Merry Christmas."

The twinkling lights of the Christmas tree reflected in his eyes as he waited for Sasha to say something, but the line was silent.

"So, how are you spending your Christmas?" she finally asked.

"Amazingly enough, I got Christmas off this year. I'm at my parents' place for dinner."

"Oh gosh. I'm interrupting family time. I shouldn't have called. I'll let you go."

"Don't hang up. You aren't interrupting. Your timing couldn't be more perfect. What about you? How are you spending Christmas?"

A moment of silence carried over the line followed by Mr. Chen's voice in the background. "Most of my roommates don't have family nearby, so we decided to have our own Christmas dinner here. We got a turkey and everything. We've already eaten and I'm so stuffed and the kitchen's a mess, but I don't care. It was worth it for the great meal."

"That sounds amazing. Maybe I need to come over and sample some of your leftovers."

Sasha let out a light, forced laugh. "Sorry, but I've already divvied up the food to all my roommates. There's nothing left for rogue friends. Anyway, they're setting up the karaoke machine and are bugging me to sing the first song. I've got to go. I just wanted to wish you a Merry Christmas."

"Sasha, wait. I want to have Christmas with you," Cole blurted out, pushing himself from the wall.

"I'm sorry? It's already after six on Christmas. I think we kind of missed it."

"I don't care about the date on the calendar," Cole said as he paced the hall. "I want to have Christmas with you."

"Okay… But I don't really know what you mean."

"I picked up an extra shift tomorrow, but I have the twenty-seventh off. Come to my place in the morning and I'll make us breakfast. Stay for supper, stay the night. I'll make a nice meal, and we can spend the day hanging out, doing whatever we want to do, even if we want to do absolutely nothing. I want Christmas with you." Cole's heart hammered. He could already feel Sasha beside him as they gorged on Christmas cookies in the glow of twinkling lights.

"I don't know. I'm so busy and I… I don't know."

"It's been forever since we've seen each other, and I hate it that we only talk every few weeks."

"Well… I guess that could work. Craig gave me the entire week off. I don't go back until the second."

"Perfect." A dancing smile stretched across Cole's face as he shoved Sasha's comment about Craig aside. "I can pick you up first thing."

"I'll take the bus."

"It's no hassle at all, and it'll save you bus fare." Cole glanced into the dining room where his sister was eyeing him.

"I want to come to your place, but I want to take the bus. Please. If not, then…"

"Okay, fine. You win. But you're not allowed to eat breakfast before you come as I'm going to make us a lot of food."

"All right. I really must go. Merry Christmas."

"Merry Christmas, my Sasha. Take care of yourself." Cole kept his ear to the phone until he heard the click of Sasha ending the call. The dead air was a chasm with Cole on one side and Sasha on another.

"You're all smiles now," Lori teased as Cole slid into his seat across from her. "Do you have a girlfriend you're hiding from us?"

"Nope, no girlfriend." Cole beamed as he sliced into his turkey. "That was Sasha Cooper."

The room went silent, other than Mike's knife scraping across his plate and toddler dump truck noises as Lori's son pushed mashed potatoes around with his spoon.

"Sasha Cooper?" Cole's mother, Helen, choked out.

Cole smiled at his family as he chewed the turkey, little fireworks exploding inside of him.

"For real?" Lori said, her eyes wide.

"Yeah, for real."

His family stared on, cutlery paused and mouths agape.

"Who's Sasha Cooper?" Mike asked dully as he spooned potatoes into his mouth.

"But... when... how..." Cole's father, Jim, stared at Cole as various noises sputtered from him.

"How is she?" Helen asked.

"She's uh..." Cole's smile faded to worry lines as a busted house in the Sax flashed through his head. "She's all right, I guess."

"What happened to her? Where's she been?" Lori asked, her empty fork dangling from her fingers.

Mike looked around the table at the shocked faces. Resting his fork on his plate, he said, "Who's Sasha Cooper?"

Lori turned to her husband. Her words came fast, her tone important. "Sasha used to live next door. She's the same age as Cole and the two of them were super close. They hung out from when they were barely walking, all the way through high school. They'd walk to and from school together, they'd hang out afterwards... Then one day..." Lori turned to Cole. "When did she disappear? Were you guys still in school?"

Cole shook his head as he chewed.

"It was the day after their high school graduation party," Helen said. "Cole was devastated. For the first while, he thought she just went on vacation. Reality eventually set in, and Cole realized she wasn't coming back. He'd drag himself around the house and he spent a lot of time looking out his bedroom window at Sasha's yard. He would sit on the front porch on Sundays with the Scrabble board set up and just wait for Sasha to come home. It broke my heart."

"Scrabble?" Mike asked.

"It was the cutest thing," Lori said. "Every Sunday, Cole and Sasha would sit on our front porch and play Scrabble. It didn't matter what the weather was like—they were out there, even in full winter gear. This went on for years."

"He even knocked on her parents' door one day to ask about Sasha," Helen said. "The day I learned Cole did that, I knew he was desperate for answers."

Mike looked from Helen to Lori, his face twisted in confusion.

"Sasha's home life was... complicated," Lori said, stealing a glance at Cole. "Her dad was... difficult, let's say."

"She had troubles at home," Helen said.

Cole's cutlery clattered to his plate and his face darkened. "Why are we tiptoeing around this issue?" Turning to Mike, he said, "Sasha's dad was an abusive bastard to both her and her mother, and her mom was too weak to protect herself or her own daughter. He treated them like crap for years. For her entire childhood."

"Cole." Lori glared at her brother and covered her son's ears. "Language."

"Sorry." Cole snatched his knife and sawed his turkey.

"But Cole was her knight in shining armor," Lori said. "He was always there for Sasha when she needed someone, and he was a constant friend to her through all those years."

"Is her family still next door?" Mike asked.

"No," Lori breathed, her eyes widening. "Years ago, Sasha's dad suffered a serious stroke and was moved to hospice. I'm not sure about her mom, but rumors are she found the nerve to leave her husband, remarried, and now lives down east. When their house sold, poor Cole completely lost all hope of ever seeing Sasha again."

"She disappeared but is now back?"

"*Apparently!*" Lori said as she gaped at Cole.

"Cole, please," Jim said. "We're all wondering the same things. What happened to Sasha, where has she been, and how did you manage to find her after all these years?"

Four sets of eyes bored into Cole as turkey and cranberry melded in his mouth. His nephew picked up a squishy handful of potato and threw it on the floor.

"She got on a bus and headed west. Needed a change, I guess. Needed to get away. She went all the way to the coast and spent the next nine years working gardening-type jobs. She found herself back in Lashburn this past spring and was hired on by the city."

His family stared at him. Cole picked up his fork and pushed a carrot away from his gravy lake. His nephew squealed.

"Good for her," Jim said. "It's good to hear she's made her way in life."

"Yeah." Cole clenched his jaw and stabbed a carrot.

Lori, open mouthed, stared into Cole. "She headed west? That's it? Nothing *happened* to her? Why didn't she tell you? She left you broken-hearted, a pile of mush, and she didn't even say goodbye? I thought she was nicer than that."

Cole strangled his fork. "I wasn't a pile of mush. And you have *no* idea what she was going through. She needed to get away and I don't blame her for leaving." Cole threw his fork on the table, swigged his eggnog, and slammed his empty glass down.

Lori stared at her brother; her lips barely parted. The bawls of a three-year-old pierced the air.

"Calm down, everybody," Jim said. "This information comes as a shock to all of us and we don't need to be making any judgements or getting our backs up. It's Christmas and I'd prefer if we could be civil and enjoy our meal in peace."

"Sorry," Lori muttered, glancing sideways at her dad. Cole glared at her as he picked up his fork and stabbed another carrot.

"But you *were* a pile of mush," Lori said.

"Mike, you'd love her," Helen said. "She's such a nice girl. Very quiet but very sweet."

"Is she married?" Lori asked.

Cole glared. "No."

"Are you guys dating?"

"We're just friends." Cole ripped apart another bun and slammed it into his gravy, misting the tablecloth with grease.

"Hang on a sec," Mike said. "Were you guys dating before she left, or were you friends?"

"Just friends."

"But they *so* could have been dating," Lori said. "They were *adorable* together."

"Seriously, Lori?"

"Enough, you two." Turning to Cole, Jim said, "That tells us the mystery of what happened to her, but you still haven't told us how you found her."

"I didn't *find* her. I stopped looking for her ages ago, and I haven't thought of her more than a handful of times in the past year. We just happened to run into each other at a party in September."

"A party?" Lori said with raised eyebrows. "So, what... You were breaking up a party and she was there?"

"No, I was *at* the party, and we ran into each other."

"*You* were at a party?"

"I can have fun too, you know."

"You can, but you usually don't."

"I can't really picture Sasha at a party, either," Helen said. "She's always been very introverted. I just never saw her as a party girl."

Groaning, Cole looked up at the ceiling before pulling his eyes back to his family. "I was at a party, she was at the same party, we got to talking, and we left because, as you all noted, we are not party people. Satisfied?"

"Look, Cole," Jim said. "I'm sorry we have so many questions. We just never thought you'd hear from Sasha again and we're all surprised. I apologize if we've said anything to upset you. One thing we can all agree on is we are pleased to hear she's doing all right, and we're happy you've found your friend again."

"This is quite the revelation," Mike said. "I think we should drink to Cole's and Sasha's reunion."

Cole, groaning again, dug the heels of his hands into his eyes while his family clinked glasses in his honor.

The flickering of Christmas tree lights danced across the living room as Cole sat on the floor and swatted the tree's ornaments. His dad and Mike were deep in conversation on the other side of the room and his mom and Lori were still trying to settle the boys in their beds after an overly stimulating day.

"Hey," Lori said as she plopped down next to Cole.

Cole turned to Lori before returning his gaze to the tree. "Are your kids finally asleep?" he asked as he turned a sparkling snowman around.

"No, but Mom sent me away anyway. What are you doing?"

"Just looking at our old ornaments. Trying to remember where we got them all."

Lori pulled her knees to her chest and gazed at her brother. "So, Sasha, hey?"

The ornament fell from Cole's fingers and bobbled on the tree—a snowman hanged for his crimes. "What do you mean?"

"Sorry if things got out of hand at supper. I'm just shocked and thrilled to hear that Sasha's back and I got carried away."

Cole shrugged as he reached for a golfing Santa. "It's all right. It is shocking news, I guess."

"What now? Are you guys going to pick up where you left off and be best buds again?"

"I don't know. Life is different now. We don't live next door to each other, so we don't see each other every day, and we have responsibilities and commitments now. It's tough for her to find work in Lashburn, so she's thinking of heading west again."

"Oh. That sucks."

Cole shrugged. "She has to do what's best for her, right?"

Silence hung in the air and Cole focussed on the golfing Santa—his look of concentration, the shiny gray of the club, the minute dots covering the tiny ball.

"You're falling for her."

"What?" Cole said, releasing the Santa from his grasp. "No. Like I said, we're just friends."

"I can tell by the way you talk about her, but it's okay to pretend otherwise." She scooted closer to Cole and rested her head on his shoulder. "Sometimes we need to lie to ourselves to get through the reality that is life."

Chapter 15

Sasha pressed her back to the brickwork and drew in cold morning air. "One day," she said. "You're allowed one day with Cole, and then you need to go." With a steadying breath, she slipped around the corner and into the vestibule.

As the elevator quivered under her feet, Sasha glued her eyes to the floor, her knees bouncing as she edged towards seven.

Stepping from the elevator, she turned the corner and slammed into a body. A gasp squeaked from her as she stumbled backwards and crashed into the closing doors. "Oh my gosh, Cole. You nearly gave me a heart attack," she said, whipping Cole with her mitts.

"Come here, you goof." Cole laughed as he pulled Sasha from the elevator. "You're going to get squished in the doors."

"That's impossible."

"I'm sure you'd find a way to do it."

"What are you doing out here anyway?" she said as she shoulder-checked him. "Trying to scare me?"

"I was too excited to see you and couldn't wait in my condo any longer. Merry Christmas, my Sasha," he said as he pulled her into a bear hug.

"Merry Christmas, Cole." He smelled like fresh laundry and body wash and Sasha dug her nose into his shirt.

With his arm draped over her shoulders, Cole led Sasha into his home. As he tossed her coat on a hook, Sasha gaped at the green boughs decorated with ornaments and lights. "You have a tree. It's beautiful."

"I got it special for today. Just this morning, I overheard two of the bulbs talking. The green one asked his buddy if he was working over the holidays and the red one said, 'Off and on.'"

"Seriously, Cole?" Sasha said, following him to the kitchen. "You have a terrible sense of humor."

"Admit it already—you love my jokes. Anyway, take a seat at the table and help yourself to coffee. Mugs are in this cupboard here. Milk is in the fridge and sugar is in the pantry."

Sasha pulled out a mug that read, *10-4, Coffee That*. As she poured coffee, steam floated from the mug and disappeared into thin air. Lumps of sugar dissolved to nothingness and milk lightened the dark.

Taking a seat at the table, Sasha wrapped her hands around the mug, its warmth soaking into her palms. "I love your place," she said. "It's so comfortable and warm."

Turning from the stove, Cole smiled. "I'm glad you find it cozy. You're welcome to stay any time."

"You always say that. Thank you."

"And I mean it. I'd rather you be here than... I just like it when you're here."

The coffee's aroma wafted up, tingling Sasha's nose. She closed her eyes and sipped soft hazelnut and cocoa undertones. "Do you remember that time we convinced the guy at the tree lot to sell us that Charlie Brown tree for five dollars?"

"That tree was amazing." Cole laughed as he sliced open a package of bacon. "And the strings of popcorn we made were the finishing touch."

"Which the birds ate, and then they pooped all over our beautiful little tree."

"Best tree I ever had. Plus, we got to feed the birds."

"Always the altruist…"

As bacon popped and sizzled, Sasha looked out the balcony window at the sprawling city. Training her gaze west, she narrowed her eyes until the horizon blurred and looked like whitecaps playing on the ocean. "I decided to go back to the coast."

Cole paused over the pan. Bacon sizzled and the air held its breath. "When are you leaving?"

"I don't know," Sasha said, tucking her hair behind her ear. "I keep going back and forth about when I should leave. A lot of jobs start in March, so I should be out west by mid-February at the latest, but I might go earlier."

"Where are you planning to go, exactly?" Cole said as he flipped a piece of bacon.

"I don't know. I guess I'll see where I end up, see where I can find a decent job." Sasha hugged the mug to her chest and stared at Cole's back.

"There's nothing in Lashburn for me," she said. "I need to go back west. I don't think I can survive here. The office work is killing me."

His shoulders twitched. He rolled his neck.

"I wasn't even going to tell you. I'm not really sure why I'm talking about it right now."

Cole spun around, his face twisted and lined. "What do you mean, you weren't going to tell me? You were just going to disappear again?"

"I don't know," she mumbled as she inched her hands into her sleeves. "It's hard to say goodbye. I figured it might be easier to just go."

"Easier for who? You? You have no idea how hard it is for someone to leave you without warning."

"Look, I'm sorry I left the way I did when we were kids, but I needed to get away. I knew you'd be upset, but you got over it."

"I got over it, did I? You have no idea. I spent weeks staring at your house, waiting for a sign of you. And when I couldn't handle looking into your empty yard anymore, I started scouring the newspaper for stories of a rotten corpse found dumped in a field."

Sasha's breath stuck in her throat. Her nails scraped the sides of the mug. "I had to leave. I thought you'd understand."

"I totally get that you needed to leave, but you should have told me."

"I was scared you'd try to talk me out of it."

"We could have come up with another plan. I could have come with you."

"Really? Barely out of high school, a great future ahead of you, an awesome family, and you'd leave it all to jump on a bus with no idea where you'd end up?"

"Yes. Or... I don't know... At least it would have been an option. At least I would have known."

But then I couldn't have disappeared...

"And do you mean it when you say that there's nothing in Lashburn for you?"

"There's not. There's my job, which I only like a few months a year. I have no family, no real friends, and there aren't many places that I like to spend my down time."

"Seriously? Did you think of me at all over the past ten years? Or did you just leave the memory of me in the dust?"

"What are you talking about? I thought about you a lot, but what does that have to do with anything?"

"Maybe it has to do with the fact that I thought I was something. A friend. Someone to lean on. Anything."

"But you are. You are my friend, and I like spending time with you, and you've been there for me more than you could ever know. Why are you so upset?"

Bacon grease splattered the countertop as Cole threw the spatula down. "Seriously, Sash? You just said there is nothing in Lashburn for you. What about *me*?"

"Yeah, of course. That's a given. You're the only thing in Lashburn that would make me contemplate staying. I didn't think I needed to say it. Do you really think I don't care about you?"

"Sasha–" Cole's phone screamed, cutting him short. Shaking his head, he plucked the phone from the counter. "Hello? … Oh hey, Frankie… No, not really… Sasha's here but give me a sec and I'll grab it for you." Turning to Sasha, Cole said, "Sash, watch the bacon for me. I have to grab something."

Cole disappeared down the hall. Sasha's nail beds whitened against the table as air rushed through her nostrils. Her eyes darted from the fake ocean on the horizon to the front door—twenty easy steps away.

Cole's voice carried from the bedroom.

Suck it up and shove it down.

Sasha stepped towards the stove and picked up the greasy spatula. The bacon popped, sending an arc of hot grease onto her arm. "Oh my gosh," she shrieked, jerking her hand back. She stared down at the strips, their edges growing dark and brittle. Sasha hesitated, then pressed the spatula into the center of the pan.

"Sorry," Cole said as he took the spatula from her, somehow instantly by her side. "That was Frank looking for some notes from a file we dealt with yesterday. Would you mind making the toast?"

Sasha fumbled with the tie on the plastic bag until a warm, heavenly smell floated out. "I thought you and Frank had the day off."

"We do. Frankie's just at the station cleaning up some paperwork."

The coils of the toaster glowed red. Cole magically transformed the bacon from a rubbery mess to crisp harmony.

"You're important to me, you know," Sasha said. "I thought it was obvious that you were the only thing in Lashburn for me. You've been such a great friend, just like when we were kids. And I honestly didn't think I had hurt you so much by leaving the way I did. I thought you'd figure out that I had to go."

"Don't worry about it," Cole said as he dumped pancake mix into a bowl. A dusting of powder floated out and stuck to the grease splotches on the counter. "I probably overreacted. I know you struggled with your homelife, and I know Lashburn is difficult for you now. I get that you need to find work out west, but that doesn't mean it doesn't suck."

"Pancakes, too?" Sasha asked as Cole mixed in water.

"I wasn't going to do pancakes, but I promised you a big breakfast."

The toast popped and Sasha switched it out for two slices of bread. "I can't stay here, and you can't leave. We're grownups now and we each have our own places to be. I'm just trying to be rational."

Cole's arms were suddenly around her—an old blanket, a strong shield. He tucked a strand of hair behind her ear, his touch leaving a lingering heat on her cheek. "Being rational sucks. I never thought I'd see you again, but here you are in my kitchen, and you're telling me you are leaving again."

Maybe I don't need Magda. Maybe I can stay.

"Promise you'll keep in touch. We can set up weekly phone calls or something."

I'm a fraud. She twisted from his embrace and reached for the toast. "Yeah, we can do that, I guess."

"You gotta promise me, Sash."

"Okay," she whispered.

The crunch of knife on toast filled the dead air. Sasha glanced sideways at Cole, but he kept his back to her as he poured batter into the pan. "Being an adult is hard," he said as bubbles appeared on the surface of the pancakes. "Being a kid is way easier."

They are both overwhelming.

Sasha gaped at torn wrapping paper and boxes scattered across Cole's living room. Snuggled in her new hoodie, she could not keep her fingers from caressing her shark's fuzzy eyeball. She looked across the chaos at Cole in his matching pair of shark slippers that happily chomped his ankles. "I still feel like an idiot for not getting you anything," she said.

"I already told you that I didn't want you to get me anything. You being here is exactly what I wanted for Christmas."

"I still feel dumb and insensitive."

"Seriously, don't. There is absolutely nothing you could have wrapped in paper that could compare to the gift of you joining me today. Now stop grumbling or you'll ruin my fun of watching you open the rest of your presents."

"You are insane, you know. Why would you buy me so much? It's kind of ridiculous."

"Because you deserve it," Cole said as he reached for a box. "Plus, you are way too fun to shop for and I couldn't help myself." With a wink, he shoved the package into Sasha's arms. "This one is for us to share."

The box heavy in her lap, Sasha slid her finger under the break in the wrapping and let the paper fall away; an old friend emerged from the folds. "Scrabble. You remembered."

"Of course I remembered, and I've been dying for a rematch. And look," Cole said, pointing to the game. "This version has fancy tiles and the board spins, so now I can finally see the words right side up. Maybe now I'll have a chance of beating you."

"You beat me lots. Anyway, I haven't played since I left home, so I'm likely pretty rusty."

"I guess there's only one way to find out. But first..." Cole snagged another parcel from under the tree and tossed it to Sasha.

"I don't deserve all these gifts."

"But you do."

Pursing her lips, Sasha undid the ribbon and pulled the lid off the box. A toothbrush lay nestled within fuzzy pajamas, a lighter cotton sleep tee, and matching shorts.

"So, you have stuff for when you stay over," Cole said. "And even though you're going away, I'll keep them in my drawer, so you know you'll always have a safe, welcoming place if you are ever in Lashburn."

Sasha lifted the toothbrush from the box like it could crumble to dust if mishandled. "You actually *want* me to stay over?"

"Absolutely." Cole slipped his hand onto her knee and gazed into her eyes. "Don't doubt that for a second."

"But I'm such a pain in the butt. I keep showing up unannounced and take up space on your couch and eat your food..."

"And I love those days. I want more of those days."

"Cole..." Tears tried to break free, but Sasha forced them down as she clasped the toothbrush to her chest. "Only you could make a toothbrush more valuable than pirate booty."

"What?" The corners of Cole's eyes crinkled as a chuckle burbled out of him. "Pirate booty?"

"Yeah. Treasure. I'd take this toothbrush over gold and jewels a million times."

A laugh erupted from Cole, and he was suddenly upon Sasha, tackling her to the ground. "You're hilarious."

The rug tickled the back of Sasha's neck as the fire glowed warm on her skin. Cole's body was comfortably heavy upon hers, his brown eyes soft and penetrating. A smile split her serious face.

"I love it when you smile," Cole whispered, brushing his nose to hers. "I don't see a big smile from you often, but when I do, I know I'm going to have a good day."

"This is a very good day." Sasha closed her eyes as electricity arced between their lips.

I'm a sham.

The smile evaporated. Snapping her head to the side, Sasha stared into the pit of flames.

Cole collapsed his face into her neck, his warm sigh condensing on her skin.

The fire burned her retinas; Cole's body was hot on hers. "I can't do this," she said, pushing Cole off.

"It's just a hug, okay?"

"No." Sasha's eyes darted around the room, and she raked her hands through her hair. "I'm going away. I'm moving. I can't..."

"Hey," Cole said, his hand on her knee again. "What if you don't go? What if you stay in Lashburn?"

Pulling her knees to her chest, Sasha flopped her forehead onto them. "I can't. I just... My life is out west."

"Yet you own a house in the Maples."

Sasha's eyes flew open, and she pressed her forehead into her knees. "Uh... Yeah but I've already lined someone up to rent out my room. Even if I wanted to stay in Lashburn, I have nowhere to go."

"But you don't even know what town you want to move to. Stay here. Stay with me. I can take care of you."

"I'm sorry?" Sasha lifted her head and glared. "I don't need to be babysat. I can take care of myself, you know. I've been doing it for ages."

"That came out the wrong way. I only meant we can lean on each other."

"No, we can't."

"Why not? It's okay to let someone help you out. No one expects you to do it all on your own. That's what friends are for."

"Believe me, Cole, you do not need to get wrapped up in my messy life," Sasha said as she picked at a piece of tape caught under her fingernail.

"Sasha..." Pursing his lips, Cole pushed the paper storm aside and slipped his arm around her waist. "Come here, you," he said, leaning his forehead on hers. "I know... I know that you live... I mean, I know you're... Ugh. How do I say this?" he said, looking to the ceiling for answers. "I know life can be messy and that's okay. I'm here for you in whatever capacity you need. No judgements."

Sasha shrugged out of Cole's embrace and zipped the hoodie up until the zipper told her pulling it further would do no good. "Don't go all policey on me now," she said with a stutter-laugh.

"Sasha..."

"Oh, look," she said, plastering on a smile and reaching under the tree. "One more present."

Cole snatched the gift away. "Would you just talk to me?"

Sasha's hands froze, clutching air where a present used to be. Her stomach twisted and her fingers curled into fists. "I thought you invited me here for Christmas, not to pick apart my life."

"I did, but–"

The phone pierced the air. Sasha snapped her head towards the sound springing from the kitchen.

"Sasha, hear me out. I can't handle this anymore. I'm going crazy–"

"You'd better get that."

The phone rang again, a warning bell in the tense space.

"But Sasha."

"It could be important."

"Gawd, Sash. It's not as important as…"

Sasha inched away. The phone rang again.

"Dammit, Sash. Fine." He pushed himself from the floor and headed to the kitchen. "Hello?"

Heart hammering, Sasha kicked off her shark slippers and scrambled from the rug. She scurried towards the door but was stopped by the framed pencil sketch—sweeping lines melded with jagged ones, coming together to create a story. She bit her lip. Her muscles relaxed in front of the picture.

The sketch was of a policeman and a little girl. The perspective was from behind, with the two walking away. The officer held the girl's hand, and he was looking down at her at an angle that allowed only a glimpse of his face. The girl was looking up at the police officer as a doll hung limply from her other hand.

"Sorry about that," Cole said, stepping into Sasha's bubble. "Sandy needed some info on a prisoner so she can process him for remand."

Sasha narrowed her eyes and cocked her head, her eyes glued to the sketch.

"Sash?"

"I love this picture," she said. "It says so much."

Cole inched closer until his shoulder was brushing hers. "What do you like about it?"

"It shows the softness and empathy of the police officer. I can see that he cares about this girl and is trying to help her. She trusts him and she knows that life will turn out okay."

"That's exactly what I was going for when I drew it."

"Wait, what?" Sasha said, turning to Cole. "*You* drew this?"

"Yeah."

"It's amazing. I had no idea you were this talented."

"Look," Cole said, slipping his hand around hers. "I'm sorry I was sticking my nose into your life. When you are ready, tell me what you need from me, and I'll be here. I'll help you."

Her fingers tensed around his. Dropping her gaze, she leaned her weight into him. "I like you."

"And I like you," he said, planting a kiss on top of her head. "A lot. How about you open your last present and then I beat you at Scrabble while we pig out on supper?"

"I would really like that. Except the part about you winning Scrabble."

"Come, my Sasha." Wrapping his other hand around hers, Cole pulled Sasha to the couch and pressed the gift in her hands. "Merry Christmas."

Sasha slipped her hand under the wrapping and pushed a corner of paper aside. When her eyes spied the swooping *H* on the box, her heart stuttered, and she ripped through the rest of the paper.

"Hammerkin?" She turned the box over, her eyes probing the logo and pictures. "Is this seriously Hammerkin or is it just the box?"

Cole shrugged, a smile playing on his lips. "Open it."

Sasha eased open the flap and pulled five gardening tools from within. "Cole, these are top of the line. You spent way too much on these."

"I got them on sale, so don't worry about the cost. Anyway, I would have happily paid full price to see the expression on your face right now."

"How is it you are so wonderful? I just... I wish I could..." Sasha bit her lip as she clutched the gardening tools meant for someone who was not a fraud. As if the tools had caught fire, Sasha's hands sprung open and the gift crashed to the floor. "I can't take these. It's too much. I don't deserve these."

As she stared at the forbidden fruit, Cole's hands enveloped hers, their warmth settling her jitters. "The joy that crossed your face when you opened these..." he said. "That's what I wanted for Christmas. Take them, Sasha. Give me the gift of using these gardening tools and loving them. Grow something beautiful. Grow something that makes you smile."

"Oh man, I am so full," Cole groaned as he shuffled from the kitchen with bags of chips in his arms.

Sasha, snuggled in her new pajamas, said, "Then why are you bringing chips out?"

"Because a *Die Hard* marathon is not complete without chips." Collapsing next to Sasha on the couch, he threw a blanket over them and wrapped his arm around her. "Thank you for sharing Christmas with me," he said and placed a kiss on her cheek.

"Thank you for having me." Her fingers grazed her tingling cheek as she leaned into Cole. "But maybe I should go. I'm really tired and I should get out of your hair."

"No way. I'm not watching this marathon without you. Plus, you're nice and warm and I'll be cold and lonely if you go."

"Oh my gosh." Sasha giggled and elbowed Cole in the ribs. "You know, I've never seen any of the *Die Hards*."

"You are in for a treat, but I have to warn you, I have a tendency to comment on the ridiculousness of these movies."

"How so?"

"Let's just say if my work life mirrored John McClane's in any way, I'd be able to repeatedly cheat death while I go badass on the bad dudes. Also, the amount of paperwork he's creating…"

"Oh yes. The paperwork. How could I forget?"

"You know what, my Sasha? You are my favorite person in the whole world."

Sasha pursed her smiling lips and played with the hem on the blanket. With a quick nod, she nestled into Cole's embrace. "This is like old times," she said, resting her head on his chest.

"This is better than old times."

"Maybe I…"

"Maybe what?"

"Maybe I can put off going west for a bit longer."

"I'd really like that."

Chapter 16

Cole attempted to combat breathe but the air was heavy. Suffocating. He stared at the bedroom ceiling as the stress of Sasha's smokescreen haunted him.

...*Gunfire from* Die Hard 3 *rippled through the condo and Cole tightened his embrace around Sasha as her spring plans haunted him. He had become John McClane, doing everything in his power to hold his world together.*

"You're squishing me," Sasha said as she pushed against him. "You have to sleep in your bed."

"I don't want my bed."

Sasha pulled the blanket around herself. "You need to be rested for work tomorrow. Get off or I'm going home."

At the word home, Cole's stomach knotted. He tightened his hold. "You can't."

"I certainly can, especially if you continue to smother me. Now get off."

As Sasha shoved Cole, a rush of cold air swept into the space between them. Flashes of shifting lights and shadows danced on her face. She raised her eyebrows, cocked her head, and yanked the blanket from Cole. He reached for Sasha as a bomb went off on the TV.

"Don't go west. Stay here." Cole's hand hummed as he tried to erect a forcefield around Sasha like he had when they were eight. "Long-term, I mean. You'll be better off."

"I... What?"

Another **kaboom** ricocheted off the walls. In the time it took Sasha to perform a heavy blink, the shape of her eyes had narrowed; the sparkle in them had become an inferno. "Don't tell me what's best for me. You have no idea what kind of shit I've had to deal with in my life, so stop treating me like a princess who needs your care."

Shivers ran across Cole's skin like an army of ants had descended on him.

"What's it going to be, then? Do you want me to stay the night, or shall I leave?"

"Uh... Stay. Of course."

"Then don't tell me what to do. And you'd better get off this couch before I do something I'm going to regret."

Cole grasped for words but the girl on his couch shut him up with her glare...

As Cole stared at the ceiling and massaged his temples, the sound of the television drifted into the room. He pushed himself to sitting, his head throbbing with the change of position.

He shuffled into the bathroom, braced his hands on the sink, and looked in the mirror—a pasty complexion with dark circles stared back. "You've got to put an end to this, Dawson. She's killing you." The rattling of pills pierced his head as he shook a couple of painkillers into his palm.

Voices, applause, whirrs, and dings of *The Price is Right* reverberated in Cole's ears as he dragged himself into the living room. "Mornin'," he said, rubbing his eyes.

Sasha turned from her breakfast. "Good morning. I hope you don't mind I helped myself to cereal. I was really hungry and didn't want to wake you."

Cole eyed Sasha for anything off-character, but she sat in her usual one-leg-tucked position, a slight smile brightening her face. "That's fine," he said. "Did you make coffee?"

"I wasn't sure if you'd want me messing with your coffee maker, so I left it for you to do."

"Seriously, Sash. You need to stop this thing you do."

"What thing?"

"You think that every little thing you do is somehow bothering me. I don't know if this stems from your childhood or from your ten years away, or for some other stupid reason, but it's really annoying. The only thing that bothers me is when you tiptoe around me, so stop it."

"I'm sorry," Sasha whispered. Cole dragged his feet to the kitchen.

While coffee brewed, he grabbed a bowl and spoon and headed back to the living room. Flopping on the couch, Cole reached for the box of cereal that sat open on the coffee table. "Did you finish the box?" he said, rattling the crumbs around as he peered inside.

"Sorry." Sasha looked up with only her eyes.

Slumping into the couch after retrieving a fresh box, Cole watched a contestant jump up and down, clapping, while the audience cheered and yelled prices. He glanced at Sasha. She was balled up on the far end of the couch, her spoon and bowl clutched in her fists.

"How'd you sleep?" Cole asked as he spooned cereal into his mouth.

"Quite well, thank you. I thought I might sleep longer because of the late night, but I guess not."

Cole swallowed his mouthful and looked over at Sasha. "We need to talk."

She froze, spoon hovering mid-air. "We talked lots yesterday."

"This is a different kind of conversation."

Like an antelope spooked by a predator, Sasha launched off the couch and raced towards the bathroom. "I actually have to go," she said and slammed the door behind her.

"For frick sake." Cole slammed his bowl on the coffee table, sloshing milk over the side. "Sash!"

Cole's head rattled as he pushed himself to standing. Once the headache had settled to a steady thump, he positioned himself outside the bathroom door. "I need to leave for work in an hour and I hoped we could... visit... before then."

"I remember I have to do something," Sasha said through the door. "I have to go. Now."

"What do you have to do?"

The door flew open, and Sasha pushed through Cole. "Just something," she said as she fought with her coat sleeve.

"Stop it." Cole clamped onto Sasha's arm. "You're not going anywhere."

"Excuse me?"

"You can't go to that—"

Sasha stiffened. Her lips performed their haunting dance as her eyes began to narrow.

"Sorry," Cole said, shoving the rest of his sentence down. His throat tightened as he pictured Sasha being swallowed up by the Sax forever. "Just stay here another night."

"I'm going." Sasha yanked her arm from Cole and tore the door open.

"At least let me drive you."

"Leave. Me. Alone." Sasha rushed down the hallway and jammed her finger to the elevator button.

"Your Christmas gift to me."

Sasha's finger quieted from its incessant jamming. "I'm sorry?" She peered over her shoulder, her face barely visible behind the winter layers she had enclosed herself in.

"You said you feel bad you didn't get me a Christmas gift. Give this to me. Give me an hour and then let me drive you home. If you don't want to talk, we don't have to."

As though holding herself together, Sasha hugged her body.

"Don't leave like this."

The light on the elevator button snuffed out and the sliding doors creaked open. Sasha glanced into the getaway box.

"Please, my Sasha."

The doors closed. Eyes glued to the tacky patterned carpeting, Sasha made the slow walk back to Cole. Her coat fell to the floor, and she settled into the couch like she was a delicate leaf that had made its decent to earth.

Cole rubbed his forehead as Drew Carey called up the next contestant. "Promise to stay, Sash. Give me this gift and don't slip out while I'm in the shower."

Sasha sunk into the cushions, hunched her back, and became a ball.

Leaving his heart on the couch, Cole filled his mug with coffee before closing himself off in his bedroom. The pain in his head pulsated like someone was using the back of his eyeballs as drums.

Hot water pounded Cole's shoulders, and he rolled his neck, but when he stepped from the shower, his muscles were still made of gravel and his mind had been twisted into a coil.

As he shrugged his jacket on, he could not make eye contact with Sasha but when she reached for the doorknob, a wrecking ball dropped in his stomach. He grabbed the sleeve of her coat and pulled her close. "I'm sorry I'm such an asshole today," he whispered as he held her in a heartbreaking hug. "I'm really worried and stressed and I don't want you to go. Please stay one more night."

"I'm sorry, but I have to go. I can't explain why, but please understand that I can't stay."

Feeling like a swatted fly twitching for life, Cole opened the door. He wandered through his building and to his car in a daze with Sasha trailing behind.

"Why won't you open up to me?" he asked as he pulled his car onto the road. "Why don't you trust me?"

"I trust you," Sasha said as she stared at passing cars. "And I tell you lots about myself. I also respect you a lot, which is why…"

Sasha's sudden silence infected the air.

"Which is why… what? Do you think I'm stupid? Do you not realize what I do for a living? I investigate. I solve puzzles. I help people." Cole glanced at Sasha, but she just stared out the window and chewed her knuckle.

He swallowed the lump in his throat. He gripped the wheel tighter. He combat breathed. Nothing helped. "What house am I dropping you off at?"

"What do you mean?"

"I mean, am I dropping you off at your make-believe house in the Maples, at your parents' old house whose address you use on job application forms, or at your real home in the Sax? If you can even call that dump a home."

"Cole…"

"Where's it going to be, Sasha? Or is it Magda? Or Jane? Or Hayley?"

"I'm sorry?"

"I've known for months. I was patient. I waited for you to open up to me and tell me that you are struggling with something. I practically *told* you I know about your lies. I know you haven't been working for the city since September and that you're somehow getting by with only a handful of hours a week as a dishwasher in Chinatown."

Sasha trembled. The lamb morphed into a lion, an inferno blazing in her eyes. "How *dare* you stick your nose into my business. I trusted you."

"*You* trusted *me*? You're the one spewing lies. You have no right to talk about trust."

Sasha doubled over, her hands pressing the sides of her head. Cole's narrowed eyes and rigid jaw stuttered, then relaxed. *Dammit, Dawson.*

"Look, Sash. It's all out in the open now. I know I sound mad, but I'm not. I'm worried about you, stressed about the whole situation, and frustrated as hell, but I'm not mad *at* you. Clearly you have some stuff going on that needs attention. I'm here for you. You can move out of the Sax and in with me until you get your feet under you again. I'll help you find a real job, we'll set up a bank account for you, and when you're ready, I'll help you find a decent place to rent. Let me help you."

Cole turned back to the road—a long line of brake lights glowed ahead of him. He slammed on the brakes, his seatbelt holding him back from complete destruction as his head pitched forward.

Traffic was at a standstill. He was in the middle of three lanes and cars were backing up behind him. Jamming his car into park, Cole rested his pounding head against the headrest and closed his eyes. "What do you say, Sash? Let me into your world and I'll help you."

The sound of the passenger door opening and slamming shut cut through Cole. His eyes flew open. The seat where Sasha had been sitting a moment ago was empty.

Clambering out of the car, Cole scanned the street and spotted Sasha weaving between vehicles. "Sasha!" he called as he darted around cars. "Come back! I'm not mad! Sasha!"

The honking of cars blasted his headache, and he looked back to see his vehicle, driver's door open, abandoned in the middle of the street while traffic inched forward. Cole turned in the direction of Sasha and saw her running down the sidewalk. "Sasha! Call me! I will come for you! I will always come for you!"

With the honking becoming incessant, Cole climbed into his car and moved it forward until he was at a standstill again. The quietness of the cabin gripped him. He scanned the area where he had last seen Sasha, but she had vanished.

Cole's hands shook as he reached for his phone and pulled up Frank's number.

"Hey, Daws. What's up?"

"She's gone. She left. I think she might be running."

"Sasha?"

"She took off. I don't know... I just..."

"Calm yourself, Daws. You're not going to be of any help to anyone if you work yourself up. Once you've collected yourself, tell me what happened."

In, two, three, four... Hold, two, three, four... Out, two, three, four... Hold, two, three, four... Cole scanned the streets and sidewalks again. "I was driving her home. I was in a crap mood, stressed and worried, and I didn't mean to have the conversation with her yet, but I did. It just came out. I told her I wasn't upset, but she freaked on me and took off."

"How did she take off? I thought you said you were driving."

Cole pinched the bridge of his nose and tried to breathe but his lungs felt stuck. "I'm in a traffic jam and am completely blocked in.

Sasha took off while we were stopped. I tried to chase her down, but she got away."

"Is she injured?"

The sensible question flicked a switch in Cole's brain. His breaths evened as the police officer in him stirred. "No."

"Is she in danger?"

"No. Not that I know of, anyway."

"So, you told her you know the secrets she has been trying to keep from you, she got upset, and she left."

"Yeah, that's basically what happened," Cole said as he inched his car forward.

"You said she might be running. What exactly do you mean by that?"

"She took off nine and a half years ago, she disappeared from my place a few months back, and she recently told me she wasn't even going to let me know about her plans to head west again. She makes herself scarce when she's upset, and I'm scared that I've screwed up and she's going to leave town today and I'll never see her again." As the words poured from his mouth, he choked down a wave of nausea.

"She's a functional, capable adult who left on her own volition, so if she disappears, she won't be considered a missing person. I know I'm sounding cold, but I'm trying to be practical here."

Cole stared at the red lights of the car ahead of him. "Yeah, but I caused this and if I never see her again, I won't be able to live with myself."

"We'll find Sasha, but you need to keep a level head. If you truly think she's skipping town, then how is she going to leave?"

"By bus. She always travels by bus."

"And you said she's heading west. Anything more specific than that?"

"Just west. To the coast, possibly, but that's not a guarantee. Orchards, vineyards, or any town out that way is what she'll be looking for. No cities."

"And you think she's on her way to the bus station now?"

Cole closed his eyes. Imprints of brake lights flickered in his head amid images of Sasha running down the street. Away from him. "She needs her stuff from her place. She has nothing on her except some gardening tools and whatever is in her pockets."

"Then that's where we'll start. I'm just about to leave for our shift. I'll head to the station, gear up and grab a car, and meet you at her place. How far are you from there?"

"About fifteen blocks, but traffic is barely moving."

"She can't go too fast on foot. We'll catch her before she leaves."

Cole inched his car forward as he played Frank's plan out in his head.

"Daws, you still there, buddy?"

"Yeah, I'm here."

"Call me if anything changes, otherwise I'll see you at her place. What's the address?"

With a steadying breath, Cole forced himself to spill Sasha's secrets. "Fifty-one Saxton Lane."

There was a heavy pause on the line.

"I know, Frankie. She's dug herself into a deep hole and I feel that it's up to me to help her out of it."

As Cole turned onto Saxton Lane, his stomach clenched. He powered through the neighborhood and pulled up behind the parked police car. Frank stood on the sidewalk, his elbow resting on the butt of the gun nestled in his belt.

"She really lives here?" Frank said as Cole stepped onto the sidewalk.

"Yeah." Cole looked towards the yard riddled with broken lumber, abandoned clothing, a doorless microwave, and piles of garbage. The wooden front steps were missing a board, and the screen door was lodged askew. Peeling paint plagued the house, and one pane of the front window was busted, with a board stuck in place of the gaping hole.

The officers approached the house. Cole knocked on the door and waited. Frank looked sideways at Cole.

"She's home. I know she's home." He knocked again. Another minute crawled by.

Finally, voices echoed from inside. The doorknob jiggled and turned, and the door opened a crack. A young man with a bald head narrowed his eyes through the busted screen door. *Ian.* "What do you want?"

"We're looking for some information on a young lady," Frank said.

"Who's this guy?" Ian asked, jutting his chin out at Cole.

"Sorry." Cole tried to keep his voice steady as he flashed his police badge. "Officer Dawson. We're concerned for the safety of a woman who lives here, and we were wondering if you know of her whereabouts."

"Her name is Sasha," Frank added. "We know she resides here, and we were wondering if you've seen her today. Is she presently at home?"

The skin between Ian's eyebrows wrinkled and his mouth turned down. "There's no–"

"Magda, actually," Cole said, squaring his shoulders. "The woman we are looking for is Magda."

Frank shifted his stance and stared into Cole, but Cole kept his eyes trained on Ian.

"Magda?" Ian said, his creases smoothing. "Nah. No Magda here."

Cole's hands curled into fists. Frank cleared his throat and shot Cole another look.

"Is someone asking about Mags?" a woman's voice called from inside the house.

"Don't worry about it, Gina," Ian yelled. "I'm handling this."

The door was pulled wide and the woman from the party who had undressed Cole with her eyes lolled on the other side of the screen. "Hey," she said as her gaze lingered on Cole's face. "You look familiar."

"I have that kind of face, I guess. Do you know Magda?"

"I know Mags."

"And? Have you seen or heard from her today?"

"Well... We used to have someone named Magda living here."

"What do you mean, she *used* to live here?"

Gina looked at Ian. Moving her gaze back to Cole, she ran her tongue across her teeth and smiled. "Magda was here about fifteen minutes ago. She packed up her stuff, left her key, and told us to rent out her room."

Gina's words were a knife in Cole's guts, twisting as his eyes searched the messy house with peeling wallpaper.

"Did she say where she was going?" Frank asked.

"She just took off. Seemed upset about something. The way I figure, it's her life and she doesn't need me poking around in it."

"Can I see the room where she stayed?"

"Daws..." Frank warned under his breath.

"I need to know for sure," Cole whisper-growled. Turning to Gina, he said, "We're not trying to dig anything up on you guys. Our only concern is Magda's whereabouts. I promise that is the only reason why we are here."

"I guess I can let you in," Gina said. "But only her room. Everywhere else is people's private spaces."

Cole nodded as he wrapped his hand around the screen's handle and pulled, but it would not budge.

"You have to push the button in and pull up on the handle."

Cole tried again but the door only rattled under his grasp.

"You're just like Magda." Gina pushed the door open from the inside and stepped aside.

The subtleness of rot and must hit Cole's nose as though he had stepped into an old closet decorated with apple cores. A barefoot, shirtless, heavily tattooed man stood in the tiny kitchen to the left and poked at something in a pan on the greasy stove. Cole glanced right, into a small living room with a worn floral couch, a worn and stained rug, and a fairly new big screen television.

"It's up here," Gina said as she led Cole up the narrow staircase and fit a key into a door down the hall.

As the door swung open, the dankness of the room sucked the air out of Cole. A grungy window let in minimal light while yellowed walls stifled the space. A stained and sagging twin mattress covered most of the splintered wooden floor, and empty wine bottles littered the rest of the room.

"Can I keep this?" Cole asked as he picked up a healthy plant from the windowsill.

"Sure. I'd just toss it otherwise."

Gripping Sasha's plant, Cole shuffled down the stairs and out the door. "Thanks for your help," he said as he wrestled the screen open. Turning his back on the house, he wandered to his car.

"What's with the name Magda?" Frank asked. "And what's with the plant?"

"It's a messed-up situation. She has a handful of pseudonyms that she uses for different situations. I don't know why she does it, but it makes it all that much harder to track her down."

Frank nodded as he stared at the dirty snowbanks. "Are you going to work today?"

"Yeah, I'm going to work," Cole said, the base of his skull pulsing with pain. "What time is it anyway?"

"Quarter to one. Our shift started almost an hour ago and you're not even geared up."

Cole stared into the distance and squinted at the glare of the sun lurking amongst clouds. "When I was sitting in traffic, I looked up bus schedules heading anywhere west of here. Their website is terrible, by the way; it took me forever to find what I was looking for. Anyway, it looks like there are four busses out of Lashburn today heading to either Beachport or Ellison, with multiple stops along the way. Two busses already left, one is due to leave at one-forty, and the other at three."

"Take the day if you need it, but if you're working, you can gear up and then we can head to the bus station in time to catch the one-forty bus."

Cole nodded and looked around the neighborhood. He felt for his gun, his muscles tensing when his hand sliced the air where it should sit.

"I'll do this with you, but you need to be prepared to respond to calls. If you can't guarantee that you can be a police officer today, then I don't want you working with me."

"I'm working today, Frank. The next bus doesn't leave for almost an hour. If Sasha's on that bus, I'll catch her in time. If not, we'll try for the three o'clock bus."

"Why don't you take Saxton through to The Maples and hook up with One-Hundredth. I'll go the opposite way and meet up with

Ninety-Sixth. We'll look for Sasha along the way, and we'll meet at the police station and head out from there when you're geared up."

Cole slumped into his vehicle. He felt like a used punching bag as he nestled Sasha's abandoned plant in the cup holder. As he drove, he searched every bus stop he passed, his phone clutched in his hand, but the phone sat eerily silent.

Cole scanned the bus station crowd again as travelers rushed past.

"I've walked the length of the station twice, but haven't spotted her," Frank said as he met up with Cole. "Any luck with the ticket agents?"

"No one recognized her picture, and they've only had four cash payments in the past two hours—three of them by men and one by an older woman."

"It's one-thirty," Frank said, glancing at his watch. "She might be on the bus already."

Cole climbed aboard the bus, his limbs shaking with lingering adrenaline. Passengers stared as he side-stepped the narrow aisle and peered into the empty restroom. At one-forty, the doors closed, and the bus pulled away, leaving Cole and Frank breathing exhaust fumes.

Busted pens littered the floor at Cole's feet as Frank pulled another vehicle over for a seatbelt infraction. His teeth madly worked the plastic casing when a suspicious person complaint came in, and again for a domestic violence call. He rolled his neck and tried to shrug out his shoulders when voices crackled over the radio, offering to pick up the files.

"It's two thirty-five, Frankie," Cole said, bouncing his leg as he stared out the window.

"I know, buddy. We're on our way."

Cole raced through the bus station, searching every corner and canvassing the ticket agents again. He held out his phone and scrolled through pictures of Sasha, but the agents shook their heads.

"No?" Frank asked as Cole stepped from the three o'clock bus.

"It's the last bus. She's got to show up. She has to."

Frank glanced at his watch. "Two fifty-three. She still might show."

"Come on, Sash..." Cole said under his breath. He bounced his knees and scanned the crowds.

"Shots fired! Shots fired! Officer down!" Both radios erupted to life. Cole's knees stiffened.

"We have to go, Daws!"

"I know! I know!" Cole burst into a sprint behind Frank, pushing through the crowd towards their car.

"I think that was Potansky's voice," Cole said as Frank pulled from the curb, lights flashing and sirens wailing. "That means it's Freson. Freson's down."

"We don't know anything yet. Don't go jumping to conclusions."

Horrid images infected Cole's mind: His friend and colleague lying in snow stained red as he gasped for air and clutched his stomach, thick blood oozing through his fingers.

"Focus, Daws. Run through the scenario of what we need to do next."

Shaking the gruesome image from his mind, Cole picked up the radio as a worn backpack made its way through the crowd.

Cole's long, even breaths cut through the stillness of the police car. He kept his forehead pressed to the steering wheel, his car a barricade to public traffic. *You chased her away. If you had only... Then maybe...*

"Dammit!" he yelled, smacking the steering wheel with his fist. He steadied his gaze on officers outside his window, some in uniform, some in suits. Another police car—lights and sirens intense—swept past and turned down the next street.

Cole plucked his phone from the dash and reread the latest texts from Frank.

> FRANKIE: Freson will be all right. The bullet only hit his shoulder. Lucky bastard will get a nice paid holiday out of this.
> DAWSON: Your black humor needs work. What's the status of the shooter?
> FRANKIE: In cells. Likely won't be remanded till tomorrow sometime. Apparently, he's got quite the rap sheet.

Cole dumped his phone on the dash and slumped his head on the steering wheel. *You missed her calls for help ten years ago and you failed her again today. You're no friend.*

"Pull yourself together, Dawson," Cole said, raking his hands through his hair. "Rehashing all your mistakes will not bring her back. You need to track her down."

Grabbing his phone and punching in an internet search for vineyards, Cole navigated his way to an alphabetical listing for the region. "Where will I find you, Sash?" he murmured. "Where will you be hiding?"

"What the...?" Cole's eyes refused to blink as he stared at the long list of vineyards and wineries he held in his hand. He scrolled. And scrolled. Over two hundred entries.

"Orchards." Cole pulled up a list of orchards in the grower cooperative, but the sunny quote at the top of the page steamrolled him, leaving him a pulpy mess: *"With over 430 grower families in the cooperative..."*

The phone dimmed, then blackened. Cole stared at the empty screen. As much as he tried to hold on to a thin ray of hope, he knew in his heart that Sasha was gone.

Chapter 17

July

Sasha rested her head on the window of the empty conference room and hugged her knees to her chest. Her eyes were red and puffy, her cheeks glistening with drying tears. Cars rolled past the Campbell Police Department and families stopped at an ice cream truck. Sasha stared through the scene and thought of Cole.

"Dumpy home... stupid reason... your lies..." His words, his anger, had engulfed her like a tidal wave, churning her underwater, raking her across the bottom, and forcing her into the vast sea.

Ashton, she had reasoned. *I'll go to Ashton and beg Curtis to take me back.* Yet, as she pushed her cash towards the ticketing agent, she said, "One way to Ellison, please."

Ellison was wet and gray, and her winter clothes hung heavy and damp off her body. Her hand had become a calcified claw gripping the baggy deep in her pocket, the stack growing thinner with each passing day. "Suck it up and shove it down," she said as she tossed another application form in the trash... as the smell of freshly roasted nuts wafted from a street vendor... as she watched a man get down on one knee in the middle of a park.

155

Relief, finally, at a vineyard. She embraced every corner of her room as she unpacked her backpack but when she looked out her window, an image of Lashburn from Cole's balcony slapped her in the face.

In the fields, hiding between rows of vines, she pushed her muscles to prune, hoe, fertilize, and stake. She ignored tired arms and aching legs as she worked long days and weekends, but Cole was always with her. *What is he doing? What is he thinking? Is he glad I left? Is he sad I left? Maybe one call...*

She punched in the first five numbers, then hung up and buried her face in her hands.

The new name would not stick. The new name took work. "You are Katie," she said with eyes closed. "Fun, spirited, easygoing Katie. Now go have fun with your co-workers." She opened her eyes and forced a smile for the mirror, but Sasha stared back. She crumpled to the bathroom floor and hid her face under a stack of towels.

The early morning sun was beating down as she clipped a leaf above a cluster of grapes. She tipped her water bottle back as a welcome breeze ruffled the drawstring on her sunhat. A tickle on her arm attracted her gaze and she stiffened.

Black widow.

Fingers tingling, she brushed the intruder off. It disappeared.

"Where are you?!" She danced around, searching her clothing for the beast. The sensation of fifty spiders crawling on her skin sent the vineyard spinning. Bracing her hands on her knees, she gulped for breaths.

"Are you all right, Katie?" a co-worker yelled from another row of vines.

"I'm not feeling well. I need to go back to the house."

In her room, she ripped off her clothing and searched every inch of her naked body. She showered, scrubbing her skin until it was red, but tiny spider legs continued to scurry over her skin, tearing pieces of Katie away until only a shell of a human was left.

She shoved her room into her pack, quit her job, and staggered down the road in the direction of the nearest town. Tears swelled in her throat and her airway tightened to a pinhole.

Suck it up and shove it down.

Shoulders aching under the weight of her pack and skin hot from the sun, she dragged herself to a gas station on the outskirts of town. She dreamed of a cold bottle of water but when her eyes landed on an old payphone on the far side of the lot, she stumbled towards it.

She slid the pack off her back, shoulders singing relief, and squeezed into the box. The air was hot and humid and smelled like a sweaty sock had farted. The floor was littered with the brittle husks of a hundred dead flies. She wrapped her hand around the sticky receiver and watched her fingers punch out a number she had memorized almost a year ago. As she mumbled the name *Sasha* into the phone, the pressure in her throat snapped. The dam burst.

Shaking, she slid down the wall and crumpled into the corner. With the receiver pressed to her ear, a decade's worth of tears streamed down her face.

"Hello?"

At the sound of Cole's voice, her breath caught in her throat. Curling into a tight ball, she listened to the automated voice ask Cole if he wanted Sasha back in his life. When he said yes, Sasha choked out a sob.

"Sasha?"

She stuffed the blubbering mess inside as tears fell to her shorts.

"Sasha? Are you there?"

"Yes," she squeaked out.

Cole was quiet, hesitant. "Where are you?"

"Campbell."

"Campbell. I don't know Campbell. Sash, where is Campbell?"

"About two and a half hours southeast of Ellison."

"How are you?"

"…I… I'm… … …" She bit her knuckle, stifling the cries.

"Are you hurt? Did someone hurt you?"

"No… No, I'm okay."

"You don't sound okay. What's going on?"

Sasha scrambled for a lie, but there were none. "I don't know. I just don't know who I am anymore."

"Do you have a job?"

Hiccupping in a sob, she squeezed her eyes shut. "I did. I've been at a vineyard since March, but I quit this morning."

"Why did you quit your job?"

"I just… I just… I can't…"

"Do you have a home?"

"I left that this morning, too."

"Do you need me to come for you?"

Gripping her stomach, Sasha coiled herself into a tighter ball. "It's a ten-hour drive."

"I have Campbell pulled up on my phone and I can be there in nine hours."

"Cole…" She grasped for words, grasped for anything to keep her from being pulled under the swamping waves.

"Where are you right now? I mean, exactly. Where are you calling from?"

"A phone booth," she hiccupped. "Southern edge of Campbell. Costline Gas."

"Do you have a friend you can stay with until I get there?"

"No."

"I'm going to send a Campbell police trooper to get you."

"No, please," she said between ragged breaths. "I don't want to bother the police."

"Sasha, listen to me. You will not be bothering anybody, I promise. This is what police do. They help people. You have nowhere to go, and I won't let you sit in a phone booth for the next nine hours. I will contact the Campbell Police, and a trooper will come for you. He or she will take you to the station where you will wait for me. You will be safe, you will have people to help you out, and I will be able to find you, okay?"

Okay.

"Sasha, did you hear me?"

"Yes."

"I'm going to hang up now, Sash. Stay where you are, and a trooper will be by for you as soon as one is available. I'll see you tonight."

Sasha nodded and hugged the phone to her face.

"Sasha, are you there?"

"Yes."

"Stay there and wait for the police. Please. I'll see you soon."

"Okay."

She heard the click of Cole ending the call and then let the ocean take her.

Sasha twitched at the knock on the conference room door and lifted her head from her knees. Cole, stubble-faced and hair a little longer than she remembered, hovered in the doorway. Tears leaked down Sasha's face as Cole's harsh tone and kind smile reverberated in her head.

"Come here," Cole said, stepping around the table.

Sasha rose from her chair. The moment her hand touched his, warmth swept through her like sunshine rippling through her veins. He pulled her in and wrapped her in his arms.

Pressing her hands to his back, Sasha dug her nose into his chest. She breathed in a hint of sweat and dryer sheet as a wave of tears sputtered from her. "Sorry I left."

"It's all right, it's all right..." he whispered as he stroked her hair, her tears staining his shirt.

When her ragged breaths evened to quiet snuffles, Cole pulled back enough to look at her. "How about we get out of here?"

The sweet scent of evening primrose floated in the air as they crossed the lot to Cole's car. "I saw a Thai place on my way through town," he said as he pulled himself behind the wheel. "What do you say we pick something up from there to take back to the motel?"

"The motel?"

"There's one off the highway on the other side of town. I had just come off night shift when you called. I haven't slept in over twenty-four hours, and I'm bagged. I need food and I need a bed."

Warm wind whipped Sasha's hair through the open window as Cole pulled from the station.

"And I'm not going to let you apologize for calling me. It was my choice to drive out here."

"I wasn't going to apologize," Sasha said as she watched kids run through sprinklers on front lawns. "I needed you to come. I don't know what I would have done or where I would have gone without you. My life is out of options, and I don't have the energy to figure out what to do next."

Cole, lips pursed and forehead creased, glanced at Sasha. "We'll figure this out. I need to know what you're dealing with so I can help you, but I'm too tired to do that tonight. We'll grab some food and a room, and we'll have a long drive to talk it all out tomorrow."

"Where are you going to take me?"

"You mean tomorrow?"

"Yeah."

"I was hoping to take you home with me. Get you settled at my place until you get your feet under you again. When you're ready, we'll find you your own place. A good place. A decent place."

Sasha propped her elbow on the windowsill and gnawed her knuckles.

"But that's a long time away. One step at a time, and you're not going to be on your own until you're ready." Cole reached across the seat and squeezed Sasha's hand.

As they drove through town, Sasha stared ahead at everything and nothing. She felt like a hollow shell with enough cracks and fissures that she should no longer be intact. Cole took charge of finding food and a room as Sasha withered in the car.

"Second floor," Cole said as he opened the back door of the car and hauled out their bags. "Can you grab the food?"

Sasha's legs were lead as she dragged them up the stairs. "What room?" she asked, shuffling along the balcony, passing door after door.

"This one here, right in front of you. Two-oh-nine." Cole reached around Sasha and fiddled with the key card, the hem of his t-shirt brushing the skin of her arm.

The door swung open. "Only one bed?"

"It's all they had," Cole said and nudged Sasha into the room. "I don't mind sharing a bed, but if you're uncomfortable with it, I can take the floor."

"No... You don't need to sleep on the floor. We can share."

Cole kicked off his sandals and zipped open his overnight bag. "I'm hungry, I'm tired, and I haven't showered in ages. Do you mind if I have the first shower?"

"Go ahead." Sasha placed the boxed food on the table near the television and flinched when Cole's hand settled on her back. He stepped around her and pulled her to his chest.

"I'm so happy you called," he said, his voice hauntingly close as his lips grazed her ear. "I was tortured over you leaving and I'll always be sorry for the way I acted that morning. Thank you for calling."

As though testing for a trap, Sasha inched her arms around his waist. When he gathered her in a deeper hug, she relaxed and pulled in a full breath. "Go for your shower. And thank you for driving all the way here to get me."

"You're my Sasha, and no matter the time of day or the distance, I will come." He planted a kiss on her temple and relaxed his arms from around her.

As the bathroom door clicked behind Cole, Sasha's eyes drifted closed. The scent of garlic, curry, and pork wafted through the muggy room. She flopped face-first on the bed and let the mattress carry her load as the sound of running water on the other side of the wall relaxed her clenched stomach.

She did not hear the shower turn off or the bathroom door open, but Cole was suddenly sitting beside her. "Why aren't you eating?"

"Hm?" Sasha lifted her head. Cole's hair was damp, and he looked like he had plugged himself in and recharged. "I was waiting for you."

Cole smiled and rubbed Sasha's back, his hand loosening some of her muscles. "If you are planning on showering, do that now and we can eat together afterwards."

Sasha pulled herself from the bed and rummaged through her pack. As the silkiness of her little blue nightie brushed her fingertips, she paused. She dug around for a t-shirt, but the thought of the thick cotton brought on a wave of sweat. She steadied her breath, gathered her things, and slipped into the bathroom.

With sweat, sunscreen, and dust shed, Sasha gingerly stepped from the bathroom. Laughter erupted from the television where a comedian was walking around on stage, yammering into a microphone. Her eyes shifted to Cole. He was sitting up in bed, the boxed food unopened beside him.

Sasha scuttled across the room and slipped into bed. As Cole's gaze lingered on her profile, she tightened her grip on the blanket. The bed creaked, the mattress dipped, and Cole's peppermint shampoo settled over her. Sasha glanced sideways and when her eyes met his, her sun-kissed cheeks burned a shade pinker. The audience laughed.

Tearing her eyes away, Sasha focused on the floral pattern of the blanket. The comedian's voice bounced off the walls, a car passed outside, and Sasha's heart drummed. Her nail traced the outline of a rose, then faltered and slipped into a pit of peonies as Cole's fingertips grazed her arm. He caressed the skin along the top of her shoulder, spawning a cascade of goosebumps, and slipped a finger under the spaghetti strap of her nightie.

"What are you doing?" Sasha whispered, tears brimming her eyes.

Cole's hand froze. "I just..." His fingers slinked away. "Sorry. I misread your signals."

"My signals?"

"Yeah." Cole shifted on the bed and turned to the comedian. "I just thought... I'm sorry. I know you're struggling, and I shouldn't have jumped to conclusions."

"I'm sorry?" A tear rolled down her cheek.

"You just look so damn hot in that. I'm tired and not thinking straight and I thought there was a particular reason why you put it on."

Sasha's eyes grew wide, and her jaw dropped. "Cole!" she said, shoving him away. "Just because I slept with you once doesn't mean it's going to happen again."

"Sorry. I'm tired, not thinking straight, and you walk out of the bathroom looking like that. I just assumed…"

"Oh my gosh, Cole!" Sasha pulled the blanket higher on her body. "I'm going to go put on a t-shirt."

"Sasha, don't." Cole grabbed Sasha's fist. "I'm sorry, okay? What I meant to say is you look really pretty. I'll feel horrible if you change because I acted like an ass. Let's rewind the last five minutes and I'll pretend I glance up at you when you come out of the bathroom, and then I turn back to the TV without another thought of how gorgeous you are. You cuddle in beside me—as friends—and then we pig out on cold Thai food before passing out into a deep sleep."

Sasha stared at Cole, her mind a tangled mess.

"Look," Cole said, his voice growing quiet. "Twelve hours ago, I thought I was never going to see you again, and now we're together in a crummy motel in the middle of wine country. You're my best friend and the most important person in the world to me. I would never intentionally do anything to tarnish your trust in me, and I'm really sorry I misread the situation. What I want to do with the rest of the evening is exactly what I just said—pig out on Thai food and pass out beside each other so when I wake up in the morning and see your face, I will know that today wasn't another one of my dreams about you coming home."

Sasha tried the swallow the lump that had formed in her throat.

Keeping his eyes locked on hers, Cole brought his fingers to his lips, then brushed them to Sasha's cheek. Her skin tingled under his touch. With a sweet smile, he repositioned himself on the bed and reached for the boxes. "I am well past famished."

Chapter 18

Cole changed the radio station and glanced again at Sasha—her head stayed glued to the window, her body pressed to the door.

"A new bowling alley opened up in Lashburn," he said. "We should check it out sometime."

Sasha stayed a ghost.

With a sigh, Cole turned the volume up, the singer's lyrics drowning out the rumble of tires on asphalt.

Rolling hills with sprawling vineyards and orchards gave way to twisting mountain roads before the landscape evened out to bright yellow canola fields. Cole pointed out deer and sheep, laughed at his own jokes, and asked questions, but Sasha was gone. By the time they pulled into the city, Cole felt like the fraying Velcro on his police vest's pocket.

Dumping their bags onto the floor in the front entry, Cole said, "I don't work tomorrow, so I'll clear out some space for you to store your stuff then. As for tonight, you'll have to live out of your pack."

"That's okay." Sasha looked around Cole's home. "I'm used to living out of it."

As Cole headed to the kitchen, he called over his shoulder, "I have some leftover pork and a bagged salad in my fridge, and we can supplement it with noodles or something. I don't really feel like cooking a big meal."

Sasha padded along behind. "That's okay by me."

Cole pulled two beers from the fridge before hauling the leftovers out and putting water on to boil. Sasha sat at the table, meticulously peeling the label from her bottle. Like a ghost come to visit again.

Sliding into the chair across from her, Cole reached for her hand. The beer's iciness lingered on her skin as he laced his fingers through hers. "This is your home now. I don't have a bed for you, but we'll make you comfortable."

As Sasha focused on her beer, Cole finished putting their dinner together, the sound of bubbling water and the hum of the microwave echoing through the quiet home. They ate in an eerie silence, quietly cleared the table, and slipped into their pajamas. Shuffling out of the bathroom in her sleeping shorts and tee from Christmas, Sasha eased onto the couch. A moment later, Cole flopped down beside her.

"Sharks?" he said, handing Sasha her slippers and sliding his feet into his pair. She tentatively took the slippers and pulled them onto her feet, her blank frown not shifting.

"I'm not upset with you, you know," Cole said. "I'm sad that life has been difficult for you, but I don't blame you for anything that's happened to you. I'm still here for you."

Sasha adjusted the slippers on her feet.

"What is making you so sad?"

"My life is so screwed up," Sasha whispered, wiping a tear away. "I have no idea what to do."

Cole frowned as he searched Sasha's face. "Come here," he said. He put his arm around her and pulled her close. Her rigid body softened, slackened... relaxed. She rested her head on his chest and burrowed into him.

"You're not alone. Tomorrow we can make a plan of where you want to be in life, and we'll get you there. Together. You can get a job, a place of your own, a phone. I'll help you get an ID and bank account, and I can teach you to drive so you can get a driver's license. It's completely doable with a plan and a little direction. If you give yourself a year to figure things out and build a foundation for your life, then you can head back west if Lashburn isn't working for you."

Cole searched Sasha's face, but she remained stoic and silent.

"We'll put your life back together, okay?"

"I don't know how I can get to that point if I don't even know who I am."

"Oh, Sash." Cole sighed and wrapped his other arm around her. "Why do you say you don't know who you are? Is it because of the different names you use?"

Sasha stiffened. She collapsed her face in her hands.

"Why do you use names? I promise not to judge. I just want to know so I understand you better."

"I can't."

While he held Sasha, Cole's gaze drifted around the room. Scrabble was tucked on the bookshelf. The little potted plant sat on the coffee table. The blanket that had cocooned Sasha—and sometimes Cole—was splayed across their laps.

Sasha was everywhere.

She was in the lines of every sweep of his pencil on the framed sketch. Cole studied how the girl's hand sat in the officer's—fragile yet trusting. "You hold a lot inside," he said as he relived drawing that piece. "You always have. Let this go. Lighten your load like you did when we were kids. I promise to not spill a word to anyone."

She gripped him tighter and stuttered in a breath. "I've never told anyone."

"Then who better to unload on than me? You know you can trust me."

"I just needed to get away. From everything. From myself."

"You mean after prom?"

With a deep breath in and a long breath out, Sasha traced the soft eyeball of left shark. "You don't get it."

"I'm trying, Sash, but you're not giving me anything to work with."

"You want to know why I use names? Where this all started from?"

Cole held his breath, fearing that the slightest noise would seal her lips again.

"I grew up being told I was useless. Worthless. I still believe it."

"It's not true though. It never has been."

"But I was suffocating. Losing my mind." Hugging her knees to her chest, Sasha hid her face in the ball of herself. "Thinking really dark thoughts."

The air in the room had grown hot, as though the fireplace was roaring. "Why didn't you tell me?"

"I couldn't tell anyone. My mind was a terrifying place, and the fear of saying anything aloud was overwhelming, but something needed to change, so I left. I put Sasha and Lashburn in the past and started fresh. New name and personality. New backstory." She raised her head, silent tears marking her face, an ocean of memories swirling in her eyes. "I had the entire story built up in my head. My name was going to be Sarah Reed, and I actually thought that I could simply create a whole new identity. Gosh, I was dumb. I completely lost it when I realized I was stuck being me."

Cole watched Sasha's face as she relentlessly picked her nails. She started to sink back into the blanket, back behind her wall of secrets. "What did you do?"

"Ha." An oddly wicked smile crossed Sasha's features. "It snowballed. Got out of control until I didn't know any better. My new normal."

The words of his interview instructor bounced around his head: *"Keep them talking."* His heart raced. "Snowballed?"

Sasha picked at the fuzz balls that clung to Cole's pajama bottoms and began to create a small mountain of pilling on his leg. "People don't like runaways, and they don't like stories of a sucky homelife. I was an outcast before I even had a chance."

"Come on, Sash."

"You have no idea." She pushed back from Cole, scattering her pilling mountain to the blanket creases. "Your life is so freaking easy."

Cole's jaw clenched and he bit his tongue before words could fly.

"So here I was, out on my own, freaking out that all my glorious plans were proven ridiculous. I refused to head back to Lashburn, and I was too stubborn to not keep pushing for a new life. I met a guy at a bar one night and when he asked my name, I made something up. It just came out. And you know what? That was the first time someone looked at me like I had something important to say. I will never forget that moment. I needed to hold on to that moment, so I started telling people what they wanted to hear rather than the truth. *'Hi, I'm Roxanne and I come from an amazing family. I moved out here for life experience.'* And guess what?" She turned to Cole, her features a mix of delight and fierceness. "It worked. I got a job. I made friends. I got my first boyfriend. And when that life fell apart, I picked up a new life. I knew I couldn't completely escape the name, so for nine years, I was Sasha only on paper."

"And you've been keeping this up for a decade?"

"My new normal. I faked my way through a third of my life and I've made up so much stuff about myself that I don't really know what is real anymore."

Cole laced his fingers in Sasha's and searched her face, her body language, her nuances. Sasha was in there. But so was Magda... Jane... Hayley...

"And to top it all off, I'm a criminal."

His hand slackened in hers. "What?"

"I'm a fraud. Giving out false names and stuff?" Sasha turned to Cole, tears ready to spill down her face. "I didn't mean for it to get out of control like this."

"Don't scare me like that. If you're just talking about making up names, then it's not illegal, it's just lying. Those lies are huge and deep, but that's all they are."

"Oh." Sasha leaned into Cole and traced the letters on his t-shirt. "I guess that's not so bad."

"They are still lies, Sash. Big ones."

Sasha shrugged as her finger swept around the S. "I actually was happy living like that. I wasn't hurting anybody by pretending to be somebody else, and it worked for me. But then Curtis destroyed who I had reinvented myself as. And then, as I was finally feeling like I was handling life again, you came along and turned me back into Sasha."

"I didn't turn you back into Sasha. You've always been Sasha."

"No, I buried Sasha years ago, but you unearthed her. As hard as I tried, I couldn't maintain my personas around you; I could only be Sasha. After spending my entire adult life trying to be anyone but myself, everything got jumbled up in my head. I left Lashburn again with the intent that I'd leave Sasha behind forever, as she only confused things. I wanted to get my fake life back, but I couldn't. You got under my skin and as much as I tried to be someone else, I kept reverting back to being me. And now, after trying to run from myself for so long, and no longer being able to fit into a new persona, I'm trapped. I'm not really Sasha, but I'm not anyone else, either. I'm a hundred different names and none at all."

Cole's head filled with the disturbing swears that had spilled from Sasha's mouth on Christmas. He buried his face in her neck. She smelled like Sasha. She *was* Sasha.

"Sasha," he said, lifting his head and looking into her eyes. "I know you feel like you don't know who you are, but I do. I see you and I know exactly who you are."

Sasha looked at Cole as he ran his fingers through her hair.

"You're Sasha Cooper. You're my Sasha. You are the fun, quiet, quirky girl from next door, and you're my best friend. Sometimes you get lost in yourself, but you always come back."

With a trembling lip, she tucked her head under his chin.

"Our Christmas day was my favorite day of the entire past ten years. On that day, you had moments where you broke away from whatever holds you down and you were wholly and completely Sasha, and you were perfect. I want you to find that person again and hold on to her for longer and longer periods of time until that is who you are all the time. Forget Magda or Jane or whoever else is stuck in your brain. Be Sasha and know that, despite what your dad said, Sasha has value and Sasha is a good, smart, compassionate, fun person. She's someone worth being."

Pushing herself from Cole, Sasha stared ahead at the pencil sketch. A tear rolled down her cheek.

"The stuff you're saying is scaring me. It's not healthy to be all these different personas, and it's not safe. I'm scared for the day that you lie to the wrong person. I think there is value in seeing a doctor."

Her eyes glazed over, and her voice lost all emotion. "I'm not crazy, you know. I *know* what I'm doing. I create my personas, and I use them like an actor uses a character."

"I didn't say you were crazy. What I meant was that clearly there are issues going on inside of you that you really should address. Life is an adventure to be lived, not to be acted."

"I'm not seeing a doctor."

"Fine," Cole said with a sigh. "If you think you can do this—find yourself—on your own with my help, then we'll try that first."

She stayed motionless, her body rigid.

"You are a good person, and you have value, Miss Sasha Cooper. Believe it."

Like a slowly deflating balloon, she let out a long sigh. Collapsing to the side, she laid her head on Cole's lap. As he stroked her hair, his pajama bottoms dampened with tears that leaked down Sasha's face.

Chapter 19

Cole pulled a box of Cheerios from his pantry as the mew of a gull drifted in through the screen door. He could not help but steal another glance into the living room where Sasha lay curled up on the couch, a light snore rumbling from her.

Settling into a chair with cereal bowl in hand, he typed *horticultural jobs Lashburn* into his search bar and sighed at the lack of useful results.

The whirr of traffic in the streets below and the hum of the fridge were Cole's companions as he downed his second cup of coffee and read through the day's news. Flipping the screen closed, he wandered into the living room. Sasha was a blanketed lump with glazed eyes poking out from the folds.

"Hey." Cole smiled and settled himself on the rug. "Good morning, my Sasha."

Sasha's gaze refocused. She stared at Cole like he was a fascinating piece of art.

"Can I get you a coffee or some breakfast?"

She looked away.

"Today we'll unpack your bag and find a place to put your stuff. We can also talk about jobs if you want, although we don't have to do

173

that right away if you're not ready. I'm back at work tomorrow, but I have nothing on the go today." With a kiss on Sasha's cheek, Cole pulled himself from the rug and poured a coffee, sliding in mountains of sugar.

"Here," he said, planting himself beside her. "Drink some coffee and then I'll get you something to eat."

"Thank you," she said and grunted to sitting.

"You're tough, strong, and resilient, Sash. You'll find yourself again. What can I get you to eat?"

"Nothing, thank you. I'm not hungry."

"Your body won't work if you don't fuel it. I'll make you some toast with peanut butter."

After watching Sasha nibble half of her toast and push it away, Cole suggested she unpack her bag, but she shook her head. He offered her a bath, but she flopped onto her side. "How about a game of Scrabble?" he asked. She buried her face in the cushions.

With a frown creasing his features, Cole tucked the blanket around Sasha's shoulders and smoothed her unruly hair. "I need to get groceries. Why don't you come with me? Get out of the condo for a bit. A change of scenery might do you some good."

"No, thank you."

"Do you just want to spend the day here?"

Sasha nodded and pulled the blanket over her head.

Breathing out pent up air, Cole stared at the lump of blanket. "If you're planning on sticking around here all day, then maybe I'll head to the gym as well. Do you mind if I'm gone for a few hours?"

"No," she said from her burrow.

"Is there anything you want me to pick up?"

"No, thank you."

Bending to a crouch, Cole eased the blanket down, shadows slinking from Sasha's face. "You're not going to run from me, are you?"

"No."

"Remember," he said, grazing his thumb across her cheek. "This is your home now. Make yourself comfortable. Feed yourself, watch TV, whatever. Later today, I'll dig out my spare key so you can come and go at your leisure." Cole paused and looked at his lost friend. "I'll be back in a few," he said and kissed the top of her head. "Take care of yourself, my Sasha."

Sweat rolled down Cole's back as his feet pounded the treadmill and his abs burned with crunches, yet his mind buzzed as he pictured Sasha's blank expression, glazed eyes, and monotonous tone. The more squats he did, the deeper his question to Sasha pressed down on him: *"You're not going to run from me, are you?"*

Stomach in knots, Cole abandoned the end of his workout and soaped himself down. He raced down grocery store aisles, throwing cheese, coffee, and eggs into his cart, and drummed his fingers on the cart handle as the woman ahead of him yakked to the cashier about her cat.

The overfilled grocery bags cut into Cole's hands as he pushed through his door. "Sasha?" he said, looking towards the living room. The couch was empty, the blanket tossed to the side. Cole's heart jumped to his throat.

"Sasha, I'm back!"

His home was quiet. He glanced at the floor—her shoes and pack, like a shining beacon, were jammed behind the door.

"Sasha," Cole called as he pulled the groceries into the kitchen. Dumping the bags on the floor, he uncurled his hands. Blood rushed back into his fingers. "Where are you?" He looked to the bathroom, but the door was wide open and the light off.

"Sasha?" His heart thumped as he hurried to the bedroom. At the sight of the empty bed, his grip tensed on the doorframe.

"Sasha!" Cole dashed into the kitchen. His home darkened as a cloud drifted in front of the sun. "Sasha!"

The silhouette of Sasha nestled in a patio chair on the balcony caught his eye. Collapsing his body against the wall, he trembled as adrenaline dissolved from his system.

Shaking his hands out, Cole slid the balcony door open and breathed a smile. "Hey. It took me a bit to find you. I'm glad you're enjoying the sunshine."

Sasha stared at the building across the street.

"Let me put the groceries away and then I'll come join you out here. I bought cinnamon buns."

As he plunked the milk into the fridge and tossed the bread on the counter, Cole glanced at Sasha through the screen door. She scratched her arm. She tucked her hair behind her ear. She watched the world.

Cole smiled.

With Sasha's pack balanced like a boulder on his back, Cole stepped from the coolness of the kitchen into the warm July air. "It's time to move you in," he said, dropping the pack at her feet. "I've opened up some space for your things in the linen closet. It's not ideal, but at least it'll be your own."

"I'm not really up for it right now."

"Too bad." Cole pulled up a chair and reached for the pack. "I want you moved in, so we're doing this now. I'll do all the work if you want, but you need to let me know if I'm about to find something you don't want me seeing."

Resting her cheek on her knees, Sasha said, "There is nothing left to hide from you."

Cole's fingers stiffened around the zipper pull. His eyes stayed on Sasha as he drew the teeth apart.

"It's weird to be here, to see this view," Sasha said as she gazed out over the city. "But I'm happy to be here. Thank you for letting me stay."

A smile swept across Cole's face, smoothing his creased features. "You're welcome. I hope you find comfort here."

Peering into the first layer of Sasha's life, Cole found her sunhat, sunscreen, and a plastic baggy with a few bills and coins inside. He put each item on the patio table as Sasha looked on.

Cole freed the winter boots and water bottle from the front of the pack before releasing the main buckles and drawstring. As he unearthed a light jacket, an image of Sasha, frozen and shaking, flashed through his mind and turned his guts.

Shrugging off his shivers, he reached into the pack's mouth and paused. "How much do you have in here?" he asked as he pulled out a baggy thick with bills.

"Just over twenty-seven hundred."

"Wow," he said, leaning back in his chair. "You've been making good coin since I last saw you."

"I try to save what I can for when I'm out of work."

"You really need to put this in the bank."

With a huff, Sasha dropped her forehead to her knees. "You seem to think that I never wanted a bank account. I'm not dumb, Cole. I know how valuable it would be to have a bank account, but our government wants to keep struggling people struggling rather than helping them out."

"What do you mean?"

"I *tried* to get a bank account years ago. They told me I needed two pieces of ID, and one of them had to be photo ID, which I didn't have."

"I thought you had an ID back then."

"Not at that point. I went to the DMV, and they told me that to get an ID, I needed to bring in a utility bill or some other official piece of mail with my name and address on it." Sasha crossed her arms and creased her forehead as words flew from her mouth. "That didn't help me in the slightest, as my utilities were included in my rent. And apparently a General Delivery mailing address doesn't cut it. They said I could show them my rental agreement, but my rental contract was essentially a conversation: *'Can I rent a room?' 'Yes, you can.'* That's it, so I couldn't use that. They wouldn't even take a letter from my landlord, as anyone can drum up a letter."

"Your rental agreement was a conversation? That doesn't sound very legal."

"Oh please, Cole. The whole world doesn't necessarily follow every little rule."

"No kidding. That's why I have the job I have."

Sasha rolled her eyes. "Anyway, they said I could show a pay stub proving that I worked in the area, but I didn't have one on me. As I was living over half an hour away and relied on others for rides into town, I couldn't spend all day at the DMV. Each time I was in town, I'd stop in, but the line was always so long. I got used to managing my money without a bank and I never needed an ID for anything else, so I eventually gave up trying."

"But what about your expired ID that you had on the night you were locked out of my place?"

"I got that a couple of years later. I was living in another town and the DMV wasn't too far from my place, so I got an ID then."

"But you still didn't get a bank account?"

"It's not that easy," Sasha said, swatting at a fly. "I finally had all the identification I needed, but then they tell me that if I didn't keep a minimum of a thousand dollars in my account, I'd get charged twelve fifty a month in service fees. *A thousand dollars.* Can you believe it? I'd much rather eat for a week with my twelve dollars than throw it at some rich bankers. I'm so freaking tired of their stupid system. If you don't fit into their perfect mold, they find a way to keep you out of their snooty club."

"Banks aren't snooty clubs, you know."

"Easy for you to say. You're a member."

Cole bit his tongue. "So, you never got a bank account?"

"No, Cole, I didn't. Please don't judge me."

"I'm not judging. I'm just trying to understand. Why didn't you renew your ID when it expired?"

"That stupid ID did nothing but sit in my pocket. What a waste of time. I just let it lapse."

"We'll get you an account," Cole said, his eyes following an explosion of startled pigeons across the street. "Not today and not tomorrow, but soon. As for now, what do you want to do with this money?"

Sasha stared at Cole.

"Until you get a job, I insist on paying for everything. There's no need for you to burn through all this cash when I'm making good pay. Save this to put in the bank so you can start with a nice amount. If you want, you can put it in my bank account, and we'll transfer it over when you get your own account."

"That's what I did with Curtis," Sasha said as she picked at dirt under her fingernail. "He put all my money in his account and told me that one day we'd change it to a joint account, but he never did. I never got my money back from him."

The muscles in Cole's jaw tightened. "I'm not like him and your money would be safe in my account, but considering your history, I'm no longer comfortable offering that as an option. You need complete control of your money."

"He's not as bad as you make him sound. He told me not to get a job digging in the dirt, but I went behind his back and got a job anyway. If I wasn't so stubborn, then maybe it would have worked between us."

"Don't you dare try to tell me that what he did was okay, because it wasn't—not any of it. He tried to change you into someone else and when you resisted, he hit you so you would comply. You were smart and got yourself out of a dangerous situation, for which I'll always be grateful."

"It wasn't a dangerous situation. I already told you he only hit me once and I brought it on myself."

Cole dropped his head and rubbed his hands over his face. Bringing his gaze back to Sasha's, he slipped her hand over hers. "I believe you loved him, and he loved you, but he was hiding his true self from you until you guys were comfortable in your relationship. He tried to mold you into what he wanted you to be, rather than who you really are. You can tell yourself that if you only did what he asked, then he wouldn't hit you again, but the truth is, guys like that will always find a reason to hit. That blow he gave you, Sash... that was going to be the first of many. You beat the odds and got out early."

"It's not like that. I'm not a statistic. I just didn't want to be his girlfriend anymore, so I left."

"Look, Sash... I've been to far too many domestic violence calls and I've seen it all, and your situation isn't all that different. Many women in your position stay in the relationship for years and nothing ever changes. Their lives don't get better, and their man doesn't stop abusing them. You are one of the lucky ones, whether you see it or not."

"He's not one of those guys, though. He was good to me. He just... I don't know..."

"Don't make excuses for him, no matter how charming he was or how much you loved him. He doesn't deserve it."

Pulling her hand from Cole's, Sasha stared off into the distance. "You make me sound like a victim, but I don't feel like a victim. I just feel like someone who pushed her boyfriend too far. Anyway, I don't want to talk about him. He's in my past. If you think it's best to put my money in your account, I'm fine with that."

"Tell you what. I'll put it inside for now and after we're done out here, you can decide what to do with it. You're decision, not mine."

Sasha glanced sideways at Cole, the corners of her eyes crinkling with a soft smile.

With the cash stowed in the kitchen, Cole turned back to the pack and made piles of her things on the patio table and along the deck of the balcony. "So far, we have clothes, food, dinnerware, and toiletries. Can I keep going?"

Sasha nodded as she looked on.

"Let's see… this towel is done. You can have one of mine. My mom gave me too many, anyway. Same with this blanket unless it has sentimental value." He glanced at Sasha. She shook her head.

Cole returned his attention to the pack. "What the…?"

"Put it down."

"Why do you have a —"

Sasha popped up from her chair, her hands in fists. "Put it down or we're done."

"But I thought you said —"

"That's it. We're done. Give me the bag."

"Sorry." Cole dropped the bag and threw his hands up.

Sasha wrenched the bag away and began shoving her life back inside. Cole grabbed the jacket that Sasha gripped in her claws. "Stop," he said. "Please."

"I said, we're done."

"I promise not to ask you questions you don't want to answer. Promise." His hand slipped over hers.

She paused. Her chest heaved.

"We're almost done," Cole said. "Let's just finish it. Power through, okay?"

Sasha stared at the collection of her things on the table as she shifted her weight from one foot to the other and back again. She nodded and, releasing her pack back to Cole, fell into her chair. "You're not allowed to ask."

"Okay." Placing Sasha's secret beside a half-used tube of toothpaste, he dug into the pack again.

"Oh... These really should be replaced." Cole fingered the thin canvas slip-ons that now had a hole in the right toe.

Twisting her body away from him, Sasha flipped her hoodie over her head.

"They're nice shoes, but you deserve to get something new with good support."

"Whatever," she said into the breeze.

With a half frown, Cole turned back to the almost-empty pack, using his fingers as eyes. His hand brushed over smooth fabric, and he withdrew the top piece of a small black bikini by one of its teensy strings. Cole's eyebrows shot up. "What is this?" he said with a laugh, holding the bikini high, the strings swaying in the breeze.

"Oh." Sasha's face sprouted the color of a tomato. She snatched the top from Cole and thrust her hand deep into the pack. As she yanked her hand out, Cole smirked at the matching bottoms clamped in her fist. "You don't need to worry about that," she said, sinking into her chair and stuffing the bikini behind her back.

Cole raised his eyebrows again and chuckled before turning back to the bag. "This is nice," he said as he pulled out a crumpled red cocktail dress and black pumps. "Miss Cooper, I never would have guessed."

"Leave me alone, Cole."

"I'm just teasing. This is a really nice dress, and I don't doubt you need to dress up from time to time. It's just that I've never seen you in a dress, other than the grad dinner, and I can't imagine you wearing heels. Are you able to walk in them?"

Lip quivering, Sasha pushed herself from her chair and stormed towards the sliding door.

"Sash," Cole said, reaching his arm out to stop her. "I was only teasing. You probably turn every eye in the room when you wear this. Please sit."

Sasha shook her head and looked skyward.

"I'm really sorry. We're almost done, and I promise to cut it with the stupid jokes."

With a sniffle and a huff, she turned from the door and slumped into her chair.

"Thank you. Sorry. May I continue?"

Sasha crossed her arms over her chest. Peering out from the side of her hood, she shot Cole a death glare. "Yes."

After placing the dress and shoes on the table, Cole reached into the pack and fished out a small makeup kit. Setting the makeup next to the dress, he glanced at Sasha—her face was buried in her tucked-up knees.

"You know what?" Cole said to the top of Sasha's head as he hauled out her winter gear. "You are truly amazing. To be able to fit all this in a single pack... It's really something."

She lifted her head, her wet eyes poking out from behind her forearms.

The bag was light and shrunken, its heart and bowels spread across the balcony. Cole was about to lean the pack against the wall but a small square of paper at the bottom, bent and frayed, caught his eye. When he pulled it out, a half smile stuttered across his face. He was staring at himself at age sixteen, his cheek pressed to Sasha's. A goofy, open-mouthed grin popped from him while a smile tried to squeeze from Sasha's sealed lips. Cole held the photo up to Sasha. She cocked her head, and a sliver of a smile crossed her face.

"And that's it," she said. "That's all that I've amassed over the twenty-eight years of my pathetic life."

"Your life is not pathetic, and life is not about the stuff you have. It's about the experiences, adventures, people, and memories made, and I'm fairly certain you've amassed many of those."

Sasha chewed on her lip, her gaze drifting out over the city.

"How about I toss your clothes in the wash to freshen them up, I'll add your food to my pantry, and I'll put your toiletries in the bathroom."

Without saying a word, Sasha pushed herself from her chair and crawled into Cole's lap. Curling herself into a tight ball, she wrapped her arms around him and buried her face in his neck. "Thank you," she said as warm tears dampened Cole's skin. "Thank you for everything."

Chapter 20

Cole leaned against the elevator wall and flipped through the application forms in his hand.

"Sasha's lucky to have you," Frank had said when Cole stepped from another restaurant. *"You're a good friend."*

But as Cole looked at the stack he had collected throughout the day, he could only picture Sasha with a smile if she was snipping deadheads from petunias. "She doesn't need another freaking dishwashing job," Cole said as the doors parted, and dumped his hard work into the hallway's trashcan.

As he closed the distance to his door, he pretended to see through the walls to Sasha. She would be smiling, and she would tell Cole all about the garden she had planted. Vases bursting with flowers of every color and texture would crowd his shelves, and life would be perfect.

As he reached for the knob, muffled voices from the TV drifted through the door. Cole's daydream was swept away like glitter into the wind, and reality took up residence in his gut.

"Hey, Sash. How was your day?" Cole said as he pushed the door closed behind him. An old rerun of a sitcom played while Sasha slumped into the couch. As though a convenience store had exploded in Cole's living room, the floor was littered with granola bar wrappers, empty microwaveable popcorn bags, a couple cans of pop, and the packaging from the pepperoni sticks that Cole had bought in Campbell. "Have you just been watching TV all day?"

Sasha stared at the television.

"Considering you're still in your pjs, I'm guessing you didn't get out today."

She replied with only a shrug.

"You know, I do have healthy food options in my fridge. And speaking of food, how's stir fry sound?"

Canned laughter filled the room.

"Let's clean up this mess," Cole said as he picked wrappers up off the floor, "and then you can join me in the kitchen, and we can spend some time together."

With a groan, Sasha rolled off the couch and reached for a popcorn bag that had yellow-orange grease oozing over its list of chemicals.

"I'm here to help you, but I'm not here to wait on you," Cole said as they headed to the kitchen. "I'll do the chicken. You find some veggies and chop them up."

"What veggies?"

Cole yanked the fridge open and pulled out a selection of vegetables. He threw them on the counter before finding a cutting board and knife. "These veggies. Any other questions?"

"How do you want them chopped?"

"Seriously?"

Sasha stared at the pile of produce like it was going to attack.

"We're making a stir fry. Cut them a good size for a stir fry."

Cole pulled the chicken from its packaging and hacked it into chunks. He glanced over his shoulder—Sasha stared at the vegetables.

"We need them in bite-sized pieces, but I honestly don't care about the shape. Be creative."

Sasha drifted towards the sink with carrots in hand. "How many of each kind of vegetable do you want?"

Cole bit his tongue and readjusted his grip on the knife. "We can make enough for both of us to have leftovers for tomorrow's lunch. With four meals to prep, four of each type of veggie should do it."

Knives thumped on cutting boards, plastic wrap ruffled away from celery, the tap turned on then off. Cole rolled his shoulders and stretched his neck. "You're welcome to use my computer while I'm at work if you want to search out potential jobs or just play around online or something. And it wouldn't hurt to touch base with Craig Patterson in case he's short staffed or something. Maybe after supper I'll help you create an email account that you can use for correspondence with your job search."

Cole glanced at Sasha, but her back was turned to him. With a stifled groan, he poured oil into the pan and turned the element on. As a trail of oil inched its way across the dark surface, soft sniffling filled the air.

"What now?" Cole peered around Sasha. Her face was lined with tears. The rock in Cole's gut shifted to a pain in his heart.

"Hey," Cole said softly. He slid the knife from Sasha's hand and pulled her into him. "What's going on?"

Clutching clumps of Cole's shirt in her fists, Sasha collapsed her weight into him.

"Did I say something to upset you? I'm sorry if I did. Please tell me what's wrong."

With another sniffle, Sasha relaxed her hands and snuggled into Cole's arms. Wrapping her up in as much warmth and sunshine as he could send through his pores, Cole pressed his lips to the top of her head and stroked her hair while she whimpered.

"Onion," she finally murmured.

"What?" Cole pulled back and looked into Sasha's wet eyes. "Onion?"

Her face relaxed and her mouth bubbled into a smile. "The onion. I was chopping the onion, and it made me cry."

"That's it? You're not sad or upset or anything?"

"It really hurts." Sasha sniffled as she wiped her eyes. "Ow. I shouldn't have touched my eyes. Now they hurt more."

"Why didn't you tell me that when I first asked what was going on? You let me hug you for ages because I thought you were really upset about something."

Sasha shrugged and another smile spread across her face. "I was really enjoying that hug, so I let you think that."

"My Sasha," Cole said with a laugh as he pulled her to him again. "I have a solution to your onion problem."

"A solution?" Sasha said as Cole disappeared down the hall and into his bedroom.

"A solution," he said a moment later, sauntering into the kitchen with a huge grin.

Sasha's mouth hung open as she stared at Cole—a giant bug with big, black, glistening eyes. "What are you doing?" she asked as he picked the knife up off the counter.

"Chopping onions. They keep the tears away."

"Oh my gosh, Cole. You look ridiculous. Do you honestly wear your swim goggles every time you chop onions?"

"No, but I thought it might crack another smile out of you."

"You're a dork, Cole Dawson," Sasha said, failing to stifle a smile as she took the knife from him.

With a chuckle, Cole popped off the goggles and searched the fridge for teriyaki sauce. "I'm just about ready for those veggies," he said, nudging a bottle of sriracha out of the way.

Without a word, Sasha slipped the bowl of chopped vegetables onto the counter in front of him.

Cole moved the vegetables around with his finger, his mouth turned down as he analyzed the odd shapes and sizes. "Why did you…"

"Why did I what?"

"Uh… nothing. Never mind. Thanks for doing the veggies."

For the fifth day in a row, Cole arrived home to a darkened living room punctuated by flickering light from the TV, and Sasha doing her best impression of a couch cushion.

"Hey, Sash. How was your day?" Cole kicked the door closed behind him while balancing a pizza box in his hand. "Did you have another relaxing day on the couch?"

"Yeah, it was okay," Sasha said, fumbling for the remote and flicking off the television. She rolled off the couch and landed on the floor with a thud. The pizza box warmed Cole's hand as Sasha crawled around on the floor, gathering granola bar wrappers.

"I didn't feel like cooking tonight, so I picked up a pizza on my way home," Cole called as he headed to the kitchen. "I'll leave it on the counter. Feel free to grab yourself a few slices."

Cole slid the box onto the counter and cracked the lid. His stomach let out a soft growl as the smell of warm cheese and pepperoni wafted out. After plopping slices onto a plate and pulling out the Scrabble box, he pushed the balcony door open and sank into a chair.

Pushing his plate to the edge of the table, Cole set up the spinning board, pulled out two letter racks, and shook up the bag of tiles. A flash of movement from inside caught his attention and he smiled as Sasha searched for a plate. With the game set, Cole leaned back in his chair and bit into the gooey cheese and crispy pepperoni as he looked out over the city.

"What's this?" Sasha said, stepping out onto the balcony.

"Pizza. Because you'll always have a pizza my heart."

Sasha paused. She stared at Cole. "You're going to drive me insane, you know." Settling in the chair opposite him, she said, "Scrabble. I was talking about Scrabble."

"It's Sunday. Our Scrabble day. I know it's later in the day than when we usually play, but better late than never, right?"

"It's Sunday? Huh. I don't know if my brain is up for Scrabble."

"Too bad," Cole said and reached for the cloth bag. "Nothing gets in the way of Scrabble Sunday. And considering your brain may be snoozing, I have the advantage and just might beat you."

"I might be able to warm my brain up." Sasha twisted the cap off Cole's water and put the bottle to her lips.

By the time half the tiles were on the board, Cole had taken the lead by thirty-four points. As Sasha studied her letters, Cole mindlessly shifted the tiles around his rack. "Tomorrow's the last day in my set, so why don't we spend Tuesday hammering out a decent resume for you, putting in a call to Craig, and searching online for jobs?"

Sasha looked up at Cole with only her eyes. Dropping her gaze, she searched the board for open spots.

"I'd love to live in my pajamas too, but it's been almost a week, and things need to change. Eating junk food all day, spending your days on the couch, never getting out… It's not healthy. For the mind or body."

"It's as easy as that, is it?"

"Come on, Sash. I'm just looking out for your wellbeing. If you're not ready for major changes yet, that's okay, but it doesn't hurt to spend a day in front of the computer to see what's out there."

"You're just trying to distract me from getting a bingo, aren't you? It's not going to work, though." Leaning forward, Sasha grabbed all seven of her tiles and dropped *attempt* into slots on the board.

"What the...?" Cole moved his eyes from Sasha's word to the smug look on her face and back to the board. He scrawled Sasha's points on the notepad, easily pulling her into the lead. "I thought I finally had you."

"You will never get me, Mr. Dawson."

Chapter 21

Cole stepped in from the balcony, dirty dishes in hand, and breathed in the lingering smell of breakfast sausage. "Get changed," he called through the screen. "I'll throw your pjs into the laundry and then we can get started on your computer work."

Sasha tucked her leg under her and nestled in her patio chair, her hands wrapped around a mug. As Cole loaded the dishwasher, he kept his eye on her, but she stayed put.

"Come on, Sash," Cole said, poking his head out the door. "I'm not kidding. I'm excited to do some computer work with you and help you find your focus."

"Can we do it another time? I'm really cozy in my pajamas out here."

"No, we can't," Cole said and stepped onto the balcony. "I've given you a week to decompress, but it's time you put some real clothes on." He pried the coffee mug from her hands and, abandoning it on the table, scooped Sasha up in his arms. "We're doing this."

"Cole!" Sasha grasped for the doorframe as he lifted her into the kitchen. "Put me down."

"No." Cole laughed as he carried her kicking, flailing body down the hall. "We're doing this. Now get dressed," he said and dumped her onto his bed.

"You're really annoying, Cole," Sasha shouted as he left the room.

"But you still love me."

With laundry quietly spinning in the machine and steam rising from full mugs on the coffee table, Cole flopped on the couch next to Sasha and propped his laptop on her lap.

"Ah... no," she said, pushing the computer away. "I'm not into technology. I agreed to do this, but you have to do all the computer work."

"No way." Cole set the laptop on Sasha again. "This is your life, your future, and you will do all the work. I'm just here to coach you along."

"You're so freaking annoying, you know that?" Sasha said as she adjusted the angle of the screen.

After helping Sasha create an email account and giving her a crash course on how to use it, Cole opened a fresh document, blank pages ready to be filled with Sasha's life. Sasha's hands flew over the keys as she loaded the screen with work experience but when she typed *Education*, her fingers curled away. "I'm so uneducated it's embarrassing."

"You have your high school diploma, which is more than a lot of people have, and you can pursue higher education down the road if that's important to you."

"Yeah, right. Me? College? Stop being ridiculous."

"Seriously? You're one of the smartest people I know. You're the reason why I passed calculus. College is completely doable if it's something you want."

Sasha shook her head. "Whatever."

"It's an option for your future. As for now, your high school diploma is all you can list, so let's tackle your personal information." He reached over and moved the cursor to the top of the screen.

Sasha paused, her fingers resting on the keyboard. *Hayley Cooper* emerged on the screen, the font dark and bold.

"Nope," Cole said as he hit the backspace. "No more names. Names are what got you into this mess in the first place."

Sasha shrugged, her index finger hovering over the H.

"You are Sasha Cooper, you have value, tons of great qualities, and people like you for who you are. Now type out your name. Your *real* name."

The S appeared. Finally, the A, and the rest of the letters.

"Next, you can include your email address, and you can use my phone number and address until you get your own."

"Anything else?" she asked after popping the numbers under her name.

"It wouldn't hurt to have a few references to give a potential employer during an interview. You'll need to contact your references in advance to get the okay that they are willing to speak for your character. And when I say *character*, I don't mean your made-up personas. I mean your personality and skills. Sasha's good stuff."

"Who am I going to use for a reference? Everyone knows me as somebody else."

"Let's start with Craig Patterson." Cole plucked his phone from the table and handed it to Sasha. "You need to call him about a job anyway."

"And say what? I can't do this."

"Yes, you can. It might feel a bit awkward, but Craig already knows your legal name is Sasha. Just tell him you are now going by your legal name instead of Hayley. He might wonder why but he won't ask, and on the off chance that he does ask, just tell him it's for personal reasons. Nothing shuts up curiosity better than the word *personal*."

"I don't know…"

Cole snatched the phone from Sasha, pulled up Craig's number from the City of Lashburn website, and handed the phone back to her. "It's ringing. Now have the conversation before I strangle you."

Sasha threw Cole an angry look as she put the phone to her ear. With a deep breath and the slightest movement of her lips, she closed her eyes. Her tense features relaxed and her nervous voice softened to one of confidence and poise. Cole looked on, his mouth twitching between a smile and a scowl.

After an assertive goodbye, Sasha curled into a ball and buried her face in her hands. "That was awful. I'm so embarrassed. Craig is probably laughing at me right now, thinking I'm a pathetic fool."

"You were amazing," Cole said, gaping like he had just watched a magician pull a dove from her sleeve. "That was an absolutely perfect phone call. I could not have done it better myself. What did Craig say?"

Sasha slid her hands down her face just enough to reveal her eyes. "He doesn't have a job for me, but he said he'd call if something opened up."

"You clearly had a successful phone call. You're being way too hard on yourself. What did he say about being a reference?"

"He said he'd be happy to do it," Sasha said through her fingers.

"And what did he say about your name?"

"Nothing. He said nothing, as if changing my name was no big deal."

Cole grinned and squeezed Sasha in a hug. "That call could not have gone any better. Listen to Craig's words instead of the negative thoughts in your head. You did awesome and Craig clearly likes you."

With a stuttering breath, Sasha stretched out on the couch and laid her head in Cole's lap.

"You did great, my Sasha," Cole said as he stroked her hair. "Today was a big day for you and you did really well. I think we deserve an evening out."

Chapter 22

Cole lounged in his chair as conversation and the clatter of cutlery on plates buzzed across the restaurant's patio. Cars whipped past and a couple of sparrows chirped from the railing that separated diners from pedestrians. Leaning across the table, Sasha dragged her garlic bread through the smear of marinara sauce on Cole's plate.

"See?" Cole said as he smiled at Sasha through his sunglasses. "Going out with me isn't so bad."

"I never said I didn't want to go out with you. I just didn't have the energy to leave your place."

"It's all in your mind, Sash. If you are in a funk and tell yourself you don't want to do anything, then that's exactly how you'll feel. But now that you are out in the world, I can already see your energy levels perking up. We clearly need to get out more often."

"Maybe." Putting her lips to her straw, she sucked up the rest of the margarita. "These are delicious."

"I'd get you another, but we need to get going." He flicked the lime wedge from the rim of her glass into her drink. "I draw the lime at two drinks."

"Oh my gosh," Sasha said as the slippery lime tried to escape her fingers. "That one was truly terrible."

"Let's go. I don't want to be late for the movie."

With Sasha's arm looped through Cole's, they weaved between tables, sidestepping waiters, and popped out onto the street. As they wandered down the sidewalk towards the theater, Sasha clung onto Cole and chatted about pasta and the cold sweetness of margaritas while he smiled at the zest in her voice.

"Cole, wait." Sasha pulled Cole to a stop. "Sorry," she said to an old man sitting atop a worn blanket, "but it's all I have." A handful of change and a single bill fell from her hand and clattered into the man's tattered coffee cup. "It's a beautiful night, isn't it?"

"Sash," Cole said, tugging her backwards.

"The lights of the city are pretty bright," Sasha said, turning her back to Cole, "but there's a meteor shower happening this time of year and you may get lucky and spot one. I always loved sitting outside on nights like this, hoping to see a meteor."

Cole shoved his hands in his pockets and hovered behind Sasha. He shifted his weight from one foot to the other as he listened to the easy conversation and watched Sasha's relaxed mannerisms.

A toothy smile cracked out from under the man's beard, followed by a hearty laugh that echoed down the street. Cole kicked a loose pebble. It bounced along the sidewalk and disappeared down a storm drain. Stealing a glance at the man's smile, Cole thought of the many times he had dealt with homeless people as part of his job. They never smiled or laughed.

With a wave and well wishes to the man, Sasha grabbed Cole's arm and pulled him along the sidewalk. "Mm... I can still taste the strawberry on my tongue. I think that's my new favorite drink."

"Sasha," Cole said, glancing behind them at the homeless person. "That man back there... I was surprised by the way you spoke with him. You were very compassionate."

"What, him?" Sasha said, twisting her body around as they walked. "Compassionate? I was just having a conversation with another person. I hate when people judge others without knowing their story."

"Well, I see it as compassion. Most people wouldn't have given that man the time of day, but you were very kind to him."

"He's a person with a heart and not a piece of garbage to be stepped over. I've had people pretend I wasn't there, or worse, when I was in a similar situation."

"What?" Cole stumbled and his heart rate ramped up. "What do you mean, a similar situation?"

"They would call me all sorts of awful names, judging me or laughing at me without even knowing me or my situation. They'd tell me to get off my lazy butt and look for a job, not realizing that I hated asking others for money. They didn't bother to find out that I would only collect enough to feed myself, and then I'd spend the rest of the day looking for work."

As though hit by a blizzard, a deep chill washed over Cole and prickled his skin. "Hang on," he said, stopping in his tracks. "You *what?*"

Sasha yanked on Cole's arm until he fell into step with her. "You have no idea how hard it is to find work when you don't have a phone number or address, but I couldn't afford a phone or a home without a job. It's a vicious circle. All these people ever saw me as was a lazy bum rather than someone who was doing everything in her power to stay afloat."

Staggering over a crack, Cole gaped at Sasha. "You were on the streets?"

"It's not that big of a deal."

"Like, sleeping outside and stuff?"

"It was only for a bit, but yeah."

"What about soup kitchens? Or women's shelters?"

"I could get by without."

"How can you say that? You were literally living on the streets. Begging for money so you could eat."

"I *did* get by, didn't I? I survived. I'm here. And I did it without going to those places."

"But why didn't you go where people could have helped you?"

Sasha stopped and turned to Cole. The sun had sunk behind the high-rises, but Sasha stood in the single beam of sunshine that stretched between buildings. Planting her hands on her hips while the sun illuminated her like a spotlight, she said, "Because I *could* get by without, whereas a lot of other people couldn't. How could I possibly take a bed from a woman with little children? Or a meal from an elderly lady? Or from someone who was sick? I'm young and healthy, and I knew I could make it out there on my own, so that's what I did, and I left the shelters for those who had no other option."

Cole searched Sasha's face as his lips tried, then failed, to formulate words. "Sash..." he sputtered, collecting her in his arms.

Wriggling from Cole's embrace, Sasha grabbed his arm and pulled him down the sidewalk. "It's really not that big of a deal."

The conversation lulled. The theater came into view, but Cole stared at the sidewalk, his thoughts a tangle of fraying fibers.

"Movies are one of the few things I miss about city life," Sasha said. She pulled Cole through the crowds as the smell of fresh theater popcorn hung in the air.

Popcorn, scattered and soiled—food stepped on without a second thought—crunched under Cole's shoes.

"Are we going to get tickets?" Sasha asked, shaking Cole's arm. "And a big, buttery popcorn to share?"

"What? Oh, uh… yeah," he said, forcing a smile. "It's a perfect night for a little humor." As he punched in their movie selection, he studied Sasha from the corner of his eye. She hung off his arm and bounced as she soaked up the energy of the theater lobby.

With tickets in hand, they navigated their way through the crowded lobby towards the concession stands, peeling their shoes from the sticky floor with every step. "This line here," Cole said, but was yanked to a halt. Sasha, frozen in place, stared at the young woman who blocked their path.

"Hayley, how have you been? It's been ages."

Cole looked at Sasha. Her eyes were lightly closed. A moment later, she blinked to attention, dropped Cole's arm, and smiled. "Leanne, it's so great to see you. It must be almost a year since we've seen each other last."

"I know," Leanne said. "Since last September, I guess. I'm working with the city again this year and was hoping you'd be on the crew as well. What are you doing for work?"

Angling her back to Cole, Sasha locked her focus on Leanne. "I headed to the coast. Wine country. I'm the foreman at a vineyard and am back in town for a few days for a visit."

"Oh, my gawd, Sash."

With a swift kick, Sasha jabbed her heel into Cole's shin.

"Hey, Sasha," Cole said, moving his throbbing leg away from her trajectory. "I'm going to get our snacks. I'll see you over there." Turning his back to Sasha, he stormed towards the concession. Once in line, he shot a look at her. She was laughing at something Leanne had said.

A group of teens cut Cole's view of Sasha. Their voices rose above the crowd as they bombed each other with popcorn. A blonde giggled and swatted a gangly boy while his friends guffawed. Cole strained to look around the annoyance only to see Sasha giggling like the blonde.

A few minutes later and two people closer to the cashier, Sasha slipped into line beside Cole. "Please don't do that again," she said under her breath.

"Do what?"

"Call me Sasha in front of my friends."

"What?" Cole said, snapping his head to look at her. "You mean, you don't want me to call you by your name?"

"You know what I mean. It was really awkward when you called me that."

"Yeah, because it wasn't awkward for me when you allowed yourself to be called a fake name, and then you go on about a fake job, and then start laughing when you keep telling me you have nothing to laugh about."

The couple at the counter collected their snacks and Cole and Sasha inched forward. "You have no idea..."

"I thought we agreed that all this name stuff was in the past," Cole said, trying to keep the conversation between them. "That you were going to be yourself from now on."

"What was I supposed to do?" Sasha glared at Cole, her eyes wet and twitchy. "I haven't seen her in almost a year and there's a good chance I'll never see her again. Was I supposed to tell her that I've been living as a fraud and that my name is completely made up, and that I force myself to laugh so others feel more comfortable around me, and that a mental breakdown made me call you to rescue me and my single pack of worthless possessions, and now I'm living off my boyfriend, spending my days stuffing my face full of junk as I lie in front of the TV? Is that what you wanted me to tell her?"

"Your boyfriend?" Cole's legs were suddenly marshmallow.

Sasha crossed her arms and turned away. "My friend who's a boy. A guy. My guy friend."

"What can I get you?" the perky girl working the counter asked.

Cole looked up to see an empty space between him and the till. "Sorry. Um... Popcorn, root beer..." Cole stumbled through their order while Sasha stewed beside him. When the cashier slid the drinks across the counter, Sasha stabbed a straw into each lid.

"Careful, Sash. You're going to spill."

"*Don't* tell me what to do," she said and snatched up the drinks.

As they stepped into the theatre, Sasha hugged the shadows and slinked into the back row. She slumped into a seat and became one with the fabric. Trailing behind and balancing popcorn in his arms, Cole settled into the seat next to her.

"Look, Sash," he said, plopping the popcorn on her lap. "I didn't want you to tell your friend your life story and your struggles. I'd never expect you to share your personal history with anyone unless you chose to. What I hoped was for you to tell her that you are now using your legal name and that you're between jobs. You weren't the foreman of the vineyard, so why tell her that? Why exaggerate something that is already not true?"

Shifting her body sideways and hugging the popcorn to her chest, Sasha sunk her head into the back of the seat and jammed her knee up against her cup holder. "Because I'm a nobody and if I tell people interesting things about myself, then maybe I'll feel like a somebody."

Cole studied Sasha's silhouette in the theater's shadows and tucked a strand of hair behind her ear. The softness of her skin made his fingertips tingle, and warm embers glowed down to his core. "You *are* a somebody. If only you could see yourself for the amazing person you are."

The theater lights dimmed, the screen lit up with the first advertisement, and Cole gazed into Sasha's eyes that flickered with reflections of movie trailers. He stroked her sun-kissed cheek, and the glow of the embers grew. He shifted in his seat and leaned in until he could count the tiny freckles on the bridge of her nose.

She blinked. She chewed her lip.

"Sasha, I–"

Sound boomed from the speakers. Sasha jumped, sending a wave of popcorn cascading over her lap. "Oh my gosh. I'm so sorry." As she picked up pieces of popcorn and jammed them in her mouth, Cole reached for her hand, but she pushed him away. "I can do this myself."

"But Sash…"

"Just leave me alone."

Cole shifted his body to face the screen but kept his eyes on the flickering pattern of light that danced across Sasha's features as she continued to stuff fugitive popcorn into her face.

Chapter 23

Cole's head was heavy on his pillow, weighed down by the descending spiral of Sasha's mood last night and the slow reveal of secrets from her past. As the morning sun streamed through the window, stabbing Cole right in the eyes, he grappled for another way to get Sasha off the couch and into the world, but he was out of ideas.

Trying to come to grips with his new normal, he rolled out of bed, wandered to the living room, and stopped short. "Sasha?"

The condo was still. The TV screen was black. The couch was deserted.

"Sasha!" His ears trained for the sound of her voice—for the sound of something. Anything. "Sasha!" He rushed through the condo, tripping over his gym bag and her shark slippers. "Sasha!"

The edges of the balcony railing marked lines in Cole's palms as he sucked in air. "This is not a bad thing. This is what you wanted. Her pack is still here. She's just gone out for a bit." But as an image of Sasha climbing onto a west-bound bus flashed through his mind, his body tensed.

Hours passed. The silence of the TV became deafening. Cole spent his day fumbling from one task to another, the clock taking most of his attention. As he mindlessly stared into the fridge, past half a grapefruit and leftover fried chicken, the sound of a key in the door hit him like a jolt of electricity.

"Sasha." Cole rushed to the door where Sasha was kicking off her shoes. His muscles begged to wrap her in a hug, but he shoved his hands in his pockets. "Where uh... Where have you been?"

"I went out. That's why you gave me a key, isn't it? So I could go out if I wanted?"

"Yeah. Absolutely. I just didn't expect... I'm so used to you spending your days on the couch."

"I just went out, but thanks for your concern."

Cole rocked back on his heels, his arms locked to his sides. "Concern? Nah. I'm happy you got out. Have uh... have you eaten? We can throw on some burgers if you want."

"You're funny," Sasha said as she walked him to the kitchen. "You were totally worried about me. It's kind of cute."

"Fine. I was worried," Cole said as he hip-checked Sasha. "You kind of have a history of running away from me, so when I find you missing, that's where my mind goes."

"It's not you I run from," Sasha said, sinking into a kitchen chair. "Anyway, I'm not going anywhere. You don't have to worry about that."

Cole stared at the empty couch for the third morning in a row as he rubbed scratchy stubble. Blinking away sleep, he dragged himself to the kitchen. As he measured coffee grounds, he stole glances at the bowl in the sink—dried milk had glued residual cereal flakes to the sides.

Rolling his neck, Cole watched drip after drip of coffee fall into the carafe. He tried to run the upcoming court case over in his head once... twice... but could not focus in his too-quiet home. He wandered into the living room, turned on the TV to the last channel Sasha had been watching, and rumpled the neatly folded blanket on the couch.

The day in court dragged. Hours pacing the lobby were interspersed with hours of being grilled on the contents of his notebook.

Leaning his body against the condo door at the end of the day, Cole jiggled the key and tried to ignore the headache that pressed into the back of his skull. Foggy images of dinner ideas drifted through his head alongside glowing pictures of takeout menus. As he pushed open the door, he jolted upright. His nostrils filled with a strong burning smell and Sasha's frantic words echoed off the walls: "Oh my gosh! Oh my gosh!"

"Sasha!" Cole ran through the smoky haze and into the kitchen. A gray cloud swirled around Sasha's hand as she fanned a pan. Chunks of blackened something smoked and stank on the stove. Cole pushed open the balcony door as the smoke alarm went off over their heads.

"I'm sorry, I'm sorry." Sasha slammed her hands to her ears as tears streamed down her face. "I wanted to surprise you by making you dinner, but I totally screwed up. I don't want to burn your building down."

"Turn the element off and take that pan off the stove," Cole said as he hopped onto a chair and fiddled with the blaring smoke detector. "And open the bedroom window to get some air flow." He jammed his finger to the button, then slammed his fist to the stubborn alarm. Sasha ran around the condo, following Cole's instructions and wiping her face. Twisting the detector from its holdings, Cole dumped out the batteries. The instant silence softened the pounding in his head.

"You made a lot of smoke, but you weren't anywhere close to burning the place down," Cole said as he jumped off the chair. "What were you making, anyway?"

Sasha slunk behind the table and towards the counter, her face red and splotchy, and collapsed against the counter. "I didn't mean to."

"I'm not upset. I'm thrilled that you wanted to make us dinner. Sometimes it just doesn't work out."

"But I'm just... can't... I try and try but..." Her face scrunched like she was trying to keep an entire lake from breaking through her dam.

"Sasha," Cole said, stepping close. "It's okay."

Biting down on her lip, Sasha peeped at Cole with reddened eyes. "But I wanted it to be perfect."

"My Sasha," he said as he moved a stray hair from her cheek, "you're here, so it is perfect." As he gazed into her ocean blue eyes framed by wet lashes, burned dinner and long court cases became a distant thought. All that mattered was Sasha.

Cole slid his hands around her waist and pulled her close; her heart hammered against his chest. He traced the tear lines on her cheek and slipped his fingers through her hair. Her breath, warm and hypnotizing, mingled with his. As his nose brushed hers, a thousand electric sparks passed between them, sending ripples down his spine.

She tore her eyes away. Dropped her head. Stared at the floor.

The earth started turning once again.

With a steadying breath, Cole pressed his lips to Sasha's temple. "Okay," he whispered.

"Okay? Okay what?"

Cole sighed heavily. "Okay, let's find something else to eat." He hesitated before stepping from Sasha. "What were you planning on making, anyway?" he asked as he poked at the charred remains in the pan.

"Stir fry, like we made before. You made it look so easy, but I clearly have no idea what I'm doing."

"Did you use oil?" Cole said, dumping the blackened meat into the garbage. The empty pan clattered in the sink. He jammed the tap to cold, sending a wave of sizzles through the kitchen.

"No."

"What heat were you cooking at?"

"High."

"Next time, add a splash of oil to the pan and cook at medium heat. And you'll have to stir and flip the meat regularly." Fumbling around in the freezer, Cole found some forgotten farmer's sausage and popped it in the microwave. "Thanks for taking the initiative with supper, though. It's a nice treat." He turned to Sasha and forced a smile.

"I wanted to celebrate. I got a job today."

"You what?" Lightning shot through Cole, and he grabbed Sasha by the shoulders. "A job? Where?"

"A flower shop. I dropped off my application on Monday, but the manager wasn't working, so they asked me to come in today. I chatted with the manager, and she offered me the job. I start tomorrow."

"That is fantastic!" Cole pulled Sasha into a tight hug and spun her around. "Wait…" he said, stopping mid-spin and dropping her to her feet. "What name did you use on your application form?"

"My own name, okay? I used Sasha."

"And you didn't pretend to act like anyone but yourself?"

Propping her hands on her hips, Sasha narrowed her eyes. "No, Cole, I didn't. Happy?"

"I am happy." Cole laughed and pulled Sasha into a long hug. "This is definitely a call for celebration."

"I bought wine," Sasha said, breaking from Cole and pulling a bottle of red from a paper bag. "I had to go to three places to find a store that didn't ask to see my ID."

"Wine?" Cole's smile faltered as an image of Sasha's room in the Sax flashed through his head. "I didn't know you were a wine drinker."

"I'm not, but people drink wine to celebrate things, don't they?"

"They certainly do." Cole looked at Sasha, pride smeared all over her face. "You know what? I'm thrilled to toast your new job with a glass of wine. This is awesome," he said, turning to the microwave. "When you get your first paycheck, we can get you that ID, and then we can get you a bank account. And in time, a phone as well so I don't have to freak out when I can't find you."

"So, you're going to start stalking me with constant phone calls?" Sasha teased, coming up behind Cole and looping her arm through his while he sliced the sausage.

"You promised me you weren't going to run, so maybe I can hold off on the stalking." He nudged Sasha out of the way and reached for a fresh pan from the cupboard. As her energy radiated beside him, he focused on swirling oil around the pan. Sasha's shoulder brushed his arm, and the smell of lavender wafted from her hair.

"Can you set the table or something? You're kind of in my workspace."

"Oh... Sorry..."

Aromatic spices wafted from the sausage as the heated pan began its magic. Cole raised his eyebrows as he dumped Sasha's peculiarly shaped vegetables in the pan. The onion and bell pepper, hacked to random bits, sizzled as hot oil singed the edges.

"Do you not own wine glasses, or am I just missing them?" Sasha asked, opening cupboard after cupboard.

"I've never been a wine drinker, so I never had the need to buy any."

"I guess we can just use regular glasses," Sasha said as she pulled two tumblers from the cupboard.

Sasha's eyes sparkled as she settled into her chair while Cole plated the food and poured the wine.

"To your new job and the start of something great," he said, raising his glass and clinking it to hers.

"It's a bit tart, but not bad," Sasha said as she pulled the glass from her lips. "Maybe with my first paycheck I'll buy us some stemmed glasses so we can pretend to be a real couple who does things like drink wine."

Cole froze mid-sip. As he steadied the glass on the table, he stared into her. "But we're not a couple."

Sasha rolled her eyes and stabbed a piece of sausage with her fork. "That's why I said *pretend*."

"I don't pretend. I've built myself a stable life that I quite enjoy, so I don't have to lie about being someone I'm not. I don't have to run from who I really am."

Sasha's fork clattered to her plate. "I'm trying, Cole. Why would you say that?"

"That came out the wrong way," Cole said, rubbing his thumping forehead. "I just want to see you succeed instead of falling back into your old ways, and a comment like that touched a nerve."

"I can survive in this world without you, you know," Sasha said, hiding her face behind her glass. "I might be a train wreck, but I can get by."

Chapter 24

Sasha smiled as she added sprigs of baby's breath to the bouquet. "I'm supposed to add a curl of ribbon to you," she said as she ran her fingers along the delicate leaves, "but I don't think the world understands that your beauty stands alone."

Dropping her hands to the workbench, Sasha studied the rolls of ribbons that created a rainbow of color on the wall ahead. "They say I'm to add some flair, and you know what happens when we don't listen to the rules. Such is life, Ms. Hydrangea." She put her nose to the bouquet and breathed.

As Sasha unrolled equal lengths of pink and green ribbon, her mind drifted to burning dinner two nights ago. Pausing with ribbon cascading from her fingertips to the floor, she closed her eyes and replayed the feeling of Cole's hands on her back, his body pressed to hers, his warm breath on her face.

Sasha's eyes flew open, the space between her eyebrows intensely creased. "Stop it," she said and clipped a sprig of baby's breath.

The bell on the front door of the flower shop tinkled as Sasha added another sprig to the arrangement. "Hi. Can I help you with something?" she heard Darla say.

"I'm here to pick up a bouquet."

Sasha froze mid-snip. Her heart leapt at the sound of his voice.

"But I was also wondering if Sasha is in."

Unable to hold her smile in, Sasha abandoned the baby's breath on the workbench and pushed through the hanging plastic curtain. And there he was—Cole, dressed in uniform, looking completely lost and out of place amongst all the flowers.

"What are you doing here?" Sasha beamed as she took Darla's place at the counter.

"Hey, Sash. Nice place you work at."

Sasha followed Cole's gaze around the shop at the colorful arrangements, stacks of cards, and plush toys.

"I was hoping I could make Monday plans with you," he said.

"What kind of plans?"

"Since our schedules are completely opposite this week except for Monday, I was thinking it'd be nice to spend that day together. We could start with the DMV and the bank, and then we could pick up some lunch and have a picnic in the park while we play Scrabble, since we're going to miss Sunday's Scrabble match."

Sasha's face fell and the muscles in the back of her neck stiffened. She snatched a pen from the counter and stared at her fingers fiddling with it. "Scrabble in the park sounds like a lot of fun, but I don't know if I'm ready for the other stuff. DMV and stuff."

"Come on, Sash," Cole said, resting his elbows on the counter and leaning in close. "It's just an ID and somewhere safe to keep your money. You wanted to do this years ago, so why the hesitation now?"

"I don't know. I haven't used my name in so long. It feels weird to have it permanently etched on some cards."

"One step at a time. We'll start with the DMV and depending on how you feel afterwards, we can either go to the bank or we can put the bank off for another day."

Nodding her head and breathing deeply, she trained her eyes on the pen's silver clip. "I guess we can try that."

"And then Scrabble in the park afterwards," Cole said, pushing himself from the counter. "Now that we have Monday planned, I'm also here to pick up a bouquet that I ordered."

"A bouquet?" Sasha wilted like the clippings on her workbench. "I didn't see your name on the orders list."

"That's because I used my brother-in-law's name so you wouldn't be suspicious. Mike Barrows."

"I think I remember that one. Let me check the back."

Getting momentarily tangled in the plastic curtain, Sasha glanced over her shoulder. Cole, looking sharp in his uniform, grinned at her before she disappeared to the solitude of the workspace.

"Yeah, this is the one I was thinking of," she said as she pushed the curtain aside again and averted Cole's dancing eyes. The bouquet glowed in Sasha's arms, the rainbow of color matching the warmth in her chest. "It was fun to put together."

"You built this one, hey? It's gorgeous. You have a real knack for this stuff."

Heat rose in Sasha's cheeks as she pushed the bouquet towards Cole. Dropping her head, she focused on her hands fiddling with the pen. "It's not that hard. Anyone could do it."

"I'm sure anyone could toss some flowers in a vase, but not everyone can arrange it like this. Everything is spaced so perfectly but it still looks natural rather than deliberate, and the colors are amazing together. It's really stunning."

"Thank you." Sasha glanced up with only her eyes. "So… who's it for?"

"Someone special," Cole said as he flipped through the stack of greeting cards on the counter. He selected one with a purple butterfly in the corner and pushed it towards Sasha. "Can you write something on this for me?"

Swallowing the lump in her throat, she said, "You can write it yourself."

"I'd rather you write it. My penmanship is terrible, and I want this person to be able to read the message."

"Okay, fine." Sasha pulled the card towards her and clicked open the pen. "What do you want me to write?"

"Start with, 'To my Sasha.'"

The tip of the pen hovered over the card. "I'm sorry?"

"You heard me." He propped his elbows on the counter and leaned in close. "To my Sasha."

Sasha pulled the pen from the card and stared at Cole.

"I paid good money for these flowers, and I expect to get good customer service as well. Are you this difficult with all your customers?"

She slowly shook her head and smiled at Cole's smiling eyes. "Fine," she said with a laugh, returning the pen to the card. "To my Sasha. Is that it?"

"Nope. You can also write, 'Congrats on the new job. I hope it makes you happy because you deserve to be happy.'"

The sweet smell of freesia wafted over Sasha as she wrote Cole's words in lovely, flowing script. Clicking the pen closed, she stole a glance at Cole. He grinned back. She reached for a floral pick, but her fingers fumbled the jar and dozens of picks scattered across the counter.

"Oh, shoot. Sorry," she said as she frantically scooped up picks and tucked them back into the jar.

As she fished around for a single pick, Cole's hand wrapped around hers. "I'm not done, you know."

"Not done?" The heat of his touch sent Sasha's heart racing.

"With my message. My note on the card."

"Oh... Okay, what else?"

"You need to know who the flowers are from."

Sasha blinked at his eager face. "Oh my gosh. You're such a dork. I get the hint. Thanks for the flowers."

"I'm serious. I'm not done with my message. You don't need an upset customer to talk to your manager about how difficult you are being, do you?"

"Fine," Sasha said, putting pen to paper again. "I'll write 'From Cole.'"

"Wait." Cole grasped her hand. "That's not right. I want it to say, 'Love, Cole.'"

The pen in Sasha's hand began to tremble. "I'm sorry?"

Cole leaned in close, dropping his voice to almost a whisper, and looked into Sasha's eyes. "Not only do you deserve to be happy, but you are *allowed* to be happy." He stroked the back of her hand with his thumb. A wave of warmth rippled through her. "And you're allowed to be loved. Believe it."

The police radio on Cole's vest crackled to life and Sasha flinched, sending the jar of floral picks sailing again. Cole's attention was diverted to the staticky message as Sasha gathered the picks into a pile. She tried to focus on the mess, but her eyes were set on Cole as he concentrated on the message blaring over the radio.

"I've got to go," Cole said, backing away from the counter. "But believe my words. I'll see you Monday. Bring your bouquet home with you."

The door to the flower shop sighed to a close behind him, the tinkling of the bells echoing to silence. Glued to the spot, Sasha watched the red and blue lights speed away, the shrill sound of the siren fading in the distance. The hammering of her heart filled her head.

"Your boyfriend is hot," Darla said as she slid up to the counter. "I've always liked a man in uniform. I had no idea you were dating a cop."

"Oh." Sasha tore her eyes from the door. "He's not my boyfriend. We're just friends."

"I totally thought you guys were a thing. Is he single?"

"Yeah," Sasha said, her brow furrowing.

"Do you think you could set me up with him?"

"With who? Cole?"

"He's cute, he's single, I'm single. Why not?"

Chapter 25

Sasha, nestled in a patio chair on Cole's balcony, stroked her cheek with the fluffy sleeve of her winter pajamas.

"Well, this sucks." Cole's voice broke the steady sound of rain beating down on the world. "So much for our plans of Scrabble in the park," he said, stepping onto the balcony. "But we can still hit the DMV and possibly the bank, and then have our Scrabble match back here."

"Sure. Sounds good," Sasha mumbled. She turned back to the view and breathed in the fresh mist. A car passed below, breaking the steadiness of the rain with a whoosh of tires on wet pavement.

Slumping into the chair next to Sasha, Cole said, "You okay? You're quiet."

"Just enjoying the rain. It's such a dreary day. Maybe we should stay in."

"This is actually the perfect day for errands as we won't be wasting a sunny day inside. Remember," Cole said, squeezing Sasha's hand, "you're not alone. We're building you a life, together."

Maybe I don't want a life. Maybe being Sasha is too hard. Maybe I want to go back to being nobody at all.

"I'll grab a quick coffee and breakfast and then we can go." Cole patted Sasha's arm and pulled himself from his chair.

"Mm-hm..."

Sasha stared at the letter tiles in front of her, but they may as well have been in Greek. Cole was already up forty-seven points, and she was drowning.

As Sasha moved tiles around on her rack, plastic cards whispered in her ear. She stole a glance into the kitchen where the new wallet that Cole had surprised her with sat on the table; the bank card and her government issued identification pulsated from within. She had plastered on a smile when she slid her Social Security card beside her ID, and Cole had excitedly pointed to all the empty slots that were waiting to get filled. And when he had hauled out the trash, Sasha waved a secret goodbye to her plastic baggy.

Sasha's chest tightened. *There's no way out*, she thought as she blinked back tears. *If you need to leave, you're going to have to take Sasha with you. And if you do that, then you're not really leaving. You are just relocating with the same sucky life.*

Sasha moved her D to the front of her letter rack. The word *date* materialized. "Hey Cole," she said, keeping her eyes focused on her letters. "The girl that I was working with on Friday when you stopped by the florist was wondering if you'd be interested in going out with her." Sasha pursed her lips and kept the lump jammed in her throat.

"What?" Cole looked up from the board and stared at Sasha.

Sasha shrugged, her eyes intent on the game board. "She thinks you're cute and asked me to ask you."

Cole returned his gaze to his rack and moved his letters around. "What do you think?"

"I don't know. I barely know her, but she seems nice."

"Do you think I should go out with her?"

"It's up to you. I told her I'd ask, so I did. It's really none of my business." As Sasha moved her letters around, *angst* popped up. Shifting around the letters some more, she finally settled on *staged*.

"None of your business, hey?" Cole muttered as he pushed himself from the rug. "I need a drink. Do you want anything?"

"No, thank you," Sasha said, reaching into the bag for six new letters.

"Tell her that my life is complicated enough right now without throwing dating into the mix," Cole called from the kitchen.

Sasha cringed.

The crack of a beer can being opened cut through the air. Sasha shifted her tiles, but her face was deadpan, her unfocused gaze directed at the leg of the coffee table. The muggy air was cut again with the piercing ring of Cole's phone.

"Hello?... Yeah, sure. I'll be right there."

Squeezing her eyes shut, Sasha swallowed a fresh crop of tears.

"Hey, Sash," Cole said from the edge of the living room. "I've been called in to work. I need to get going."

"But it's your day off."

"A suspicious package was found at the bus station and it's sucking up a ton of resources," he said as his thumbs punched out a message on his phone. "We have a lot of officers on scene, and they need to free up some bodies to respond to calls."

"But..."

Looking at Sasha, he sighed. "It's part of my job. I can get called out anytime."

Sasha hugged her knees to her chest as Cole disappeared down the hall. A moment later, he was back, heading towards the front door. "Sorry our plans of Scrabble in the park didn't pan out. I guess it wasn't meant to be." As Cole slipped his feet into his shoes and reached for his keys, he said, "You can have my beer. Keep the Scrabble board set up and we can finish our game later."

"When you will be back?"

"I don't know. Depends how long it takes with this suspicious package. It could be only a couple of hours, or it could be late. Don't wait up for me." Without looking at Sasha, Cole slammed the door behind him.

Chapter 26

Sasha stood at the railing of the balcony and stared into the night; she clutched the prepaid phone in her hand. *Throw it as far as you can. I dare you.* She lowered her gaze and opened her hand—the phone stared up at her mockingly. Closing her eyes, she said, "You are Sasha. You are Sasha. You are Sasha."

She slumped into a chair; her hand hovered over the patio table. A malicious smile crept onto her face and she opened her fingers in a freeing release. The heavy *clunk* of the phone hitting the table killed the smile. Tension pressed back into her.

Sasha picked up the wallet that lay next to her phone and flipped it open. The cards tucked inside each slot smirked at her.

"ID," she said as she removed the card and laid it on the table. It glowed like a neon sign in the shadows, the moon's radiance highlighting the silver letters of her name. "Social Security." She placed the card beside the ID. "Bank card. Bus pass. Mobile minutes card. Library card..." With each card she laid down, her chest constricted a little more, a boa slowly crushing the life from her. "No, Magda. I don't need you," she said through gritted teeth.

Leaning back in her chair and staring at the cards spread out before her, Sasha tapped the corner of her phone which sent it spinning in a slow circle. She tapped it again and watched it spin around and around as Cole's words echoed in her ears: *"If you give a smartphone a chance, you'll learn to love it. You can absolutely afford the monthly plan, and you deserve to have a good phone, but it's ultimately your decision. If you'd rather have a cheap pay-as-you-go, then get that."*

Sasha sent the phone spinning again as she looked at the multitude of cards with the name Sasha Cooper on them.

She swept her hand through the cards, scattering them into chaos.

The boa squeezed.

Sasha staggered towards the railing, the hard rectangle pressing into her palm. As she looked at the phone in her shaking hand, a siren in the distance pierced the night. Sasha's trembles subsided, her breath evened, and her hand relaxed around the phone. The siren continued its wail.

Chapter 27

Sasha smiled as strawberry-lemonade vodka played with her taste buds and bubbles tickled her tongue. Pressing the bottle to her lips, she watched Cole tear apart a head of lettuce and chuck it into a salad bowl.

"I stopped by the library after work today," Sasha said, propping herself on the barstool at the island. "I must admit, I'm enjoying the benefits of the library card you convinced me to get."

"That's great. I knew you'd like it."

"The library has their fall crafting programs advertised. They have a fall-themed wreath class next month that I'm thinking of taking."

"That sounds nice. I think you'd enjoy that."

"We just have to figure out how to hang the wreath on your front door."

Cole grabbed a cucumber and hacked it half. "Mm."

"And as much as I told you the bus pass was too expensive, it's really nice to not have to search for change every time I ride."

"Don't forget you'll save money in the long run with it, even if it doesn't feel that way."

"You are so good to me," Sasha said and tipped more pink liquid into her mouth. "Thank you for being there for me."

Cole glanced up from the cutting board and gave Sasha half a smile. "You're welcome. You know I'll always be there."

"I know." Sasha breathed deeply and relaxed into the back of the seat.

"Hey, Sasha. Tomorrow is the last day of my shift schedule. On Monday and Tuesday, I think we should look for an apartment for you."

A wrecking ball flew through the kitchen and knocked the air out of Sasha. "I'm sorry?" she said, fumbling her drink onto the island. It wobbled then steadied. "Already?"

"Look, Sash. This was never supposed to be a permanent arrangement. I opened my home to you so you could get your feet under you again. You now have a steady job, money in the bank, an ID, a phone... You're ready."

"But... I don't know if I'm ready."

"You're ready. You are a strong, capable woman and you need your own space."

"But..."

Throwing the cucumber slices in the salad, Cole said, "I want my couch back. I didn't mind you sleeping there for the past month and a half, but now that you are in a position to get your own place, there's no need for you to sleep on my couch."

"You want me gone?" Sasha said, the foundation she had been building crumbling beneath her.

"I don't want you gone. We'll still see each other lots, we'll call each other lots, and you can crash at my place occasionally. Or I can crash at yours. I like having you around, but my place simply isn't big enough for two single people. If we were together, then yeah, we could share my bed and there'd be no need for you to move out, but if all we're ever going to be is friends, then it's time for you to go."

Sasha's mouth went dry. Tears pricked at her eyes. Cole hacked the celery to bits.

"What happens if you meet a guy and want him to come over? Are you going to have him hang out on the couch? And what if I bring a girl home and we find you sleeping on the couch or even in my bed? What am I going to tell her then?"

"I'm sorry?"

"You'll always be my best friend, and we'll still hang out, but it's time for you to go."

The kitchen started to spin. Sasha gripped the counter, her nail beds turning white. "I'm... I... I need a shower." She steadied her feet and turned from the kitchen.

Air rushed in and out of Sasha's lungs as she fumbled with the bathroom lock. She was suddenly out of her clothes and hugging the shower curtain for support. As the edges of her vision darkened and blurred, she spun the tap to as hot as she could stand. "You can't run. You can't run..." she said as water stung her skin. "Stay in Lashburn. Make Cole happy."

Hot water pounded her back, numbing her body and turning it bright red. "Find someone. Sasha can't do this. Find Magda, Erin, Kendra... Just find someone. Be someone else. Be someone better."

Sasha's eyes flew open, the terror of the nightmare still having its hold. She stared into the darkness of Cole's living room as her heart pounded in her ears and her breaths stuttered out in fragmented pants.

Monsters lurked around corners and hid in shadows as Sasha hurried to Cole's bedroom and slipped into his bed. The air was warm, the sheets were warm, and everything smelled like sleeping Cole. As panic began to release its icy fingers from her soul, she closed her eyes and steadied her breath.

"Hey." Cole's hushed voice cut the night. "What's going on?"

Rolling to her side, Sasha's widened pupils searched Cole's face. Shadows morphed the angle of his nose and stubble altered the shape of his jaw. "I had a nightmare and didn't want to be alone. Sorry I woke you."

"That's okay," Cole whispered, pulling his blanket over her shoulder. "Do you want to talk about it?"

"No. Well, maybe. I was in an alley and a guy was pushing me into his car. I tried to call for help, but I couldn't find my voice. I kept looking for someone to help me, but I was alone with the scary guy."

Cole rested his hand on Sasha's arm and drew small circles on her skin with his finger. Chewing her lip, Sasha inched her body closer to Cole. "And then you were there. You were in your uniform, and I tried to call out to you, but I couldn't. You were only a few feet away and you were watching me struggle with this guy, but you didn't help me. You pulled your notebook from your vest and asked me to describe the guy. I kept looking at you, desperate for you to help me, but you kept asking me the same questions, saying you needed the information to be able to do anything. As much as I didn't want to see the guy's face, I finally turned to him in hopes that if I could tell you what he looked like, you'd help. So, I turned around and saw that it was Curtis who was on top of me. That's when I woke up."

Cole glided his hand down Sasha's arm, leaving goosebumps on her skin, and laced his fingers through hers. "Are you scared Curtis is going to find you?"

"No. I don't know why I dreamed of him. I'm not afraid of him and I'm no longer worried about him coming to Lashburn or anything."

"You do know that if it was real life, I'd get that bastard away from you, don't you? I wouldn't watch you struggle."

Sasha nodded, her head pressing into the soft pillow. "I know you would. It was a silly dream and now that I think about it, I don't know why it scared me so much."

"It's not silly." Cole moved his hand to Sasha's hip and pulled her near. "And I'm here for you now. I'll always be here for you, no matter where life takes us. You're safe."

Sasha rolled to her other side and nestled her back against Cole's chest. He wrapped his arm around her, and Sasha relaxed into his warmth as the stress of the nightmare drifted into the night.

As they lay together, Sasha thought about the dream, about Curtis, about Cole's friendship, and about how she did not want to get her own place yet. The room was quiet, and Sasha listened to the sounds of the city happening outside the bedroom window: the odd car passing in the night, a dog barking, the distant sound of a siren.

"I'm not ready to get my own place. Not yet," Sasha said. "I'm trying to embrace this new life you are helping me build, but it's a lot to take in. I know my ID and bank account seem trivial to you, but it's a huge step for me and I need to slow down a bit. You said you want me off your couch and I get that, but I'm scared that if I leave too soon, I'll drop back into my old ways."

Sasha waited for a response, but all she heard was the quiet, rhythmic sound of Cole's breathing as he slept.

Chapter 28

Sasha grabbed the napkin that tried to take flight and shoved it under her glass of water. She glanced at Cole as he poked at ice cubes with his straw.

"We need to find something," Cole said as he reached for a loaded nacho and dunked it in salsa. "We don't get another day off together until the end of the month and by then it'll be too late. If we don't get you something today, then you'll have to search on your own next week."

"What about evenings?"

"I'm on nights next week."

Sasha sighed as she picked a jalapeno off a nacho and tossed it to the side. "I still don't see what the big deal was with the first place."

"I know that one is appealing because of the cheap rent, but I refuse to let you live in a dank basement with black mold and mouse turds."

"I've lived with mouse droppings before, you know. Rodents are kind of hard to escape when you live on an orchard."

"That's not my point. Maybe you should rethink the third place we looked at. It was nice, clean, well maintained, and the price was decent."

"Yeah, and then I'd have to leave for work an hour earlier because of the sucky bus routes in that area. Anywhere I'd want to go would require a lot of transfers. Not that you'd understand, with your fancy car that can get you wherever you want to go."

"I've already told you, when you're ready, I'll help you get a license and a car, but you keep telling me that you prefer the bus. I don't care if you want to ride the bus, but you don't get to be jealous of those with cars."

"I still think we should at least look at the basement suite near the bus station. It might be exactly what I'm looking for."

"No." Cole shook his head as he tossed the straw to the side and sipped from his glass. "Sanchez confirmed that the alley behind the house is a mecca for drug deals. It's simply not a safe place to live."

Sasha rolled her eyes as she dipped a nacho in sour cream. "It's not like I'd hang out in the alley or anything."

"Again, that's not the point. You might need to bite the bullet and look at places with higher rental prices. If you want to live in the real world, you have to adjust your idea of what things cost."

Sasha rolled her eyes again. *Maybe I don't want to live in the real world.*

The three-storey walk-up stared at Sasha as she stepped from Cole's car. Large trees at the front of the property either waved merrily or loomed menacingly—she could not decide which.

"It's freshly painted, and these carpets are only two years old," the landlord enthused. "The kitchen and bathroom were both redone within the last five years."

"It's not bad," Cole said, swinging open the bedroom closet. "It's the best one so far and the price is within your range."

"I don't know," Sasha said as they left the bedroom and wandered through the tiny living room. "There's no balcony, and the window looks out over a parking lot."

"If those things are important to you, then you're going to have to pay over a thousand. That's just the reality of it. This place is only six blocks from the florist and about a half hour walk from my place. You're a block away from a main bus route, plus there's that community garden just down the street."

Cole headed into the cramped kitchen and opened the fridge, then the dishwasher. "These appliances are in great shape as well." He looked at Sasha expectantly. She looked back stone-faced.

"So?" Cole said. "I don't have the energy to look at any more today. It's either this or you need to find something on your own next week."

Sasha wandered over to the window and pressed her forehead to the cool glass. An old Honda and an older Mitsubishi sat in the parking lot amongst weeds pushing through cracks in the pavement. The corner of Sasha's mouth twitched as she stared at weeds defying asphalt and reaching for the sun.

"What'll it be, Sasha? Yes? No?"

The air sat on her like an elephant. "Okay," she said. "I guess I'll take it."

Cole wrapped his arms around her and gave her a tight squeeze as she stared out the window in a trance.

While Cole chatted with the landlord, Sasha wandered back to the bedroom. She looked out the window that shared the same view as the living room—cement and other people's cars. She closed her eyes and tried to steady her quivering nerves.

"Hey, Sash?" Cole called from the kitchen. "We've got the contract ready for you."

The air squeezed Sasha. She shuffled from the bedroom and when she saw Cole and the landlord smiling at her, she forced one in return.

"In addition to the first month's rent, I'll need one month's rent for the damage deposit," the landlord said. "After the six-month lease is up, we can renegotiate for a longer term if you are interested."

"Six months?"

"They wanted a year," Cole said, "but I negotiated down to six months. I know a year is a long time for you, so I thought you'd appreciate a shorter lease. You can stay longer if you want, but at least you aren't committed."

Sasha stared at the papers and tried to keep them from shaking in her hands. "I thought it would be month-to-month."

"Those dives you've lived at in the past may have been month-to-month, but if you're going to build yourself some stability, you need to make a longer commitment."

Tears brimmed at the edges of her eyes, but Sasha held them back and forced them deep inside. As she closed her eyes and searched for someone within, Cole's hand, solid like his handcuffs, slipped around hers. "I know you can do this."

She opened her eyes at pages blurry through stubborn tears while the talents of a dozen personas jockeyed for position to push Sasha out of the way. Her fingers cramped as she clutched the pen, and she watched her hand glide over the spaces on the prison sentence, the blanks filling in with the signature of Sasha Cooper.

Chapter 29

She slapped on a smile one day and swore the next. She laughed when she was supposed to, tied her hair up for a few hours, then shook it out. Hayley worked on arrangements at the back of the flower shop whereas Crystal dealt with customers up front. Magda was in charge of difficult conversations, and Grace and Whitney pulled together any loose ends.

And Sasha smiled and hugged Cole when she was in his home.

You can do this, Sasha told herself, managing her heart rate with deep breathing while she filled a mug in Cole's quiet kitchen. *And once you're locked away in your own place, you can have a full mental breakdown. As for now, get someone else on board and play the part the world expects you to play.*

As Sasha wandered from the kitchen, her eyes fell on the couch. *...your last night here...*

The world dropped away.

Panic engulfed her as ocean waves crashed over her head. She gulped for air as the walls crushed her from all sides. Trying to control her frantic breathing, Sasha stumbled onto the couch; the room spun, tilted, and pulsated. As she ditched her shaking mug on the end table, spilling coffee onto her hand, she was gripped with a familiar, all-consuming terror, and crumpled to the floor.

You can do this. You've been through a lot worse. She pressed her forehead to the floor and tried to breathe.

Who are you kidding? Sasha can't do this. Sasha only knows how to run.

Her head shot up. Adrenaline swept through her veins as her mind grasped for the drug that she suddenly, desperately craved.

She tore from the living room and wrenched her backpack from Cole's storage locker. As she pulled her clothes from the linen closet and dumped them into her bag, she was hit by a notion of déjà vu, feeling herself go through the same hysterical motions six weeks ago in Campbell, eight months ago in Lashburn, a year and a half ago in Ashton, and countless other times over the past ten years.

As she tossed her toothbrush in her bag, Sasha sobbed to the empty condo. "I'm sorry, Cole, but I have to. It's not forever this time. I just need to sort some things out in my head. I'm sorry, I'm sorry, I'm sorry."

Sasha stuffed her wallet and phone in her pack and stumbled to the bus station with no plan of where to go, only knowing she needed to get out.

Chapter 30

Sasha jolted awake, whispers of a dream sliding away. She stretched her eyes open to passengers gathering their bags and coats. "Where am I?"

The woman in the aisle eyed Sasha and turned away.

Using her sleeve to wipe away drying drool, Sasha peered out the window but all she was given was the side of another bus. In a daze, she shrugged on her jacket, climbed down the steps, and gaped at unfamiliar buildings.

Sasha drifted past tall buildings and across busy streets, barely paying attention to red and green lights as people bumped into her as though they hadn't noticed she was there. A lump sat in her throat and her pack pressed down on her shoulders. She dragged herself past parks, shops, and restaurants, following cracks in the sidewalk.

A singed, earthy aroma stirred Sasha's senses. Pulling her gaze from gum stains on the pavement, she looked through the window of a coffee shop. Carafes lined the counter. Muffins, scones, and quiches smiled from the glass display case. Sasha breathed the smell into her lungs and imagined her hands wrapped around a warm mug of serenity. Her grumbling stomach tried to push her inside, but as she watched friends and couples talk and laugh, she stayed cemented to the sidewalk. Those people lived in another world—a world on the other side of the glass where life was happy and always smelled like fresh coffee and friendship.

"Suck it up and shove it down," Sasha said, turning from the window and pressing towards the unknown. *Suck it up and shove it down. Suck it up...* The lump that she had been holding erupted into a sob. Pressing her fist to her mouth, she slumped to the side of the building.

Sasha dug her fingers into the wall, her nails scraping the brickwork as she gulped for air. *Control yourself. Suck it up and...* The mantra was useless. Panic was taking hold, swamping Sasha's body. Cars and gawking faces blurred and darkened. She clung to the wall as swirling currents tried to pull her under.

"Cole," she wheezed, her body swaying. "I need Cole." She dropped her pack and thrust her hand inside, seeking the solidity of her phone. As her fingertips nudged the soft leather of her wallet, the pressures of Lashburn slammed into her and she froze.

Falling onto her bottom, she closed her eyes. "You're in a garden. You're in a garden..." Petals and leaves emerged and enveloped her as she strolled down a path of steppingstones. Twittering birds and a babbling brook calmed her breathing. The scents of honeysuckle and gardenia slowed her heart rate.

Sasha opened her eyes to city life bustling around her—busses, street signs, legs rushing past. With a steadying breath, she heaved her pack onto her shoulders. *You can do this, and it starts with finding food and a bed.*

She pushed herself from the building, but tears tried to claw their way to the surface. *Stop it. Stop it! You are Magda. You. Are. Magda. Deep breath. Press on.*

She lifted her chin and flipped her hair over her shoulder, but every street was still the same. Every face still looked through her. Magda's feet ached and her shoulders cried. Shop owners gave her conflicting directions and the two-dollar burger sat like a grease pit in her stomach.

As the sun blinked behind a building, Magda stumbled up the stairs to a hostel. A headache pulsated behind her eyeballs and a musty smell sat in the air as she wandered down the cramped hall.

"How much for bed?" Magda said to the ponytailed man as she slid her pack off her shoulders.

He flipped the page of a large daily planner. "Thirty-two a night, but we're all booked up for tonight, I'm afraid."

"I'm sorry?" Octopus tentacles wrapped around Magda's legs, dragging her under.

"There's a huge music festival in town and everything's booked solid. If you don't have a reservation, I'm afraid you're out of luck."

"What do you mean, everything's booked?"

"I've been on the phone with other hostels all day trying to find room for people, but the city is full."

"So… there's *nothing*? Nowhere in this city to stay for the night?"

"Not for hostels. You could try a hotel, but I wouldn't hold out much hope."

Sasha stared at the man, her voice failing her. *I need a swear word. Magda, where did you go?*

Inhaling ragged breaths, Sasha left the hostel. Echoes of guitar notes and hoots of a crowd drifted from another world. As she turned the corner, a parking lot paved the trail to a cookie cutter building where a bright green hotel sign winked at her.

Sasha edged up to the building. As if invited, the doors parted. With a deep breath and a silent plea, she stepped into the pristine lobby.

She meandered to the front desk, gawking at the vaulted ceiling and contemporary art that adorned the walls. Her stomach tightened and her heart leapt as her mind tried to remind her of wonderful and awful days.

As she waited in line, she flipped her hoodie over her head and shifted her weight. The guests ahead of her draped their jackets over their arms and rolled their matching suitcases away. Sasha looked down at her old shoes and adjusted her dirty pack on her shoulders.

"Ma'am?"

Her head snapped up, knocking her headache around. She shuffled up to the desk and found a smile for the guest services agent.

"Good afternoon, ma'am. My name is Jeffrey. How may I help you?"

"Hi. I know there's a big music festival in town, but I was wondering if there's any chance you have a room available for tonight."

Jeffrey pursed his lips as his fingers danced across his keyboard. "I'm sorry, ma'am, but we are completely full. Is there anything else I can help you with?"

Squeezing her eyes shut, Sasha gripped the desk as her mantra instinctively rolled through her head. When the waves settled, she lifted her gaze. "Do you by chance know if there are any rooms available anywhere in..." She glanced around the lobby before turning back to Jeffrey. "What city am I in?"

"What city? You are in Denover and the city is fairly full. If you'd like, I could call around to a few places for you."

"You'd do that for me? Oh, my goodness. You are very kind."

Suppressing a chuckle, Jeffrey reached for the phone and punched in numbers. Sasha leaned into the desk, knees bouncing, as she listened to him ask the same question before he hung up and tried another number. As he worked his way down the list, Sasha's knees stopped bouncing. Her heart rattled in her chest.

The room started to spin. Sasha propped her elbows on the desk and buried her face in her hands. *Get a grip. You've managed worse before. What are your options? Hop on a bus to another town, do the street thing in Denover, or call Cole...* Sasha cringed and flopped her forehead onto Jeffrey's desk with a thud.

"Ma'am? I found one."

Sasha blinked at Jeffrey.

"It's at the Baronial across town," he said, covering the receiver with his hand. "Beautiful, grandiose hotel. Absolutely stunning. It's a single room with a king-size bed, Jacuzzi tub, and private balcony. Five hundred and fifty a night, and they require a minimum two-night stay."

"Five hundred *dollars*?"

"It's a high-end hotel with a spa, three restaurants, a pool and hot tub, golf course, and casino. Considering Denover is as busy as it is this weekend, five-fifty is a steal."

Slumping her forehead on the desk, Sasha ran the other options through her head once more.

Why does life hate me?

Her hands curled into fists, and faces flashed through her head: Dad, a ball of rage; Mom, too sick to care; Curtis, with a deadly smile; Gina, with a key to every room.

Sasha stewed at the desk, the line of guests growing behind her as Jeffrey patiently waited on the phone.

Enough of this pathetic life. Enough struggling. Enough poor choices. And enough of trying to jam myself into a reputable life.

"Ma'am?"

She lifted her head from her forearms, fire in her eyes. "I'm so sorry, Jeffrey," she said with a classy smile. "If that room is available, I will gladly take it."

Victoria flopped onto the king-size bed and sank into the fluffy folds. Even with a worn backpack slung over her shoulder and with no credit card to put on file, Victoria's fluid movements, graceful confidence, and generous tips wooed the Baronial guest services agent into believing she was someone who belonged.

A warm breeze swept in through the open balcony door while Victoria turned the tap of the Jacuzzi tub. A giggle erupted from her as she drizzled bubble bath into the swirling water below. Sinking into the steaming water, she disappeared into the bubbly world while stuffing a complimentary cookie in her mouth.

Victoria lingered in the tub, the hot water soothing her muscles until her fingers and toes pruned and the bubbles had dissipated into a soapy film. Snuggling into a luxuriously soft bathrobe, Victoria hung the red cocktail dress in the bathroom with the hot shower running, steaming the wrinkles out of it. With a contented sigh, she twisted off the cap of a water bottle and stepped onto the balcony to survey the city of Denver as it stretched out before her.

"Hey, Sash," Cole called as he closed the door behind him. "Sorry I'm late. I was stuck at the hospital trying to get a blood sample."

Cole listened for Sasha, but the condo was silent. "Sasha? You here?" He glanced down—no shoes.

"You here, Sash?" he called again, wandering through his home.

Pulling a beer from the fridge and sliding the balcony door open, Cole flopped into a patio chair and fished his phone from his pocket. He searched up Sasha's name and hit her number. His brow furrowed when it went directly to voicemail.

"Hey, Sash. Just wondering where you are. I'm home and was wondering if you wanted to make something here or go out to eat. Call me."

Cole studied his phone like it was missing a piece. Setting it on the table, he put the bottle to his mouth and looked across the city as a warm breeze swept over him. Cars passed below, people waited for the walk light to change, and Cole picked at the label on his beer.

The bottle drained, Cole lingered on the balcony, his fingers madly drumming the table. He picked up his phone.

"Hey, Sash. Me again. It's getting late and I haven't heard from you. Just wondering where you're at. Please call."

Cole bounced his leg as he watched the sun disappear behind a building. He glanced at his watch—two hours overdue.

"Where are you, Sash?" Cole said and pulled himself from his chair. As he passed the balcony's storage locker, he froze. "You wouldn't." He reached for the door's handle. "Please be there." The door creaked open.

An empty hole stared Cole in the face.

"No, no, no!" he yelled, slamming the door shut. He burst into the kitchen, tore through the condo towards the linen closet, and threw open the door.

Empty shelves.

"Sasha! No!"

Cole ran to the front door. He pulled it open and looked left and right down the hall. "Think, think… Work. The flower shop."

With the phone pressed to his ear, Cole paced the living room, but the florist's impersonal recorded message reminded him that the shop had closed hours ago.

"Where did you go, Sash?"

Chapter 31

Victoria crossed her legs and leaned back in the stylish barstool while the strum of a guitar floated around her. After hours of lounging in her room, she had slipped into her cocktail dress, curled her hair, and created her face using half a dozen pencils and brushes.

"Victoria, you are striking," she had said as she smoothed her dress in the full-length mirror. With one last smile at her reflection, Victoria grabbed her wallet and headed to the lounge.

"Here you are, ma'am," the bartender said as he set a chicken salad in front of Victoria. "Is there anything else I can get you?"

"No, thank you." Victoria smiled and placed a napkin on her lap. Low lights glinted off her glass as she tipped a splash of cosmopolitan past her lips. Reaching for a fork, she gazed out the window—the moon's glow shimmered on the surface of the inky swimming pool.

"Your best rye, straight up."

Victoria glanced up to see a man pull up a barstool a couple of seats from her. He turned to her with a smile and a nod before moving his gaze to the phone in his hand. Victoria smiled back and pierced a leaf of lettuce.

"You're a cosmo girl, hey?"

"A cosmo?" Victoria asked, glancing at him again.

"A cosmo. You know, cosmopolitan," the man said, pointing to Victoria's drink.

"Oh... uh... Yes, that's my signature drink. If I can't decide what I want, I'll always fall back on a cosmo." Victoria sipped the sweet pinkness, pleased with the bartender's recommendation.

"This guy is fabulous," he said, looking across the lounge where a man sang quiet folk songs into a microphone. "He was here last night. I didn't see you here. Is this your first night at the hotel?"

"It is." Victoria pierced another leaf and slid it off her fork with her teeth.

"What brought you to Denover? You don't look like the kind of lady who's in town for the music festival. Are you at a conference or something?"

Locking her eyes on his, Victoria smiled while vinaigrette serenaded her taste buds. She shook her head, faux curls tickling her exposed back.

"You're on a holiday with a boyfriend, husband, or friend?" he asked, glancing around the lounge.

"No," she said, reaching for the cosmo. "Keep guessing."

The man chuckled and leaned back in his seat. "You're here alone. A solo vacation."

Crossing her legs in his direction and dipping forward an inch, she said, "You figured me out."

"And why would you be on a vacation by yourself? It seems an odd thing to do. Don't you want to share your experiences with someone?"

"It's actually a fabulous thing to do. I can do whatever I choose without having to please anyone." Looking around the lounge, she said, "What about you? Are you here alone?"

The man shook his head and took a sip of the drink that the bartender had placed in front of him. "I'm on a holiday with my dad. He wanted to stay in the room tonight, but I needed to get out for a bit."

"Your father? How interesting. It's marvelous that you're traveling with him."

"He's always wanted to see this part of the country, so I decided to treat him to a holiday while he's still able."

"That's very bighearted of you. You don't meet a lot of men taking their father on a vacation. Where have you been so far?"

"We spent some time north of Ellison…"

"I lived near Ellison for a couple of summers," Victoria said as she stabbed a slice of chicken.

The guy smiled and swirled his rye. "It's beautiful country. You get the best of both worlds with ocean and mountains. We also went to Prairie Roots. I don't know if you've been, but it certainly wasn't what we expected based on the name. I figured it would be bare prairie, but we couldn't believe how lush it was."

Victoria smiled as she nibbled the chicken. "I lived there as well."

"Seems like you've lived everywhere. What brought you to those places?"

"Various reasons. I traveled around quite a bit for a number of years. Followed people, followed dreams…"

The man sipped his rye, a smile playing on his lips. "Where do you call home now?"

"A few hours east of here. A quaint place," Victoria said, lighting the fire in her eyes.

"Does this place have a name? Or are you going to keep that a secret?"

244

"It does have a name." She wrapped her lips around the fork and slid the chicken off, her eyes locked on the guy. "What about you? Where are you from?"

"Chicago."

"That's quite a ways away. And what do you do in Chicago?" Victoria knocked the rest of the drink back, letting the final drops kiss her lips.

"Advertising. I'm with a firm."

"Advertising... Fascinating." She reached into her glass and fished out a slippery cranberry.

"Can I get you another?" the bartender asked as he slid Victoria's martini glass away from her.

Victoria gazed at the pilfered glass; three cranberries were left behind. "I may later this evening, thank you, but nothing at the moment."

"I'd like to buy the lady another drink," the man offered. Turning to Victoria, he said, "Another cosmo?"

Victoria smiled lazily. Pressing her napkin to her mouth, she softly burped vodka and cranberry essence into her nose. "I suppose I could. Thank you."

"So," the man said, pulling himself from his barstool and sliding in next to Victoria. "What kind of work do you do in your quaint little place that apparently has a name that you don't want to share?"

Victoria propped her elbow on the bar and rested her chin in her hand. She gazed into his brown eyes while soft notes from the guitarist floated across the lounge. "I do this and that. Whatever falls into my lap, I guess."

The man half-smiled and swirled his rye. "You're not going to tell me where you live, or what you do for a living, or what caused you to move from place to place so much?"

"Are those details really that important?"

"They are if you're trying to get to know someone. Is there anything about yourself you are willing to share?"

"Well, you see... um... ah... I..."

The bartender set the new drink in front of Victoria and she snatched it up, knocking some over the side. Gazing at the man, she pressed her lips to the glass and slurped back a mouthful. As the alcohol warmed her chest and the sweetness fondled her mouth, she cranked up the fire in her eyes.

Moving his gaze from Victoria to the puddle of spilled booze, the man pulled his phone from his pocket. As he swiped between screens, Victoria stared at him, lips pressed to her glass. "Checking your email?"

He glanced at her, then to his phone. "Ah... no."

Victoria craned her neck and watched the guy swap pieces of animated candy on his screen. "I have stories you wouldn't believe."

"I'm sure you do..."

Sinking into the back of the barstool, Victoria chewed her lip and fixated on the liqueur bottles behind the bar.

The man stuffed his phone in his pocket, knocked back the rest of his drink, and pulled some bills from his wallet. Turning to Victoria, he said, "It was nice to meet you, my friend. I hope you enjoy the rest of your solo vacation."

And then he was gone.

Victoria sputtered garbled words as she watched him waltz across the lounge and vanish around the corner.

"Ugh." Victoria turned back to her salad. *What is with you? Stories are all you have, so you'd better pull yourself together.*

Victoria plunked her fingers into the cosmo and fished out a cranberry. She sucked the alcohol from it, turning it in her fingers to access all angles and crevices. As her lips worked the berry, her mind concocted captivating answers to the guy's questions.

Grinning at her plan, Victoria drained her glass and thanked the bartender. She hopped off the stool, smoothed her dress, and strutted through the lounge, exaggerating the sway of her hips and smiling at all the gentlemen.

"I am fantastic," Victoria said as she left the lounge and followed the dark hardwood flooring to the elevator. Passing a mirrored wall, she smiled at the way the red dress hugged her curves but when her eyes drifted to her face, she paused. Goosebumps rippled across her skin. The ocean swelled and undulating waves sent a rush of nausea through her. She brought her hand to her face and looked past the foundation, lipstick, and eyeliner. She gazed into her ocean blue eyes, not recognizing the woman who stared back.

Chapter 32

Cole held his head in his hands, elbows on the table. The stove's clock was the only light that penetrated the dark kitchen. His heart thumped in his ears, his mind a mess of fragmented thought patterns...
... *names... makeup... predators, rapists...*
...*my Sasha... Please be safe. Please be okay. Please be alive.*

Chapter 33

Victoria spooned raspberry yogurt into her mouth as the morning sun warmed her face. With feet propped on the balcony's railing, she looked over rooftops and leafy trees to the grassy hill in the distance. Ant-like humans peppered the hill, and an echoing guitar tune floated on the clouds.

Draining the last of her coffee, she stretched her arms over her head. "You have full day of vacationing ahead of you, Victoria. Let's start with a visit to the pool."

After painting her face, Victoria slipped into the little black bikini and turned sideways in the mirror. "Bryn may have felt self-conscious in this thing, but if Curtis had bought it for you..." With a spin and a giggle, Victoria pulled the hotel's plush bathrobe over her body before gliding out the door.

Victoria strutted through the hotel, smiling at guests and firing up her eyes for the men. Rounding the corner into the spa, she breathed in the scent of lavender, eucalyptus, and relaxation as harp chords strummed overhead. Pool signs told her where to go and when she pushed through the glass doors, the summer sun kissed her skin.

The smell of freshly cut grass and chlorine swept around Victoria as she sashayed across the pool deck with head held high. Slipping her bathrobe off, she lowered herself into the water, purring as the warmth enveloped her toes, ankles, knees. She pushed from the edge and glided under the water as gentle currents caressed her torso. She popped her head out of the water for a breath before diving under again and swimming a few laps. Muscles glowing, Victoria pulled her dripping body up the pool ladder and strutted towards the hot tub.

The hot tub burbled softly, inviting Victoria in. She eased into the steaming water and gazed out at the Baronial Golf Course and city beyond. As a jet massaged muscles stiff from her pack, her mind drifted to the dwindling numbers in Sasha's bank account.

Repositioning the other shoulder against the jet, a familiar face jumped out at her from across the fence. Victoria leapt to her feet, splashing the elderly lady sitting across from her.

"Chicago!" Victoria yelled as she bounced down the steps that joined the hot tub to the pool deck. "Chicago!"

The man slowed, turned, and looked around.

"Chicago, wait up." Victoria waved her arm as she trotted towards him.

"Hey," she said when she reached the low fence separating pool from golf course. "I wanted to talk to you."

His eyes swept over Victoria's bikinied body. "It's the lady with the great smile but no answers."

"That's what I wanted to talk to you about. I know I was really vague last night and that wasn't fair to you. You were looking for a nice conversation and I wasn't giving you anything. I wanted to apologize."

The man shook his head and watched a golfer sink a long putt. "Don't worry about it."

"But I wanted to tell you why I was being so elusive."

"It's okay," he said with a shrug and turned to go.

"Wait." Victoria reached over the fence and grabbed the man's arm. "I want to explain myself."

The man glanced at the line of water dribbling from Victoria's hand and down his arm, and raised his eyebrows.

"I feel bad about how I acted."

"Look, it's all right. We don't know each other, and you aren't obligated to tell me anything."

Victoria sighed and pulled her hand back over the fence. "I just don't want you going back to Chicago and telling your friends how you met this woman in a bar, but she turned out to be a weirdo. I'd rather you have a nice story to tell about me."

His face relaxed into a perplexed smile. Brushing the droplets from his arm, he chuckled. "Are you here to tell me the name of your town? Or what you do for work?"

Summoning her Victoria eyes, she said, "Do you have a few minutes?"

The guy puffed his cheeks and let the air out in a rush. Glancing at his watch, he said, "I'm meeting my dad for golf in half an hour. How long is this going to take?"

"Just a few minutes. I promise."

"All right, I'll humor you."

"Thank you." A breeze swept across Victoria's belly, sending a cascade of goosebumps along her skin. "Come sit."

Hands on his hips, the man looked across the golf course again. A golf ball cracked in the distance, muffled voices carried from the hot tub, a gull cried overhead, and the man let himself through the pool's gate.

"I'll be right back," Victoria said as she trotted off, leaving the man alone on a teak lounge chair. She grabbed a towel and wrapped it around her body before bouncing back.

"All right," the man said as Victoria perched herself on the edge of a chair. "What is it you need to tell me?"

"I've had some... misfortunes in my past, and sometimes, if I'm dwelling on that part of my life, I have trouble opening up about aspects of myself. I suppose one could say I feel guarded at times."

"That's fair," the man said, shifting in his seat. "Sorry you had difficulties, but it's not my business. I'm sorry if you feel you have to tell me."

"I don't mean to make you feel uncomfortable again, but I wanted you to know that I'm not a stuffy person who is too good to share things about herself."

The corners of the man's mouth tipped down. His eyes darted around the pool as if he was trying to find an excuse to get up and run away. "Is that all you wanted to say?"

"I'm married," Victoria blurted out. *Crap. Stick to the story, dummy.*

"Oh..." His back straightened like someone had shoved a stick up his shirt. "Okay... Not sure what I'm supposed to say to that."

"I love my husband, and I didn't mean to flirt with you last night. I was simply enjoying your company, and the cosmos were making me a little carefree. My husband is actually the one who sent me on this trip. He knows I need my own space, and he sends me on vacations a couple of times a year so I can defuse."

The man pursed his lips and looked over his shoulder at a group of golfers.

"To answer some of your questions..." Victoria continued. "For work, I used to be a wine rep. That's why I traveled around so much. I spent a lot of time in wine country and lived in a lot of different places. A few years back, I was at this vineyard not far from Ellison and I got mixed up in some bad business. It wasn't my fault, but I found myself in the middle of this mess. The more I tried to pull myself away from the situation, the deeper I found myself. Finally…" Victoria paused and stuttered in a dramatic breath. "Things got really bad. I knew too much about deals and stuff, and I ended up getting trapped. Literally. These people—these really bad people—kept me captive. I was terrified and I tried to figure a way out of there, but I couldn't." Victoria's words were puking from her mouth as the story started to write itself.

"One day, I got my hands on a phone, and I called the cops and told them I was being held against my will. The cops showed up and, well, they rescued me."

Victoria let out a rush of air and pressed her hand to her chest. She dropped her head and, facing the cement, glimpsed up at the guy. His forehead was creased, his eyebrows so tight they were almost one, and his mouth twitched. He scratched his head and opened his mouth.

"There was this one cop in particular," Victoria blurted. "He helped me a lot. He pulled me from that pain and from that misery. He…" Her breath caught in her throat. Blazing eyes were doused by a teary film and her gaze drifted out across the golf course. "He saved me. He was so good and kind. He didn't have to come all that way, but he did without question. I had no one in my life—no friends or family—and I had no home, so he took me in. He told me I could stay with him until I got my life back together." Sasha wiped a tear. Her gaze fell to the chlorinated puddle forming under her feet. "And then I fell in love with him."

"And did you marry him?"

"I'm sorry?" Sasha asked, looking up at the man.

"The cop. Is he your husband?"

"Oh." Sasha wiped her eyes with shaking hands. "Oh, uh, yes. We fell in love and got married." Steading her breath, she looked past the man. "And we lived happily ever after."

"I'm sorry I left you in the bar last night. You were right that I thought you were a bit vague and maybe a bit odd. Or that you were hiding something that I didn't need to be a part of."

Sasha knotted her arms around her stomach, feeling like she had just been caught cheating. "Thank you for listening. You'd better go meet your dad."

The man looked at his watch, then back to Sasha and reached his hand out. "I never got your name."

"Sash– Victoria," she stammered. "It's Victoria."

"Matt," the man said, taking her hand. "It was a pleasure to meet you."

"Enjoy your golf game." Sasha hugged the towel around her body as her teeth chattered.

"I hope you enjoy the rest of your vacation, Victoria. It sounds like you have a very kind, understanding husband."

Sasha bit her lip and gave Matt a wave as he turned to go. Shivering, she made her way back to the hot tub and slid into the water. Her gaze drifted, unfocused, to the rippling water of the swimming pool. A cloud floated in front of the sun, casting a shadow over Sasha and darkening the glint of the pool's surface. Closing her eyes, Sasha sunk to her ears in the steamy water. Her plans to spend the day at the pool fizzled.

Sasha rummaged around in her pack for a t-shirt as her wet bikini hung limply over the side of the Jacuzzi. "Where is it?" she said, pushing aside Cole's granola bars and an open pack of disposable razors. Spying the blue hue of the shirt she wanted, she yanked it out.

Something hard fell on her foot.

Her phone, like a discarded friend, stared up at her accusingly. Her stomach hardened to stone.

Sasha pulled the shirt over her head and collected the phone from the carpet. It was cold, hard, and oddly heavy. She crawled across the bed and nestled into the suffocating sheets; every thought turned to what waited inside the phone.

She powered it up.

Her heart stopped.

Eleven unheard messages.

"Hi, Sasha. This is Beverly from Thorns. I was wondering if you will be coming in to work today. If something has happened and you cannot make it in, I need to know."

"Hey, Sash. Just wondering where you are. I'm home and was wondering if you wanted to make something here or go out to eat. Call me."

Sasha drew her lips in and swallowed hard.

"Hey, Sash. Me again. It's getting late and I haven't heard from you. Just wondering where you're at. Please call."

"Sasha, where are you?" The panic in Cole's voice sucked the air from Sasha. "All your stuff is gone and you're not picking up. Call me. I'll have my phone on me all night. Call any time. Please."

"Sasha, please call." The lump in Sasha's throat hardened as Cole's voice broke. "I'm worried about you. I'm guessing you needed to leave because of the apartment. I'm sorry if it was too much to take in. Please come home. I'm scared that something bad has happened to you."

"What are you up to, Sash?" Cole's voice sounded like an echo lost in a valley. "I'm just lying in bed. It's three in the morning. I can't sleep. I'd love to hear your voice. I'd love to know you are safe. Please come home."

"Sasha, it's Beverly again. I'm sorry, but not showing up for work without an explanation is not acceptable. Please come by the shop to pick up your final paycheck." Sasha squeezed her eyes shut, forcing the tears to stay inside.

"Morning, Sash. Still wondering where you're at. I didn't sleep last night. I hope you had a great sleep. Wherever you are."

"I should probably stop leaving these messages or I'm going to eat up all your minutes, but I keep holding out hope that you'll actually pick up one of these times."

The next message was simply a heavy sigh.

"Just let me know you're safe. That's all I ask." A long, staticky pause before a click to silence.

Sasha's hand trembled as she pulled the phone from her ear. "I'm so sorry, Cole," she whispered. "I was in a bad place and wasn't thinking. I'm so, so sorry." Taking a deep breath and steadying her nerves, she punched in his number.

One ring.

"Sasha?"

"Hey." Sasha pressed her hand to her mouth and tried to keep the tears from spilling over.

"I was so worried. Are you okay?"

"I'm okay. I'm sorry I didn't call or tell you I was leaving. I didn't know I was leaving until… until I was gone…"

"Where are you?"

"At a hotel in Denver. I needed some space. I needed to get out." A sob broke through the crack in her voice.

"Are you in a room at the hotel?"

"Yes. I got myself a room."

"I'll call you in your room, so we don't eat up all your minutes. What hotel are you at?"

Sasha sunk deeper into the sheets. "The Baronial. Room eight-five-one."

Silence infected the line. Sasha held her breath.

"The Baronial? Isn't that a really luxurious hotel?"

"Yes," she squeaked.

"Seriously, Sash? Okay. I'll call you right away on that line."

The click of the ended call sounded like Cole had shot a hole through her tattered picture of them.

Rolling to her side, Sasha stared at the hotel phone on the bedside table. It rang loud and shrill, echoing throughout the room. "Hello?"

Silence. Then, "I can't do this anymore, Sash."

"What can't you do?"

"I can't be friends with you if you keep taking off when life gets hard, without letting me know where you are."

"It won't happen again. I'm ready to come home. I need to come home."

"That's what you say now, but the moment that things start stressing you out, or when you don't want to be yourself anymore, you're going to get on another bus and take off. It's what you do, and I can't handle it."

"But I won't." Sasha pulled herself to sitting and hugged her knees to her chest.

"You need help. I thought I was enough to help you but now I know I'm not. Let me take you to a doctor."

"I already told you I don't need that."

A heavy sigh carried over the line. "How many names have you used since you left yesterday?"

"That doesn't matter."

"It does matter!"

She flinched. Cole's tone scuttled across her skin.

"How many?"

"A few." Sasha pulled the duvet over her head. "But I don't see what that has to do with anything. I'm not hurting anyone by changing my name now and then."

"And changing your personality. I've seen you do it and it's freaking weird. It's not normal and it's not healthy. And you *are* hurting people because you are breaking their trust. You may not have seen any consequences yet, but that doesn't mean they aren't there. One of these days, your lies are going to catch up with you."

Sasha bit her lip and stared at the dark wall of her duvet cave.

"Let me take you to see someone professionally. I know you don't see the need, or maybe you are scared, or you don't want to admit that you have issues, but you need to talk to someone."

I'm not crazy.

"Sasha, talk to me. Please say something."

As Cole's dependable voice swept through her body and hugged her soul, the stone in Sasha's stomach softened. She clutched a pillow to her chest and pressed her face into it. The words she needed to scream aloud stayed trapped inside. *I want to be Sasha. Just Sasha. Only Sasha.*

"I want to come home," she said. "I want to see you and I don't want to be here anymore. Please come for me."

"Are you going to let me take you to a doctor?"

"I told you I don't need that."

"Then I can't come for you."

"I'm sorry?" Sasha pulled the duvet off her head. Staticky hairs stuck to her face and sucked into her mouth with every rapid breath.

"I can't give you what you need. You need professional help, and if you refuse to seek that help, then I can't have you in my life. I'm sorry, Sasha. Take care of yourself."

The sickening click was followed by a deep, dark, empty silence.

"Cole!" Her voice plummeted into the chasm left by Cole. "Cole!"

The numbers on the phone's base blurred through tears. Sasha frantically punched in Cole's number, but it would not connect. "Why is this not working?" she cried as her eyes scanned and rescanned the instructions on the phone's base, but they may as well have been written in French.

Under dark, swirling skies, Sasha's ocean began its swell. She dropped the handset and scrambled for her cellphone, gasping for air as the current tried to suck her under. Four rings, then voicemail.

"Cole, please," Sasha begged through her sobs. "Please come for me. I want to go home. I want to see you. I'm sorry I left. I'll never leave again. Please come for me."

Sasha pleaded into the phone until the recorded voice, cold and emotionless, told her she had run out of time. Hugging the phone to her chest, she collapsed into the bed, staining the pillowcase with mascara.

When her breathing settled and the sobs quieted to whimpers, Sasha turned to the hotel phone and calmed her voice.

"Good afternoon, Miss Cooper," the guest services agent answered. "How may I be of service?"

"I was wondering if you'd be able to tell me when the next bus to Lashburn is."

"Please allow me a moment and I will find that information for you."

Quiet sounds carried through the phone—fast typing and the distant chatter of guests in the lobby. Normal sounds. Everyday sounds.

"Here we are," the agent said. "The next bus leaves the Denover station tomorrow at eleven a.m.. There is another bus at three-twenty."

"Nothing today?" Sasha's fingers twisted into a fist around her hair and her lungs forgot how to breathe.

"I'm sorry, but there are no other busses to Lashburn today. The next one is tomorrow at eleven."

"Thank you," Sasha mumbled. Releasing her hair, she flopped face first into the bed and let the sobs rock her body. Rolling to her side, she reached for her phone and punched in Cole's number.

"I'm coming home tomorrow," Sasha cried into his voicemail. "I'm taking the eleven o'clock bus out of Denover. I should be at your place late in the afternoon. I'm not going to turn my phone off anymore, so please call. Please, Cole, call me. And then I'll see you tomorrow."

Chapter 34

Sasha lay in bed as the brightness of the sun slowly faded to muted pinks and oranges. When her bladder refused to be ignored any longer, she dragged herself to the bathroom.

As burning water stung her hands, she looked at her reflection in the mirror; the darkness around her eyes from her ruined makeup echoed the hollowness inside.

"You are a terrible person," Sasha said. "You've always been useless, and you chased away the only person willing to put up with you." She dropped her clothes to the floor and turned away from the freak in the mirror.

Hot water beat down on Sasha's shoulders as dark makeup swirled down the drain. Gravity winning the battle, Sasha curled into a ball on the shower floor. Water pounded her body without relief and pulled her hair towards the drain. *Take all of me,* she thought as a lock vanished into the pipe.

With a towel wrapped around her body, Sasha steadied the black eyeliner pencil in her pruned fingers. She leaned into the mirror, averting her gaze until she was close enough to focus only on the detail of the eye. "Thank you, Victoria, for being someone who wears makeup," she said as she darkened the border of her eyelid. As Victoria emerged, a fire lit in her core, burning brighter with each stroke of the mascara brush.

When the last curl bounced from the curling iron, she slipped into the cocktail dress and stepped in front of the full-length mirror. She turned to inspect her angles and smiled at her firm, round bottom. "You are Victoria, and you are extraordinary."

Spinning away from the mirror, Victoria stepped into the hall with head held high and hips swaying.

Rings and dings of the casino reverberated in Victoria's ears. She weaved between slot machines while flashing lights and screens of charging buffalo tried to steal her attention. As she rounded another group of slots, the casino opened to rows of tables.

Propping her hand on her waist, Victoria sashayed down the line, her eyes on the bar at the other end, but the sweep of a craps stick pulled her to a halt. Like a bottle of champagne uncorked in her veins, a long-forgotten tingling sensation bubbled up inside. The roll of the dice, the excited cheers, and the calls from the dealer oozed into her pores and settled in her core.

Victoria smoothed her dress, squared her shoulders, and shimmied up to the table. Flipping open her wallet, she fingered the smooth fibres of a twenty while eyeing up the competition: two serious-looking businessmen, a young couple hanging off each other, and a group of men who laughed too loudly as they guzzled beer and stole glances at Victoria.

Directing a flirtatious smile at the men, Victoria laid her twenty on the table. The moment the money touched the green felt, her muscles stiffened, and her smile fell away. She stared at her fingers pressing down on the bill as a voice sucked the fun away. *This is your bus money, idiot. You can't risk anything if you plan on seeing Cole again.*

Her fingernails scraped the felt and her hand curled into a fist, crumpling the bill inside. She tore herself from the table, glancing longingly at the dice bouncing along the felt and off the table's wall. A loud cheer erupted behind her as she hurried away.

Smoothing more imaginary wrinkles from her dress, she collapsed into a barstool and closed her eyes. *You're Victoria. Classy, elegant Victoria. And Victoria does not feel Sasha's pain.* With a steadying breath, she looked at the bartender and forced a smile.

"What can I get for you?" the bartender asked as he squeezed a lime through a juicer.

Victoria stared at the desiccated lime that the bartender had plucked from the machine and tossed aside. Its skin looked lifeless; the sweet juiciness had been crushed from it. "What are the limes for?"

"All sorts of drinks. Mojitos, cosmopolitans, daiquiris, margaritas..." The bartender pulled down the handle on the juicer and watched the juice flow into the jug below.

"That looks like a lot of work. You must go through a lot of limes. Why not just use lime juice from a bottle?"

The bartender chuckled to himself and glanced at Victoria as he pulled another shrivelled rind from the juicer. "Because there is nothing like the real thing. You can taste the difference in quality when you use a genuine ingredient rather than faking it or taking the easy way out."

She dropped her gaze to the lacquered bar as background noise of the casino buzzed in her head. Biting her lip, she traced the wooden grain with her finger. A mix of lipstick and blood sat on her tongue.

"The key to getting the most from your limes," the bartender said, "is to warm them up before you squeeze them. Let them sit in warm water for ten minutes and you'll get ten percent more juice from them, if not more."

"Really?" Victoria cleared her throat and focused on the bartender's smile.

"It makes sense if you think about it. Limes and other citrus fruits grow in warm climates, so they'd naturally be at their peak performance at those temperatures." The bartender squeezed the last lime and grabbed a rag to clean up his workspace. "Apples. Now those are interesting fruit. Did you know that there are over seventy-five hundred cultivars, yet they are all the same species? And for the most part, cultivars are propagated by grafting onto rootstalks rather than grown from seed."

"You taught me something new about limes, but I already knew about the apples. I used to work at an orchard, so I'm well versed with that fruit."

"Very nice, very nice. Where did you work?"

She tried to ignite the fire in her eyes, but her lighter was out of juice. Slumping in the barstool, she said, "Orchards around Stanley and Pointon Bridge, mostly. I also spent some time at Delburne Orchards near Ashton."

"Very nice. Beautiful places. Is there a drink or something else I can offer you this evening?"

"Yes, please. One final drink of my vacation. Let's make it a cosmopolitan."

"Sure thing. One cosmo coming up."

"Actually, since it's the last drink of my trip, I think I'll do something different. What would you recommend?"

"Our mojitos are popular. Or maybe a sangria? I can whip up just about any drink you dream of." The bartender slid the wine list and drink menu to Victoria. She perused the selections, but nothing jumped out at her. Glancing at the rows of bottles lining the wall behind the bar, her eyes stopped at a single bottle in a glass case by itself.

"What's that?" Victoria asked, pointing to the case.

The bartender smiled. "That is our finest Scotch. Single malt, smooth as silk, aged twenty-six years. If you're a Scotch drinker, it's a treat."

"And if you're not? If you've never had Scotch before?"

"It's still a treat, although most people try their hand at Scotch with something a little less… select. But if you are in the class of people who can imbibe in something of this league without worry, then I think it's worth a shot."

She stared at the bartender like he was speaking gibberish as Cole's words filled her ears: *"I can't have you in my life."*

You're Victoria. You're Victoria! Remain classy… "If it's a good Scotch, then I think I'll give it a try."

The bartender raised his eyebrows and smiled. "Fantastic. Do you want to know the price per glass before I pour it?"

"Oh. Okay… How much?"

"Two fifty. Are you still interested in having some?"

"Two fifty a glass? I can handle that. I'll try it."

"Are you staying at the hotel?"

"Yes. Room eight-five-one, but I'll pay for my drink here."

"Very well." The bartender pulled a key from the cash register and slid it into the lock on the case. "Interesting fact: Scotch evolved from a Scottish drink, *uisge beatha*, which means water of life…" The bartender continued with the history of the Scotch, the bottle it was in, and the story of the twenty people worldwide who could make the type of glass that this Scotch was drunk from, but she looked through him.

"And there, ma'am, is the finest Scotch you may ever drink. Enjoy." The bartender placed the glass holding the amber liquid in front of Victoria and smiled.

Victoria put the glass to her lips. Her nose wrinkled as the aroma wafted out, reminding her of bandages. She tipped a teaspoon of liquid into her mouth and froze. Imagining she had the grace of the Queen of England, Victoria set the glass on the bar and talked her muscles through the motions of swallowing. The whiskey burned her throat while its smokiness floated into her sinus cavities. Victoria forced a straight face as the bartender looked on expectantly.

"So?" he asked. "How's your first Scotch?"

"It's not what I expected," Victoria choked out.

"Some people say it's an acquired taste. Give it a chance. This is a fine drink." Seeing an older couple take a seat at the other side of the bar, the bartender excused himself.

Victoria sipped the Scotch again and cringed. She put the drink down and looked at her phone lying on the bar. Victoria was sputtering out like a lost satellite signal.

"This is much too lovely of a hotel to be looking so miserable. Did you lose all your money at the casino or something?"

Sasha looked up from her phone. A man was toying with a coaster a few seats away.

"No, I lost all my money a different way."

"Really?" the man said, shifting one seat closer. "And how did you manage that?"

"I guess you can call it poor life choices."

"I've had my fair share of those." Getting the bartender's attention, the man called out a drink order before turning back to Sasha. "How bad is it? Are you talking about all your life savings or just a big chunk?"

Sasha picked up her phone and cradled it in her hand, running her thumb across the screen. "When you're talking about someone like me, it's hard to differentiate between the two."

"Sounds like life is pretty rough."

Sasha stared at her reflection in the phone's screen. She tried to look past Victoria's face, past her own dull eyes, and into the inner workings of the phone, as if she could find Cole there.

"You look like you're trying to get that thing to ring," the man said as he reached for the rum and Coke that the bartender had placed before him.

"I'm sorry?" Sasha said, looking up. "Oh, yeah. Sorry. I'd love for it to ring, but he's not going to call. He's done with me."

"Boyfriend troubles?"

Shaking her head, Sasha took a sip of Scotch, cringing as it burned her throat. "He's not my boyfriend. He's just a friend. My best friend. I guess I should say he *was* my best friend, but he doesn't want anything to do with me anymore."

"And why is that?"

"You know that thing I said about poor life choices? Let's just say it has something to do with that."

"What happened?"

"I don't really want to get into it. It doesn't matter anyway. He won't answer his phone. He was the only good thing in my life, and now I've screwed that up too. I'm almost out of money, I have no job, no friends, no family, and now he's gone as well. Without him, I really have nothing, other than an empty apartment for the remainder of the month, but I don't even have anything to fill the apartment with."

"That's rough. Anything I can do to help?"

"That's very kind of you, but there's really nothing to do. I just keep screwing up my life, and I don't know why. It's like I don't want to be happy or something, so I push the goodness away." With a heavy sigh, Sasha took another sip of Scotch and cringed. "He is so good. He's kind and thoughtful and patient. And he helped me. When everyone else was turning their backs on me or pushing me away, he was there. He always came for me when I needed him, without question and without judgement. I've known him my entire life and we *get* each other, you know? He makes me feel important. And we had fun together. He bought me these stupid shark slippers for Christmas and a matching pair for himself. He can be such a dork, but I love when he does stuff like that. And his jokes. Oh my gosh… don't get me started. They are groaners, but I secretly love his sense of humor. We'd spend our days off together, watching movies or playing games or going to the park…"

"You love him."

Sasha glanced at the guy before returning her gaze to the phone. She placed it on the bar and pushed it to the side. "I shouldn't. I'm not supposed to. He's my friend."

The man smiled and took a sip of his drink. "But you do. I can tell."

A breath stuttered into Sasha as she tightened her grip on the Scotch glass.

"Does he love you?"

"Yeah, right," Sasha said with a laugh. "As if someone like him would love someone like me."

"Well, why not? You are best friends, you clearly like to spend time together, and from the sounds of it, he was there for you when you needed help. He obviously cares for you. Is it really that much of a stretch for him to be in love with you?"

Images of Cole tumbled through Sasha's head. She could smell the rain on his skin from their rapturous night on his couch; feel the heat of his hands on her back the day she turned from his kiss in the kitchen;

and hear the nervousness in his voice when he bought her flowers signed, *Love, Cole*.

Sasha traced her finger around and around the rim of her glass, its smoothness barely calming the knocking of her heart. "I need to get back to him," she said as tears welled up in her eyes. "I need to fix what I did but I don't know how."

"He still loves you. If he loved you and if you were best friends, then those feelings are still in him. You can fix this, and you can get him back."

Nodding, Sasha dabbed at her eyes with her napkin, blotches of black staining the white tissue. "I'm going back tomorrow. I'm catching the bus at eleven and I'll go to his place as soon as I get back. I know he won't turn me away, no matter how upset he is." She picked up her glass and took another sip, wincing at the flavor.

"What are you drinking? You certainly don't look like you're enjoying it."

"It's horrible. It's Scotch from that bottle in the glass case. I don't know if I can finish it. It's like I'm swallowing a snake."

The man's jaw dropped. "I thought you said you had money troubles. What the hell are you doing drinking that stuff? You certainly know how to go out with a bang."

"It looks fancy, but it's only two fifty a glass."

"*Only* two hundred and fifty a glass? What kind of world do you live in?"

Sasha shook her head and took another sip. "Two fifty a glass. Two dollars and fifty cents."

The man stared silently into Sasha, not moving a muscle. Finally, he said, "Seriously? Oh, shit, girl. Are you being absolutely serious?"

"The cheapest thing on the menu. I have no idea why they have it looking so regal in that case and with these special fancy glasses. It's terrible stuff."

"Oh, shit." The man leaned his elbows on the bar and covered his mouth with his hand. "I'm guessing you haven't paid for that yet."

"Nope. I might get a second drink to wash this swill down."

"How much money do you have left?"

Sasha wrinkled her brow. "I don't think that's any of your business."

"Humor me. You said you lost most of your money. How much do you have left?"

"Just over two hundred and fifty dollars."

"Oh, shit."

"Why do you keep saying that?" Sasha asked, swirling the Scotch in her glass.

"That Scotch you are drinking… the *swill*, as you call it… it's not two dollars and fifty cents—it's two hundred and fifty dollars."

Sasha stopped swirling the liquid and looked up at the man, her fingers tingling as panic filled her veins. "No, it's not. The bartender clearly said it was two dollars and fifty cents. No one in their right mind would pay two hundred and fifty for this." Sasha stared at the man, but he just stared back with pursed lips.

The glass case, the key, the specialty glass… No, no, no. There's no way…

"You okay? You're kind of pale."

"Um, bartender? Bartender! Excuse me. How much did you say this drink was?"

"Two fifty a glass. Three thousand if you want to purchase a full bottle."

Sasha's focus drifted to her drink. "I think I might be sick," she mumbled. "I can't possibly pay that much for a single drink. The fact that it even costs that much is preposterous. Who would buy this? Why would the hotel even have a drink with that price tag? Oh my gosh." Sasha moaned and hid her face in her hands. "Here I go again, screwing up my life, as usual."

The bus ticket.

Her head snapped up and her eyes went wide. "I'll have less than fifteen dollars left," Sasha said, tears hovering on the edge. "How can I get to Lashburn with only fifteen dollars? I need to get there."

"Whoa, whoa, whoa." The man chuckled and shifted to the seat beside Sasha. "Did you say you need to get to Lashburn?"

"That's where he lives. I need to get to him."

A wide smile stretched across his face, and he clapped his hands together. "I will drive you to Lashburn tomorrow."

"I'm sorry? Why?"

"I'm going to Lashburn tomorrow. I have a car I need to deliver to a friend there. He's expecting it just after lunch. I plan to leave here before nine. I can't promise I'll take you to your friend's place, but I can at least get you to the city."

"You'd do that for me? You'd drive me to Lashburn?"

"It would be my pleasure. By the way, my name is Dan."

Grabbing her balled napkin, Sasha dabbed at tears that had breached the rim. "I'm… Victoria. You are so kind. I don't know how to thank you."

"No thanks required. I'm more than happy to help you out. If you'd excuse me for a moment, I need to make a quick call. Don't leave. We need to make plans to meet up in the morning."

"I will stay right here." Sasha beamed through her sniffles. "Thank you again."

As Dan excused himself, Sasha turned back to her drink. She stared it down like a matador facing off a bull. Determined to choke down every last drop of the most abhorrently priced thing she knew she would ever consume in her life, Sasha took another sip and cringed. As the liquid burned her throat, she nestled her fingers around her phone, knowing that fate had brought Dan into her life.

Chapter 35

Sasha traipsed across the park's grass, leaving a trail through the early morning dew. Tapping her hands to the sides of her legs, her eyes zoned in on the black car parked by the tennis courts. The butterflies in her stomach clenched their wings as Dan's plan rolled through her head.

As Sasha neared the lot, her eyes narrowed. The driver was slumped forward like a ragdoll, head resting on the wheel. Slowing her gait, she looked around, but the only movement was a robin scurrying across the grass. As her shoes scraped gravel, she paused. "Dan?" she said across the lot. The driver looked like he was asleep. Or dead.

Shaking out jittery hands, Sasha inched across the lot until she was standing in front of the driver's door. The sun's rays glinted off the shiny metal while the man wilted on the wheel. With legs fired up ready to run, Sasha tensed her hand into a fist and rapped on the window.

Dan rolled his head and cracked his eyes. He peered at Sasha through slits. Looking like he was pushing through molasses, he moved his hand from the wheel and shoved open the door.

"Dan, are you okay?"

"I'm so sick," Dan whispered. "I think it was the crab cakes I had for dinner."

"Are you going to be all right?"

"No." Dan fell from the car and staggered to a nearby garbage can. He braced his arms around the can and stuck his head inside. Loud heaving echoed from the garbage as his body rocked in rhythm. When he was done, he wiped his mouth before sliding to the ground.

"Um... Dan?" Sasha slid her pack from her shoulders and let it slump to the gravel. "Are you able to drive?"

Eyes closed, he shook his head. "I barely made it here, but I needed to meet you. I know how badly you have to get to Lashburn, and I couldn't leave you hanging."

"That's... That's so nice of you..." Sasha tucked her hair behind her ear and shifted her weight. "But... You'll be able to drive. You *have* to drive. If we just wait for a bit, you'll feel better and then we can go."

"I'm not going anywhere today."

"But... No..."

"You can still go, Victoria. You need to find your guy as soon as possible and fix things with him. And I promised my friend I'd have the car to him by this afternoon. You can take the car, drop it off for me, then get your man back."

"I'm sorry?"

"Take my car. Please."

"Hang on," Sasha said. "You want me to take your car? Without you? You don't even know me. Aren't you scared I'm going to steal it or trash it or something?"

Without warning, Dan pulled himself to standing and stuck his head in the garbage, making the awful heaving sounds again. When he was done, he sunk to the ground, flopped onto his side, and closed his eyes. "I don't care," he groaned. "Anyway, there's a GPS in the car so I can always find you if you take off with it. And then I'll come after you and mess you up." Dan opened his eyes a crack and half-smiled. "Kidding. You're a nice girl and I trust you. If I didn't, I wouldn't offer you the car."

"I can't take your car. It wouldn't feel right."

"For my sake, take the car. My friend is counting on me to get the car to him today and I can't let him down." Dan moaned and clutched his stomach. "I'd go with you if I could, but I can't even stand up. Being in a moving vehicle is not going to go well for me. I've offered to help you with your troubles. Please help me with mine."

Sasha squeezed her eyes shut and pressed her hands to her head. "I don't know. I'm too nervous. Maybe I'll come up with another plan."

"You need to get to your guy as soon as possible. The longer you leave him alone, the easier it'll be for him to keep you at a distance. If he's important to you—the most important thing in the world—then you have to act while he's still recovering from the breakup. Get to him while his emotions are raw."

"Yeah," Sasha whispered as air rushed in and out of her lungs. "Maybe..." She dropped her head between her knees and forced a slow breath in. *Okay, okay... I can do this. Like driving on an orchard. Keep to the speed limit and obey all traffic laws. Just this one time, for a very good reason. No one will find out. But what if...*

Sasha pulled herself upright. Dark edges and twinkling bursts made her sway. "What about you? I can't leave you here."

"Yes, you can," Dan said, his faced pressed into the gravel. "I'm not getting back in the car. I'll crawl onto the grass and lie down under a tree. When I feel better, I'll manage my way home."

Sasha turned and looked at the car. The metallic paint sparkled as though embedded with diamond dust. The rims looked like turbines, ready to pulverize anything that came near.

Sasha breathed deeply. Oxygen flowed through her body, swimming in her cells and tricking her brain into thinking she had control. "I don't even know where to drop it off."

"At my friend's house. Chad. Twenty-five Grovedale Ave. Do you need to write it down?"

"I have a good memory. But what happens if the car breaks down or something? I wouldn't know what to do."

Dan groaned again and curled into a ball. "The car's in great shape and the fuel tank is full. Nothing will happen, but in case you need to get a hold of me, I'll give you my number. Can you remember it?"

Sasha nodded. "Yeah, but..."

Dan coughed and burped and pulled himself up again. Doubling over and hugging the garbage can, he choked out his number between heaves.

"Thank you for your help," he said as he sunk to the gravel. "You have no idea how much this favor means to me. I'd go with you if I could, but..."

"It's okay," Sasha said. "I appreciate the offer. It's just that..." Her body quivered.

"The keys are on the dash. Chad will be waiting for you."

"What about you? I can drop you off at your home."

Straining to his knees, Dan crawled across the gravel towards the grass. "No, I'll manage. I really appreciate your help. I wish you the best with fixing things with your guy."

As Dan crawled away, Sasha inched towards the car. She stumbled over her pack and bumped into the door. The exterior, already hot from the morning sun, burned her skin.

"But... Dan, I can't..." she said, turning around. Dan was a hundred feet away, collapsed on the ground in the shadows of the trees.

Closing her eyes, Sasha sucked in a lungful of air. *But Magda can.*

An image of Cole lounging on his balcony, smiling and telling a stupid joke, flowed into her. She breathed deeply and waited for her heart rate come down.

Magda popped open the back door and tossed the pack in before she climbed into the driver's seat. She pulled the seatbelt across her body; its securing *click* sounded like a deadbolt.

Chapter 36

Sasha scanned the highway as the drone of tires on asphalt buzzed in her ears. She felt like a goat making its way over a rickety bridge, Eden in the distance, and a troll waiting to sneak out and pounce.

"I shouldn't be here," she said, flexing her hands cramped from clenching the wheel. "I should have turned back." As she passed another mileage sign with Lashburn's name, she rolled her shoulders and pulled her fingers through her hair. "Come on, Magda. Where'd you go? I only need you for an hour more."

The highway dipped and curved. Cars passed by her window. She rounded a corner before an overpass and as her eyes landed on a group of police cars ahead, ice swept through her veins. Her trembling foot slammed the brakes.

Sinking low in her seat, Sasha cleared her throat and shook out her shoulders. "Never mind them. They won't worry about you. They're dealing with a dirtier criminal than you." She pulled her hood over her head and hovered just below the speed limit. The police cars blurred through her tears.

As her car hurtled towards the trolls, Sasha searched the highway for the helpless goat caught in their claws, but there was nothing. No cars pulled over. No police officers talking to anyone. The cars were simply sitting there, side by side, facing the passing traffic, with a cop behind the wheel of each.

Sasha's hands were welded to the wheel and her eyes were glued open as she passed the gauntlet. The row of police cars grew smaller in her rear-view mirror. Rushing blood pounded in her ears. *You are Magda and you are tough.*

Sasha rolled her head and focused on her breathing. *Just like Cole taught you. In… two… three… four… Hold… two… three… four…*

Red and blue lights glinted in her periphery. Sasha's controlled breaths crumbled into disjointed wheezes. "Oh my gosh, oh my gosh. You need a story. Suck it up and shove it down." As her foot quivered on the gas pedal, the police car closed the distance, its siren sounding like a pack of trolls chasing her down.

"It's up to you now, Magda," she said, voice breaking. "The cops need a good, calm, confident face."

As she pulled to the shoulder, red and blue flashes bounced off the car's mirrors and reflected in her wet eyes. The gearshift was a strange combination of solid and liquid in her hand as she slid it into park. Adjusting the angle of the rear-view mirror, she looked into her eyes. "Suck it up and shove it down," she said while wiping tears away. "You can do this, Magda. You are strong, tough, and confident, and no one can push you around. Suck it up and shove it down." She closed her eyes and breathed deeply.

Worry lines smoothed, eyes narrowed in confidence, and her mouth turned up in a smirk. Relaxing into her seat, she kept her eyes trained to the mirror.

The officer exited his car and strolled up to her window. He hovered at the door, his baton, Taser, and gun staring her in the face.

Magda locked her eyes on the word POLICE that was plastered across the cop's vest.

She thought of Cole.

Don't let go, Magda. She shifted her gaze to the officer's Velcro name badge—V. Lao.

You are Mag—

He rapped on the window. Magda jumped, knocking herself from her daze. She looked through the window at Lao; his eyes bored into her. He rapped again, although the knocking seemed to come from her heart.

Magda's eyes darted across the collection of buttons on the door. Her finger hovered over one button, then another, as Lao's shadow shifted on her body. She pressed down on a random button and breathed relief when the driver's window slid down.

"Good afternoon, ma'am," Lao said, scanning the car's interior. "Do you know why I pulled you over?"

"Hey, Officer Lao. Sorry, but I don't know why I was pulled over. I wasn't speeding."

"It's Trooper Lao, and no, you weren't speeding."

Pursing her lips, Magda moved her gaze to the logo of silver wings cushioned in the center of the steering wheel.

"I pulled you over for tinted windows."

"Huh?"

Lao pointed to the passenger window. "Your windows. They are tinted, which is illegal."

"Oh, that." The tiny muscles in the back of Magda's neck relaxed. "No one told me it wasn't allowed."

"According to the traffic code, this vehicle is not allowed on the road with these windows."

"Tell you what. I'll be home in an hour, and I'll get it fixed right away. You can go back to finding speeders and I can get this little glitch sorted out. Thanks for letting me know. I'd better get out of your hair." Smiling at Lao, Magda slipped her hand around the gearstick.

Lao grunted and squared his stance. "May I see your license and registration?"

"What?" Prickles swept across Magda's skin. The tiny neck muscles seized.

"Your license and registration."

Magda dug her fingernails into the soft leather of the gearstick, her eyes glued to Lao's gun nestled in the holster on his hip. "Ah... My license is in my wallet which is in the backseat."

"What about registration?"

"Registration...?"

"Your vehicle's registration. You have the stickers on your plate, but I'd like to see the actual documents."

Magda's eyes darted around the vehicle. She wrenched open the center console and rifled through, tossing aside burger coupons and unopened air fresheners.

Lao's voice broke her from her mantra. "Where are you headed?"

"Lashburn," Magda said, pulling out an empty Doritos bag and tossing it over her shoulder.

"What's in Lashburn?"

The console now empty, Magda's eyes drifted across the vehicle's interior. *Think, think.* As she brushed a rogue burger coupon from her lap, she said, "My home."

"And what do you do for work in Lashburn?"

"I work at a flower shop."

"No registration in the console, hey?"

Ugh. Just let me go. Magda flipped down the visor and plucked a gas receipt from behind the mirror.

"Where are you coming from?"

"Denver. A weekend getaway." Magda hucked the receipt into the backseat and slapped the visor closed.

"Denver, hey? Did you go to the music festival?"

"I thought about going but I ended up just hanging out in the city."

"Where did you stay?"

Geez, RoboCop. Enough questions, already. Magda snatched a paperclip from the cup holder and worked at uncurling it from its spiral pattern. "The Baronial."

"Hm. Nice place."

"Uh… yeah…?"

Lao glanced at vehicles passing on the highway before turning back to Magda. "Who did you vacation with?"

"Just myself. A solo vacation."

"Just yourself? Most people who go on vacation meet up with others or travel with others. What made you go by yourself?"

Beads of sweat cropped up on Magda's forehead. Like shifting through Scrabble letters, she searched her brain for the right answer. "I just needed to get away. Get some me time."

"Whose vehicle is this?"

"Mine." Her fingers fumbled the paperclip. It bounced off her knee and landed on the floor.

"And you don't know where the registration is?"

Magda stared at the paperclip between her feet. "Well," she said, nudging the paperclip with her foot. "The thing is… my boyfriend looks after all the car stuff. I know he put my registration in here somewhere, I'm just not sure where."

"A lot of drivers keep theirs in the glove compartment."

The glove compartment. Dammit. Pulling her eyes from the ruined paperclip, Magda leaned over and popped the latch. She pulled out a vehicle manual and a bunch of papers.

"You passed it. The one you just put down. The one in that little plastic folder."

"I know." Magda snatched up the folder and handed it to Lao. He flipped it open and studied the paper within.

"What's your name?"

"Magda. Magda Cooper."

"Well, Magda Cooper, you say this is your vehicle, but your name isn't on the registration."

"My name? Oh... Whose name is on it?"

Flipping the plastic sleeve closed, Lao stared down at her. "Why don't you tell me?"

Suck it up... Steady yourself... "Oh, that's right. I forgot that my boyfriend said he registered this vehicle in his name. It's basically my car. I'm the sole driver of it, but he looks after all the technical stuff."

"Huh. Interesting. What's your boyfriend's name?"

"Uh... Dan. Daniel."

"What about a last name?"

"Jones. But he recently changed his last name. Something about not wanting any connection to his father or something. I don't remember his old name because he changed it before I met him. If there's a different last name on the registration, that's why."

"Interesting." Lao snapped the registration closed and glared at Magda. "You say this vehicle is registered to Daniel Jones, or Daniel Something. If that's the case, then who's Ivan?"

"Ivan?" Blood drained from her face.

"Ivan Janicki. That's the name on this vehicle's registration."

"Oh, him." Magda laughed and swallowed the rising nausea. "He's my boyfriend's friend. My boyfriend bought this car from him a while back and I guess he forgot to take his registration out."

Lao stared down at Magda and puffed up his chest. "Miss Cooper, we could go around like this for hours, but I've frankly had enough of your bullshit. Where's your license?"

She bit down on her tongue. *You are still in control.*

"Miss Cooper? If you haven't already figured it out, I've had enough of you. I suggest you tell me where your license is or I'm going to arrest you for obstruction."

Fighting back tears, she licked her lips and swallowed hard as she dug her nails into her palms. "It's in my wallet."

Lao glared. "I'm not going to play one hundred questions with you. Where *exactly* is your license?"

"My wallet is in my pack, top pouch."

"May I?" Lao asked, pointing through the window at the pack. She nodded.

The back door of the car opened. The zip of the pack being breached penetrated her ears. Lao was back the window, holding the wallet out to Magda. "Your license, please," he said. "And in case you haven't figured it out yet, I don't like lies. You will be in a lot more trouble if you keep feeding me tales rather than telling me the truth."

Flipping open the wallet, Magda ran her finger over the cards. Bus pass. Library. Social Security… "Shit," she said. "I must have left it at home. Here's my ID, though." Magda slid out the identification and handed it to Lao.

"What's this?" Lao asked, holding the card up to Magda.

"It's my ID. I told you I forgot my license at home."

"And why am I not surprised that the name on your ID is different than the name you gave me?"

"Because my legal name is Sasha, but everyone calls me Magda. I've been called that for so long, I don't even remember where the nickname came from."

"And when you got your supposed driver's license, why did you not turn in this ID card?"

Shrugging her shoulders, Magda confidently stuttered, "They never asked me for it."

"You really enjoy the taste of bullshit, don't you? I'll be right back."

As Lao turned from the car, Sasha's hands flew to her face. She gulped in ragged breaths and peered between her fingers into the rear-view mirror. Nausea rose again as she watched Lao strut to his vehicle. She glanced at her pack in the backseat and saw the corner of her phone sticking out from the unzipped pouch.

She turned back around.

Minutes crept by at a snail's pace. *Give me tickets, give me a lecture, I don't care. I just need to get to Cole. He'll forgive me and I'll never leave him again.*

She caught movement in the side mirror and, seeing Lao approach, wiped her eyes. *Magda, please come out.*

"Miss Cooper. Not surprisingly, you do not have a driver's license. I thought my little warning about lies would have clued you in to stop trying to talk your way out of this, but you just can't help yourself, can you? Please exit the vehicle. You are under arrest for obstruction and for operating a motor vehicle without a subsisting license."

"I'm *what*?" Magda slipped under the crashing waves.

Lao opened the door and stared her down. "You are under arrest. Out. NOW!"

Flinching, Sasha stumbled from the car. The ground beneath her was Jell-O. She tried to steady her legs, but the edges of her vision darkened and blurred. Lao's voice was gruff and unsympathetic, his words fading in and out. Cars zipped by but Sasha only saw streaks of color.

Lao's heavy hands turned Sasha around. "Put your hands on the hood of your car."

She felt her muscles comply.

"Do you have anything sharp in your pockets?" he asked as he ran his hands down her legs. "Knives, needles?"

"No."

Lao's gloved hands were on her arms, pulling them behind her back as legalese rolled off his tongue. The *click-click-click* of handcuffs tightening made her sway. The cold metal dug into her skin.

"...the choices you made... back of my car... detained for a drug investigation...'

Words and questions were flung at Sasha, but they sounded mixed up, like they had been thrown into a blender.

"...speak with a lawyer?"

"Sorry?" she whispered.

"Miss Cooper, do you wish to speak with a lawyer?"

"... ... ...no..."

Lao's grip was locked on Sasha's arm. She stumbled along the asphalt as he walked her to the police car and dumped her in the backseat. "Is there anything else you need to tell me? The truth is your friend right now, and you need all the friends you can get."

Sasha shook her head as tears rolled down her face.

"So, when we search your vehicle, we will not find anything out of the ordinary? There is nothing you are hiding?"

Sasha shook her head again, her voice lost in the currents.

"Very well, then," Lao said and closed the door.

As Sasha stared through the scratched and smudged window that separated her from the front of the police car, she drifted from her body.

Sounds muffled and a loud hum filled her head. Flashes of movement shifted in her periphery. She told her eyes to blink, then blink harder as silhouettes of more cops and a dog surrounded Dan's car.

As if the air that held her up suddenly let go, Sasha crashed back into her body. The loud hum was gone, and voices blared over the police radio in erratic bursts, shaking Sasha's skull. She writhed in her seat, trying to free her hands to cover her ears, but the handcuffs tore into her wrists.

A salty tear rolled over Sasha's lip and onto her tongue. Through the wetness, through the window, a chocolate lab sniffed Dan's vehicle—hood, windows, tires... anywhere on the car where the handler tapped. The dog sniffed and snuffled along the side of the vehicle and when he put his nose to the back bumper, he sat on his rump and stared at the trunk. The dog handler rubbed the lab's head with loving pats before he and the dog disappeared from view.

Straining her neck to find the dog, Sasha jumped at the sound of Lao opening his door. As he settled in his seat, the bars on the windows seemed to thicken, and the last bit of air was sucked from her lungs.

"That dog that sat beside your vehicle just told me what I already knew," Lao said as he looked at Sasha using the rear-view mirror. "You have drugs in that vehicle. In addition to the obstruction and driving arrests, you are also under arrest for possession of drugs."

Sasha lifted her eyes to meet Lao's. His gaze bored into her like she was a squashed insect that he was inspecting through a magnifying glass.

"I've already read you your rights. Do you want me to read them to you again?"

Sasha closed her eyes and tried to tuck her knees to her chest. "I need to talk to Cole," she said. "Cole can fix this."

"Pardon me?"

Sasha slowly shook her head. "I'm supposed to be... How did I end up here?"

The sound of the car door opening and slamming shut cut through Sasha's stupor and her eyes flew open. Craning her head around the headrest, she watched Lao laugh and talk with the other officers. She watched him pop open the back door of the car that was supposed to bring her to Cole. And she watched as he pulled out her pack and started going through her things.

"No," Sasha whimpered. Her purple t-shirt fell from Lao's hands and crumpled into a pile on the asphalt. "That's my stuff."

While Lao turned Sasha's phone over in his hand, other officers swarmed the vehicle like flies on a dead bird. Police boots poked out from the open back door, another officer crawled underneath the car on his back, and a fourth was examining the interior of the trunk.

Sasha sat and waited and observed, then waited some more. The reality of what was unfolding in front of her seeped into the recesses of her brain.

The rumble of power tools snapped Sasha to attention. Their roar carried through the police car, sawing and drilling into Sasha's skin.

Seconds... minutes... maybe hours passed. The sun had shifted, and the glare hit Sasha in the face.

The cops crawled out from their corners of the car. A cold sweat ran over Sasha as they lifted their tools in victory, slapping each other on their backs while laughing.

A satisfied smirk oozed from Lao as he strolled towards the police car. He settled in his seat, his confidence turning the air thick. Sasha tried to draw in the heavy air, but her lungs felt like they had given up.

"I warned you," Lao said as he pulled a notebook from his vest. "I told you the truth was your friend, but you didn't take my advice. You have a good system there—one of the better ones I've seen—but we beat it. We got you." Lao glanced at Sasha using the mirror and his eyes crinkled in a smile. Turning back to his notes, he said, "As I expected, you have a load of what looks like bricks of cocaine. On top of obstruction and the license offense, you are also under arrest for possession of narcotics for the purpose of trafficking. Once I am done here, I will read you your rights."

Sasha stared ahead, her eyes drying as her lids refused to blink. A whisper from deep inside told her to say something, but she had no voice. She could not even begin to try to formulate a coherent sentence. She vaguely heard Lao read her rights, but the words drifted in and out of her head, distant and muffled. Closing her eyes, Sasha searched for someone who could pull her from this mess, but all she found was an empty hole.

Chapter 37

Cole stared blankly at the half-filled computer screen. Dark circles hung under his eyes after a second sleepless night. Legs weary from pacing the length of his home, he had hauled himself into the office to plug away at his task list.

He reread his scrawled notes—again—and typed in the name of the witness from the hit and run. His fingers quieted on the keyboard as his thoughts swirled with yesterday's conversation with Sasha.

The bus schedule called to him constantly—an hourglass with every grain bringing him closer to the beginning or the end of everything. He tapped his phone, and the bus logo lit up his screen.

Denover to Lashburn – on time

Sucking back the rest of his cold coffee, Cole flipped a page in his notebook and chewed his third pen of the day down to the ink chamber.

"Dawson."

With a crushed pen sticking out of his mouth, Cole looked up from the screen. Deputy Chief Straddle stood in the doorway of his office, his salt and pepper hair combed flawlessly in place and his mouth set in its usual straight line.

"Sir?"

"My office," Straddle said before disappearing into his office.

Flipping his notebook closed and chucking the pen in the garbage, Cole pulled himself from his chair and wandered across the bullpen.

"Sir?" he said as he stepped into the room.

"Take a seat. Close the door."

The buzz of the bullpen became a dull hum behind the door as Cole fumbled into a chair under Straddle's watchful eye. Cole smoothed his wrinkled shirt and pulled on his shorts until they sat evenly across his knees, but he still looked out of place in the pristine, ordered space. Identical bookshelves filled with law and criminology literature framed the room, with Straddle's cherry desk centered between the two. A silk plant stood like a sentry in one corner, and a floor fan of equal height stood in the other. Policing certificates and awards bordered the window—three on each side, all in matching frames. And Straddle sat in the center of the formation, slowly swiveling back and forth in his leather throne.

"Dawson," Straddle said. "Can you tell me who Sasha Cooper is?"

"I'm sorry?" Cole blinked to attention. "Uh, yeah. She's a friend of mine."

"How well do you know her?"

"Really well. We grew up together and have always been close, other than a few years when we lost touch. I'm sorry, sir, but why are you asking about her?"

"We'll get to that in time. You said you two are close?"

"She has been my best friend since we were kids, and we lived together for a couple of months until recently. Not *lived* together as a couple, but I gave her a place to stay while she was between homes. Why do you need to know?"

"Just answer my questions."

"Sorry, sir," Cole said, wiping his sweaty hands on his shorts.

"And what's her relationship with the law?"

"The law? I'm not sure I know what you mean."

"Is she a law-abiding citizen, or does she skirt our laws?"

Cole swallowed hard and his eyes darted between bookshelves. "Sir, I can assure you, Sasha is as straight as an arrow when it comes to the law. She sometimes follows a different code than most of society, but she would never do anything illegal."

Straddle picked up a pen and started twirling it in his fingers. "What do you mean, she follows a different code?"

"She prefers to lay low—under the radar. For years she went without an ID, she only recently got a bank account, and she's never had a credit card. She'll pick up odd jobs here and there, and find a room to rent until it's time to move on. It's not a typical lifestyle, but it works for her and it's completely within the law."

Straddle raised his eyebrows as he continued to swivel his chair and fiddle his pen. "I did a bit of research on your friend, and it looks like she's had contact with the police a few times."

"She has," Cole said, the skin between his eyebrows furrowing, "but only as a victim. She came from an unstable home, and she should have reported her abusive boyfriend as well, but she didn't. The only file where she's not a victim is when she was loitering in the vestibule of my building, and that was because she needed a safe place to stay for the night and was waiting for me to get off shift. I'm sorry, sir, but what is going on? Why all the questions about my friend?"

"I just got off the phone with the Metelyk Police." Straddle silenced his chair and returned the pen to his desk. "They have your friend in custody. They laid a number of charges against her."

"What? What kinds of charges?"

"Well," Straddle said, flipping a page in his coiled notebook, "obstruction and operating a motor vehicle without a subsisting license, for starters. Also," he added, looking up from his page, "possession of narcotics for the purpose of trafficking."

"That's not possible. Maybe it's a different Sasha Cooper. My Sasha wouldn't do that."

"They say she's been pretty tight-lipped since they arrested her, except that she keeps asking for you." Straddle laced his fingers together and rested his hands on his stomach as he leaned back in his chair, his eyes boring into Cole.

"I know her better than anyone and I *know* she wouldn't do that. During her darkest times, when she couldn't afford to eat, she'd refuse to get help from a women's shelter or soup kitchen because she didn't want to take from others. She always puts everyone before herself. She's a good person and there is no way she'd transport drugs."

"She has financial problems?"

Cole looked around the office, his gaze bouncing off dark furniture and framed credentials.

"Dawson?"

"She did. Does. But that doesn't matter. She wouldn't do that."

"You'd be surprised what people do for money when they get desperate."

"Not Sasha. She has issues, but she's a good person to the core. Something is wrong with this situation."

"Look, Dawson. You've seen through our job how people's emotions can cloud their judgement. You clearly care for this person, and you don't want to believe she's involved in criminal activity, but it's apparently a pretty cut and dry case. *My* concern is that one of my officers is affiliated with a drug courier."

"With all due respect, sir, Sasha is not a drug courier. I don't care what the evidence says, I *know* she would never do that." Cole's bit his tongue, forcing his tone to stay controlled as his fingernails dug into the armrests.

"Yet the evidence says she would. I am relieved to know this comes as a shock to you. If you were aware of Sasha's activities and you withheld the information, that would be grounds for dismissal. Now that you know, I expect you will take steps to distance yourself from her."

Cole leaned forward and buried his face in his hands as his scrambled brain tried to keep up. "Sir," he said, looking up at the Deputy Chief. "If the Chief told you that your wife has been transporting drugs, what would your reaction be?"

Straddle pursed his lips, his eyes locked on Cole. "I would say there has been some mistake. My wife would never be involved in something like that."

"Exactly. You understand where I'm coming from. Sasha's not my wife, but she's my best friend who I care about deeply, and whose character I can speak of with absolute certainty. I know she has flaws, and a hell of a lot of them, but being involved in an illegal activity is not one of them. There's something else going on, sir. She's been framed or duped or something. She may have been the one holding the smoking gun, but I guarantee she didn't pull the trigger. Not on this."

The leather chair creaked as Straddle started swiveling again. He snatched the pen from the desk and twirled it in his fingers as he studied Cole. What felt like hours ticked by as Straddle continued to swivel and twirl, twirl and swivel.

"Suit up," Straddle commanded without warning. "Take a PC."

"Sir?"

"I trust you, Dawson. If you genuinely believe that there is more to this story, then you need to act. Your friend needs you. Find out what's going on. I doubt they'd let you talk to her dressed as you are, but if you go in uniform, they might give you a chance. I'll call ahead and see if I can arrange for you to meet with her."

Cole nodded as a hundred different scenarios bounced around inside his head. He squeezed and opened his eyes, exhaustion clawing at his brain while his heart bounded like he had just chased down a criminal.

"Here's the name and number of the lead investigator I spoke with earlier." Straddle picked up a piece of paper and handed it to Cole. "I'm not paying your time for this, but I'm letting you use one of our cars. Don't make me regret my decision."

"Thank you, sir." Cole gripped the doorknob, his hand shaking as he turned it.

"And Dawson."

"Sir?"

"Good luck. I hope she's worth it."

Cole paced the concrete pad at the back of the Metelyk Police Department, his baton clinking with every step as long shadows stretched across the parking lot. A loud click and a muffled thud came from the door before it was pushed open from the inside. "Cole Dawson?" the trooper said. "Vince Lao. Come this way."

Cole followed Lao through the door and up a few steps to the bullpen. The drone of the photocopier scanning and spitting out pages of bad decisions filled the air.

"Is she here?" Cole said as he glanced around the workspace. With low ceilings and only five desks crammed into the space, it felt more like a holding room than the bullpen of a police station.

"She's in cells. I'm trying to get a bail hearing done but I won't get that until tomorrow, so she'll have to spend the night."

"Why not just issue a Promise to Appear?"

Lao crossed his arms and stared into Cole. "Are you aware that one of the charges against Miss Cooper is obstruction?"

"Yeah."

"Her stories are all over the place and after the crap she's pulled with me so far, I don't trust her to show for court. I can't get her to talk but I'm gathering she's broke, so I'm going for a non-cash bail. Hopefully that will persuade her to appear for her court date."

"Can I see her? None of this makes sense, as it's completely out of character for Sasha, and I want to know where her head is at."

"She's not talking to me but if you think you can pull some answers from her, I can set you up in the interview room. I normally wouldn't do this, but your deputy said you might be able to get her to talk so we can finally get a statement."

"Thank you," Cole said, rubbing the back of his neck. "Do you mind filling me in on the file first? I know she has these charges against her, but none of it makes sense. If I could get a better picture of what we're dealing with here..."

"We can talk in the interview room, but I'm going to have to take your gun and search you before we go in."

After a quick pat-down, Lao led Cole down a narrow hall and into a small room. Everything was gray—walls, floor, ceiling, table. Cole fumbled the empty space on his hip where his gun should be.

"Just so you're aware," Lao said as the door clicked closed behind them, "I'm going to have to video record our conversation as well as your conversation with Miss Cooper. Anything said in this room can be used in court."

Cole nodded and pulled up a chair. With a steadying breath, he brought his eyes to Lao. "What's going on here?"

"I'm not sure what you're asking," Lao said, taking the seat opposite Cole. "You've already been informed that Miss Cooper has three charges laid against her."

"Yeah, I got that part. What I don't understand is why. What happened to lead to those charges?"

"Look, from what your deputy told me, you are close friends with the accused and had no idea she was involved in the drug trade. You are understandably upset but I can assure you the evidence is strong. I didn't allow you in my building to have you try to convince me of your friend's innocence, because she's not. You are only here to get her to talk."

"Something's not right. Tell me what happened so I know what we're dealing with."

Lao leaned back in his seat and crossed his arms. Flicking his wrist and checking his watch, he sighed. "I initially pulled her over for tinted windows, but I quickly realized that there was something else going on. She was exhibiting the classic signs of nervousness, and she kept changing her story to make up for the flaws I was pointing out. She was quick on the ball with her lies, but it was easy to tell she was hiding something."

"Hold on. Sasha was driving?"

"Of course. Solo occupant. She said she owned the vehicle even though the registration didn't match, plus she was using a false name. She kept changing her story and tried to convince me that she had left her license at home."

"What name did she originally give you?"

"Magda Cooper. She said Sasha is her legal name and everyone calls her Magda, but I don't buy it."

"Freaking Magda again," Cole muttered under his breath.

"Anyway," Lao continued, "she was giving me the run-around and I eventually got tired of hearing her talk, so I arrested her for obstruction and not having a license. I seriously don't get why some of these people think lies are going to work, especially after I flat-out tell them they won't."

"She's a pathological liar."

"Pardon me?"

Digging the heels of his hands in to his eyes, Cole said, "She's a pathological liar. It's what she does." He pulled his hands from his face and stared into Lao. "She had a screwed-up childhood and has been running from herself ever since. She lies as a coping mechanism, and I don't think she even understands that it's wrong. Sasha wasn't lying to evade detection of drugs; she was lying because she's deeply troubled. She was probably terrified you'd find out she didn't have a license, and that's what was making her act all nervous. I swear, she freaks out when her library books are going to be overdue. I can't imagine how stressed she'd be if caught driving without a license."

Lao narrowed his gaze. "Has she seen a psychologist?"

"No," Cole said, rubbing his stubbly cheek. "She knows she lies, but she says it's not harming anyone, and she doesn't see the validity in therapy. But some of the stuff... it's weird."

"She's aware that she lies? She's not delusional?"

"It's a deliberate act, but not with illicit intent. She's got issues but her mind is sharp, and she knows what she's doing."

"Everyone's got issues, but you can't use them as an excuse to break the law. If she's a pathological liar but has no underlying mental health issues, then I just see her as a liar and the charges stand."

Cole knocked his chair back and pressed his hands into the table instead of around Lao's neck. "You're missing the point. She was lying because she was stressed out, not because she was hiding any drugs."

Shaking his head, Lao chuckled and looked at the blank wall behind Cole. "I don't know if you are aware," he said, refocusing his gaze on Cole, "but this is my expertise—taking traveling criminals off our roads. I've stopped thousands of vehicles and have arrested people carrying all sorts of contraband, from guns to illegal cigarettes to exotic animals, but what I find most often is drugs. No matter what the criminal is carrying, they have the same reaction to me, only with varying degrees of severity—some are better at hiding their stress than others. Sasha is textbook. Her driving behavior, nervousness, lies, changing stories... I'm an expert at what I do, and this is a slam dunk file."

Cole rubbed his face as a low growl emanated from his core and rippled through his body. "About the drugs... I'm assuming you found them after arresting her on the other charges?"

"I read Miss Cooper her rights, put her in the back of my PC, and then we started the drug investigation. The narcotics dog nailed off a confirmation almost instantly, but then it got trickier. Your friend has a sophisticated compartment that would fool most police, but we found it. We haven't processed the six bricks we seized yet, but I'd bet my house they're kilo bricks of coke."

Cole fell into his chair as Lao's words sliced through him. The table went in and out of focus and Cole pressed his feet into the floor, grounding himself. "What did Sasha say when you told her about the drugs?"

"She didn't deny it. In fact, after nattering on early in the investigation, once she realized she wasn't going to win, she shut right up. Except she kept asking for you, that is. The criminal befriending the cop. Very clever."

"She's not a criminal," Cole growled. "I can't explain why she was driving, and I know the lying is bad, but the drugs? Not Sasha. She's a blind mule or something. She's been tricked."

"If she was blind, her demeanor would have been completely different. She absolutely knew what she was hauling. I know you don't want to open your eyes to reality, but get your head wrapped around the idea that I'm going to lock her up."

Chapter 38

Cole paced the interview room, shoulders rigid. His hands curled into fists as he tried to figure out how to smack some open-mindedness into Lao. "And why were you driving, Sash?" he said to the blank walls. He snatched a pen from the table and gnawed on it furiously.

The sound of the doorknob being turned cut through the tiny space. As Lao ushered Sasha into the room, his hand clamped around her arm, Cole swayed. "Oh, Sash..." Sasha, looking like a mouse in an owl's talon, raised her eyes to meet Cole's.

"Take your time," Lao said, "and give a knock on the door when you are done."

As the door closed behind Lao, Cole staggered across the space and wrapped his arms around Sasha. "Sasha," he whispered, pressing his nose into her hair. "What have you gotten yourself into?"

"Fix it, Cole," she whimpered. "Please fix it."

"I don't think I can. This thing is bigger than me." Cole cupped Sasha's face in his hands and looked into her wet eyes. "This is scary, Sash. We're talking jail time here and I don't know if there's anything I can do to pull you out of this mess."

"But I didn't do it."

"I believe you, but no one else does. The evidence is stacked so high against you... I don't know if there's a way out of this. Why aren't you talking to them? Why not tell them the car and drugs aren't yours?"

Her face crumpled into her hands and her shoulders shook.

"You need to tell me what happened. No stories, no lies. Tell me exactly what led to you being here." Slipping his hand around hers, Cole settled into his seat. Sasha, splotchy-faced and lashes clumped and glistening, slumped into the chair opposite him.

"How did this all start?"

Wiping tears, Sasha said, "If it wasn't for that drink, then I would have gotten on the bus, and I'd be at your place already."

"What does a drink have to do with this?"

Sasha's icy fingers tightened around Cole's hand. She took in a steadying breath and flicked the chewed pen, sending it careening across the table. "Last night, at the bar in the casino, I ordered a drink. A Scotch. The bartender told me it was two-fifty a glass, which to any reasonable person means two dollars and fifty cents."

"You don't seriously..."

"Turns out, it was actually two-hundred and fifty dollars. For a single glass. And it wasn't even good. Can you believe that? Someone would actually pay two-hundred and fifty dollars for a single drink? Just think of how many months I could eat for with that money."

"Were you able to pay the bill?" Cole said as he massaged his forehead.

"I did, but it only left me with just over fifteen dollars. Once I realized I didn't have enough money to buy my bus ticket, I freaked out. I started adding up how many days I needed to panhandle for to raise the bus fare. I *needed* to get to Lashburn." Sasha's voice broke and she hiccupped in a sob. "I destroyed the only thing in this world that matters to me—our friendship—and I was desperate to get home to you."

His words from yesterday's phone conversation slammed into him: *"I can't come for you... I can't have you in my life."*

"I'm sorry," Cole said through his fingers, but his words were drowned out by Sasha continuing her story.

"There was this guy I was chatting with at the bar. I poured my heart out to him, telling him how I needed to get back to you, and he offered me a ride. He had a car to drop off at a friend's place in Lashburn, so it's not like he was going out of his way or anything, but it was still a very kind gesture."

Cole's hands dropped from his face. He stared at Sasha.

"We decided to meet at a park this morning but when I got there, he was so sick. He said it was food poisoning and couldn't drive. He just lay on the ground and kept throwing up into the garbage can. He told me to take his car, drop it at his friend's house, and then I'd have to make my own way to your place."

Cole's heart hammered. He could almost see the thin thread of hope that was dangling in front of him like a spider's shimmery silk line. "Sasha," he said, his tone slow and steady, "did he give you the address of where to drop the car?"

"Twenty-five Grovedale Avenue."

"Did he give you any other information? Names or numbers or anything?"

"Well, his name is Dan, and he gave me his cell number in case I needed to talk to him about anything. And the friend's name is Chad, but that's about it."

"Sasha, you need to provide a statement, and you absolutely need to include that information. It might be just what you need to get yourself out of this mess."

"No." Her eyes were like dinner plates as if Cole had suggested she throw herself into a volcano. "I don't want to talk to him. He hates me and he's not going to help me. He's so happy to have me locked in his police station."

"Who, Lao?"

"He's the one who arrested me. I won't talk to him."

"It's his job to investigate all information. He *has* to listen to you and if you have information that will help your case, then he is required to take it into consideration."

"I won't talk to him. He'll only make things worse."

"Seriously, Sash. How much worse can it get?"

Looking as though she had seen a ghost, Sasha hugged her legs to her chest while tears hovered at the surface.

"Sasha," Cole said, softening his tone, "I'll see if I can get someone else to take your statement, but you need to talk. You need to tell your story to someone other than me."

"You're a cop. Why can't I just tell you?"

"Because I'm not on the file and me taking a statement from you is a conflict of interest." Cole waited for Sasha to say something, but she just hugged her knees and stared at the table. With a resigned sigh, he said, "Tell me more. You said the guy was sick and told you to take his car. Why would you do that, especially knowing you don't have a license?"

"I needed to get to you," she said, wiping a tear away. "The guy convinced me that if I waited any longer, you'd get over us and I'd never get you back. He said I needed to get to you while your emotions were raw. I figured as long as I obeyed the traffic laws and didn't speed, I'd be fine."

"Sasha," Cole said, forcing his voice to stay level, "do you realize this guy is a drug dealer?"

Moving her eyes to meet Cole's, Sasha creased her brow. "No, he's not. He was really nice. Plus, he didn't look like a drug dealer."

"Oh, my gawd, Sash," Cole groaned, compelling himself to not yell at her. "And do you know what a drug dealer looks like?"

"Well, no... But I'm assuming he'd look scary and shady, and this guy was really nice and looked... normal."

"What about his car? How do you explain him hauling six kilos of coke if he's not a drug dealer?"

"I don't know... I never really thought about the drugs being his."

Cole buried his face in his hands and counted his combat breaths. "What about the lies? I know lying is kind of your thing, but don't you think it's irresponsible to lie to the police when they stop your vehicle?"

"You don't get it." She exploded, fire in her eyes. "I was freaking out because I knew I didn't have a license, and then I wasn't even sure if I should be driving a stranger's car, and I didn't know how else to answer the cop's questions. I just told him what I thought he wanted to hear."

"You thought Lao wanted to hear your made-up version of events rather than the truth?"

"I don't know," Sasha said, a stream of tears running down her face. "There was so much happening, and I was freaking out and I needed to get to you, and I just wanted the cop to go away. Telling the truth didn't make sense."

"Seriously?" Cole pushed himself from the table. He paced the room, his head in his hands. "How stupid can you be? Do you not understand that lying is bad? Don't you know that when the police ask you a question, the correct response is *always* the truth? I'm putting myself on the line for you, Sash. I know those drugs aren't yours, but all these lies certainly aren't reflecting well on me. Do you think it's a good idea for a police officer to be standing up for someone who vomits lies all the time?" He pressed his hands into the wall and dropped his head.

"What's going to happen to me?"

"I don't know," Cole said, pushing himself from the wall. "But you need to make that statement. You have to stay here overnight but you'll be released tomorrow. I'll take you back to my place where we can figure out how to get you a lawyer and whatever else to get you out of this mess."

"I'm scared."

"Which is why you need to make that statement."

Sasha's face was wet as she hugged her knees in close. She looked like a wildflower, picked then tossed aside, vibrant colors fading as she was left to wilt.

Body heavy and brain fried, Cole collapsed into his chair. He reached for Sasha's hand and laced his fingers through hers. Her fingers were ice, her nails chewed down, her skin like silk. Laying his head on his outstretched arm, Cole gazed at Sasha and took in every detail of her beautiful, shell-shocked face.

A knock at the door was like a cleaver cutting their connection. "I need to get Miss Cooper back to her cell," Lao said, standing over them.

With a nod, Cole slid his hand from Sasha's, but she clasped his fingers and held on. Her grip tightened and her ocean eyes filled with tears.

"I'll be back for you tomorrow," Cole said and wrenched his hand away.

As he stumbled past her, Sasha grabbed his arm and yanked herself to standing. "Don't leave me." She hugged her arms around him, her body warm and quivering against his. "I can't stay here. I need to go home with you."

"You can't, Sash. Your lies have finally caught up to you. You have to spend the night here, but I'll see you tomorrow."

"I'll die here." She squeezed her arms around him and buried her face in his chest. "I need you to stay with me."

Cole gripped Sasha's wrists and tried to peel himself from her, but she clung on like he was a life raft.

"Please. I love you."

"What?"

"I love you, Cole. Please don't leave me."

Cole's face twisted and creased. Ripping Sasha's hands from around his waist, he blinked back tears and looked into her miserable eyes. "It's too late for that." He jerked his arm away and pushed past Lao.

"Cole!" Sasha lunged after him, her fingernails carving white scratches on his arm, but Lao held her back. "Cole, I love you. I need you. Please. Cole!"

As Cole stumbled through the station, Sasha's screams and Lao's commands to stop resisting echoed off the walls. Shoving the door out of the way, Cole burst from the station and gulped in the cool evening air.

With ragged breaths, Cole looked back at the station. He pictured Sasha's cell door slamming shut as she continued to scream his name. He took a step towards the station, then turned away and dropped his head between his knees.

As his heart rate slowed and the haze in his mind began to clear, Cole pulled himself upright. His heart and mind beat him up, twisting and pushing against his skull until he could no longer hold onto any tangible thought.

Leaving the darkness of the parking lot, Cole dragged himself into the building to retrieve his gear. As a trooper handed Cole his duty belt, Lao strolled into the bullpen.

"She's a bit worked up," Lao said as he approached Cole.

"You think?" Cole glared and clipped his belt around his waist. "She's innocent, you know. Not for the obstruction or license, but for the drugs. She's completely innocent."

"Look, man. I'm not going to keep going over this with you. The evidence is strong and I'm going to lock her up."

"Why do you need to do that? Why do you have to sneer at me when you tell me that Sasha's going to jail? This isn't a game, you know. It's her life and I wish you'd look past what seems obvious and do a better job investigating what is actually going on. She has good intel. An address, name, and number. She was a blind mule. Watch the video of my conversation with her. Get a statement. Some criminal pegged her for the trusting, naïve, good person she is and duped her into running his load for him. And now she's taking the fall and he's getting off."

Lao crossed his arms over his chest and smirked. "If she starts talking, then I'll listen to her story. But honestly, after what she pulled at the vehicle stop, it's going to take a miracle for me to believe anything she says, including some made-up address."

"She's innocent of the drugs. Have someone else get a statement because she won't give it to you. She knows you're out to get her and she believes talking to you will only cause her more harm." Turning to the other trooper, Cole said, "*You* take Sasha's statement. Don't let this narrowminded prick do it because she won't talk to him, and that's what he wants." Glaring at Lao, Cole added, "We are supposed to protect victims, not throw them to the wolves."

"A *victim*?" Lao laughed. "Miss Cooper is hardly a victim. Face the facts—your girlfriend is a drug runner. She had six kilos of coke in that compartment. She's going to jail for a very long time."

"She's a blind mule, you idiot. Have someone who's unbiased listen to her and you'll learn the truth."

"The truth? Who knows what the truth is with her? I have all the evidence I need. The question is, how much are you willing to sacrifice for her? Are you going to believe the facts or are you going to believe the ravings of a pathological liar?"

Cole squinted as the fluorescent lights of the police locker room cut into him. As he crumpled onto a bench, the clink of his baton hitting the metal seat echoed in the empty space. He grabbed his phone and pulled up Frank's number.

"Hey, Daws. How are you doing?"

"I... I can't."

"Straddle called to ask about Sasha. He wanted to know if I had ever met her and asked what you've said about her. He told me she's been charged with possession with intent, but that's all I know. What's going on?"

Cole tried to stifle his tears, but the floodgates burst open. "I failed her," he wept. "I keep failing her, over and over, and this time it's... it's just so screwed up."

"Listen, Daws. This is not your fault. Sasha made her own choices and she's the only one responsible for what's going on. You can't take the blame for this."

"I should have insisted she see a psychologist. I shouldn't have pushed her into getting an apartment. And when she called yesterday needing a ride, I should have gone to her. I promised I'd always come for her when she needed help, and yesterday when she made that call,

I turned my back on her. And now she's... I made a promise years ago that I'd always watch over her and keep her safe, and I've failed. Her life is over because things got hard, and I gave up instead of keeping my promise."

"Where are you?"

"At the station. I just got back from Metelyk." Cole closed his eyes and wished the world would go away.

"I'll come get you. You shouldn't be alone tonight. Maria and I will make you dinner and you can have the guest room. If you need to talk, I'll be there for you. If you need your space, I'll leave you alone."

"I want to be alone tonight. I'm going back to my place, but thanks."

"When you're up for it, we can talk it out and we'll make a plan for what to do. You tell me what Sasha needs and I'll be there for her."

"I don't know anymore," Cole said as he pushed himself from the bench. "I just don't know. The lead investigator on her file is dead set on laying the charges. The evidence is stacked against her, but the truth is under there. I'm just not convinced there's any way of pulling it to the surface. She's screwed herself. If only I was there for her like I was supposed to be."

"This sounds like a bigger conversation than we can have over the phone. You sure you don't want me to get you? I'd feel more comfortable knowing you were with someone tonight."

"No. I'm going to bed right away anyway. I need to get up early to head back to Metelyk to get Sasha. They're doing a bail hearing, and she should be released in the morning."

"All right. But call if you need to talk. Even in the middle of the night."

"Thanks, Frankie. Thanks for listening." Cole hit end and peeled his uniform off. His police armor crumpled to the floor, leaving his soft center exposed.

Chapter 39

Sasha burst through the doors of the police station and gulped in a lungful of fresh air. Scanning the street, she stumbled down the steps and disappeared around the corner.

She hurried from alley to alley, weaving away from busy streets and neighborhoods, with only cats and house sparrows to witness her escape. As she rushed past peeling fences and dented garbage cans, backyards fell away and the call of children playing disappeared. She popped out of a side street and, finding herself in the industrial area, slowed her pace and steadied her ragged breaths.

The throaty croak of a raven carried through the air and gravel crunched under Sasha's feet. She pulled her hood over her head and her eyes darted from one dilapidated business to the next.

With the buzz of highway traffic a distant hum, the sound of a vehicle creeping across the gravel from behind flipped her stomach. She held her breath as the whirr of the engine drew near.

The car slinked along like a lost dog following her home. Sasha's hair stood on end, but she pressed forward, eyes locked on gravel passing beneath her feet.

"Victoria!"

The slam of the car's door pierced Sasha. She froze.

"Victoria."

Swallowing hard, Sasha turned. "Dan?" A smile spread across her face, then vanished as Cole's warning played in her head: *"...this guy is a drug dealer..."*

"Hey," Dan called with a smile, walking towards Sasha. "I can't believe I found you."

Sasha slowly shook her head and started walking backwards.

"When I got over my food poisoning, I called my friend to make sure he got the car, but he said you never showed. I got worried so I decided to see if I could find you. I knew it was a long shot, but I owed it to you to help you if you were in a bind. I was running low on gas, so pulled into Metelyk to fuel up and then I spotted you. I can't believe it. It must be fate."

Sasha stumbled on loose pebbles as she continued to back away. Her eyes darted from Dan to the car. It crept along, keeping pace beside her. She stumbled again as Dan's words replayed in her mind: *"And then I'll come after you and mess you up."*

"What are you doing out here? Why aren't you in Lashburn?"

Sasha opened her mouth, but her voice stayed trapped inside.

"We need to get you back to your guy. I know how much it means to you to see him again. I'll give you a ride the rest of the way to Lashburn. It's the least I can do."

"That's really nice of you, but I'm okay now. I talked to him over the phone, and we patched things up. He's actually on his way here now. He should be pulling up any minute."

Dan looked around the industrial area before his mischievous glare met Sasha's wide eyes. "He's picking you up *here*? That's an unusual place to meet."

"Yeah... his... uh... He blew a tire on the way here, so he's getting towed in. I'm meeting him at the towing place."

"That's not going to do him much good." Dan leered as he kept coming at Sasha and the car inched along beside them. "He should get dropped off at a tire shop or garage."

"Yeah, but... you see... he's... he... I..."

"I know he's not coming for you. Let me give you a ride to Lashburn."

"Leave me alone," Sasha said as she searched the road behind Dan. "He is coming. I know he is."

"I'm giving you a ride. It's the least I can do."

Sasha spun on her heels and burst into a run. Her vision pulsated with each frantic beat of her heart. Dan's feet pounded on the gravel behind her. In an instant, she was jolted backwards. Her writhing feet stirred up clouds of dust as she was dragged across the road. Shrugging out of her pack, she exploded with weightless speed and sprinted towards the distant highway.

Movement flashed in Sasha's periphery. A surge of adrenaline gushed into her veins as the driver sprang from the vehicle and raced towards her. Her legs burned as she turned off the road and across an open lot, her heart ready to burst from her chest, but the driver was quick. His sandpaper fingers wrapped around her arm and yanked her towards him. She dug her heels into the gravel and twisted her body as she tried to wrench herself from his grasp, but his arms were suddenly around her, binding her tightly. Sasha opened her mouth to scream, but all that came out were wild, high-pitched squeaks. She struggled to pry herself from his grasp as he hauled her, kicking and flailing, towards the car.

"Get in the car!" he yelled, pushing Sasha into the backseat. Her head smacked the opposite window as Dan crawled in behind her.

The contours of the door fading in and out, Sasha clawed at the handle. She yanked it again and again. The unlock button jumped out at her and she mashed it with shaking fingers.

The lock popped.

"I don't think so," Dan said as he reached around Sasha and grabbed her wrists. "Help me with the cable ties."

Stiff plastic bit into Sasha's flesh as it tightened around her wrists. Gravel spun under the tires and her body slammed into the back of the seat. Her forehead throbbed with every frenzied thump of her pulse and the edges of her vision darkened and blurred. Closing her eyes from Dan's uneasy smirk, Sasha curled herself into a quivering ball and sobbed.

Chapter 40

Cole's eyelids were pierced by the sun's rays that streamed in through the bedroom window. As he stretched his arms over his head, an image of Sasha, red-eyed and trembling, slammed into him. Bolting upright, he looked at the clock: ten forty-seven.

"No, no, no." Cole scrambled from the bed and patted his shorts for his phone. "Think."

He scoured his bedding, tossing pillows over his shoulder and throwing the blanket to the side. The phone smiled up at him, the glint of the sun reflecting off its shiny surface. Lunging across the bed, Cole grasped the phone and, tearing out of his room, pulled up the Metelyk Police's number.

With the phone pressed to his face, Cole sprinted out the door and down the seven flights of stairs. As he pushed through the door into the parking garage, Sergeant Heather Lane came on the line.

"I'm on my way," Cole said. "I'm coming. Let her know I'll be there soon."

Cole pushed the limits for speed as he raced to Metelyk, the mileage signs not flying by fast enough. Pulling to a stop in front of the police station, he bounded up the front steps, wrenched open the door, and launched himself into the lobby. "Cole Dawson from the Lashburn Police. I'm here for Sasha Cooper, your prisoner from yesterday."

The woman working behind the glass cocked her head and frowned. "I think she has been released already but let me check for you."

As Cole paced the lobby, Sasha's *"I love you"* bounced around in his head and swirled around his heart. A moment later, the sergeant pushed through the door into the lobby.

"Hi, Heather," Cole said, shaking her hand. "What's going on with Sasha's case? Did she provide a statement?"

"She did, and it was pretty much bang-on with what she told you in the interview room yesterday. I watched both videos last night—the one of you with Lao and the one with you and Sasha—plus Lao's in-car video of the traffic stop."

"Who took her statement?"

"I did. She was very composed and told me exactly what happened."

"Did she tell you about the address and phone number?"

"She did, and we did some digging. The phone number brought us to a mattress store, so that was a bust, but the address was good intel. I talked to the Lashburn drug section this morning and they have been keeping an eye on that house for a while. It sounds like they haven't had much movement on that file in a few months, so Sasha's info is exactly what they needed. Not counting Lao, everyone on the file believes that Sasha was unaware that there were drugs in the vehicle. With her statement, the intel, and the fact that she has never been convicted of anything before, we dropped the drug charges."

"They're dropped? Completely?"

"They are, and Lao wasn't too happy about it, but that's his problem. He can be overconfident at times, but he's a great investigator and has pulled millions of dollars' worth of drugs off the highways over the years. As for the obstruction and license charges, they will stand. Sasha has a court date on those."

"That is fantastic," Cole breathed, raking his hand through his hair. "Thank you."

"You are welcome. We're still trying to uncover some information on the owner of the car, but that's none of Sasha's concern."

"She can go, then? She's been released?"

"Well, yes… Sasha has been released. I told her you were on your way, but she chose to leave on her own."

"What?" The smile dropped from Cole's face. "What do you mean?"

"We had no reason to keep her any longer. She knew you were on your way, but she wanted to leave even though I told her she could wait here for you. I offered her a phone to call you, but she declined that offer as well. She seemed very anxious to get out of here. I'm sorry."

"So… she's… gone? She left?"

"I tried to get her to stay, but she wouldn't. But she asked me to give you this." Heather held out a folded piece of paper.

"Where'd she go? When did she leave?"

"She didn't say and it's not my place to ask. We released her about half an hour ago. I'm truly sorry."

The paper slipped from Heather to Cole. He stumbled to the door in a daze. "Thank you for all your help," he said, turning around. "I appreciate all you've done for Sasha. She's a good person."

"I gathered that."

Cole drove up and down every road in Metelyk a half dozen times, peering down alleys and into shops, and racing through the library. He scoured parks, the industrial area, and nearby highways and sideroads before he pulled to the curb and cut the engine.

A dull pain crushed his chest. As he rested his forehead on the steering wheel, he glimpsed the paper lying on the seat next to him. With a steadying breath, he picked up the note and unfolded it. His heart split when he saw Sasha's writing.

Dear Cole,

I'm sorry that I'm leaving without saying goodbye, but I knew that if I waited for you, there was no way I'd be able to go, and I have to go. I've proven to myself and to you that I'm no good at living a "normal" life. I keep messing things up. You have been so good and kind and patient with me, and I do not know why, for I do not deserve your kindness. You are a true friend.

You were right when you said it doesn't look good for a cop like you to have a friend like me—someone who somehow finds her way to a drug charge, and someone who can't help herself from lying, no matter how hard she tries. I do try, Cole, I really do, but when things spin out of control, my stories and personas are a way for me to feel like I have a say in what's happening in my life. Am I proud of how I live? No, but it's what I have to do to keep my head above water and to keep going. I refuse to let my troubles negatively affect you and your career. You are too good of a cop to be bogged down by me. I wish you all the best in your career. I know you will go far, and you will help so many people.

I wish I didn't have to leave as I feel at home when I'm with you, but we have to be honest with ourselves and see the situation for what it is—my life choices will only lead to more anguish for the both of us. Anguish. Now there's a great Scrabble word! I will miss our Scrabble Sundays. You always complain you can't beat me, but you are a better player than you give yourself credit for.

I hate to leave our friendship this way but it's the only way I know how to do it. I hope you find joy and success in your career, and I hope you meet someone who makes you happy and loves you the way you deserve to be loved.

I'm not going to tell you where I'm going, for two reasons. First of all, I don't want you to find me. We need to face the fact that me being in your life causes you pain, and I don't want you to suffer because of me anymore. You deserve so much more than that. Secondly, I won't tell you where I'm going because I don't have that answer yet. I'll just have to see where the road takes me. And please don't try to call me. My phone is powered off and I will not be turning it back on. When I eventually find my way to a major center, I'll sell it at a pawn shop. But be sure that wherever life takes me, I will never forget you, I will always love you, and I will look back on our friendship with happy memories. You have given me the happiest memories of my life.

Take care of yourself, Cole, and please don't worry about me. I can fend for myself, and I will find a place in this world where hopefully I fit in.

I will always love you,
Sasha

Cole read the note over again, tears bleeding Sasha's words across the page. He pressed his nose to the letter and breathed deeply but all he smelled was paper and ink.

When the page had dried into a crustier version of itself, Cole put his car in gear and made the drive back to Lashburn, the empty seat beside him a black hole.

The condo was quiet.

Cole sat at his kitchen table and reread the letter. He plucked a wilted freesia from the vase and pressed it to his nose as he pulled up Sasha's number. At the sound of her voicemail, freesia petals broke from the stem and fell, lifeless, onto the table.

"Hey, Sasha. It's Cole. I know you likely won't receive this message, but I wanted to call you anyway. I got your letter. I wanted to tell you that you are wrong. I'm not going to be better off without you. I don't care that you have turned my world upside down. Without you here, I feel empty. I want you back. The stuff that's happened to you doesn't impact me or my job negatively, and even if it did, I wouldn't care. I'd give up my job a thousand times over if I could have you back here with me. So, if you do actually listen to this message, please call and I will come for you. I will always come for you, no matter the time of day or the distance. I will always regret not coming for you when you asked me to the other day, until the day I die. If I could have my way, you'd be back here with me, and we'd play Scrabble while wearing our shark slippers. Maybe we'd sip wine from tumblers, or maybe I'd buy some stemmed glasses so we could drink wine like real couples do. And maybe we could be a real couple. You'd stay here with me, and we'd share my condo and I wouldn't care that it's only a one-bedroom place because one bedroom is all we'd need. Sasha, I lo–"

An automated voice came over the line, telling Cole that he had reached his time limit and asked if he would like to rerecord the message.

He clicked end.

Cole brewed a pot of coffee but after a few sips, abandoned the mug on the counter. He drizzled too much dish soap into the steamy water and as the sink overflowed with bubbles, he walked away from the dirty dishes. He turned the television on but stared through the screen at the blank wall behind.

Lying on the living room rug, his eyes drifted to the framed pencil sketch of the police officer and little girl. He turned away and downed the rest of his beer. Cole tossed the empty can on the coffee table. It tipped and rolled to a stop when it hit his phone, foamy drops splattering the screen. Cole reached out and pulled up Frank's number.

"Hey, Daws. How are things with Sasha? Has she been released?"

His fingers pressed into his eyes. His voice cracked. "She's gone. For good this time. I slept in. I failed her again. Always failing her. Always. She was released and took off before I arrived. She left me a letter telling me she was disappearing for good because she didn't want to be a drain on me anymore. She's gone into hiding and I know she's not coming back. She's not going to call, she's not going to show up at my building... She's just gone and it's all because of me."

Cole waited for Frank's encouraging words and advice, but the line was silent.

"I have to face the fact that she's not supposed to be part of my life. I have to stop chasing her. I have to stop hoping that she'll call or come home to me. I need to convince myself that she has her life, and I have mine, and they don't mix. We are destined to take different paths, and I need to get my mind around the idea that I have to put her, and our friendship, behind me and move on. But the thing is, I don't know how to do any of those things. I don't know how to let her go. How do I live with the choices I've made? How do I accept that I'm not what she needs? That she thinks her only option is to go into hiding and change who she is—a choice and a lifestyle that might land her in jail again, or beaten, or dead? How do I head into the future and leave her in the past?"

The silence on the line smothered Cole.

"Frankie? What do I do?"

"I don't know, Daws. I really don't know."

Chapter 41

Sasha's hip dipped into the bare mattress while the mustiness of the small room clung to her hair and clothing. As she traced the cuts and bruises on her wrists, her shoulders still aching from the position they had been bound in, a tear rolled down her cheek.

Snuffling in a stutter-breath, Sasha stared at the wood veneer walls, having long since given up hope of finding a break in the finish. Her eyes shifted to the barred-up window, and she wished she had the strength to rip the metal bars from the studs.

And the voices. The voices. Sasha sniffled in a cry and trained her eyes on the door. For three days, the voices outside the door talked about The Jackal. His authority. His impending arrival. His decision on what to do with the girl who ruined his shipment.

The front door slammed, shaking the cabin. Sasha bolted upright as her fraying nerves sparked.

"What the hell happened?"

Ice-cold dread filled Sasha's veins as the voice echoed throughout the cabin.

No.

Gripping the threadbare blanket in her fists, she strained to hear the muffled conversation going on in the living room.

"It was the girl. She's the one who somehow allowed herself to get pulled over."

"And who picked her to be the mule?"

"It was Jared. He picked her out in the casino in Denover."

"She was perfect. Fresh and innocent looking, out of cash with a desperate need to get to Lashburn, and naïve as hell. I don't know what went wrong. The cops must have been tipped off or something."

"Did she snitch?"

"She spent a night at the police station, so she may have said something."

"Where is she?"

"In the back room."

Sasha's every cell vibrated as the click of shoes on hardwood grew louder. Closer. She scrambled off the bed and pressed herself against the wall farthest from the door, her breaths wild and ragged.

The door burst open.

He stepped into the room, sucking the air out of it with his presence. As his eyes landed on Sasha, his face faltered and slackened.

"Bryn? Pumpkin?"

Sasha hiccupped back a sob.

"*You* are my mule?" Curtis laughed, his mouth cracking into a disjointed smile.

"Her name's not Bryn, it's Victoria," Dan said, coming into the room behind Curtis.

"Actually, it's Sasha." A man with bulging biceps filled the doorway as he flipped through Sasha's wallet.

"What?" Curtis said, turning to Biceps and ripping Sasha's ID out of his hand. He studied the card before looking at Sasha. His eyes narrowed and his jaw tensed. Sasha's plastic image snapped in his hand. "Pumpkin? Is this true? Your name is *Sasha*? You were *lying* to me?"

Voice jammed in her throat, Sasha trembled as she waited for her legs to give out.

"Out," Curtis said, turning to the men. He paused as though gaining momentum, but rather than throwing a chair, he turned around slowly. He stared Sasha down, his narrowed eyes stripping away her dignity, and waited until the door clicked closed behind the men.

"A mule... a snitch... a liar... a fraud..." Curtis clucked as he walked the length of the room. "I had no idea you had it in you. You are a very curious enigma."

He stopped inches from Sasha and studied her face. "Who are you?" Traces of musky aftershave wafted over her, pounding her with memories, both wonderfully entrancing and dreadfully chilling. His charismatic voice, dark eyes, and mischievous smile stirred desire and nausea.

The dark lapel of his suit coat brushed her t-shirt. She tried to press further into the wall, but Curtis leaned into her, his body heavy on hers. "Pumpkin, why so quiet? Aren't you happy we're finally reunited?" He ran his fingers across Sasha's cheek and through her hair. His touch burned her skin.

Sasha turned her head away and closed her eyes as Curtis continued to stroke her like a cat.

"Why did you leave me? I loved you and you broke my heart. I made sure you wanted for nothing, yet this is how you repay me?"

A whimper escaped from Sasha as she tried to curl away from him, but he pressed his body, hot and sticky, to hers, pinning her against the wall.

"We can get back to where we were," Curtis whispered in her ear, the warmth of his breath leaving condensation on her neck. "You'll learn to love me again. You will move back into my house, and I will give you everything you need and anything you desire. And we will be happy forever."

Silent tears streamed down Sasha's face as Cole's warning echoed in her mind: *"That blow he gave you, Sash... that was going to be the first of many."*

"Do you know what I do to people who mess up one of my operations?" Curtis said, madness returning to his voice. He grabbed a fistful of Sasha's hair and jerked her head back, forcing her to look at him. His pupils were so dilated, they looked like black holes. "You don't want to know what I do with those people. Lucky for you, I love you too much for that to be your fate. This was meant to be."

Curtis released Sasha's hair and grabbed her arm, yanking her across the room and out the bedroom door.

"Change of plan," Curtis said as he dominated the living room. "I will leave *Bryn* here with you for one more night. I have business to deal with elsewhere, but I'll be back for her tomorrow. Keep her comfortable. She's one of us now. I want her locked in that room overnight, but she can have free rein of the place during the day. Take shifts guarding the front door and her room when she's in there, and she doesn't go anywhere alone. And nobody lays a hand on her. She's mine to deal with if she steps out of line."

"Jared," Curtis said, turning to Dan. "I'm uncertain what to do with you. You are the one who sabotaged my shipment and one of my best cars by choosing a fool to run the load, however, because of you, Bryn is back in my life. Let's call it even, but you are out of chances."

"And you..." Curtis pressed his lips to Sasha's ear and squeezed his hand around her arm. "I'll be back for you tomorrow, and we can start our lives together again." He kissed Sasha on the cheek the way he had every morning when they were together, then grazed his nose along her hairline as though trying to find her scent. "And clean yourself up. You look disgraceful."

Releasing his lock on Sasha, Curtis disappeared out the front door. The walls shook as he slammed the door behind him. Sasha and the men stood frozen in place as the noise of tires spinning on gravel and the familiar hum of his BMW speeding away carried through the windows.

Sasha quivered as she stared at the door, the scent of Curtis's aftershave stuck in her nose. A man with more tattoos than bare skin stepped in front of the door, crossed his arms, and smirked.

The dry cereal from the morning turned in Sasha's stomach. Plastering her hand to her mouth, she ran to the bathroom and made it to the toilet just in time. She sunk to her knees on the linoleum and hugged the sticky bowl as she heaved again and again.

When she had nothing left, she slumped against the wall. Feet appeared in the doorway, and then a glass of water on the floor next to her. Sasha looked at Dan through her tears. "Why did you do this to me?"

"It's nothing personal. It's just business."

Sasha scuttled from the floor, knocking over the glass and drenching her sock as she stumbled past Dan. She staggered into the bedroom and, slamming the door behind her, collapsed onto the bed. Sobs rocked her, shaking the bed, breaching the walls, and drifting to silence in the deep, dark forest.

Sasha lay curled up on the mattress, dried tears marking her face and putrid acid from her vomit stinging her throat. "I'm going to die," she whispered to the walls. "My life is over. There is no escape from here and Curtis will kill me."

Shifting on the creaky bed, Sasha palpated the tender lump on her forehead and stared at the yellowed ceiling. "What are you doing right now, Cole? Do you think of me? Do you miss me?"

She thought of strawberry margaritas and movies, warm coffee and soft blankets…

…the smell of a book and the hard edges of a Scrabble tile…

…Cole's smile, voice, hands…

Sasha's throat clenched and tears burbled out, leaking down her temples and soaking the pillow as she listened to the voices outside the door: Dan, who betrayed her trust and bound her wrists; the driver who seemed to enjoy shoving her around; the man with arms as thick as a gorilla's; and the fourth man, tattooed and pierced.

She closed her eyes and whispered her mantra.

Stay with me, Magda. They will call you Sasha or Victoria or Bryn, but you are still Magda.

She steadied her nerves, opened the door, and stepped into the hall.

Chapter 42

Magda held her stance and gripped the doorframe. Biceps engulfed a chair outside the room, swallowing the cabin's space with his presence.

"I haven't brushed my teeth in over three days," Magda said, steadying her voice. "Can I have my pack?"

The man moved his eyes from his phone and looked Magda up and down. "Maybe," he said and headed to the living room.

"Jared, you went through her stuff," he said, digging through the pack. "Is there anything she can't have?"

"Let me check." Dan popped up from the couch and stuffed his hand inside. Magda held her breath as Dan pulled out the Hammerkin set and cutlery. He rummaged around some more and snatched her phone from the top pouch.

She swallowed back tears.

"She can have the rest," Dan said, dropping the pack on the ground and kicking it to the side. "I'll lock up these other things."

Hoisting the pack onto her shoulder, Magda brought it to her room and dumped it in a corner. After fumbling for her toothbrush, she wandered to the bathroom and sealed herself in. The tattooed man followed her at every turn.

Magda stared at her reflection in the mirror—dark circles under her eyes, cracked lips, pale skin, and a purple lump on her forehead. "This isn't the end," she whispered. "Find a way."

Treading lightly towards the living room, Magda glanced at the only outside door, barricaded by Biceps who was playing on his phone. She wandered through the kitchen, the men's eyes always on her, burning holes through her clothing. As she took a cookie from an open box on the counter, she scanned the space for knives. The wooden drawers fought back as she opened one after the other, but only spoons remained. The fridge—the color of mustard left out in the sun—held a tub of margarine, a pizza box, and beer.

"What are you looking for?" Dan said as he sauntered across the living room and joined Magda in the kitchen.

As she vigorously nibbled the cookie, the ginger essence biting her tongue, Magda stole a glance at Dan. "Just familiarizing myself with the kitchen." She opened a cupboard above the fridge and was hypnotized by a clear bottle, half full of transparent liquid, with a black top and the telltale label. The scent of the raki, reminiscent of black licorice, swept around her and a wave of sweat ran down her back. The vigorous notes of Vivaldi played somewhere in her mind.

Her hand slipped from the cupboard door, and she curled away from the bottle, willing the scent and the song out of her psyche. With a stuttering breath, Magda forced a raised chin and looked Dan in the eyes. "Curtis said I could make myself comfortable, so I'm checking out the space so I can make something to eat."

"There's no leaving here, you know. I've already screwed up by letting you lose the load, and there's no way I'm letting you get away before The Jackal gets back."

"Why do you call him that?"

"It's his business name. I don't know where the name comes from, and I know better than to ask. Number one rule is you don't ask him anything personal. Until just now, I had no idea his name was Curtis." An impish grin played on Dan's lips as his eyes caressed Magda. "Did you and him really have a thing going on a while back?"

"A thing?"

"I find it hard to believe you guys used to be together."

Magda cringed and popped the rest of the cookie in her mouth. "I didn't know who he was, and he didn't know who I was, but it worked for a while," she said as she chewed. "But then I discovered what an asshole he was, so I left."

The thought of Curtis's licorice breath on her neck made her stomach turn. She blinked back tears and cast her gaze to the cookie box. *You are Magda. Don't crumble.*

Edging from the kitchen and away from Dan, Magda wandered around the living room, every footstep accompanied by a creak. A chessboard set up flawlessly on a shelf made her pause, but it was the fleck of green beside it that stopped her in her tracks. "How is this…" she whispered as she reached for the leaf, '*…handmade and mouth-blown from the highest quality crystal in Italy by master artisans.*'

The leaf, broken off at the base where only a hint of orange kissed the green, weighed a ton in her hand and the smooth edges burned her fingers. She returned the leaf to the shelf, taking care to place it upside down. A rebellious smirk crossed her face.

Putting the game and leaf behind her, she scanned the bookcases that took up every wall. Books in Italian and Turkish filled the space and when her eyes landed on a shelf dedicated to Whitman, Gray, and Dickinson, she turned away.

The tattooed man's eyes were on her. Dan leaned against the counter and chuckled. The driver scowled from the kitchen. Biceps played on his phone.

Magda tucked herself into a tight ball in the corner of the sagging couch and focused on the windows, analyzing their latching mechanisms.

"Game time," Biceps said as he stood from his chair and shoved his phone into his pocket. "I've been on door duty for two hours. Someone else take over."

As he drew near, Magda's skin prickled as though tiny fireworks were going off inside her veins. He grabbed the remote from the coffee table and flipped through the channels. Magda hugged her body as the man's bulk squished the air.

As he lowered his weight onto the couch, the cushions caved in, taking Magda with them, as though the man were a blackhole and his gravitational force was pulling everything into him. Magda gripped the armrest, digging her nails in as tears sprung to her eyes. She glanced sideways—he was close enough that she could touch the scorpion tattooed on his neck.

When he leaned back and adjusted himself, something hard knocked against Magda's foot. She looked down and when she saw what lay in the crack between the cushions, her breath stuck in her throat.

Bicep's eyes were glued to the pre-game show. Dan and the tattooed man laughed in the kitchen and the driver stared at the TV from his perch at the door. Biting her lip, Magda snagged a blanket from the loveseat, settled into the dip of the couch, and draped the blanket over herself. Her heart hammered as voices of sportscasters filled the air. She probed the crack.

Crumbs of potato chips caught under her nails and the smooth packaging of an old soy sauce packet squished between her fingers. When she hit hard plastic, goosebumps sprung up across her body. She wrapped her fingers around it and shoved it down the back of her pants.

"I need a shower," Magda said. Tossing the blanket aside, she wriggled out of the couch's pit and shuffled towards her room.

Magda pressed the door closed and pulled the phone from her pants.

Wi-Fi.

Battery.

Access.

With a shaking finger, she punched in two numbers but a thump at the door sent the phone tumbling from her hands. Magda grabbed a change of clothes from her pack and buried the phone deep in the bundle. She cracked open the door. A quiet yelp escaped from her lips, and she stumbled backwards. Dan loomed over her.

"I'm going for a shower," Magda said, lifting her chin. "I haven't showered in days."

Dan's mouth turned up in a wicked smile as his eyes stroked her body. "Need help?"

Hugging the clothing to her chest, Magda shook her head. "No."

"Hm. A shower. I guess I can allow that," Dan said, barely moving aside.

Magda eased past him, his body like a slug as she brushed against it. She rushed to the bathroom and locked the door behind her. She spun the tap on the shower and turned the phone to silent. The numbers blurred through her tears as her thumbs worked the screen. Pressing the phone to her face, she sank to the floor and listened to it ring… and ring… and ring…

Chapter 43

Cole typed the offense into the computer and glanced at the clock — the minute hand seemed to be moving in reverse. He groaned and rubbed his eyes.

"You good to go on a patrol after we finish this court package?" Frank asked.

"Sure," Cole mumbled.

"Come over for steaks before our shift tomorrow night. It'd be good for you to get away from home and work and do something different."

The thought of food made his stomach turn, and an invitation was just one more thing to stuff into his mind that was already bursting with pressure. "I don't know." He read his last entry, forcing himself to dive completely into work and never come out.

A gentle vibration in his vest pocket pulled Cole's eyes from the screen. At the sight of an unknown number on his call display, he held his breath. "Hello?"

Heavy breathing carried over the line, followed by a voice quieter than a mouse. "Cole?"

"Sasha?" He jolted upright, all senses firing. "Did you get my message? Where are you?"

333

"Please, Cole," she cried, barely above a whisper. "Help me. They have me."

"What?"

"He's coming back for me tomorrow."

"What are you talking about?" He looked at Frank. Frank stared back.

Muted sobs and sniffles emanated from the phone as Sasha fumbled words. "The... The drug dealers. They have me trapped. In a cabin. Curtis is their boss or ringleader or whatever and... Cole, he's... he's coming back for me tomorrow."

The bullpen vanished around Cole as his phone became the only thing in the world. "I don't understand. Are you serious or are you making this up?"

A haunting whisper drifted over the line. "I'm scared to go with him."

Cole launched from his desk and dashed across the bullpen to the Deputy Chief's office. As Cole barrelled through the closed door, Straddle looked up from his desk—his phone pressed to his ear—and shot daggers at Cole. "Dawson. Martinelli. Exit my office immediately."

"No." Cole set his phone on Straddle's desk and put Sasha on speakerphone. "You need to hear this."

"Sasha," Cole said. "What's this about Curtis? Do you mean your ex? What is going on?"

"Yes. Curtis. They call him The Jackal. I didn't know he was into drugs—into selling them or whatever—but he was here and told me he'd be back for me tomorrow."

Straddle looked from Cole to Frank to Cole's phone and ended his own call. He placed a recording device beside the phone and snatched his coiled notebook and pen.

"Whose phone are you calling from?" Cole said, leaning his hands on Straddle's desk while trying to keep the tremor from his voice.

"One of Curtis's guys. A big, scary guy. His phone fell out of his pocket, and I picked it up when he wasn't looking. I'm hiding in the bathroom. They think I'm in the shower. Can you please come?"

"Where are you? I need to know so I can come for you."

"I don't know," she said, sobs and sniffles mixing with her words. "In a cabin in the forest somewhere, but I don't know where. I'm sorry I don't know where."

"It's okay, Sash," Cole said as a teardrop splattered on his screen.

"I can't leave. They are guarding the door, and they follow me everywhere unless I'm in my room or in the bathroom, but there are no ways to escape from either of those rooms." Sasha's voice steadied and terror hovered in the pauses between her words. "I'm doomed. Curtis says he's going to take me home with him. He's different than I remember. He's scary."

"Do they have guns?" Cole's voice cracked.

"I don't know. I haven't seen any, but I don't know."

"Sash–" A hiccupping breath silenced him. Unable to get words out, Cole stepped from the desk. He wiped his eyes and pushed stale air in and out of his lungs until his breaths evened.

"Sasha, I can find you if you send me a pinned location of where you are."

"I have no idea what that means."

Cole forced calm into his voice. "You need to listen carefully and follow my instructions. Can you do that?"

"Yes."

"Go to the main screen on the phone. You won't lose connection to me. Find the *Maps* app and click it."

Cole gripped the edges of the desk until his fingers throbbed. He closed his eyes and whispered a prayer.

"Okay, I got it," Sasha said, her voice evening out.

"You should see a button that has an *information* or *location* symbol that you need to click. You are looking for something that says *mark my location* or *pin my location*."

As Cole stared at the phone, officers assembled in Straddle's office, and more were gathering outside the door. Frank and Straddle were busy on their phones, their eyes and ears directed to Cole's conversation.

"I see it."

"Click on it. Then look for something that says *share*. You might need to scroll up on the screen. Can you find it?"

"I got it."

"Click *share* and then select *text* or *message*. That will take you to the texting screen where you will type in my phone number and hit send. Do you understand?"

"I think so."

Cole listened to Sasha's heavy breathing and quiet whimpers, each second an eternity. "Come on, Sash. You can do this," he murmured as tears hovered in his eyes.

When a *ping* sprung from Cole's phone, his breath caught in his throat. A map with a little teardrop arrow pointing to Sasha a million miles away glowed on his screen. Cole choked out a sob. The other officers let out a muted cheer.

"I got it," Cole said, clearing his throat. "I got your location. I can find you." Shoving the rising nausea down, Cole took a screenshot of the location and sent it to Frank and Straddle.

"Listen, Sash. I'm coming for you, but it'll take time. You're a couple of hours from Lashburn and I need to assemble a team. This is too big of a job for just me, but I promise I'm coming for you. You need to be patient."

"How long–" A sob robbed the rest of the sentence from her. Between breaths, she stuttered, "How long will you be?"

The office tilted and swayed. Gripping the desk, Cole closed his eyes, and a tear ran down his cheek. "I don't know. I wish I could be there instantly, but I can't. Depending on the tactics that we need to take, you might not see us until the morning, but I promise we will be there. I will be there. How many people are in the cabin with you?"

"Four men plus me. And Curtis is coming back tomorrow."

"Do you have somewhere to wait?"

"I have a room."

"Within a couple of hours, I want you to close yourself off in your room. When you hear us arrive, find somewhere to hide. It might be easy for us to come inside the cabin, but it also might be extremely difficult and dangerous, and I don't want you caught in the middle of anything. You absolutely cannot under any circumstances leave your hiding place until we come get you. Do you understand?"

"Yes."

"I'm going to hang up right away because I don't want you on the phone any longer than necessary. The text you sent is going to be visible to anyone who looks at that phone, so you need to delete this message and hide the phone so it can't be found. When I hang up, power down the phone. Do you know how to do that? Completely turn it off?"

"Yes."

"Good. And don't hide it in your room, because once he discovers his phone is missing, that's the first place he'll look."

"I can't do that," Sasha wailed quietly. "Someone is always watching. I'm going to screw up and he'll find his phone and then he'll do something horrible to me."

"Sasha, listen to me," Cole said as tears streamed down his face. "I'm going to ask you to do something that I will never ask of you again."

Sasha sniffled into the phone.

"Sasha, you need to be Magda."

"Magda?"

"Yes. Find all of Magda's courage, confidence, and grit, and get rid of that phone. Between your amazing brain and Magda's daring, you can do this. Hide the phone and wait for me. I'm coming."

"Okay," Sasha whispered, sniffling back tears.

"Are you ready to do this?"

"Yes."

"I'm coming for you, Sash. Be brave and be patient and I'll see you as soon as I can."

"Okay."

Cole's finger hovered over the *end call* symbol. Sasha's frantic breathing, her quiet whimpers, disappeared to a dead line.

Chapter 44

Sasha hugged her knees on the bathroom floor as though the world would crumble if she let go. With a deep breath and a reaffirming nod, she swiped the *power off* prompt on the phone. The screen flickered to black.

"Suck it up and shove it down."

As a referee's calls drifted through the door, Sasha pulled herself to her feet, wiped the tears from her face, and stared into the mirror.

"You are Magda. You are tough and confident."

The woman in the mirror narrowed her eyes. Her forehead smoothed and her lips curled into a growl.

"You are Magda, and nobody can push you around."

She twisted her fingers around the phone and slunk her hands up inside her hoodie's sleeves. Squaring her shoulders, she wiped the remaining tears, took a deep breath, and opened the door.

"What are you up to?" the driver said as he stood from his chair. "You've been in there forever, but your hair isn't even wet."

"None of your business," Magda said and headed towards her room.

"Like hell it's not my business." His hand locked on her arm, and he spun her around. "If The Jackal finds out you've been up to something, we're both done for."

Magda breathed deeply as the man's grip burned her flesh. Fire erupted in her eyes, and she glared at the driver. "If you must know, I got my period just now. Menstruation. Aunt Flo. Surfing the crimson wave. Shark week."

The driver's eyes went wide, and his mouth clamped shut.

"I made a bloody mess in the bathroom, quite literally, and I've spent the past ten minutes mopping the floor. I'm on my way to find a tampon from my bag if that's okay with you. If not, then I'll continue to bleed from my taco all over this cabin. If that's what you want."

The man's mouth was set in a perfect line.

"Is that what I should do? Go exactly where you say I have to go and leave a red trail, so you'll always know where I am?"

"No. No, get what you need." Red in the face, he turned towards the living room, suddenly engrossed in the football game.

Magda stepped towards a bookcase and glanced into the living room—all the men were glued to the TV. Quick as a snake strike, she dropped the phone behind a row of books.

In her room, she dug through her bag and pulled out a tampon before she scurried to the bathroom. She slammed the door behind her and twisted the lock. Fumbling with the wrapper, Magda freed the tampon from its captor, flushed it, and left the wrapper in the garbage.

As iron-smelling water washed over her and swirled down the rusty shower drain, Sasha let the sobs come. The stress of what she had set into motion curled around her muscles and bones, sending a deep ache into every inch of her body.

Cole's stomach was empty, its contents left in a bush in the parking lot. With his back pressed against the conference room wall, he listened to the section heads make a plan. Maps were spread on the table, notes scrawled on the whiteboard, and Cole languished on the sidelines like a rookie football player aching to feel the ball in his hands.

As Straddle traced his finger along a sideroad on the map, Cole wiped away another tear. His gaze fixed on the circle in the center of the forested area. When Straddle marked an X through it, Cole tore out of the office to find the bush.

Sasha stepped from the shower. Grit, tears, and puke had washed down the drain, but the demons inside were unable to be scrubbed away. She pulled a t-shirt over her head, closed her eyes, and imagined snuggling into Cole.

The crash of the bathroom door being ripped from its hinges jolted Sasha back to reality. Her eyes flew open, and she spun around. Biceps, arms bulging and neck scorpion hissing, loomed in the doorway. "Where's my phone?" He shoved Sasha backwards and her head whipped back as she collided with the sink. Voice trapped inside, she shook her head.

"Where is it?" He grabbed Sasha's arm and twisted it behind her back. A burning pain deep in her arm freed her voice and a yelp sprang from her lungs.

"Mitch," yelled one of the men from the living room. "You mess her up, The Jackal ain't going to be too impressed."

Biceps sneered but relaxed his hold. "What did you do with my phone?" he said as his gorilla arms pushed her again. The back of her head knocked against the mirror and stars flooded her vision.

"I... I don't know. I don't have it."

He pressed his hands into every angle of her body. Muscles rigid, Sasha closed her eyes and tried to conjure up a peaceful garden, but the image would not stick as the man worked his fingers down her thighs. He grabbed Sasha by the shoulders and shoved her out the door before he tore the bathroom apart.

Tears streaming down her face, Sasha rushed to her room but stopped short in the doorway—her room looked like a tornado had gone through it. The blanket and pillow were on the floor, the mattress was slumped on its end against the wall, the bedside table and lamp were smashed on the ground, and the heat registers had been torn from their cavities. Sasha's belongings were strewn across the room and her empty pack laid half inside and half outside the closet. Kicking the red dress and a winter boot out of the way, Sasha closed the door.

Cleaning the room focused Sasha's mind—the tremors subsided and breaths evened. Once the room was tidy, she crawled into bed and waited.

Did I power off the phone? I think I did, but maybe I didn't.

I shouldn't have put it in the bookcase. Someone will find it there for sure. How could I have been so stupid?

They know I took the phone. They know I made a call. Someone knows what I've done. Someone will burst through that door any moment and do something horrible to me.

And then Curtis will find out and I'll wish I were dead.

Sasha woke with a start, the nightmare still fresh in her mind. In it, Curtis was moving towards her and she could not run, she had no voice, and her muscles were frozen. And he came at her again and again.

The room was roasting, but Sasha shivered uncontrollably as she stared wide-eyed at the darkness around her, the yellowed ceiling a putrid grey. The sound of footsteps in the hall sent her heart racing.

The footsteps stopped at the door before moving away. Out of energy, Sasha lay in bed and hugged the frayed blanket to her chest.

Hours that felt like days passed, the room brightened with the rising sun, and more sounds were heard in the cabin—voices, footsteps, forks on plates, toilet flushing.

And Sasha waited.

Waited for Cole, waited for Curtis.

As the shadows moved across the room with the sun, Cole's image started to fade and Curtis's face was stuck in her mind, his eyes growing darker and darker.

Cole stared blindly at spruce and aspen outside the unmarked police car, some leaves taking on a yellow hue, while Straddle typed a report into the in-car computer. Parked on an overgrown road miles from the cabin, Cole was stiff from sitting while his ears buzzed with the silence that droned over the police radio. His face was tight from dried tears, and his frantic breathing had calmed, but his heart continued to thump like a helicopter's rotors.

Finally, with the sun high in the sky, the radio burst to life: "The subject has arrived. All positions ready."

Chapter 45

Sasha pulled her knees in close and shivered under the blanket.

He's not coming. I'm not worth saving. I'm Curtis's now. I'll become Sasha Schakal. I'll be a tongue twister. Actually, I'll be Bryn Schakal. Pumpkin Schakal. Mrs. Schakal. Mrs. Jackal.

Over the voices of the men in the living room and the pounding of blood in her ears came the creak of the front door opening. Sasha bolted upright. *Cole.*

"Pumpkin! It's time to start our lives together again."

Bile turned in Sasha's stomach. She forced Cole's image out of her mind, squared her shoulders, and lifted her chin. "So be it. You gave it your best."

A thundering crash echoed through the cabin. "This is the police! Put your hands where we can see them."

The bile sputtered up into a gush of tears. Sasha flew from the bed and raced to the closet. She slid the door closed behind her and crawled as far under the dresses and jackets as she could. Shouts hurtled through the walls and unfamiliar voices swirled into her ears. The stomp of boots reverberated through the cabin and pummelled her heart.

Musty clothing draped over her shoulders and stroked her hair as doors slammed, shaking her bones. A splintering sound crashed on the other side of the wall. Something—or someone—thudded against her back and sent a tremor through the drywall. Curling into a tight ball, Sasha pressed her hands over her ears, but the clamour busted through the spaces in her fingers.

A gunshot rang out. Sasha's scream pierced the walls of the closet as an image of Cole lying in a pool of his own blood leaked into her brain. She rocked back and forth, her hands squeezing her head like a vice, and sobbed.

Cole's knuckles were white on the car door handle as Straddle pulled onto the property. When the cabin poked out from the trees hundreds of yards ahead, Cole yanked on the handle, but Straddle's hand locked on his arm. "Not yet. Let them do their job."

A gunshot boomed through the forest like a sonic wave, bouncing off trees and ricocheting in Cole's chest. His eyes darted around the property, but there was no movement. As Straddle picked up the radio, Cole leaned his head on the dashboard and squeezed his eyes shut as nausea rolled again.

Chatter blasted from the radio, but Cole could not follow the cacophony of voices. Then, silence.

Lifting his head, Cole peered through the trees at the cabin, but everything was still. "Sasha's in there."

"I know. Be patient."

As Cole lay his head back on the dash, images of Sasha flashed through his mind... brow wrinkled as she studied the Scrabble board... a sparkle in her eye while arranging flowers on the kitchen table... a smile as she stroked soft pajamas... completely relaxed as she curled up to him on the couch...

Then, images of Sasha pushing through the busted door in the Sax... shivering with blue lips and icicles in her hair... talking to a homeless man like he was a friend...

The police car was a cramped jail cell, the air hot and stuffy. Feeling like he had just stepped from a spinning carousel, Cole pressed his fists to the sides of his head. He stared at the cabin through the blur of tears, but it was as if time had frozen.

Everything was too quiet.

The radio jumped to life and broken chatter conveyed the message: "All suspects are in custody. The scene is clear."

Cole burst from the car and sprinted towards the cabin. "Sasha!" he yelled as he ran, using desperation as fuel for his burning muscles. "Sasha!"

Sasha's ragged breaths filled the closet as old clothes brushed her face. Her wide eyes stared into the darkness; her hands were still clamped over her ears. The noises from before had been replaced by an eerie silence dotted with unfamiliar voices.

The closet door creaked open, and a sliver of light pierced Sasha. Her breath seized. Heavy boots stood only a few feet in front of her.

Sasha's voice began to squeeze out of her throat, a monstrous scream about to be unleashed. Her hands clamped her mouth shut as she stared at dirty, black laces.

The legs in front of her bent to a crouch. A face scanned the closet until the man's eyes landed on her. He smiled. "Hi, Sasha. We've got all the bad guys. You're safe now."

She trembled, not knowing his face, not knowing the words that came from his mouth.

"Sasha!"

Her ears pricked at the sound of Cole's voice so close but so far.

"Sasha."

The man turned his head. "In here."

A moment later, another pair of boots stood in front of her and then there was Cole's face with pain, tears, joy, and relief playing on his features. "Sasha. My Sasha. You did it. You saved yourself."

Sasha was frozen in place, hands cemented to her mouth, eyes wide.

"Hey, Sash. You can come out now. We got them all, including Curtis. He will never hurt you again."

Sasha's quivering hands relaxed but her voice and muscles failed her.

"Come on, Sash. Come out. I promise it's safe," Cole said, extending his hand. "I'm going to take you home."

Cole's hand seemed unattainable, a million miles away, a mirage. She could not move. Nothing made sense.

"Please come out." Tears brimmed Cole's eyes and his voice cracked. "I love you, Sasha. I've always loved you and I'll never stop loving you. Come out and I'll take you home—to our home—and I'll never have to come for you again because we'll never be apart. I can sell my condo and we can buy a house with a big yard, and you can grow us all sorts of amazing things, and we can play Scrabble every day if you want, and I won't complain if I never win again. Come out, Sasha. Come share a life with me."

Sasha gulped in a lungful of air. Her petrified muscles released with a hiccupping sob. As tears rolled down her cheeks, she reached out. When her hand rested in his and he broke into a huge, tear-soaked grin, Sasha knew she was home and home was where she would stay.

Chapter 46

Nineteen Months Later

The engine roared as Sasha pressed her foot to the accelerator. Trees became a blur of greens and the broken line down the middle of the highway melded into a solid smear. As Lashburn disappeared in the rear-view mirror, she let out a freeing laugh. The turnoff for the botanical garden vanished behind her and the road stretched open ahead. "Not today, work. And too bad for you, Master Gardener class. This day is all mine."

As the miles passed, thoughts that were taking up space in her mind began to flit away. No appointments, schedules, or housework. No forced smiles or strained conversation. Zero expectations.

A police siren buzzed on her phone—Cole's text tone that he helped her install—and Sasha reached to the passenger seat.

I got us reservations at that Italian place for 7. Have a great day and I'll see you then. Love ya.

Sasha's chest warmed. She sent a heart emoji back, then chucked her phone over her shoulder where it bounced off the backseat with a thud.

"Okay, baby," she said as she rubbed the dash. "Let's see what we can get up to in eight hours."

She whizzed by busy tractors working endless fields and waved at cows that watched her pass. A flock of geese sailed over her car and she leaned forward, gazing up while she gripped the wheel. A lone goose doing its own thing outside of the V pattern flapped to keep up.

Town names plastered on signs disappeared behind her, and when a name finally caught her attention, she pulled off the highway.

The rest of the weight lifted. Painting bedrooms at their acreage became a distant thought. Psychotherapist homework left the forefront of her mind. And the oil change that Cole kept reminding her about drifted away.

She breathed.

As she drove down Main Street, her foot eased off the accelerator and she took on the pace of the sleepy town. A family gathered around a table outside an ice cream shop, a woman jostled a ladder out the door of a hardware store, and the smell of smoked meat floated through the window as she passed a deli.

Spotting a playground ahead, she pulled to the side of the road and rummaged around in the backseat.

With a fresh smile stretched across her face, she hauled her belly out of the car and strolled across the grass. Fresh spring air filled her lungs as a gentle breeze swept the hair from her neck. As the laughter of children drifted across the park, she eased herself onto a bench next to a woman who was rocking a stroller and gazing out towards the playground.

"It's a beautiful day."

"It is," the woman replied, turning with a smile. "I've been going crazy trying to keep my little boy entertained inside through last week's rains. I'm so happy he can run off his steam out here again."

"You have two kids?"

"Adam is the little guy in the green hat over there. He's four," the woman said as she pointed towards the slide. "And this is Ella. She's just shy of three months."

"They're sweet."

"What about you? Do you have any rug rats out there?"

"This will be our first."

"Congratulations. Do you know what you're having?"

She smiled and rested her hand on her belly as she imagined an ultrasound where she and Cole watched the tiny movements of the little girl she was carrying. "Actually," she said with a sparkle in her eye, "we're having twins. One of each—a boy and a girl."

"That's great. You'll definitely be busy. When are you due?"

"Eight more weeks."

"Well, who knows? Maybe next year, your little ones will be playing with Ella at this very playground."

"A whole new life, hey?"

"Pretty much," the woman said with a laugh. "I'm Karla."

"It's nice to meet you, Karla," she said, taking the woman's hand and breathing in the fresh air. "I'm Lizzie."

Acknowledgments

The journey from idea inception to you holding this book today has been long, and there are too many people to thank in such a small space, but please know, every person who I have had the privilege of meeting, whether in person or through cyberspace, has had an impact on me and deserves a thank you.

In particular, I want to thank the team at Between the Lines Publishing for taking a chance on me and my novel. My editor, Penny, was a delight from the start, and her keen eye and personal musings elevated my story and made the editorial process a joy. As well, this book would not have reached nearly as many people without the help and expertise of Julia, Jared, and the rest of the Wildbound PR team. Their joy, verve, and passion for sharing books with the world is infectious, and I am both ecstatic and humbled to have them champion me and Sasha.

Many thanks to the literary journals, magazines, and story collections that gave my short stories homes over the years and helped me grow as a writer. I want to send my gratitude to the lone man from Chicago—whoever you are—whose single question sparked the birth of Sasha and her universe, and to the bartender who taught me about apples, limes, and really expensive Scotch. Without these conversations, I never would have been hit with inspiration for this novel. As well, I would not be where I am today without the support and generosity of the online writing communities. The people I have met taught me so much about what it means to be a writer, and they have always been there for the ups and downs of this crazy industry. And you, dear reader, because without you, this book would not have found its way onto a bookshelf.

A massive thank you to my three children, Ryley, Ivy, and Holly, who always cheered me on. And finally, to my husband, Ryan, who stood by me through rejections and acceptances; imposter syndrome and those moments when I stopped mid-conversation to jot down a juicy piece of dialogue; for being my alpha reader, first editor, business writer, marketing whiz, concierge, rock, shoulder to cry on, and biggest fan. This book would not be here without you.

Laura Frost is an award-winning author of novels and short stories. She has been published in numerous journals and collections and is a returning judge for an international short story competition. An amateur baker and former wildlife biologist from northern Canada, Laura explores the world with her family, seeking out adventure to both calm and stir her writing muse. Seeking Sasha is Laura's first novel.